THE SENATOR AND THE PRIEST

ANDREW M. GREELEY

THE
SENATOR
AND THE PRIEST

FORGE®

A TOM DOHERTY ASSOCIATES BOOK

New York

This is a work of fiction.
All the characters and events portrayed in this novel
are either fictitious or are used fictitiously.

THE SENATOR AND THE PRIEST

NOV 3 0 2006

This book is printed on acid-free paper.

A Forge Book
Published by Tom Doherty Associates, LLC
175 Fifth Avenue
New York, NY 10010

www.tor.com

Forge® is a registered trademark of Tom Doherty Associates, LLC.

Library of Congress Cataloging-in-Publication Data

Greeley, Andrew M., 1928–
    The senator and the priest / Andrew M. Greeley.
        p. cm.
    "A Tom Doherty Associates Book."
    ISBN-13: 978-0-765-31591-5
    ISBN-10: 0-765-31591-2
    1. Clergy—Fiction. 2. Legislators—Fiction. 3. Brothers—Fiction. 4. Political
fiction. 5. Washington (D.C.)—Fiction. I. Title.
    PS3557.R358S428 2006
    813'.54—dc22

                                                                    2006004268

First Edition: November 2006
Printed in the United States of America

0 9 8 7 6 5 4 3 2 1

The idea for this story came into my imagination from reflections on the two Mayors Daley, neither one of whom have ever engaged in negative campaigns. "You can't do that to people's kids," the first Mayor insisted. Both men were/are by character and conviction and maybe genes incapable of attacking other candidates. It seemed to me that this trait could well be imitated by all political candidates. Hence the story is dedicated to them. As the late mayor said, "You can't do that to people's kids."

My neighbor at Grand Beach, Lawrence O'Rourke, covered the United States Senate for thirty-eight years. I am more grateful than I can express to him for his help in telling this story. He is not responsible, however, for any mistakes or errors I might have made.

AUTHOR'S NOTE

My story is set in the present with all its political stress and strain. However, all the characters, lay and clerical, are products of my imagination. None of the denizens of the Capitol and the Beltway are based on any real people, though of course they represent certain tendencies in American political life. The two United States Senators from the Prairie State are both friends of mine. Senator Thomas Moran is not like either of them save in that all three are Democrats. I take no stands on some of the arguments between the Catholic Church and Catholic political leaders. However, I am sympathetic to the dilemma of Senators like Thomas Patrick Moran and I agree with him that continued efforts to force Catholic politicians to impose the Church's teachings on the rest of the country by denying them the Eucharist will lead to the disappearance of Catholics from the country's political life. No one will remain to support the Church's traditional teachings on war, poverty, and social justice. The two newspapers bear the names of extinct Chicago journals and are not meant to represent any current newspapers in the city.

Some readers will accuse me of "partisanship" because my protagonists are Democratic—they wouldn't complain if I had made them Republicans. Rules for Republicans are different. In fact I am a Democrat and have been all my life. I make no apology for alignment with the party that, whatever its faults may have been, has always remained the party of the poor and the oppressed. Moreover, it would be difficult to write a story about the United States Senate and hide one's own partisanship.

THE SENATOR AND THE PRIEST

CHAPTER 1

✝

"YOU REALLY shouldn't be here, you know," my brother Tony jabbed a finger at me. "You have no business playing with the big kids. Never did. You shouldn't run again."

His tone was jocular, as it always is when he's reproving me, big brother laughing at silly little brother, now the big brother priest reproving the little brother who was pretending that he was a United States Senator.

We were glancing at our menus in the Capitol Grill, a hangout for Republican Senators and lobbyists. I did not want to bring Tony into the Senate Dining Room where my colleagues could hear us argue. Besides, he would want a drink before lunch.

My brother had put on weight. He wasn't obese yet, but in a few more years he might be. The tall, solid body which had served him well in his three sports career at Fenwick high school was deteriorating and the shock of long blond hair which the young women from Trinity had worshiped was thinning. He needed to see a dentist. Several times he drummed his fingers on the table. My brother was too busy with the work of the Lord to take care of himself.

"Vodka martini on the rocks," he told the pretty young waitress with his best smile. With everyone else besides me he was charming. With me he was edgy, almost driven.

"What about you, Tommy?"

The pretense was that he was the host, though I would pick up the bill. "Iced tea."

"Mary take the creature away from you?" he asked, hinting as he always did that my wife ran my life.

"She likes to be called by her full name. . . . I have work to do this afternoon. I would never come on the floor of the senate with the smell of booze on me."

My wife and my adored older brother never got along. Besides, I had learned that two drinks at lunch took the tension out of my life and made me vulnerable.

"I bet a lot of the big guys have a couple of drinks after lunch."

Always the big guys.

"That's their problem."

I felt my body tighten. I was falling apart. Every day I woke up tense. Every night I collapsed into bed tense. There were only a few moments in my office in the early morning when I could feel that I was not being torn apart, a Roman criminal tugged in four directions by wild horses. I didn't need Tony hassling me after the morning committee hearing and before a difficult afternoon session. The Senate had crushed all the joy and laughter out of my life.

"You haven't done much here, Tommy," he sipped his martini as though it was a forbidden love. "Created a lot of controversy that's all."

Why was I always thinking these days in images of forbidden love?

"We got some good legislation through," I defended myself. I had always defended myself with Tony. "Pensions, immigration, veterans."

He ordered a sixteen-ounce steak, rare. I settled for a bowl of chowder and a house salad with vinegar and oil dressing.

"Mary really has you on a short leash, doesn't she?"

It was pointless to defend my wife. He had advised me not to marry her and he was always right in the advice he gave me.

"Mary Margaret," I said automatically.

"Are you two attending Mass regularly?" he demanded, as he continued to sip his drink.

"What makes you think we're not?"

"You should think of the kids. They need your good example."

"They give us good example," I said, truthfully enough.

Before we had left the Dirksen Senate Office Building—a place which often reminds me of the Queen of Heaven Mausoleum in Hillcrest, just west of Chicago—to walk over to the restaurant I had, at his insistence, shown him my office. He had frowned as we walked by the receptionist and through the bullpen where letter openers, stenographers, writers, advisers, legislative assistants, press representatives, researchers, schedulers, interns, volunteers, and other staff functionaries were working, a scene which always reminded me of the old films about sweatshops in the garment industry. When we had entered the two small cells where Chris Taliferro, my Chief of Staff, and Manny Rodriguez, Deputy Chief of Staff and Senior Press Liaison, were working, he barely acknowledged my introduction of these lovely, exotic, and indispensable women.

In my own much more luxurious office there was a big desk, wood wall paneling with the great seal of the Senate and the State of Illinois, color photos of my family, a comfortable chair and even a couch—with a splendid view of the Capitol itself beyond the big windows. On this early summer day the crystalline dome seemed almost unreal against the clear blue sky, a postcard picture or perhaps a background for a Hollywood set.

"John," I had gestured towards the only bathroom in the office.

He had ignored me. Real men don't need to urinate.

"Why the hell do you need all those people out there?" he nodded impatiently towards the outer office.

I sat in my judicial chair, though I was not the judge at the moment but the defendant.

"The Federal system does not have precinct captains or ward committeemen to whom the people can appeal," I said with a sigh, "so they appeal to their elected representatives for relief. Much of the work out there is responding to such appeals, opening the letters or the e-mail, contacting the offending agency, passing the tough cases on to me, responding to the people."

"Most of the complaints must be silly," he had dismissed my explanation.

"Some are, some aren't. The federal government can be mindlessly oppressive. We are generally successful where the constituents have a valid complaint. . . . Some of my staff are researchers. We have a vote this afternoon on the Pension Protection Bill jointly sponsored by Senator Bartlett McCoy of Kentucky and myself. We have to be very careful about writing proposed legislation. I have three assistants who deal with the press and schedule my day, a very bright intern from Georgetown law who is drafting legislation on property rights."

He waved my explanation off as, hands shoved into his jacket pocket, he strode back and forth across the office.

"This is all a big, silly game, isn't it, Tommy?"

"The people in Connecticut who had their homes condemned for a shopping mall and the airline workers who had their pensions wiped out in a bankruptcy hearing might not think so."

He sank into couch, exasperated with my game.

"Who pays these people?"

"The Senate allots a budget to every Senator for staff. I pay the interns myself."

"A living wage?" he had demanded.

"Most of my colleagues know how much they depend on their staff. Even the Republicans don't stint on staff salaries."

"Most of them are women, aren't they? And they fawn all over you, don't they? I saw the way they smiled when you walked through the office. You're not turning into a Bill Clinton, are you?"

"I'm too busy to notice," I had said.

"You don't expect me to believe that, do you?

"Let's go eat," I had risen from my desk. "I have to be back for the session this afternoon when we're going to try to pass the Pension Protection Act."

He had continued his cross-examination as we walked down the marble corridors and out into the bright sunlight. My brother had winced every time I greeted someone, senator or staffer or guard, by their first name.

"So what kind of hours do you keep around here?" he asked.

"The Senate is technically in session on Monday, Tuesday, Wednesday, and Thursday. The various committees have their meetings in the morning and the full sessions begin at two every afternoon, more or less. Nothing much ever happens on Monday, though a few senators use the day for long speeches to which no one listens. Some of the committees meet on Monday and Friday too. The formal sessions on Tuesday and Wednesday usually end by seven, sometimes earlier. Today, Thursday, is the big day when we debate and vote on legislation. Those sessions can go on to midnight, which makes it difficult for my colleagues to catch the early plane on Friday morning."

"You mean you only work three days a week."

"Most of what we do doesn't happen on the Senate floor. Many Senators commute back and forth to their families and their constituencies where they spend a lot of time mending fences and raising money. Some of them spend their nights here in the Beltway with other senators in two-room apartments. We elected to make Washington home. Keep the family together. Maybe once a month I fly to Chicago to give a lecture."

I got no points for keeping the family together.

I wished to hell he'd leave me alone.

"It sounds like a pretty easy job, unless you're one of the big boys. And they say you're cute little Tommy Moran, the Tom Cruise of the United States Senate."

"Only if you believe the lies Leander Schlenk publishes in the *Examiner.*"

"He's an old hand in this city. He knows what really happens here."

F. Leander Schlenk was the "veteran capital correspondent" of the *Examiner* whose column "Under the Dome" was Holy Scripture to many Chicagoans, just as Mike Royko's words had been a long time ago.

"He's never mentioned that I'm the assistant minority whip and serve on three important committees: Banking, Judiciary, and Armed Services."

I had fallen into the trap I usually fall into with my brother Anthony. I was trying to defend myself.

"Tommy, Tommy!" He sighed loudly and his shoulders dropped in dejection. "How many times do I have to tell you that you don't know anything about those subjects. You don't belong here. Do you really think you are an expert on the armed services? You can't be that dumb."

"I'm the senior Democrat on the subcommittee on the service academies," I snapped back. "We're investigating the abuse of women at those places."

"Those girls must know that if they go there, they're going to be abused. You're wasting your time."

We entered the Capitol Grill and I calmed down. There was never any point in arguing with Tony. I was wrong by definition, guilty till proven innocent, only none of my proof was admissible evidence. Thus it always had been.

"So you're just about out of the Church?" he continued the case for the prosecution as he cut the blood-red steak with considerable relish. Well, a priest, being celibate, was entitled to some pleasure. As a noncelibate so was I.

"What makes you think that?"

I was being my usual passive-aggressive self when I deal with my brother.

"Well, your parish priest threw you out of Mass, didn't he?"

"He refused us Communion, all five of us. So we walked out and went over to the Jesuits."

"They'd give Communion to anyone!"

Clementine that he was, he didn't think much of the Jesuits.

"How Catholic of them."

"I suppose the kids don't go to Church, teenagers are pagans these days."

Get to the point and leave me alone. Why are you here? What's all this leading to? I have enough problems.

"They go to Mass almost every day at school—just like superstitious old fashioned Catholics. Breakfast with Jesus every morning."

I finished my chowder and pushed it aside. I noted Senator Evergreen of Oklahoma, one of the most obnoxious "Christians" in the Senate, eyeing us. He knew who my brother was. He'd come over and talk. I lost my appetite for the salad.

"You'll never be right with the Church till you get out of this job and out of this city. You can't be a good, practicing Catholic and be a Democratic senator, that's all there is to it. And besides, you're out of your depth."

He didn't look at me when he delivered this judgment since he was too busy finishing off his steak.

"Tony," I said with a sigh, "if you get rid of all the Catholic Democrats—and I think that's what you guys want to do—that will kill the social justice legislation the church has supported for decades. Poverty, immigrants, the environment, the death penalty, unions, foreign aid—will vanish. The haves and the have-mores, as the President puts it, will take over the country."

"That's the trouble with you politicians," he pounded the table, spilling some of the steak blood on the table cloth. "You always give in and compromise. If you were still a good Catholic, you would take a strong stand on every issue, represent your faith on the floor of the United States Senate."

"Compromise is what you have to do in a democratic society, especially if you're in the minority party."

The waitress lifted his martini glass from the table with an expression that asked if he wanted more. He nodded as if he scarcely noticed. . . .

The Clementines, like the Jesuits and many other orders, were content that some of their members be wild cards, men with special causes who are assigned to a minor post and left free to pursue their causes. Tony was the "prior" at a Clementine parish in an African-American neighborhood in Chicago. The work there was left to younger Brothers while he pursued his pro-life crusade—and dashed around the world to deal with Clementine crises.

"That's the problem with you, Tommy. You have no convictions, so you can't have the courage of your convictions. There are some issues you can't compromise on. As your brother and as a priest I must tell you that your immortal soul is in danger. If you wish to save your soul you must take a strong stand on abortion, homosexuality, and stem cell research."

He was devouring a dish of chocolate ice cream and adding to the mess on his clerical shirt.

"None of those issues are before the Senate during this session."

He pushed back his chair, as if he had given up.

"I have to warn you, Tommy. If you don't change your ways, if you don't stop disgracing our family, I'll have to admonish you not to seek re-election."

"Admonish" me. The two martinis must have messed up his brain cells.

"We have made no decision yet about reelection."

"Then I have to tell you that if you do run again, I will personally oppose your reelection."

I felt like he had kicked me in the balls. Even if he were dead wrong, he was still my brother. How could he ally himself with Lee Schlenk and the *Examiner* and "Senator" H. Rodgers Crispjin, men who were my bitter enemies and determined to destroy me?

Mary Margaret would say it was sibling rivalry. I had found the national audience he had always wanted.

I didn't know whether that was true or not. She also pointed out that in other contexts he was a different man. He was highly respected in his own order or he would not have the positions of responsibility to which he had been elected.

"That is, of course, your privilege as a citizen of this Republic and the State of Illinois," I murmured automatically.

"See what I mean, Tommy," he crowed, "you're too weak to be angry! No spine! No guts! You disgust me!

He rose unsteadily from his chair, prepared to walk away in disgust. If I hadn't taken hold of his elbow he might have fallen on his face. Fortunately, we managed to slip out of the Capitol Grill before the advent of the genial, heavily scented Senator Evergreen.

I felt guilty about that. He and E. Edward Evergreen would have delighted in each other, both models of charm. Authentic charm, I told myself.

CHAPTER 2

†

T<small>HE</small> D<small>EBATE</small> on the Pension Protection Bill droned on. The Senators who were hoping to catch an early plane back home for their long weekend with family and/or constituency were becoming irritable. The debate might go into the small hours of the morning. We had decided to live in the Beltway to keep the family together. Maybe we had made a mistake. Mary Margaret and I still had little time for one another. How much would we have had if I had to change reservations and wait on standby for a flight to Chicago early on Friday morning? Would our relationship have been any different? Senatorial life messes up family relationship no matter where you live. We had drifted apart not because of quarrels but because there was no time for love.

"Hat" McCoy and I had counted our votes at the beginning of the debate. We both thought we had the votes, unless there was some double cross. He had counted three more votes than I had. "You shunuff one pessimistic Irishman," he said with his mountain accent which was partially political and partially authentic. "Hat's" real first name was Bartlett, but hailing from "Bloody Harlan" County in Kentucky he claimed to be an heir to both families in the feud. He also claimed to be a "Christian" but a "laid-back" Christian. He went to the Christian prayer breakfast, but "not all the time." He also told me that he was a "laid-back" Republican. That meant that on some occasions he could work with Democrats, especially as the White House's power over

Congress waned. A slender handsome man, only an inch or so taller than I was, with thick black hair parted in the middle, and an easy grin, he and I were friends and on occasions allies. Even at a time when the Senate was more polarized than it had been since the end of Reconstruction, he and I got along "just fine, bein' as how we both Irishmen."

"Except you kick with the left foot," I had said.

He thought that was very funny.

I sat uneasily on the edge of my chair. Lobbyists were swarming in the cloakrooms (where cloaks were rarely hung) and in the corridors in search of exemptions for their firms or industries.

The legislation had two major provisions. All pension funds should be "fully funded" which means that the money had to have been set aside for payment to retirees and not based on hope and expectation. This had been the law for some time, but there were loopholes which enabled companies to create the illusion of adequate funding when in fact it did not exist. The second requirement was that existing pension funds could not be used by companies as hostage in bankruptcy court or in labor negotiations.

"Hat" and I agreed that this was legislation that the people of the United States wanted and that it would be very difficult to vote against it if we could ever get it to the floor of the Senate. It was also legislation we wanted our names on. The "McCoy Moran Act," he said. "Sounds like some left-foot kicking, Bible-thumping preacher man." We had labored for ten months to get it on the floor and we would have an "up or down" vote on it before this session ended. We needed a big vote, strong enough to overcome a veto and strong enough that the Senate leadership could not appoint opponents to the conference committee which would work out differences between our bill and the House bill—if the House ever passed a bill.

We knew the bill would pass, though I was pretty sure it would never become the law of the land until we had at least one Democratic chamber in Congress and a Democratic President.

We had agreed that "Hat" would fight off amendments exempting automobile companies from the legislation and I would fight against the airlines. He had done an effective job describing the "Neesaan" factory in his home state that made cars that did not break down and also made money and didn't have to demand "give backs" from their workers.

We beat that amendment down with three votes.

The airline amendment might be even closer.

I paid little attention to the debate. My big brother was still hassling me. And I was worrying about him. All my life I had sought his approval in everything I did. He was five years older, a "natural leader," who took care of me against the bullies in grammar school and instructed me how to cope with Fenwick High School. He was truly my "big" brother, a good half-a-foot taller, and a superb athlete while I made a fool out of myself whenever I engaged in competitive sport. Our parents, high-school teachers who married late in life, were often indifferent figures, loving but caught up in their own relationship. Big brother took care of me. I adored him.

The major disagreement in our life was about Mary Margaret. While we had "hung around" together with our respective gangs in high school, we had become an "item" in our senior year and then as freshmen at Loyola. Tony did not approve of her when he came home from his first summer at the Clementine seminary. She reacted in kind.

"You should get rid of her, bro. She's trouble. She flaunts herself."

My wife was nothing if not a modest woman. There were strict limits on our affection, much like the old days.

"She's part of the O'Malley family. You know what kind of people they are. Her father takes pornographic pictures of women."

Ambassador O'Malley is an internationally famed photo artist, who in some Catholic circles is thought to be a man who "takes dirty pictures." The spirituality Tony was picking up at the seminary—where according to some priests the Vatican Council never happened—was very negative about "smut."

Mary Margaret insisted that he didn't like her because he was afraid of women with strong opinions—which she had at least once every hour—and because she would break his domination over me. Maybe she was right. I also suspected that he might have resented the fact that I had found such a glorious woman and he couldn't have her. But that's the way my mind works when I feel cynical. She does radiate powerful sexuality, even when we are estranged as we implicitly were the day of his visit. That might frighten a man who was fighting strongly to keep his celibate promises.

It was downhill after that. My wife worked on appellate court cases and I did public defender work after we left law school. She made a lot more money than I did, which bothered me not at all. But it offended my brother. He tried to talk her into giving up her career when she became pregnant with Mary Rose. She laughed at him and said he was a male chauvinist living in the wrong century. He stormed out of our apartment. Later he spoke to me on the phone and ordered me to exercise my spousal authority over her. I told him that I didn't have any.

He blamed her for the article I wrote for the *Atlantic Monthly*. It was her fault that I decided to run for the Senate. She was responsible for the strong appeal we made for the votes of Mexican Americans. She was guilty of leading me astray on such issues as abortion, rights of homosexuals, and stem cell research. She was leading me out of the church.

I listened to his complaints and then made my own decisions. Mary Margaret supported me but the decisions were mine. Tony could never accept that. I really wasn't tough enough or big enough to make my own decisions.

"He's lost his control over you," she would say, "but he'll never stop trying."

I suppose she was right, but I still hoped that I could win him over.

A page handed me a note from the cloakroom.

"Airline lobbyists in news conference in the corridor. Robbie."

My good friend Senator Evergreen was babbling about the strength of American capitalism. I slipped across the aisle and showed the note to "Hat." He rolled his eyes and nodded. This would be the big fight on the next vote.

My heart pounded as I walked out to the cloakroom. Robbie made my heart pound and my hands perspire. I was not in love with her, but, as President Jimmy Carter once famously—and improbably—had said, I had lust in my heart for her. She was a recent graduate of the Columbia School of Journalism, a fresh young beauty with blond hair, full figure, keen mind, and an aura of shy fragility. She had a crush on me and had hinted, so subtly that one hardly noticed it, that I could have her if I wished.

Monica Lewinsky she was not.

But I wasn't Bill Clinton either. I was a pushover for vulnerable women, though none such had ever hit on me. I knew I should brush her off, but she would burst into tears if I did and I didn't want to hurt her.

As my brother would have said I was being tempted. I was in fact putting myself in an occasion of sin.

I did not think I could ever be unfaithful to Mary Margaret. I still thought that I would not. But I was not as sure as I used to be.

My wife, as I have said, is a very modest woman. On the other hand she is also a very intense woman. If we do something, she would lecture me and the daughters, we must do it well. Therefore she made up her mind that she would be a sexually attractive wife and bent all her efforts in that direction with considerable success. The blend of modesty and intensity was what made her sexy. I think. What do I know?

Tall, slender, with a flawless complexion and flaming red hair, trim with a moderately voluptuous figure, she had dazzled me as far back as I can remember. I will never forget the dance at the parish high club when we were both freshmen. She walked up to me, considered me quizzically, took me into her arms for a dance—my resistance melted immediately—and whispered in my ear, "You're cute Tommy Moran, I think I like you."

CHAPTER 3

✝

DURING OUR FIRST JANUARY in Washington, while we were
settling into our home in Georgetown (rented to us for a hundred dollars a year by Ambassador O'Malley), introducing our daughters into Gonzaga Prep and the Ursuline Academy, and trying to figure
out what the day-to-day operations of the Senate were, a very prominent Beltway power broker and his very decorative wife invited us to
supper, perhaps to discover what the young populist from Chicago was
really like. A couple of reporters were present, an editor, the German
ambassador, the DCM from the Spanish embassy, a columnist from
The New York Times, a senior Republican Senator. Dinner jackets recommended.

Big deal for two novices from the Prairie State. At first the harmless
little Senator did not garner much attention, as usual a moon-like satel-
lite, reflecting the radiance of his spouse in her white-gold dress with
her pale shoulders accented by thin, mostly symbolic, straps, her fiery
hair fashioned into a glittering crown, her smile illuminating the silver-
ware and the china and the linen and her contagious laughter enchant-
ing everyone—an elegant woman in an elegant setting. The guests of
both genders could not take their eyes off her. Kathleen Ni Houlihan,
Maeve the Magnificent, Erihu the goddess. My own imagination was
awash in fantasies of what I would do with her when we returned to

our bedroom. I had even whispered a gross suggestion into her ear as I helped her off with her wrap. She blushed and smiled.

She spoke to the German diplomat in German, mentioning that as a very little girl, the Old One (as Chancellor Conrad Adenauer was called) had praised her German. She apologized to the Spanish diplomat for her Mexican accent and answered with graceful charm all the questions addressed to her. Yes, the children were in Gonzaga Prep and the Ursuline Academy and loved it in Washington, but they were adventurers who adjusted easily to change. Yes, she would be doing appellate work of Brown, Berger, Bobbet, and Butts. Yes, she had met some of the Senatorial wives and they had been very sweet, even the Republicans. No, she would not define herself as a Christian, only as an Irish Catholic from the West Side of Chicago. Yes, it was true that the family had two Spanish days a week; even the Senator was becoming more fluent in the language. Yes, the Georgetown neighborhood seemed to be a lovely place to live, though not as picturesque as River Forest, Illinois. Yes, her name was Mary Margaret, contracted to Marymarg, but only by her parents, her siblings, her children, and her husband—but in his case only at certain approved times.

There was uneasy laughter at that last remark in the sex-drenched atmosphere around the dinner table which she had created all by herself.

Finally, half-way through the dinner, they turned to the silent Senator.

What reforms, the Timesman asked, did I plan for the Senate?

Easier to reform the Catholic Church.

But are you not in favor of the abolition of attack ads in political campaigns?

Only of voluntary abstinence.

Your campaign proved, did it not, that a candidate can win an election with little fund-raising and not attack ads?

It proved that in one time and one place a candidate did not need to vilify his opponent to win an election.

The reelection could be more difficult, the editor observed, might it not, especially with Senator Crispjin already in the running with the support of the *Examiner* and the money of the Roads family behind him?

Six years is a long time.

Office holders, our host said, have a hard time regaining a position that they have lost.

Grover Cleveland being a notable exception. To be candid—and one should never trust a politician when he uses that word—we have made no decision about running again. We'll have to see what happens.

An editorial we?

Not at all.

What's your next book about, The man from the *Times* asked.

Political trials.

What?

The constant abuse of power by federal prosecutors. Using frightened subordinates to rat out the target, often suborning perjury in the process. Destroying careers by bankrupting defendants with legal fees, using the publicity of their show trials to seek public office, charging perjury against anyone who deceives a federal officer—with nothing like a Miranda warning.

There was dead silence around the room.

Those tactics could be used against anyone in this room. As Martha Stewart or Governor George Ryan proved.

Will you be a Senate maverick, the anchor woman wondered, or will you go along to get along?

We Chicago Irish are genetically programmed to work within systems, to value coalition and compromise, to aim for achievable goals not perfection. Politics is the art of the possible. I hope to work hard to win the confidence of my new colleagues on both sides of the aisle.

You could be a very dangerous man, said the Republican Senator with a smile.

I hope so, Senator.

You can't imagine, Senator, my wife said. Beware the harmless little Irishman with the quick tongue and a charming smile.

Especially, I added, if his wife is a red-haired Celtic goddess.

We creamed them, she said later, as she clung to me on the walk down the street to our house, a pose of vulnerability which she had assumed when we thanked our host and hostess.

And I'm going to cream you as soon as we get to the bedroom.

I hope you're able to wait that long.

CHAPTER 4

†

A S THE DEBATE on Pension reform dragged on four years later, I
continued to ponder my brother. He was certainly aware of the
good notices I was earning in the national media and in the cautious
Chicago Daily News, even if the *Examiner* polls showed H. Rodgers
Chrisjin running against me in the election a year and a half away. At
the cost of enormous effort and strain I had become an effective Senator as I had promised that night at the first of many Georgetown dinners. I had many friends on both sides of the aisle, did my homework,
counted votes, arranged compromises with which people could live, attended meetings, did not grandstand nor hog the TV camera. I was, as
the *Daily News* had said, a quiet and influential member of the Senate
who paid his own air fare on the few junkets he made.

I had even remained faithful to my wife in the house of ill repute
which the Senate often seemed to be—people coupling in closets,
bathrooms, cubbyholes, anterooms, and especially in the small and dis-
creet "hideaways" which some of us had just outside the senate chamber. They were supposed to be refuges of peace and quiet to which a
Senator could retreat from the floor during a debate to read and think
and pray perhaps for a few quiet moments, away from the hubbub of
debate. I had one such hideaway now in virtue of my position as minority whip—assistant minority whip.

I used the hideaway rarely and forbade my staff ever to bother me there. I did not want Robbie slipping into it when I was unprepared.

I remembered the romp Marymarg and I enjoyed the night we had returned from that first Georgetown party. Nothing like that for a long time. No way could Robbie ever compete with her as a bed mate. If only . . .

I had paid a heavy price, both of us had, for my becoming an effective Senator. So had all our family.

I would never persuade my brother that I had played successfully with "the big guys" and indeed had won the occasional victory in the process. In his world view I had not "stood up" for my Catholic principles on the floor of the Senate. I had not denounced abortion, stem cell research, and homosexuality. I had not made them my basic issues. Instead I had concentrated on small issues like the protection of the pensions of workers, the property of ordinary folks which local governments wanted to condemn so they could build supermarkets with big block stores, the rape of women cadets at the service academy, the protection of the rights of immigrants. For Tony these were trivial issues. They were not for the people who were the victims, as I had tried to explain to him many times.

Our first Sunday in Washington we had gone *en famille* to the local parish Church. I suppose the four red heads were a give away. During the homily the pastor denounced Catholic politicians who did not sacrifice their careers for their principles.

"I think he knows we're here, Daddy," Mary Rose had whispered, a stage whisper, the only kind our exuberant daughter would attempt.

He certainly did. At Communion time he passed ostentatiously by all five of us at the rail—though the four redheads were hardly offending Catholic politicians. We promptly marched out of the Church, followed by at least a third of the congregation.

The Jesuit who greeted us at the entrance of the Georgetown chapel for the afternoon Mass assured us that we were "most welcome."

And then he added that the Monsignor was an absolute asshole.

CNN was waiting for us after Mass.

"The Jesuits let you into the Church, Senator?"

"They said we were most welcome."

"Were you aware that the Monsignor has been fighting this issue with his parishioners for a long time?"

"We're new kids in town. I must say that I am astonished that the Monsignor would deny the Sacrament to my wife and children too. That violates the Code of Canon Law."

"Why is the Church refusing the Eucharist to Catholic politicians?

"Only to Democrats," I said, "and only a few priests and ambitious bishops."

"But why?"

"I suspect that it is a way to persuade themselves that they are regaining the power they lost because of the sexual abuse mess."

"Isn't that counterproductive?"

"I would think so."

My three daughters all are gorgeous young women with red hair, like their mother, but they are not really clones, though you would know at first glance that they are sisters and, if Marymarg were present, she was their mother.

Mary Rose (also sometimes Maryro) is the oldest. She is tall, brilliant, and self-possessed. She doesn't so much argue with us as tell us when and where we are wrong. She is a power forward on the Gonzaga basketball team and very dangerous. She is authoritative rather than bossy and shares her mother's intensity, but is much more serious than Marymarg. She is as prone to tears, however, as her mother. When we stalked out of the church, she led the way, her head proudly in the air, like she was thinking of shaking the dust of the place from her feet.

Mary Ann (Maran) is our resident little mystic, quiet, reflective. Often seems to be in another world. Very sensitive to her parent's emotions. Sweet and sympathetic. She wept when we were denied the Eucharist.

Mary Terese (Marytre) is the youngest of the brood and the loudest. She doesn't mind a good fight with anyone, inside the family or out, but is as quick to make peace as she is to make war. She wanted to stay and fight the priest at the parish.

The *Chicago Examiner* carried a headline the next day which said

Church Denies Sacrament to Tommy, Family

Leander Schlenk didn't add that we later received the Eucharist at the Georgetown chapel.

My brother called me that afternoon and bawled me out.

"What kind of example are you giving to your poor children? How dare you countenance their embarrassment in public."

"I'm thinking of filing a canonical suit," I fibbed, "against the pastor for denying the sacrament to my wife and children."

"You wouldn't dare!"

"He violated the Code of Canon Law. I am entitled to seek relief."

"You'd be a laughing stock. . . . I suppose you missed Mass?"

"We went to the Georgetown chapel in the afternoon."

"They let you in!"

"Actually they welcomed us."

"They'll let anyone in," he snapped.

Lee Schlenk had yet to supply such labels for me as "Renegade Catholic," "Cute Little Tommy Moran," and "The Tom Cruise of the United States Senate." Those would come later.

When I had begun my campaign without much hope of winning, but trying to make a point about negative ads, I consulted with a certain theologian about these issues.

"What do you think about these maters, Tom?" he had asked me.

"I'm opposed to abortion. I'm not sure you can call it murder. It is also a right sustained by the law of the land. It's not going to change. The public does not want it to change. Most of my constituents don't want it to change."

"And gays?"

"I think they've been dealt a bad hand and the Church should leave them alone."

"And stem cell research?"

"I'm told that half of fertilized ova are never implanted. I can't imagine God causing that many abortions of human persons."

He examined my face silently for a moment.

"It would seem you have done your research, Thomas."

"The Church expects us to follow its orders when we vote."

"Yes, it does. Your moral decisions should be 'informed' by church teaching."

"That makes it very difficult for those of us working in politics."

"It makes it impossible, Thomas."

"The Bishops don't care. They're trying to persuade themselves that they still have power despite the mess they made of the sexual abuse crisis."

"That may well be part of it. Better say 'some bishops.' "

"All right . . . And they want to force us to use our political position to impose Catholic teaching on all Americans."

"Precisely."

"And I believe that Catholics have struggled for hundreds of years to destroy that impression of the Church."

"And your conscience tells you?"

"That, finally, I have to make my own decisions as to what is best in the circumstances."

"Then you must follow your conscience, must you not?"

"That's what I was taught in college . . . but my brother says that the Church has the right to tell me what the right prudential choice is."

"Forgive my language, Thomas, but your brother, dear sweet man that he is, is also an asshole."

The sound for a quorum call was echoing throughout the chambers, calling everyone away from their booze and their naps and maybe their women. I glanced at my watch. Eleven. Too late for the last flights. Serves them right for talking so much.

"It looks like we'uns a gonna win, Brother Tom!"

"Shunuff, Brother Hatfield."

"Brother Tom, you lookin' like hell. You a needin' time off."

Shunuff we did win.

I found a cab to take me back to Georgetown. I avoided the office, fearful that Robbie might be waiting for me in the office.

I was too dependent on my brother's opinion, I told myself. Maybe I should see a psychiatrist about that. That would take too much time. My work in the Senate had worn me out. The constant assault on me and my family was sapping what little energy I had left. Maybe I should have told Tony that I had no intention of running for reelection. That would have pleased him somewhat, but it would not satisfy him. I would never satisfy him. I remembered in the cab the experience with my wife after our first Georgetown dinner, the sheer joy of taking off her clothes, slowly, one by one, as she stood motionless, save for mischievously dancing green eyes, and lips twitching with suppressed laughter.

"Tommy, even your most lascivious fantasies are sweet."

Such love between us would never happen again as long as I was a Senator.

CHAPTER 5

✝

POOR TOMMY had lunch with his idiot brother today. That's the last thing he needs with voting this afternoon on Pension Protection and a hearing tomorrow on rape at the service academies. He's been caught between the two of us for twenty years. I'm winning. At least I think I am. Sex has gone out of our lives only because we're both exhausted at the end of the day. I don't think that's directly Tony's doing. But he is part of the reason Tommy is so tired. He and those goons at the *Examiner* and Rodge Cripsjin and Bobby Bill Roads.

I asked Rosie—my Mom—when I was twelve whether I was too young to make a decision about the man I wanted to marry. Way too young, she had said. When did you decide about Chucky? I was real old, maybe ten. No regrets. No way. Is it Tommy?

"Do you like him?"

"He's kinda cute."

"Like Chucky when you were ten?"

"Not nearly as crazy."

"Are the things that men and women do always fun?"

"If there's love and respect, yes—sometimes more than others, but that's the way of life."

"Chucky is always nice to you?"

She thought that was very funny.

"Poor dear man can't help himself. He's always nice. Nicer than I am."

I wasn't sure what that meant, so I didn't push it.

"Well, I think I've made up my mind about Tommy Moran."

"And you want my approval?"

"I guess."

"Go for it," she said hugging me. "Go for it."

That's not what most moms would say.

So Tommy hung around, my knight errant according to Chucky. We were very cool about everything, but we both had crushes and were kind of falling in love, but not quite, not yet.

Tony did not even notice that I existed, not till he returned from his first year in the seminary. The first time he saw me, he devoured me with his eyes, so openly and clinically that I felt my face grow warm. I wanted to stare him down, but I didn't have the self-possession those days to do it. All right, I'll grant him the excuse that he was just back from the seminary and the second excuse that he didn't think his little brother could possibly have collected a woman like me. But the truth was that he wanted me and instead his little bro had me. The animosity between us never went away after that moment. To be candid (a word Tommy laughs at) I find him disgusting. He still looks at me that way.

Yet he is a good and hard-working priest, respected by most of the laity who know him.

When he argues that celibacy is a good thing for priests, I sometimes say to him that it is a good thing for some poor woman that he's celibate. He turns deep red and says that I'm being impertinent.

Which of course I am.

Not that celibacy is bad, my Uncle Ed and my brother Jimmy are good arguments for celibacy, but there's a kink somewhere in my brother-in-law's soul that makes him a bad argument for it. Tommy and I went to Loyola together, living at our homes for the first couple of years. I loved my family too much ever to leave home.

So one day Rosie asked me at dinner, "So what about Tommy?"

"So what about him?"

"Shouldn't you get a ring from him pretty soon?"

Good question.

"We haven't discussed marriage," I said firmly.

"Isn't it time you should?"

"First year in law school."

"Maybe I should leave the table," Chucky said.

"Don't you dare," we both said together.

"Ring at college graduation? Wedding at end of first year?"

"Sounds good to me," Chucky observed.

"You stay out of this," we both said together again.

"Monstrous regiment of women," he said, one of his favorite phrases.

"Sounds good to me," I agreed.

"The woman has to bring closure," Rosie warned me.

"That's certainly true," Chucky said.

"I know THAT!"

So it was settled in our family. Everyone liked Tommy, my little sister Shovie said he was too good for me. Which was probably true. Well, he's mine, just the same, I snapped back at her. Tears filled her eyes and she apologized. I was only kidding. Then we embraced and both of us had a good cry.

When we graduated from high school, I changed my mind about the University of Chicago. I decided I'd attend Loyola with Tommy and then go to law school with him too. We didn't discuss my change in plans, but Tommy seemed delighted that I'd still be in the neighborhood. But then he was always delighted with anything I did. Still is. I think.

My plan was off by a year. He gave me a ring at Christmas of our junior year in college and informed me that we would be married the week after we graduated.

"It's too early!" I said, my careful plans ruined.

"No it's not," he laughed. "Now put on the ring!"

I did, quickly before he could take it back.

Most of my family has always thought that Tommy was a nice little guy who sort of hung around hoping I'd notice him. Rosie knew better.

"He's like your father, dear. He has a spine of steel when he makes up his mind. You'd better get used to it."

I had kind of known that all along. I'd never doubt it again.

Besides I was flattered that he wanted me that badly.

"He likes you," Chucky said, "because you laugh at his little jokes."

"Not the first man in history to do that," Rosie told him.

His brother, ordained that very Christmas in Rome, was furious. He persuaded Tommy's elderly parents to oppose the marriage. Tommy was too young to marry. I was not the right woman. I would ruin his life. My family were not really good Catholics. The marriage must be stopped. We were certainly sleeping together (we weren't).

My first hint of the family fight was when his mother hung up on me when I called their house, returning a call from Tommy. I called again and she hung up again. I cried myself to sleep that night.

"What's happening?" I demanded when I met Tommy on the L platform for our daily ride down to Loyola. "Why did your mother hang up on me?"

"I didn't know she did that, Mary Margaret," he said sadly. "I'm sorry. Don't worry about it."

"I do worry about it."

"Father Tony disapproves of our engagement. Mom and Dad always agree with him. I'm afraid I will have to move out of the house."

"Why?"

"Why move?"

"No! Why does your brother disapprove?"

He hesitated.

The L train rumbled to a stop and we got on.

"Why? What's the matter with me?"

"He says you seduced me."

"I've been doing that since high school."

"Eighth grade," he laughed, "that's not what he means."

"He thinks I'm an immoral woman?"

"That's one way of putting it. . . . Don't worry, I'll move out of the house and turn him off."

"He'll haunt us all through our marriage."

"I won't permit that."

Tommy couldn't prevent his brother from intervening at every major event in our life together. However, he did fight him off every time.

Father Tony behaved badly at the wedding rehearsal and at the wedding itself.

Monsignor Raven, the pastor emeritus of St. Agedius and the man who had presided over my parents' marriage, was supervising the rehearsal—which meant we were doing what Rosie and I wanted, which he cheerfully acknowledged was true. It was a wonderful nostalgic interlude until Father Tony arrived, rushing in from the back of the church.

"I'm sorry I'm late, Father," he said briskly, "Rush-hour traffic on the Eisenhower. Thanks for the help. I suppose the bride's family couldn't wait. I'll take over now."

I stopped breathing. Rosie, Aunt Peg, my two sisters, my cousin Rita (née Margaret Mary) looked liked they were prepared to riot.

My father intervened.

"Ambassador O'Malley, Father," he shook hands with Father Tony. "It's the custom here at St. Agedius that one of the parish staff does the rehearsals to make certain that all the liturgical regulations of the parish are observed."

There were no liturgical regulations for marriages at St. Agedius. Chucky is truly awesome when he puts on this ambassador face. Rosie spoiled it all by giggling.

After the rehearsal, Father Tony offered to hear the confessions for the wedding party. Monsignor Raven suavely said that it was not the custom at St. Agedius to impose confessions on a wedding party. There ensued a discussion of how the various priests in our families would divide up the work.

My groom, head bowed, shoulders slumped, face agonized, said nothing.

"I am the groom's brother," Father Tony insisted, "I should do the whole ceremony."

"Father James O'Malley is the bride's brother, Father, and Father Ed O'Malley is her uncle. They both tried to reach you several times to discuss the matter. You did not return their calls. . . ."

He dismissed that with a wave of his hand.

"We have a very busy parish, Monsignor. I don't have much time."

"In your absence we decided that you should have the honor of doing the ceremony yourself while Jim will say the Mass and Ed will preach."

"I want to preach," Tony said firmly.

"We will do it as Monsignor suggested." My beloved, in a loud, clear, and confident voice ended the conversation.

I squeezed his arm in support.

No rehearsal dinner was scheduled because the groom's parents "could not afford it."

Chucky announced that he had told the cooks over at the club to put on a few extra hot dogs, so if anyone wanted to have a bite they should come along. Everyone did except the groom's parents and brother.

"He's my brother," Tommy apologized, "my big brother. He feels he has to be in charge."

"I understand, my love, but you're really the big brother."

"I'll really be in charge in our new family," he hugged me, "subject of course to the rules the queen consort lays down."

"Naturally."

The Catholic wedding ceremony actually has three vows. The priest asks the bride and the groom separately for their consent, then they both repeat their vows, then they exchange rings with yet another promise. The Church apparently wants everyone to understand what has happened.

So Father Tony asked me if I Mary O'Malley took Thomas Moran to be my lawful wedded husband. I said yes in a loud and strong and very determined voice. Then, he asked me to repeat my vow after him, "I Mary take you Thomas . . ."

"I Mary Margaret take you Thomas . . ."

My husband, fortunately for all of us, called me by my proper name in both his vow and the exchange of rings.

"He just doesn't notice," he whispered to me when Jimmy continued the Mass. "All people will remember is your uncle's wonderful sermon."

Uncle Ed had preached about the bride and groom at the marriage feast of Cana consummating their love while Jesus was changing water into wine, lest their party be a failure. I couldn't see Father Tony's face, but I was betting he was shocked about a hint that penis was entering vagina while a miracle was happening.

But it was not true that no one would remember the contretemps between me and Father Tony. Every woman in my family would remember it in every last detail. The Irish never forget affronts at weddings and wakes.

At the wedding, Chucky, the Master of Ceremonies by acclimation, toasted us with the comment, "Every father thinks that no one is good enough to take over his daughter's life. Tommy you are more than good enough. God bless you both."

Joe McDermott, a big, blond, power forward of a man, one of our classmates from Loyola, toasted the groom in a few short sentences of which all I can remember was that we would have a wonderful family life, with cross examinations every night at supper.

We had insisted that the toasts should be brief.

Then my husband toasted me with a sonnet he had written. Modesty prevents me from repeating it, though, mind you, every word was true.

Chucky, as I've called my father since I learned to talk, was about to announce the end of talks. Father Tony took the mike away from him.

"I'm the brother of the groom," he began genially. "I want to say a few words by way of a toast to my little brother."

My poor husband cringed next to me. I put my arm around him and held him tight. I prayed that the Crazy O'Malley clan would restrain their fury. Rosie and Aunt Peg were two jungle animals waiting to pounce.

For ten minutes Tony preached about St. Paul and the relationship between men and women, the complementarities between men and women, the father's role as head of the family and the woman's as the heart. The woman could not be an effective heart unless her husband was firm in his role as the head. The husband must at all times be firm with his wife and children, though lovingly firm. These two roles were part of God's design. Tom must remember that the reason there were so many divorces these days was that husbands had abandoned their obligations to exercise authority in the family because of the pressures of radical feminism. Etc. Etc.

Etc.

It was pure patriarchalism, absolute and undefiled. Whatever they may have thought, there wasn't a husband at the dinner who didn't know that it was a pipe dream.

Finally he shut up.

I realized that I had to do something or someone in the family would grab the mike. So I did.

"There is one more toast," I began, "from the bride to the groom."

My remarks had not been scheduled because I feared I would end up sobbing or laughing hysterically. Well, I wasn't going to sob now.

"First I want to assure Father Moran that I accept completely his prescription for a happy marriage. I will confine myself to decisions about the small matters and leave to him decisions about the important ones. I'll decide where we will live, the names of our children, how many we will have, our career plans, the kind of home we will have, where our kids will go to school, where we will go on vacations. And you, Tommy dear, can make the major decisions: our stand on tax reform, Social Security, the cold war, our relations with England, and how we will vote in elections, so long as it's for the Democrats."

Laughter from everyone except Tommy's brother and mother and father.

"Tommy, my groom, my husband, by beloved, my true love, my wonderful bed-partner-to-be, I was twelve when I fell in love with you. I have not changed my mind since then and I never will. Rosie told me that I was too young to make such a choice and then admitted that she made a similar one when she was ten. I asked her if she ever had any regrets. She just laughed and said certainly not. I won't have any regrets, either, Tommy love. As long as God gives me life, Tommy dearest, I will stand by you and support you and be faithful to you and hold you in my arms every night we are together. With the help of God I will never go away and I will never let you go. I will love you and be your love always and forever and even after that."

Tommy stood up and absorbed me into his arms and we lost ourselves in a passionate kiss.

Everyone stood up and applauded. Except Tommy's family.

We didn't have the money for an elaborate honeymoon. So we went up to my parents' house at Grand Beach to consummate our marriage on the same bed where they had consummated theirs.

"Eventually, dear, when Chucky sobered up."

I had packed a bottle of Bushmill's Green in my suitcase, because everyone knew that I was something less than a strong hitter when that was present. I poured a glass for each of us after we had undressed and we drank a toast to each other. A glass of it on the dresser at night has always been one of our little hints.

One that we haven't used in a long time.

Perfectionist that I was (and am) I was determined to be the perfect lover on our wedding night. I wasn't, but neither was Tommy. We bumbled and stumbled around—which might have been a paradigm for our marriage—but we laughed at ourselves and had fun—another paradigm.

We don't laugh much any more.

CHAPTER 6

✝

GENERAL ROLFSON," I said to the commandant of the Air Force, "we have at least one thing in common. We both have three daughters of roughly the same age, do we not?"

The youthful looking four-star general with closely cropped hair and darting, angry, eyes regarded me with undisguised suspicion and distrust, an enemy agent who had violated the security of the command compound. The chairman of the subcommittee—Senator Samuel Houston Crawford of Texas—had sung his praise about the reforms at the Academy in Colorado Springs. Sam claimed to have been a jet pilot. In fact, he had washed out in training and served in the logistics department or whatever they called it. I was not about to use this information in the current context, however. If I did that I would have broken all my own rules.

"If you say so, sir," he replied.

"Would you recommend that any of them should seek an appointment to the Air Force Academy?"

"No, sir, I would not."

He had told the truth which in the present context for him was a mistake.

"May I ask why not?"

The junior officer next to him whispered in this ear.

"I must distinguish in my response to your question, Senator, between my feelings as an officer in the United States Air Force and my feelings as a father. As an officer I accept the policy of the government on sexual integration in the military. As a father, I have personal reservations about what would be proper for my own children."

"I see. You mean gender integration, don't you?"

He blushed and said in a tight voice, "Yes, of course, Senator. Thank you for the correction."

"I would share those reservations, General. I would not like to see any of my daughters at the controls of a jet fighter, as you were and as well as my distinguished friend from Texas."

"I still fly jets, Senator."

"For which I admire you greatly, General, though I will be excused, I trust, from imitating you . . . But could not young women serve well in, let us say, the logistical and supply components of the Air Force?"

I dared not look to see if the Senator from Texas had squirmed.

"Perhaps, I did not make myself clear, Senator. I support the policy of the American government but I personally do not believe that women belong in the military even when they are not in harm's way."

He was dead now, poor man. Whatever hope he had of being chairman of the joint chiefs had slipped away. Still he could retire on the salary of a four-star officer and work for some Texas oil company.

"Might I ask why, General?"

"I personally believe that the kind of men we need in the military are aggressive, dominant men, the only kind that can really fight wars. Women make it more difficult to sustain such an attitude."

"The Air Force wants warriors you mean?"

"You never served in the military, did you Senator?"

"I did not, General. But I remind you that the American tradition is that the military is under civilian control."

"I understand that, of course, Senator. The military needs fighting men, I'm sure you agree with that."

"Warriors?"

"If you wish to call them that."

"And in a warrior culture, women are more likely to be in danger of assault?"

"We will do everything we can to prevent that, sir. But it will almost certainly happen."

This exchange would make national television tonight. I felt sorry for the general, but more sorry for the victims of the culture of rape at the Academy.

"Warriors are more likely to rape women if they are available victims and warrior officers are more likely to wink at such attacks?"

"I didn't say that, sir. I said we would do everything we can to prevent such attacks. But women in the service should understand the dangers and not act provocatively."

"Women in a warrior culture sometimes seduce rapists?"

"You're putting those words in my mouth, Senator."

"Let us think a moment, General, about a company like, let us say Microsoft. Why are they not troubled by the emergence of a rape culture?"

"Because they hire different kind of men, Senator."

"Not the kind of men you need to fight a war? A little less savage perhaps?"

"The senator's time has expired," said Sam Houston, whose adulteries were notorious in the Senate.

"I thank the senator. I also thank General Rolfson for his candor. American parents will understand better the risks of a daughter enrolling at any service academy."

I sank back in my plush chair, sick to my stomach. I had destroyed a man's career and his reputation and warned people that the military culture as it currently existed tolerated a "boys will be boys" attitude about rape. That culture could change eventually, but not in the present culture of the United States Senate.

Robbie who was sitting behind me leaned over and whispered, "Will you talk to the media afterwards?"

Her perfume was enticing.

"I don't have much choice do I?"

"Are you proud of what you did to General Roflson, Senator?' the first question from the media.

"It is the duty of the committee to oversee the armed services. I ask questions with that duty in view."

"You seemed to suggest that rape is encouraged in the current culture of the military?"

"Suggest? I said it outright."

"You think this cannot be changed?"

"The difference between General Rolfson and me is not over whether we want our daughters at the Air Force Academy. Neither of us do and for the same reasons. The difference is whether we believe that some warriors are necessarily rapists. However strong the sexual urges of young males might be, I believe that a society has the duty to impose sanctions that prevent them from attacking women."

I returned to my office deeply discouraged. Our pension bill would languish in the house. Rape would continue to be commonplace in the military. I was wasting my time. Our struggle to defend private property from Wal-Mart big boxes had a chance, but why did it all have to be so difficult?

Some of my colleagues were drifting back into the office building after their return from their constituencies and families. I envied them. I didn't belong here. Maybe my brother was right. No, certainly he was right.

The headline in the *Examiner* the next day said it all.

TOMMY ATTACKS WAR HERO

CHAPTER 7

†

MARY ROSE joined us the day after I took my bar exam. I was twenty-four years old. Markam, Kean and Howe agreed that I didn't have to begin working till after Christmas. Tommy, who also passed the exam, started to work at the public defenders office. Our future looked bright and complicated, but the complications didn't seem insurmountable then. In fact, they were both brighter and far more complicated than we could imagine. Our tiny little redhead was bright and sweet and cute. We both adored her. She adored us. And, bless her little heart, she slept at night.

We were still deeply in love with one another, well matched and alert to the problems our two careers would cause. Or so we thought. Tommy was unfailingly patient with my enthusiasms and at the same time grateful for them. We were fine until his brother came around to hector and harass us. He had already become, so it seemed, an important person in his order, traveling back and forth from Rome and around the world to tend to its affairs. His parents had become reconciled to us when I announced my pregnancy and especially when they had their first peek at our little charmer. We postponed her Baptism until after the first of the year so that Father Tony could pour the water after his return from an "important inspection of the African mission." He favored us—or more precisely me—with a sermon about risking an eternity in limbo for the little girl because I didn't love her enough to bring her over to Church.

"Do you really believe in limbo, Father Anthony?" I asked. "St. Augustine cheerfully assigned unbaptized babies to hell."

This was a quote from my priestly brother Ed, who warned me that the Clementines were a particularly old-fashioned order.

"You shouldn't take chances, Mary," he insisted.

"I can't believe that God's love would be constrained by my irresponsibility."

I was now in a mode where I argued with him all the time. It wouldn't change his mind because, as my husband said, he was basically clueless. But it made me feel good.

"You shouldn't take chances," he replied, "not with people's immortal souls."

"Next time we won't wait till you return from Africa."

He ignored me but lectured us for fifteen minutes about the terrible conditions in Africa, utterly unaware that Rosie and Chuck had produced a book of photographs and essays about Africa.

He then insisted that Rose was not a "saint's name."

"Don't we call Mary 'Mystical Rose' in the litany?" I asked.

Our little darling smiled happily as he drenched her with the Baptismal water. He addressed her as Mary, just as he did me on our wedding day. Nonetheless the Baptismal records at St. Agedius tell posterity that she is Mary Rose.

"I'll send you a book that my mother and father wrote about Africa, Father," I said when the ceremony was over and I was nestling my adored child in my arms.

He ignored me. I sent him the book. He never acknowledged it. Naturally.

"I wish you wouldn't argue with my brother, Mary Margaret," Tommy said to me later after we had put the wonder child down for the night. "I know he's all wrong but he means well."

"He still has a stranglehold on you, Tommy dear."

"Only when he's around."

That was true enough. Tommy continued to live his own life and loved me far more than he loved his brother. Yet he suffered terribly during incidents like the one that afternoon. I realized that his brother would be with us for the rest of our lives and that was part of the package into which I had bought.

"I shouldn't have taken him on. I'll try not to do it again. But he is such an asshole."

I do not use such language. Never. I have banned it, along with fuck, shit, screw, and other inappropriate words from our home. Yet I had said it.

Tommy laughed, delighted that I had fallen from grace.

Our two more clones—Mary Ann and Mary Therese—arrived when I was twenty-six and twenty-eight. They were sweethearts too, though somewhat more rambunctious than their big sister. I promptly plunged into a spectacular postpartum depression after Marytre.

Markam, Kean had decided early on that I was a gold mine for income-producing billable hours, which is why law firms exist. Even though I was young and pregnant and allegedly sexy, I was very good at appellate work in both the state and federal courts. In such a context I did not have to convince juries but only judges. The arguments were with very smart lawyers, though as one of my senior colleagues said, "Few are as smart as you are, Mary Margaret, and none as charming."

I was very excited when I told Tommy that in the evening.

"Haven't I been telling you that all along?"

In the early stages of my pregnancy with Mary Therese I pleaded before the United States Supreme court—mostly an unimpressive group of narcissists, it seemed to me—and actually won a partial victory.

"Not bad for a peasant kid from the West Side of Chicago," Tommy said, as he hugged me. Struggling with the impossible job of public defender at 26th and California, he wasn't getting much emotional satisfaction. Yet it was his vocation as much as his brother's to the priesthood. At least for a time. Yet he was a rock of stability for our marriage.

It was his idea that we accept the loan my parents offered for us to buy a home in River Forest, which we could pay off at little more cost than the rent for our now crowded apartment in Rogers Park.

"I know you have this principle about being independent," he said. "But you also have one about keeping your parents happy. Besides, we want our kids to go to the same school we went to."

He was very skillful at manipulating my principles. But, as I have said, he was a very smart lawyer, even if his billable rate was not as high as mine.

He also installed a small gym in the basement of our Dutch Colonial home on Lathrop Avenue and decreed rules on how often we must both use the equipment.

We were faced with career decisions of the sort that so many families with two professionals face. Markam, Kean wanted me back. I was a cash cow, though they were careful not to use that term, even if I wasn't always around or occasionally brought a small redhead into the office to nurse. The money would be nice but I didn't want to leave my children with a baby-sitter or a nanny during these precious years.

"That's no problem at all," Tommy said. "I'll be the househusband."

"TOMMY! That's absurd."

"No, it's not. Your daughters will bond with their father and we'll all have a wonderful time, living off your income. And I'll be able to finish my book about the decline of civility in American politics."

"You'll be the laughingstock of the Chicago bar."

"And that will bother me a lot!"

"I know it won't, but . . ."

"But nothing!"

"And it will drive your brother crazy."

"Too bad for him . . . I have had it with 26th and California. Daugherty and Klein will take me on as an 'of counsel.' I'll help out on cases

I can analyze at home, maybe make an occasional court appearance, mostly talk settlement with opposing lawyers from home."

"And take care of the kids and write a book."

"No big deal."

"You want to steal my daughters from me."

"You've got it . . . but seriously, by the time mommy comes home in the evening they'll be so fed up with daddy that they'll love mommy even more."

He was right again. It was our solution, not one I'd recommend for anyone else, but then I don't recommend anything for anyone else. It's against my principles.

He was also right when he agreed that we should spend a month in Mexico every summer. It would be a wonderful education experience for them and for us. Learn a different language, be part of a different culture. Right?

It was mostly my idea because I had powerful if hazy memories of West Germany when I was a little girl and Chucky had been Jack Kennedy's ambassador there.

It would mean limiting our trips to Grand Beach, so much of my life when I was growing up, to an occasional weekend. But Chucky and Rosie, much to my surprise, insisted it was a wonderful idea. I was still dubious. How would our pale white gringa daughters with the brilliant crimson hair fit in with kids their age in a professional-class neighborhood in Hermosillo? However, I didn't realize even then that our kids were adventurers, a band of explorers. They loved the shy, sweet Mexican girls their own age who came over to our bungalow to welcome them. They delighted in new places and new people and traveled as a gang of three, leaving behind all the spats that kids, especially girl kids, have with one another. This experience would pay dividends in years to come.

And Tommy and I were still deeply in love, unshakeable, unassailable love, or so we thought.

A case rolled up on Tommy's desk in River Forest that changed our lives. It made him famous, well, a celebrity anyway in Chicago. He had to leave the house only twice, and Rosie was of course all too ready to spend the time with her granddaughters.

The case was a particularly nasty murder in Lake County, north of Chicago. The daughter of a very rich family had been beaten, raped and murdered, as was her eight-year-old daughter. The heads of both victims had been blown off with a shotgun. The husband, a somewhat unsuccessful investment broker, a dark-skinned Italian from Brooklyn, was an instant suspect. The cops, responding to the calls of neighbors who heard the shotgun blasts, found him wandering around the house in a daze, his hands covered with blood, clutching the shotgun. After twelve hours of questioning by the local police, he confessed both the murder and the rape. His arraignment was the kind of scene the media loved, the suspect sobbing hysterically, the victim's mother and father shouting curses at him and demanding instant justice to the TV cameras. Given what TV viewers apparently want to see, the story began the evening news every night for ten days.

The firm sent the papers in the case out to my house hubby.

"Notice anything in the evidence?" he asked me.

"Offhand, no DNA evidence. Surely the cops are not that dumb up there?"

"Precisely."

"They must have a semen sample somewhere."

"I called them and told them that I was acting for the defendant and asked if they could provide any data on the DNA. They said that they sent it off to a lab, but didn't have any report yet. They felt with the confession they didn't need it."

"Maybe they are that dumb . . . What are you going to do?"

"I'm going to call them twice more and then I'll go into court and ask for an order to send it to an impartial lab."

"What if it's not his?"

"We will demand that the court order his release from prison and file a civil suit against the cops and the prosecutor."

That's exactly what we did.

And he was on the ten o'clock news that night, thankfully after the redhead brood were sound asleep.

My husband is a very photogenic, clean cut, wavy haired little Mick with a bright smile and evident intelligence. He also speaks English and not lawyer or cop talk.

"I told the court that we found it strange that the DNA from the victims had not been tested and asked the judge to order that it be sent to an independent lab for testing."

"What good would that do, Mr. Moran?"

"If I were the State's Attorney I would want that nailed down in case the defense asked during the trial."

"Do you have any reason to expect that someone else might have committed the murders?"

"I just want to be sure."

"Did the judge grant the motion?"

"She took it under advisement."

"Do you expect that she will rule in your favor."

"I certainly hope so."

"Good, Tommy," I exclaimed. "You're great on camera."

"Only on camera?"

"All the time! Do you have any hints that there is another man?"

"Our private eyes have dug up the dirt that she may have had a fling with a doctor from a local community hospital, a somewhat mercurial and unstable person."

The judge turned down the appeal. Tommy's partners went into the state appellate court on an emergency basis and demanded an immediate order, which of course they got. The DNA found on both victims was not the same as that of the defendant.

My brilliant house hubby immediately made his second trip to Lake County and demanded that he be released. The State's Attorney argued that there was still the defendant's confession.

Tommy repeated for the cameras after the hearing what he had said in response, in the calm, measured tones I knew so well.

I could develop a crush on that man, I told myself.

"It is not unknown, your honor, for people to confess a crime they have not committed after twelve hours of police interrogation. I suggest to you that there is a dangerous murderer out there whose brutality makes him a threat to the community. The police and the States Attorney have failed their responsibility to the public. As for my client, patently he is innocent."

"Do you think she will rule in your client's favor?"

"If she doesn't, she'll face another possible reversal in the appellate court."

She ruled in Tommy's favor of course and, changing her tactics, denounced the incompetence of the police and the State's attorney. The victim's mother assaulted the defendant as he left the court a free man and then turned her attention to Tommy, giving him a black eye.

"I sympathize with the poor woman," he said. "But grief doesn't justify assault and battery."

"Will you file charges or sue, Tommy?"

Already they are calling my poor husband Tommy! The hussies.

I put another pack on his eye and offered him a glass of Bushmill's.

The mother's lawyer offered an apology which Tommy's firm accepted.

Tommy was too good on camera for the media to forget. They tripped out to our house twice more—when the doctor was arrested and later when he was convicted. His comments were the same.

"All I can say is that I am happy that an innocent man was not convicted. This ought to be a warning to everyone how dangerous is a hasty search for a criminal, especially when your cameras are watching every move." The kids were immensely proud of their father, especially because they had an answer now to the little bitches—a word I also forbid—who teased them that their mommy worked at an office but their daddy didn't.

Shortly after that case, both of Tommy's parents died, his mother first from a massive stroke, his father a month later from a heart attack, a broken heart Tommy had said. They were both in their early seventies, not all that old these days, but in poor health for a long time. They were shy, quiet, respectable people, the sort that almost never married. But the sting of passion had caught them at the outer limits of fertility. They produced Tony less than a year after they were married and my Tommy five years later. They were great readers, a habit Tommy had acquired very young in life. His father taught history, his mother math. Tommy told me after we had buried him that his father had worked for thirty years on a history of the Irish in America which he had burned the day we buried his mother.

"He wouldn't let anyone read it. He was afraid they would ridicule it. I read a few pages once. It was brilliant."

Father Tony was a whirling dervish during the first wake and funeral. Everything had to be perfect, the way his parents would want it—the flowers at the wake, the prayers, the liturgical details, the music. He could not eat or sleep. He had to drive himself half mad making sure his mother had the funeral she deserved. He moved his poor father around like he was part of the scenery. He said the Mass of course, but asked one of his fellow Clementines—"The best preacher in this country"—to give the homily. It was high-flown, abstract, and meaningless, a success as a homily only if you were into a rich, sonorous, and sanctimonious voice, as some of the Irish are.

My family are heavy into making wakes and funerals. Father Tony barely spoke to them at the wake and at the cemetery.

He was a different man after his father's death, a pale ghost of what he had been at the first funeral, quiet, mournful, dependent.

"Thank you for being with us during these difficult times, Mary Margaret," he said to me at the cemetery as he held both my hands. "They loved you and your beautiful daughters very much. They were never demonstrative, but they did admire your courage and your generosity."

"Uncle Tony was different this time," Mary Ann whispered to me. "Like he kind of loved us."

"I'm sure he always had, hon."

She nodded, still puzzled.

"I've never seen him like that," Tommy said later on. "I wish he were that way all the time."

I thought to myself that the energizer bunny was much nicer when his batteries ran down. I hoped the change would last but it didn't, especially when we turned to the next phase of our life.

CHAPTER 8

✝

Tᴀᴛ ᴀᴜᴛᴜᴍɴ and winter was a tumultuous one for our family. Everything happened, almost all at once it seemed. Even when I try to play the tape in my memory of those months it seems to turn into fast-forward. Tommy's success in freeing an innocent man and then filing a suit against the Lake County police and States Attorney made him a public figure, one with powerful television charisma—his fifteen minutes of fame, I told him, though I was enormously proud of him. Then the *Atlantic Monthly* published a segment from his book *Attack Politics: The End of Civility.* The publisher immediately increased his advance from ten thousand to a hundred thousand dollars, for fear another publisher might try to seduce him to back off from a contract that seemed to me to be almost unenforceable. Poor dolts, they never realized that my Tommy would never do anything like that.

The book was mostly history, Tommy's favorite subject. I often told him that he should go back to school and earn a doctorate. I'd be glad to support him. He said it was more fun to do history his way, which was certainly true. The last couple of chapters, however, talked about attack methods in contemporary American politics. He argued that the deliberate destruction of an opponent in American political life was a dangerous threat to our society, both because such a strategy was far more effective in an age of television and, worse, created a polarization which had never existed before. The people of the country, he argued from surveys, were pragmatic. However, the activity of well-organized and well-funded interest groups polarized politics. The result was that politics had become more vicious, and dislike and distrust for politics and politicians was increasing dramatically. Precisely because of the power of the media, including the Internet, attack politics was much more destructive to the fabric of the body politic than it had ever been before.

I'm prejudiced, but I think he made a very strong case.

"Be careful, Tommy love, your fifteen minutes of fame may last for a half hour."

A couple of our neighbors, more active in politics than either of us were, visited us one night in early November to suggest that Tommy make a run for the State Legislature next November. They were eager to turn the district around. Demographics, they assured us, had already made it a Democratic district. He should try out his tactics—never attack his opponent and never ask anyone for money. In such a race, you didn't need much money anyway but they'd raise whatever we needed.

Tommy looked at me. I shrugged my shoulders.

"We'll think about it," he said, "and call you tomorrow."

"Well, you didn't say no."

"Well?" he said to me.

"Tommy, one of my colleagues who served in the legislature says that Springfield is like Ash Wednesday all year long."

"I won't win."

"I'm not so sure. You have TV charisma."

"Yeah, but who sees local candidates on TV?"

"True enough . . . Still it's a chance to test your theories."

"And maybe prove them wrong."

"In this country, Tommy love, nothing succeeds like failure with the possible exception of martyrdom. If you want to do it, I'll support you totally."

We consulted the children. They thought it was no big deal.

"Can we travel with you?"

"Sometimes."

"Will Daddy be on television a lot? He's really cute!"

"Will we meet a lot of Latinos?"

"You bet."

That was that. They were adventurers.

Joe McDermott, our friend from Loyola years and Tommy's best man, signed himself on as our legal counsel. He was still the big blond power forward, even if he had put on a couple of pounds. He always cleared his throat before making one of his solemn high pronouncements. He treated me with courtly respect to which my madcap laughter often did not entitle me.

Pro bono he insisted. We were to announce our candidacy at the Unity Temple, Frank Lloyd Wright's famous church in Oak Park. Good Catholics that we were we'd never been in it before. It was a kind of creepy place.

It was the week before Thanksgiving and almost a year before the election. The primary in Illinois is in March, eight months before the election. That makes for an absurdly long campaign. We would probably not have any primary opposition, so we would not have to start active campaigning till June, still a long time.

Joe had all five TV channels there for the announcement. My friends from the neighborhood had assembled a little crowd of supporters.

Tommy was his usual adorable self—relaxed, gracious, charming. Just a nice looking young Mick with a red-haired wife and three adorable little girls. Then when he began to talk, without a podium and without a script he became magical—a decent man, with candor and integrity and honesty.

I'm announcing my candidacy for the General Assembly from the 14th district. My wife and three children are my only supporters and the kids can't vote—though if we move back into Chicago, maybe they could.

I'm making three promises today that I will keep throughout the campaign.

I will never permit a negative ad against my opponent. Attack ads which harm the candidates and their families are an evil which will disappear from American society only when enough candidates solemnly pledge never to use them, even if that pledge means losing an election.

I will never ask anyone for a financial contribution. My friend Joseph McDermott will preside over campaign finance. He will never ask for money either. Nor will he tell me who has contributed and who has not. Only when enough candidates adopt these rules will the pernicious effect of money on elections be eliminated.

Finally, I promise to make no campaign promises. In our country only a majority of a legislative body can deliver on a promise. I can promise no more than that I will work for better schools, better public transportation, better housing for the poor, fair treatment for immigrants and respect for the environment. I certainly am a Democrat and in some respects a liberal Democrat though not in every respect. I look forward to an interesting campaign.

There was absolute silence for a moment. Everyone seemed to sense that something new had happened. The kids led the applause.

"Any questions?"

The reporters asked the usual questions we might have expected—property taxes, public schools, pension reform, the influence of the Catholic Church.

To the last he replied, "My brother is a priest, my wife's brother is a priest, and her uncle is a monsignor. On both sides we've been Catholic since before St. Patrick. I have learned two things from the tradition of Catholic social teaching. The first is that we must be on the side of the poor and the needy and the oppressed. The second is that we accomplish social change by cooperation, not conflict. Neither position is incompatible with being a Democrat, not in Cook County anyway."

That broke it up.

Tommy watched as the media left, his eyes seeing something far away.

"Tremendous," Joe McDermott said shaking his hand. "You wowed them. Some of that will be on all the channels tonight. . . . Wasn't he great, Mary Margaret?"

I was also staring at something far away. I couldn't make out what it was, however.

"I think I just saw my husband crossing a river," I said.

"The Des Plaines?"

"I think they call it the Rubicon."

We shook hands with the people and thanked them for coming. The daughters joined us and they thanked the people too. Like I say, adventurers. Joe passed out petitions to get Tommy's name on the ballot for the primary.

"You were magical, Tommy," I said.

"Don't look at me with those shining eyes, woman," he said with a suggestive wink.

We met Rosie and Chuck at their favorite ice cream parlor on Chicago Avenue and celebrated with sodas and sundaes and malts.

Tommy watched me very carefully during our courtship, his eyes probing me, studying me, analyzing me. I didn't pay much attention. I thought he was just admiring me or maybe, as time went on, desiring me. I didn't understand that he was figuring me out, gauging my responses, exploring my moods, checking out my quirks. By the time we were married I had become pretty transparent to him. Then he turned the same search light on my sexuality, though he had already guessed that beneath all the crisp authority and strong opinions I was a deeply sensuous person, despite my modesty. It didn't take me long to realize that he had scoped me out and that I was in every respect naked to him. At first I didn't like that at all. Women weren't supposed to be that way with men. You lost control if you let that happen. Married women my age often discussed how you could keep your husband dangling—as though it was a woman's right and duty to do so. How could you be real power in your family if you couldn't do that? You control men by rationing sex, right?

I didn't like that strategy because I loved my husband and besides I was determined to be the perfect married lover just like I was the perfect daughter and the perfect student and the perfect tennis player and the perfect lawyer. So I read all the books about sexual techniques and was not, I must confess, turned on by them. So I was a perfect target for Tommy's careful study of me, a pushover sexually. Sometimes all he had to do was look at me with a certain faintly sinister smile and I lost all my modesty and all my ability to resist. A voice inside me suggested that I was nothing but a whore. But he was my husband and I loved him. I spoke to none of my friends about this problem—if it was indeed a problem. I asked Rosie what she thought—in an indirect and round-about way.

She laughed and said, "Hon, a lot of men and women play silly games about wanting and refusing sex. It's all foolish nonsense."

So I guess I went with the flow and began to enjoy my vulnerability to my husband, whom, like I say, I love deeply.

That night after he had announced his venture into politics, he used one insidious little trick that he knows turns me on quickly. In one continuous movement, he unzips my dress, unhooks by bra, and slips his fingers under the elastic of my pants. As my clothes fall away I change from the cool, cerebral, high powered lawyer into an aroused, groaning wife desperate for her husband. I don't know why this trick works so quickly—and so effectively. It must be some deep twist inside me. I like being in disarray, almost naked yet with my clothes still clinging precariously to my body. All the time Tommy is laughing at me, reveling in what a pushover I am. Sometimes he just has to touch the zipper and I collapse. He is so damn proud of himself that I am furious. No man has a right to do that to a woman. However, sometimes I laugh too. In fact always. Of course I have to wear a dress with a zipper for it to begin. It used to be that we'd both laugh a lot during our love-making.

It doesn't work any more. Or rather we don't do it any more. The Beltway or the Senate or something had put out the fire.

Our love-making that night, ages ago, was gentle and peaceful and wonderful. I say this because I want to make it clear that I was committed to wherever he might go across the river, no matter what happened.

"I'll never second guess you, Tommy," I said as we relaxed after our romp. "Never."

"I might second guess myself," he laughed and kissed me again.

We had not even bothered to watch the news that evening.

Joe called us the next morning. "You guys were wonderful. It was a major coup. You won the election last night."

My colleagues at work complimented me.

"Your husband is pure charisma," said the managing partner. "Can we sign him on?"

"Nepotism," I said, bantering with him.

"We could bend the rules."

"I think I can forget that."

A couple of our women partners praised the kids and assured me that they would move to the West Side so they could vote for Tommy.

"He really is cute!"

"Funny, I'd noticed that . . . He's good in bed too."

We didn't hear a word from Father Tony. Apparently he hadn't noticed that his brother was running for the General Assembly. I sighed with relief.

The day after Thanksgiving, Joe called us again. He asked Tommy to put me on the phone.

"You guys didn't go away for Thanksgiving?"

"Just to Grand Beach for the O'Malley Family bash."

"You'll be around tomorrow?"

"Sure."

"There's some people who want to talk to you. They'll come out tomorrow night. Very important people."

"Good people?" I said uneasily.

"Sure. Very good people. They want to ask you something. I'm not going to advise you on how to respond."

"We both like secrets," Tommy said.

There were three of them. We recognized them at once. Major powers in Illinois politics. The kids were upstairs at their homework.

We offered them a drink or a cup of tea. They declined. They were eager to get down to business.

"We noticed your television appearance the other day," the woman said.

"We were impressed," one of the men added, "both by what you said and the way you said it."

"We think we can beat Rodgers Crispjin next year," the third man said.

"And we think," the woman finished the pitch, "that you're the man to do it."

"Your approach to politics is new and different."

"And long overdue."

"Crispjin is a pompous phony and the people are beginning to see it."

"It won't be easy, but it can be done."

"The mayor?" I asked.

"The mayor has a policy of not intervening in a primary. But he'll pass the word that he thinks you're a winner—he really believes that. Then in the general election he'll back you strongly. You'll have no more than token opposition in the primary. Neither will H. Rodgers. The trick will be for you to get more primary votes than he does. That will make you a valid contender."

"I'd probably lose," Tommy said.

"Probably," said the woman. "But you might win."

"We can raise money for you. We'll do it your way. Who will be your chair?"

"Ambassador O'Malley?" he said, raising an eyebrow in my direction.

"He'd love it!"

"The race here in this district?"

"We'll talk to them and get them a candidate that will be a winner. They won't want to stand in your way."

"We'll give you a couple of days to think it over, not too many because we have to collect the petitions."

"I don't think we need to think it over, do we, Mary Margaret?"

"No, Tommy, we don't."

"We'll go for it," he told our guests. "Sounds like fun."

They were astonished. We were supposed to argue, they were supposed to win us over. Were we just a little crazy? We sure were.

"No promises that we'll win," I said.

The woman nodded.

"I have a strong hunch that you will."

They left as quietly as they had come.

"Did we really do that?" Tommy asked me

"I can't believe we did."

"Neither did our guests."

"I agree with what you said, Tommy. We'll probably lose."

"Yeah, but what if we win?"

"We can worry about it then. . . . We'd better go upstairs and tell the kids."

They were delighted.

"Someone has to straighten out the mess in Washington," said Mary Rose.

"We'll campaign with you," Mary Ann said firmly.

"Will we win?" Mary Therese wondered.

"Of course we will," I said confidently.

"Drat it woman, no zipper tonight!" he said when we entered the bedroom.

"That's never stopped you before."

The next day the *Examiner* had the first of many headlines.

House Hubby to Challenge Crispjin

Strategists for veteran Senator H. Rodgers Crispjin visibly relaxed yesterday when they learned that the best the Democrats could do to challenge the Senator's reelection bid was to choose an obscure suburban lawyer, Tommy Moran. For the last several years Tommy has been a househusband while his wife, hotshot lawyer Mary O'Malley, earned big legal bucks for the family. "If that's the best the Democrat party can do," said a close ally of the distinguished Senator from Illinois, "they are really bankrupt. We'll run the usual vigorous race of course, but we have no doubts about the outcome."

CHAPTER 9

✝

O UR FIRST STEP in assembling a staff was to meet with another
Loyola classmate, Dick Sanchez, or Ricardo Sanchez as he called
himself when he was being seriously Latino. Ricardo was of medium
height, taller than Tommy of course, with a pencil-thin mustache, and
a smile which revealed perfect, if reconstructed, teeth. A River Forest
dweller with kids about the ages of our own who also attended St.
Luke's school, he was movie-star handsome with bedroom brown eyes.
He reminded me of the various characters that played the Cisco Kid.
Indeed I called him Cisco that night when we were sitting in Doc
Ryan's bar on Madison Street in Forest Park.

"OK," he said, "everyone knows that Rodge Crispjin is a phony.
He's tall and handsome with his snow white hair. He looks like a Senator, but he's as lazy as sin and he's in the tank with Bobby Bill Roads
and his crowd of hypocrites from Oklahoma and sleeps with every lus-
cious woman he can get his hands on. He hasn't introduced any major
legislation during his term in Congress and doesn't have much influence. His down-state accent is phony. He's a public relations bubble
that is waiting for someone to burst."

"Ric," Tommy said, going into Spanish, "here's a map of Illinois
counties with the greatest proportion of Hispanics. Those are census
figures, so we figure they represent mostly legals."

"We believe," I continued also in Spanish, "that this is the time to mobilize the Mexican voters in the state. They belong in the Democratic party."

"You guys are really good," Ric said in English. "Tommy, a person can tell that you're a gringo, but one that knows the language well. Mary Margaret, when you go into Spanish, you become Mexican—the eyes, the gestures, the facial expressions, the body movements. Sonoran accent of course, but there's nothing wrong with that."

"Hermosillo, Cisco," I said. "The kids are really good at it."

"That should be a big asset in the campaign."

"We want you to take charge of our Hispanic campaign," Tommy continued. "Help us to mobilize the Mexican-American votes."

"The HDO has that sewed up."

"Only in Chicago, not even Suburban Cook, where your folks are all over the place," I argued. "To say nothing of Dupage. We think we can carry Dupage for the first time in any election if all our amigos turn out."

"Lake too," Ric agreed. "We don't owe Rodgers Crispjin anything . . . What's in it for us?"

"Major political power in Illinois," Tommy continued the argument, "It's time, you know, long past time."

"And an ally in the United States Senate?"

"We Irish never forget a favor. I'd advocate immigration reform anyway, but with more sense of backing back home, if the Mexican-American voters put me there."

Ric shook his head.

"You two guys have always been magic. You'll bring excitement back to politics. I'll have to talk to Tina, but I know what she'll say. What do you want me to do?"

"Co-campaign manager with Joe McDermott."

"You have the whole Loyola Law School class. I bet you signed up Dolly McCormick too, smart, pretty Black woman."

"Chief of Staff and Press person."

"Wow! You guys move quickly."

"We don't have much money yet," I said. "The party says more will be coming in, but you know our ground rules. We'll pay you something even during the primary."

"The Ambassador is the chairman of the finance committee," Tommy added.

"Hell," Ric continued in English, "I'll do it pro bono. It will be fun."

"You'll need something for secretarial . . ."

"Tina would be furious if she were left out . . . this is going to be fun!"

"Chucky," I said, meaning my dad, "says that volunteers will swarm in."

"I'm sure he's right."

"Tommy has some money coming in from book royalties, we've put a second mortgage on the house. Lake County wants to settle our suit."

"You guys are incredible! We're going to win! . . . What will you be doing, Maria Margarita?"

"Scheduler, Cisco, adviser, morale."

"And person in charge, I bet! Tina's going to love this!"

"That was easy," I said as we drove back to our house.

"You know this Tina? What is she like?"

"Well organized, smart, dangerous! Tiny, very pretty, fire in her brown eyes."

We were silent for a few moments.

"We're getting in deep, Mary Margaret," he said, sounding a little dubious.

"There has to be one rule for us Tommy: We're having fun! A magical mystery tour!"

"Speaking of fun, I note, counselor, that you are wearing a dress with a zipper."

"I thought you might notice that."

That was only four years ago. We were so young.

We announced officially two weeks after we had agreed to run, in a small room at the Marriott on Michigan Avenue, already bright with Christmas decorations. The kids all wore red dresses and green ribbons.

The room was packed with media people and supporters, the room overflowing as we had hoped it would be.

Again my delicious husband had no notes and needed no podium.

This looks like it's getting to be a habit. I may have set a record for the number of times a man has announced his candidacy—twice in five weeks. I can guarantee I won't go for three.

I'm making the same three promises today that I will keep throughout the campaign.

I will never permit a negative ad against my opponent. Attack ads which harm the candidates and their families are an evil which will disappear from American society only when enough candidates solemnly pledge never to use them, even if that pledge means losing an election. No matter how many attack ads my opponent may level at me, I will, with the help of God, honor this pledge.

I will never ask anyone for a financial contribution. My father-in-law, Charles O'Malley, will preside over our campaign fund. He will never ask for money either. Nor will he tell me who has contributed and who has not. Only when enough candidates adopt these rules will the pernicious effect of money on elections be eliminated.

Finally, I promise to make no campaign promises. Politics in our system of government is necessarily a matter of forming coalitions and winning votes. Just now it is hard to win votes for the issues with which I am concerned—fair treatment for immigrants, restraining the power of Big Oil, Big Pharmacy, and Big Insurance, protection for the pensions of ordinary people, protection of private property from condemnation by greedy local authorities, an increase in the wages of ordinary Americans, a more equal distribution of tax burdens.

That's a big order. I can't guarantee how much progress I'll make on any of them, but I'll try.

Now let me introduce my staff. My friends Joe McDermott and Ricardo Sanchez will be co-campaign managers . . . Dolly Mc-Cormick will be Chief of Staff and Press spokesperson. My wife Mary Margaret will be scheduler and morale officer and tell me what to do. My daughters Mary Therese, Mary Ann, and Mary Rose will laugh at my jokes. We hope to add others as the campaign proceeds.

We can answer a few questions . . .

MEDIA: *The Chicago Examiner* says you are nothing but a house-husband.

MORAN: I enjoyed the role and am proud of it. I did manage to win a few cases from my home office—the Lake County false-arrest case for example.

MEDIA: Did you clear your candidacy with the Cardinal?

MORAN: No. That would have been presumptuous. I believe Mary Margaret's Uncle, Monsignor Ed O'Malley, informed him unofficially.

MEDIA: It is true, is it not that you support abortion?

MORAN: I believe that abortion is wrong. However, the law of the land guarantees a woman's right to an abortion. I am not going to try to take that away, not that a Senator has much chance to be involved with the issue.

MEDIA: Do you think the Church will bar you from the Sacrament?

MORAN: Not in Chicago. I would add that my concern with poverty, racial justice, the rights of immigrants is motivated by a long study of the Catholic Church's social teachings.

MEDIA: Is it true that you support the rights of illegal immigrants?'

MORAN: As I read the declaration of independence, all men, not just citizens, have certain inalienable rights. Illegal immigrants do not lose those rights. I would rather see a policy that enables them to migrate legally. Two things should be obvious—our society needs them and they do not take jobs away from other Americans as some people try to tell you. It is criminal how many of them die down in the deserts. We must stop them or we lose all right to be considered a humane people.

MORAN: Repeats the response in Spanish.

DOLLY: Last question

MEDIA: How much money do you have in your campaign fund now?

MORAN: Not much—as I said, we put a second mortgage on our house, I added the advance royalties from my book which comes out next year.

MEDIA: Senator Crispjin has ten million dollars in his fund.

MORAN: I don't think I'll catch up with him! . . . Now we have some entertainment for the season.

We assembled our little ad hoc mariachi group. Tina Sanchez and her daughter Consuela, it turned out could play the violin. My daughter and I had some guitar experience. We did a few hand-clapping Mexican Christmas carols. We were not yet very good—we'd improve with time, but we were never very good. It didn't matter. The kids stole the show.

"Senora," Tina Sanchez embraced me, "I am more a gringa than you are. Feliz Navidad!"

I don't think our debut worried the forces of Senator Crispjin much.

HOUSE HUBBY AND CLASSMATES PANDER
TO ILLEGALS

One-time househusband, Senatorial Candidate Tommy Moran and a group of his classmates from Loyola Law School pandered shamelessly to illegal immigrants yesterday. At the announcement of his candidacy yesterday, Tommy repeated the same themes that had marked his announcement a couple of weeks go for the General Assembly with an added boilerplate in defense of illegal immigrants, which he then translated into very poor Spanish. To top the day off a couple of musicians and some children (including the candidate's daughters) with very little talent sang Mexican Christmas carols.

Partisans of the veteran Senator H. Rodgers Crispjin ridiculed this pathetic performance.

"We'll bury that little fool," one of them said.

"Will the Senator debate him?"

"Don't be silly!"

On the morning of Christmas Eve, Father Tony showed up to reprimand Tommy. He stormed into our library room in the basement which had become our campaign headquarters. He ignored me and started right in.

"What's this nonsense about the Senate? I go to Australia for a few weeks and you make a fool out of yourself! How many times do I have to tell you that you shouldn't try to play with the big guys!"

"I was asked by leaders of the Democratic party . . ."

I had not before noted Tommy's reaction to his brother when Tony is in full fight—talking and not listening. My charming, articulate husband lowered his head, bowed his shoulders and acted like a puppy dog being reprimanded by this master for soiling the parlor carpet.

"You're a sacrificial victim. Do you think you have a chance against Senator Crispjin! He's a big man in Washington! And a good man too! He stands four-square against abortion!"

"We think we can beat him."

"Who's this 'we?' You and your wife and kids? Isn't it enough that you humiliate them by forcing them to sing in bad Spanish on television?"

"It's good Spanish . . ."

I wanted to fight then and there. But for once in my life I kept my big Irish mouth shut.

"Did you get the Cardinal's permission to run?"

"No . . ."

"He will have to deny you the sacraments!"

"He doesn't do that to people."

"All the other Illinois bishops will!"

He was pacing up and down, his eyes wild, his face flushed—more like a Pentecostal preacher than a member of a religious order which emphasizes the intellectual life.

"We hear they won't, maybe only one of them."

"Your problem, Tommy, is that you've never accepted your place in life. You've always wanted to play with the big guys. You should go back to defending dope peddlers. That's where you really belong."

"I'm testing my article in the *Atlantic Monthly,* can someone run a credible campaign without using attack ads . . ."

"*Atlantic Monthly!* Who reads that! . . . Where are you getting the money?"

He turned and pointed at my poor battered husband like he was a prosecuting attorney.

"Money is coming in . . . We put a second mortgage on the house. My publisher increased the advance on my book which is coming out in the spring . . ."

"BOOK! You never told me you were writing a book! How much money did they give you for it?"

"Sixty thousand advance . . ."

"Do you realize how many children that kind of money would feed in Africa!"

"It's about the history of attack ads . . ."

"I don't care what it's about! You have no qualifications to write a book! . . . Maybe you should write about the humiliation of being a housewife while your wife supported the family . . ."

I wanted to break his neck, but I was still containing my temper.

"Maybe I could."

Finally he sagged in the couch, a man exhausted after a hard day's work.

"Do you have any idea what this does to my reputation? Do you know what priests are saying to me? My little brother trying to beat a veteran and distinguished United States Senator? I've given up trying to defend you!"

Tommy was silent.

"Please tell me that you will change your mind and renounce this folly."

"No."

Tony buried his head in his hands.

"Is there nothing I can do to persuade you that this is a great sin of pride, Satan's sin? You will lose. You will destroy your reputation. Your family life will collapse. You will have nothing left. In the name of God I beg you to give it up!"

"No."

"Then God have mercy on you . . . I will pray to our parents in heaven that you will change your mind."

A worn and defeated man, his roman collar detached from his shirt, his long blond hair in disarray, he rose from the couch and staggered out of the room and up the narrow stairs to our first floor.

"Don't expect me to support you!" he shouted at us.

Tommy and I sat silently at our big worktable, arrayed with our tentative schedule for January. Tommy's head was still bowed, his shoulders still slumped. I went to the cabinet, removed the bottle of Bushmill's Green and poured us both a drink.

"Early Christmas drink," I said as I handed the bigger one to him.

"'Tis yourself that has the heavy hand, woman," he said ruefully. "Thanks for being quiet."

"I don't quite understand . . ."

"Oh, I do," he sighed as he sipped the whiskey very carefully.

"Tell me about it, Tommy."

"I was the tagalong little brother. My mother ordered Tony to take care of me when we went out to play. I was an embarrassment to him when I pestered him to let me play with his friends. They made fun of him, called him a nursemaid. Remember I was five years younger and short for my age."

"And, as I remember, even in first grade, with a dangerously clever tongue."

He grinned at me over the Waterford tumbler, my sweet, funny lover coming back to me.

"So he had to protect me from the kids who tried to beat me up, egged on by girls like you . . ."

"Tommy, I never . . ."

"And, of course, I adored him. My big brother. He knew everything about school and about sports and about how to act. I tried to model myself after him . . . You should be more like Tony my mother used to say . . . And I wanted to be like him."

"What happened?"

"I never got over my hero worship, Mary Margaret. Even today, when I know that everything he says is bullshit . . . All right, not in this house . . . but that's the only appropriate word . . . I still want his approval. I know I'll never get it, but, God help me, I'd like to have it."

"But you stopped following him around?"

"When he went to high school. I realized that I could have a lot more fun when he was not around. I was funny, class clown, and also very smart. So the same little girls who thought I was a creep now thought I was cute. The boys thought I was funny. I had it made."

I took his hand and led him over to the couch. I put my arm around him.

"He was at Loras when I started at Fenwick, so I couldn't get in his way and he couldn't get in mine. Mom would complain to him every vacation about the fast company I was keeping . . ."

"Our crowd!"

He laughed.

"I thought it was pretty funny too. Mary Margaret O'Malley, the *Censor Morum,* 'fast.' However, I kept getting excellent grades, so that was proof that I was taking proper advantage of my opportunities. And all I wanted to do was to stare at the afore mentioned matriarch and picture her with her clothes off . . ."

"You did not," I giggled.

"We didn't like the O'Malleys very much. Your grandmother, after all, was from the South Side and that was bad enough. They had fun and that was even worse—dissolute, noise-making, heavy-drinking bunch, not at all respectable like we were. On the other hand, they were above us and we shouldn't push ourselves into their world—which of course I wanted to do so I could push the wondrous Margaret Mary into bed with me."

"You did not," I giggled again and kissed him.

"I don't blame my parents. They were good people. They never had a chance. Respectability was so important to them . . ."

"And respectable we were not."

"Heavens, no! . . . As you remember, when Tony found out we were 'keeping company'—mom's very words—he was furious. Ever since then you've been the scarlet woman who has ruined my life."

"Fair enough description!" I kissed him again, a lingering one this time.

"So we just have to live with him. He hasn't changed my mind since he tried to break us up . . . It still hurts that he doesn't understand me or support me."

"How can he get along with the other priests in his order?"

"From what I hear, he tones down his manic side with them and is sensitive and collegial, even if he gets uptight occasionally. I guess I'm the weak link in his personality."

I didn't say that there was something deeply sick about his brother. He knew that without my telling him.

Suddenly the cavalry thundered down the steps. Our eighth grader, Mary Rose, home from buying presents for us at Alioto's over on Chicago Avenue. We had put some distance between ourselves before she had reached the bottom of the staircase.

"Father Uncle wasn't very happy, was he?"

Ah, she had not just returned.

"You should not eavesdrop, young woman!" I warned her.

"Mo-THER! He was shouting so loud that I couldn't help hearing him! He doesn't think we'll win the election, does he? Well, he's wrong!"

Every time I see her, arms folded, determined face, flashing eyes, I think I'm looking into a mirror twenty years ago.

"He doesn't think we ought to run," her father said lightly.

"What's his problem anyway?" she demanded.

"His problem, hon, is that your father is his little brother and he sees him catching up and passing him."

Tommy didn't disagree.

"WELL, if that little brat Marytre ever passes me up, I'll just take credit for her!"

"I'm sure you will."

"He doesn't like you very much, does he, Mom? Why not?"

A fast, hardball pitch, for which I was not prepared.

"I mean, that's the best thing you ever did, Dad, wasn't it?"

"That's what your mom tells me every day."

"WELL, she's right! . . . I just got the most bitchin' presents for both of you. You won't believe it!"

And off she went, ready to take on the world.

I tolerate that word in the house because it is merely a teenage adjective.

"She answered the question for you," I pointed out to my husband.

"I assume that the whiskey is a prelude for something . . ."

"Not now with Ms. Big Ears around."

"Later."

We hugged each other, a pledge and a promise.

CHAPTER 10

✝

CHRISTMAS AT THE O'MALLEY'S with singing and dancing and arguing and cameras snapping all the time was its usual madcap experience. I could imagine why Tommy's respectable parents thought we were awful. But as Chucky always said, "There is a time for rejoicing and a time for not rejoicing and this is a time for rejoicing."

Everyone called my Tommy "Senator."

"Crispjin," Rosie said to me, "has taken a little too much for granted. People are tired of his Dutch solemnity and self-satisfaction. They're ready for a mischievous Mick."

What if we really do win, I asked myself. Then what do we do for an encore?

I was still upset by Tony's assault on Tommy, though not enough to ruin the Christmas fun. He was a problem that would always be with us, win or lose. The fights would continue. At some point I might have to tell him that he should stay away from my house and my kids.

The day after Christmas we sat down with Joe and Ric and Tina and Dolly to lay out our plans for the campaign up to the primary. Chucky was there of course, preternaturally quiet.

"Our goal is to win more votes against token opposition than Senator Crispjin gets against token opposition. That way we have some credibility."

"And Bobby Bill will crank out money for the attack ads," Joe said.

"If we get them really worried they may overplay their hand. Anyway we'll pick up the usual Chicago votes but we can't take them for granted. Dolly, we should be in at least one Black church every Sunday. Better more than one."

"You bet."

Dolly was a lawyer like the rest of us, but she had chosen to become a very high-priced public relations consultant. Slender with a head that was almost shaved, she was the most radical of us and a few years older. She had grown up in a housing project and had worked with grim determination to achieve success in her studies and to pass the bar exam. She had carefully crushed all traces of African-American dialect from her speech, but quit the practice of law after less than a year. She had married a very successful African-American banker and found that she hated law. Too dull, she asserted, while PR was always exciting. She took a leave from her own firm to work for us. Dolly had strong dislikes and strong loyalties.

"We will concentrate our efforts here and in the collar counties, with a couple runs down state," Tommy said, "just so they'll see our faces on TV. The Illinois Federation of Labor is meeting in Carbondale. I should be there and in some Black churches in East St. Louis. Ambassador, we will need a plane for that trip and maybe once more. Small one, just me and Joe."

Chicago pols divide the region into the city, the "county towns" (suburban Cook County) and the "collar counties"—Lake, McHenry, Kane, DuPage, and Kendall.

"And a couple of security people."

"Not so fast, white man," I said.

"And my wife," Tommy added.

"The money is coming in nicely," Chucky said. "I'll get a good plane and a good aircrew and put them on retainer. I have a friend who owes me a favor."

"Aircrew?" Tommy frowned.

"Captain and first officer, one of them a woman," I ordered.

That was that.

"Ric, we play our Latino card early, do we not?"

"The HDO won't be happy with us, but I can lean on them to turn out crowds in the city. I figure we establish that base early and then tend it carefully till November. We'll have no trouble using parish halls and the local community centers. Bring the mariachi group of course."

Idiot that he is, Chucky went through the motions of strumming a guitar.

"Kids only on weekends," Tina insisted.

"And Friday nights if they have their homework done first."

"There are tens of thousands of Mexican Americans in the suburbs and the collar counties," Tommy said, "especially out in DuPage and down in Joliet. How do we get them? They don't seem very well organized."

"There are parishes that have a Mass on Sunday," I said, "maybe some of them will let us use their parish halls. We can pass out leaflets before and after the Mass."

"Till the pastor chases us off parish property!" Dolly said with a laugh.

"And," I said, "a lot of Latino college kids have called to volunteer. We can send them out to wherever we find concentrations to ask them to come and listen. They can be part of a precinct organization later."

"Many of them in the suburbs are not legals but they may come anyhow. It will stir up interest."

"We can't afford empty houses," Ric said. "Which can happen if there's a snow storm."

"That's your job, Ric. No Hispanic empty houses."

"I hear you, Tommy. I'll get you on the Spanish-language stations too. They'll be dying to have you. Also in East St. Louis when we're downstate. And the Spanish radio stations too. Rodge Crispjin won't know what hit him."

Tommy nodded.

"What about polls?" Joe asked.

"We don't do them," Tommy said firmly. "We make it clear that we are not running a campaign based on polls. On the other hand we read very carefully every poll we can get our hands on."

"I got some friends who run focus groups," Chucky said. "They owe me some favors. Maybe they can do a couple pro bono."

"Your father has lots of friends," my good husband observed.

"He should have. He has worked all his life collecting. Now is a good time to . . . what's the phrase, Chucky?"

"Call in my markers. But I don't ask for any campaign contributions unless someone offers to make one. I know the rules."

Laughter all around the room.

"What about the media, Dolly?"

"We all watch Chicago TV news. We know whom to trust and whom not to. Since this is a new kind of campaign we will emphasize our total transparency."

"What does that mean, Doll?" I wondered.

"It means we tell the truth, a whole lot of truth, more truth than anyone expects us to tell—not necessarily the whole truth!"

We all laughed.

"Besides," Dolly continued, "your husband is the slickest pol I've ever seen. He'll tie the media in knots and laugh them off and he'd route Crispjin in a debate."

"There won't be any debates," Tommy dismissed the possibility. "Why should he give me more attention?"

"If you start to catch up, he might have to," Dolly said.

"He'll just pour more money into attack ads, most of which we will ignore."

"If you say so, Boss man . . ." Dolly said, rolling her deep brown eyes, "and when we make mistakes, when we stumble, when no one shows up, we admit that we're novices, just learning. And, oh yes, we ignore the *Chicago Daily Examiner* and Leander Schlenk. If he comes to a news conference, we answer his questions politely, no wise-guy stuff. But we do not answer anything he says in the paper. In some cases I'll issue a clarification. We don't want that crook unnerving us."

"We are polite to everyone," Tommy insisted, "even the most pushy media intern. Or ordinary folk who ask obnoxious questions. It will be Joe's job or his muscle's to keep us moving when we have to move. No temper tantrums from anyone."

"Why is everyone looking at me?" I asked.

It was great fun. The fun wouldn't last. We would grow weary and discouraged and angry. We were up against big odds. It just wasn't fair.

I was wrong that day. The primary campaign continued to be fun. So did the summer and fall campaign. It stopped being fun only when it began to look like we had a good chance of winning.

I took a leave from the firm to help "manage" my husband's campaign. I would come back for one major case in April on which I had worked and my partners said they absolutely needed me. It would also provide us with a little more cash for day to day living.

Tommy hammered out his campaign speeches and responses to questions during our winter season.

The first one was his standard populist speech. It played well with union people and Blacks. The latter seemed to identify with Tommy like he was one of them, perhaps because of his smile and his laughter. He enjoyed the cries of approval from the congregations and responded in kind.

"Be careful, Tommy," Dolly advised him tongue in cheek. "You won't never be one of us, but you might have a hard time being white."

Average family income, taking inflation into account, increased in the United States in the thirty years after the end of World War II. It kept pace with the yearly increase in the nation's productivity. That meant that ordinary folk were sharing in the nation's growth. However, after 1975 family income froze despite the increase in productivity. That meant that the rich were creaming off all the increases in the economy and leaving the rest of the people behind. The rich got richer, the poor got poorer, and the middle class was locked in place.

There are many reasons for this situation. However, in those years, especially in the Reagan and Bush administrations greed became fashionable again. Companies dropped older employees because their salaries were said to be too high. They fired men and women just before they became eligible for pensions. They outsourced jobs to companies who paid substandard wages. They fought to destroy unions. They exported jobs overseas. They canceled pension programs to escape bankruptcy. They cut jobs when they had made serious mistakes, so they would be lean and mean—though they always had been mean. They closed American factories. They cut workers' salaries but never their own. The top executives paid themselves exorbitant salaries that were unrelated to their success in leading the company. They called them golden parachutes. One man's parachute was a hundred and forty million dollars, though the company's stock went down twenty-five percent during his years in charge. They played all kinds of merger games which brought big gains to themselves but lost a lot of jobs for workers. All the time this was happening, the government did not try to stop them. Rather it encouraged them. The main villains are Big Oil, Big Pharmacy, and Big Insurance— all of which are gouging us day in and day out. It's time to stop them. That means it's time for a Democratic Congress again. This could be a turning point election, time to take government out of the hands of the rich and give it back to the people. It's time for the government to stop supporting the haves and have-mores and become concerned about those who have less.

MEDIA: Tommy are you ashamed that you were Mr. Mom for a couple of years?

CANDIDATE: Why should I be? I liked it. I got to know my children better. They got to know me better. Poor dad was so hapless and helpless that they tried to make life easy for him. I think they liked Mr. Mom. Now even when they're becoming teens they seem to like him too, which as you all know is against the rules.

MEDIA: Do you think all dads should be Mr. Mom for a couple of years?

CANDIDATE: I'm not prescribing for anyone but myself. It was the thing to do for us at that stage of our family life.

MEDIA: If you win will you continue to be Mr. Mom and a Senator?

CANDIDATE: No!

He didn't say that he became Mr. Mom because his wife was prone to a PPS syndrome. I had to do it because of my crazy wife.

MEDIA: Don't you think it's wrong to use a foreign language in your campaign?

CANDIDATE: Spanish isn't a foreign language. It was the language of vast sections of our country before English came along. Is it really a foreign language in Los Angeles, the city of Our Lady Queen of the Angels? Most Latino Americans don't want a separate culture any more than did the Irish or German or Italian Americans. They don't see a contradiction between being Americans and keeping alive the best of their heritages. I'll talk to people in any language they know.

MEDIA: Isn't the Mexican music inappropriate?

CANDIDATE: Those who aren't Latinos seem to like it too.

This was our first big surprise in the campaign. The mostly "anglo" audiences in the suburbs wanted the mariachi band. They would join in the singing with the Latinos in the crowds. We had to buy Mexican dresses and sombreros for our daughters. The winter winds kept stealing the hats.

That phase of the campaign was dense with good will and excitement. We were having a good time and so were our crowds. We ignored the *Examiner* just as Rodgers Crispjin ignored us.

Tommy and I found ourselves deeply in love again. It was the first time since the *Law Journal* that we had worked together. We didn't need the Bushmill's to find the right mood at the end of the day.

I was dragged before the TV camera to defend myself against the charge of exploiting our three beautiful daughters.

TV: Don't you think people flock to your husband's rallies so they can ogle four beautiful red-headed women?

MARY MARGARET: In the middle of winter? They could watch Kirsten Dunst on DVD in the Spider-Man films.

TV: Did you take your family to that resort in Mexico every summer because you knew you were going to run for office?

MARY MARGARET: No. My husband felt that it would be good for our kids to learn about another language and culture . . . And it wasn't a resort. It was a small bungalow.

TV: Didn't your children resent losing their summers?

MARY MARAGARET (laughter): My kids are adventurers. They love Hermosillo. We'd put it to a vote every year and it was always unanimous.

The trickiest of Tommy's talks was the one aimed especially at the Latinos. He had to praise them without seeming to pander.

Every immigrant group has made an important and unique contribution to the country. I for one am fed up with the stereotype that the bigots today use to attack new Mexican immigrants who are trying to improve the lives of their families just like the rest of us once did. We hear nothing about the long-lasting Mexican contribution to American culture—the names of cities, the mission churches, the art, the music, even the sombreros which my daughters have a hard time protecting from the winds.

I never hear these bigots acknowledge that Mexican Americans are hard workers, that they have a strong family life, excellent health, and a deep religious faith which influences everything they do. If I'm elected to the Senate I will try to bring an end to the senseless immigration policies which kill so many men, women, and children in the desert. This slaughter has to stop. It was once said of my ancestors that they could never become really good Americans. They drank too much, they were lazy, they were shiftless. Well, that wasn't true. The same things are said against Mexican Americans today. And they aren't true now either! Finally there is a tremendous contribution that Mexicans are making to American life. Their religious faith emphasizes that God comes to Mexican families and celebrates their feasts with them. Our dour country needs more of that festivity and joy!

Then we'd segue into the mariachi, often expanded to include O'Malley cousins with horns and drums and even the good Rosie with her lovely voice. The crowds sang with us. The nice thing about Mexican music is that you can vocalize along with it even if you don't know the words.

It all seemed to work reasonably well, dead of winter or not.

By the middle of March we were running on nervous energy. The primary came not one day too soon. Fortunately for us the snow storm held off till mid-evening.

We decided not to buy space in a hotel for a vote-counting party. The Moran basement was still our headquarters. The nine o'clock news on a Chicago channel reported an "upset victory" for our side. We had collected twenty-five thousand more votes in a virtually uncontested primary than Senator H. Rodgers Crispjin had piled up in his similar primary.

The anchor person was usually an airhead, but she was correct in her hasty analysis.

"It looks like Senator Crispjin has a horse race on his hands."

Tommy and I walked out in the falling snow to face the two cameras which were waiting. He was coatless, as he always was.

"As Winston Churchill said after the battle of El Alamein, 'It is not the beginning of the end, but the end of the beginning.'"

We walked back into the house, arm in arm.

Leander Schlenk dismissed the outcome in his commentary the next morning.

Tommy's "Victory"
Doesn't Mean Much, Pols Say

Veteran Chicago political observers discounted this morning the apparent "victory" in the primary beauty contest between househusband Tommy Moran and incumbent Senator H. Rodgers Crispjin. The Senator had remained in the national's capital during the campaign while upstart Tommy campaigned vigorously, if not always tastefully. "The Senator's campaign has not even begun," one pol said. "When it does, he'll bury Tommy."

"He's right," Tommy said the following afternoon. "Now the negative ads start."

"He may overkill," Dolly suggested.

"I wonder how many readers believe Lee Schlenk," Ric Suarez said. "Their circulation is way down."

"Our job is to keep pushing," I suggested. "At least they know we're around."

Congratulations and promises of support poured in from Democratic leaders all over the state. No one liked Crispjin very much.

"OK," Joe McDermott said, "we got a lot of votes from Cook County, but we did better than the Senator in the collar counties, especially DuPage. That's the first time something like that happened. Dolly, why don't you get a statement out on that."

"I'll do better that that. I'll say it on the five o'clock news tonight."

We decided we would rent a store front on Chicago Avenue, just down the street from Petersen's Ice Cream, as our headquarters—in keeping with our style of a surplus store campaign. We would at last take a breather to get ready for the main campaign which would start Memorial Day.

"We'll visit every county in the state," Tommy promised. "Let's begin with a big song festival in Grant Park—ethnic music: American, Polish, Italian, Irish, German, Korean, Chinese, and Mexican."

"One from many," Ric Sanchez agreed.

Tommy and I were supervising the work on the storefront the following week when a TV reporter caught us with the first poll.

"It shows Senator Crispjin thirty percentage points ahead of you,

Tommy, fifty-five percent to twenty-five percent. Do you have any comment."

"How large was the sample?"

"Four hundred and three voters interviewed by phone."

"I'm not surprised," he said, shrugging his shoulders. "He is after all an incumbent Senator running against an amateur. I'd comment that fifty-five percent is his maximum and twenty-five percent is my minimum. We'll catch up."

"Four hundred respondents," I said, "isn't very many."

"It's probably a good guess, however."

He sat down under a huge picture of himself, surrounded by kids of all colors.

"Do you think the other side could be faking polls?" I asked.

"Bobby Bill is capable of that," he agreed. "No one ever promised us a level playing field."

The negative ads came like the deluge. Tommy househusband versus a real man. Tommy the demagogue against a great unifier. Inexperienced Tommy against the experienced and veteran Senator, whose previous job description was a real estate developer, but it was against the rules to say that.

We hunkered down and waited. I activated some more of our volunteers to compile phone lists for October and then went back to the firm.

We took the kids to Grand Beach for a winter weekend. They pummeled us with snowballs. The TV cameras which had invaded the village caught some wonderful pictures of the kids attacking us and then of the grinning little demons throwing snowballs at the camera person. They were smart enough not to hit her.

CHAPTER 11

✝

W HILE I WAS AWAY at the firm, we hired some veteran Illinois operatives to help us understand the various downstate counties. Volunteers came pouring in. The negative ads tapered off because the *Daily News* and the TV stations were talking about overkill. A poll in early May showed that we had gained ten points and the Senator had lost six points—forty-nine percent to thirty-five percent.

"We've cut his lead in half," Tommy told the interviewers on *Chicago Tonight,* a PBS program. "We're in striking distance. Frankly we're closer than I had expected to be."

"Tommy," Lee Schlenk jumped in, "it isn't true, is it, that you've gone back to being Mr. Mom during the lull in the campaign?"

I wanted to claw my way through the control room glass.

"I think it was known all along that Ms. O'Malley had a case before the Illinois Supreme Court during the spring session. She won it incidentally."

"You don't seem to show any sense of shame at taking a subordinate role in the family during a campaign. How do you think the voters will react to that?"

"Maybe they'll understand that political candidates need to make ends meet."

"Senator Crispjin has never been a house hubby. Won't that give him an advantage over you in the election?"

"I made a promise that I would not discuss the Senator during the campaign. I will only say that for me every chance to spend some time with my daughters is a rewarding experience."

A woman reporter from the *Daily News* asked, "Your children threw snowballs at a TV camerawoman at Grand Beach earlier in the year."

"They didn't hit her. They weren't even trying to hit her as was clear from the tape."

"Proving that they are smart politicians?"

"Proving that they are well-mannered young women who have been taught that the only people you can hit with snowballs are your parents."

"Tommy," a woman from the *Chicago Defender* asked, "is your wife a smarter lawyer than you are?"

My dear Tommy beamed at the question.

"The good Mary Margaret O'Malley is a brilliant and beautiful woman. We do different kinds of law, appellate versus criminal defense, so a comparison might not be fair to me. But whoever said fair. She is a much better lawyer than I am and I'm proud of her."

Well! All right!

The host (male) asked, "Tommy, the accusation has been made that this festival of ethnic songs with which you're launching your campaign is divisive and demagogic. What do you say to that?"

"It is really the opposite. We're including every group we can find— including bluegrass and Yorkshire folk singers."

"Come on, Tommy," Lee Schlenk interrupted. "You're including criminals who have invaded the United States across its borders."

"Those criminals, as you call them, Mr. Schlenk, are human beings with the rights with which all humans are endowed. Moreover, most Mexican Americans are legally here and many are American citizens, just like you and me."

The host cut Schlenk off and ended the interview.

"Do you think he believes all that crap?" I asked him in the control room.

"Who knows what he believes," he said, embracing me, "and who cares as long as he keeps setting me up with those questions."

"Thanks for the compliments," I breathed, escaping his kisses.

"I didn't say that criminal defense is a lot more difficult than standing before relatively civilized appellate court judges!"

"Beast," I said returning to the kiss.

The other panel members congratulated him and wished him well during the campaign.

"You'll catch him," said the woman from the *Daily News*.

The ethnic festival and Grant Park was a huge success. There must have been fifty thousand people there in front of the old James C. Petrillo Band Shell, named after a "a labor guy," Tommy pointed out in his brief introduction. Several Mexican-American bands performed, proving that mariachi was not the only kind of Mexican music. Nonetheless the campaign band did perform with considerable verve, the full band backed up by assorted O'Malley cousins.

"These folks," my husband informed the crowd, "are a thoroughly American phenomenon, made up of Mexican Americans and Irish Americans who have been seduced by mariachi."

We outdid ourselves and the crowd screamed its approval. We had a lot of voters out there, most of them Chicagoans who would vote for a junk yard dog if he were a Democrat. Still there were great visuals which would appear in whatever ads we were able to pay for in late October.

Then something ominous happened as we were breaking up. The three girls had disappeared.

"Where are the kids, Tommy?

"I hear them screaming somewhere."

The Chicago cops who were maintaining order heard the screaming too and pushed their way through the crowd. We followed right after them.

The scene we came upon was horrific—and bizarre. A woman, early thirties, was clutching our nine-year-old Mary Therese on the ground.

She was screaming her lungs out. The child's sisters, furies from another world, were punching the woman and pulling her off their little sister.

As we and the police arrived, Mary Therese broke free and rushed into my arms.

"She tried to steal me, Mommy!"

"She kidnapped our little sister," Mary Rose proclaimed to all around in her most dramatic voice as she pointed an outraged finger. "We stopped her."

"Jesus told me to take her away from those terrible people," the woman sobbed. "He said that she would be damned to hell if I didn't take her."

"I'm not going to hell, am I, Daddy?"

"God loves you too much to ever lose you, darling."

The cameras were all around us. You can't even have privacy in a kidnapping these days.

"Do you think, Tommy," a woman reporter asked, "that this was a plot by the Senator to ruin your day for you?"

My husband needed a moment to compose himself.

"Of course not. I'm grateful to Chicago's finest for their prompt reaction . . ."

"What about us?" Mary Ann demanded. "We found her."

"I knew you would. But thank you too."

The police took the woman off to their headquarters and an African-American woman detective led us to a dressing room off the stage of the band shell where we could regroup.

"She tore my pretty Mexican dress," our little heroine protested.

"She was evil," Mary Rose declared. "Mo-THER, sit down, you look terrible."

I did sit down and realized that I was shaking.

"Do you have any bodyguards, Mr. Moran?"

He looked around.

"Our security guys were around earlier. I don't know what happened to them. The state police were supposed to take over today."

Joe and Dolly pushed their way into the room.

"Are these folks your security people, sir?"

"No, detective, they're my staff."

"What happened to our security?" Joe asked the whole world.

"They disappeared. Find out what the hell happened to them and to the state cops! This begins to look like a setup."

"Sir," the detective said to Tommy, "with your permission I will summon some Chicago uniformed police to escort you to your car and then escort you home."

"Thank you, detective," I said.

"It was a brilliant concert, Ms. O'Malley. I'm sorry it had to end this way."

Later that evening, the sedated Mary Therese sound asleep and the other two girls on watch at the door to her room, our crowd, including the redoubtable Chucky, were sitting glumly in our "war room" pondering what happened.

Joe had screamed at the Governor and demanded the head of the state police on a platter.

"We don't want them messing around us anywhere," he shouted. "We were set up."

We could hear the Governor promise that he would get to the bottom of it.

"I don't care what bottom you find, Governor. We don't want your idiots around us any more."

He slammed the phone down.

He had already dismissed the private security group whose boss had insisted that his men had left only when they thought the concert was over.

"Bobby Bill?" I asked.

"Would he go that far?" Tommy shook his head in dismay.

"He only had to bribe a couple of people."

"He must really be afraid of us."

The Mayor of Chicago called to "apologize." I assured him that Chicago's finest had saved the day.

"We're going to get to the bottom of this, Mary Margaret."

"It goes pretty deep."

It was all on the nine o'clock news, the success of the concert was hardly noticed. There was wonderful footage of the sisters saving Marytre and of myself and Tommy embracing them. The cops had the name and address of the woman. She was from Arkansas and still insisted, as she had on camera, that Jesus had sent her to save "the pretty girl from her terrible family." Senator Crispjin's office had issued a statement which said, "The Senator regrets any violence. However, he feels that a candidate who engages in divisive and demagogic rhetoric runs the risk of offending patriotic Americans."

Then our Dolly was on the screen.

"Has American politics deteriorated so badly that terrorism has become an acceptable part of a campaign?"

She didn't add "with the approval of one candidate." That was against our rules.

"Do you have any idea, Dolly, what happened to the state police detail that was supposed to be protecting the Moran family or the private security group that has been protecting him up to now?"

"No we don't. We feel we were set up."

"By whom?"

Dolly simply shrugged.

"They really want to drive you out of the race, Tommy," Ric Suarez said softly.

"I guess we have them scared. What do we do now?"

Chucky intervened.

"We sign on Mike Casey's Reliable Security. It's all off-duty Chicago cops, the best on the force. We tell the governor that we don't trust his cops. If he wants them around, that's fine but we have our own cops and the state police should stay out of their way."

"They probably won't try anything again," Tommy said without conviction.

The Governor called to say that he promised a police car in front of our house every day and night.

Joe told him to keep them out of our way.

That was not the last of it.

The next morning Leander Schlenk reported from Washington that some members of Congress thought that Tommy had organized the kidnapping plot to promote his "faltering" campaign.

In the middle of the following week we were going over to our headquarters to plan for the grand opening. The two Reliables, big linebacker types, joined us at the doorway to escort us towards our van.

Across the street two state policemen were apparently sleeping in their car.

Our middle daughter Mary Ann stopped us at the bottom of the stairs.

"That's a bad car," she pointed at our battered old Chevy. "Don't get into it!"

"Hush, dear," I said.

She's our psychic one and has moods like that.

"Run!" she shouted, breaking away from us. "Run!"

We followed her down the street, running to catch up, even the two Reliables.

"Hurry! Hurry!"

Then the blast of the exploding car knocked us to the ground. We were only bruised a bit. The two state police cops across the street were critically injured. A column of flame leaped from the car, closing our house off like the biblical seraphim closed off paradise in the Bible. All the front windows in the house were shattered as were the windows across the street. They were destroying our neighborhood.

Tommy rolled over and flipped open his cell phone.

"Tommy here, get out of there through the back door. NOW! There may be an explosion!"

Then he called the Oak Park Police.

"I think there may be a bomb in a car in front of it . . . I don't want to argue with you . . . Just do it . . . A bomb exploded in front of my house a couple of minutes ago . . . PLEASE DO IT!"

We heard a second explosion.

"Forget about it assholes. It just blew up . . ."

"Ambulances on the way," one of the Reliables said. "I think the River Forest Fire and Police are on the way."

"Everyone all right?" I asked.

"We're OK," Mary Rose murmured. "Aren't we lucky Mary Ann is a psychic!"

"It was a BAD car," Mary Ann said sadly. "It smelled bad."

There were two explanations the next morning for the explosions. *The Examiner's* headlined asked

Did Tommy Blow up His Own Car?

In Washington Senator Crispjin told a bank of microphones that he deplored the violence in quiet Chicago suburbs and called for an end to it. "I ask my opponent to moderate his rhetoric which I'm sure has enflamed this election."

"What rhetoric?" demanded a reporter.

"He said that illegal immigrants had the same rights as good American citizens."

"He only quoted the Declaration of Independence that all men have certain inalienable rights. Since when, Senator, is that inflammatory?"

The Senator backtracked.

"At least he ought to know that immigration is an inflammatory issue in this country."

"So he shouldn't talk about it?'

"He should be careful what he says."

"Are you going to drop out of the race, Mr. Moran?" The national news reporter asked as we watched the installation of new windows.

"No."

"Are you going to stop talking about immigration as your opponent suggested?"

"No."

"Have your neighbors complained?"

"Yes, some of them. They want us to move out of the neighborhood."

"Will you?"

"No."

"Are you worried about the safety of your family?"

"Yes . . . There is no legitimate appeal in this country from the ballot to the bullet. We're not the ones making that appeal."

Those two dialogues looked good on Chicago television. The next poll in the *Daily News* reported that his lead had shrunk from forty-eight percent to thirty-eight percent. The *Examiner* and the Senator dropped the issue. The negative ads disappeared for a while.

"Is it right for us to put our children through these risks?" Tommy asked me one night in bed. Neither of us were able to sleep. Nor were we in the mood for making love.

"They say they're not in any danger as long as Mary Ann's psychic thing is working."

"They live in a fairy-tale world. They see us as actors in a movie or a TV series. The good guys always win. We're wearing the white hats."

"The larger question, Tommy love, is whether we should be in it. Is it right to risk our lives and the kids' future in a joust with windmills?"

"What are we trying to prove anyway?"

"Exactly."

We were both silent for a while.

"Maybe," he said, "we could withdraw from active campaigning. Tell the world that the risk to our children is too great. We might get a lot of sympathy votes if we did that."

"Whoever wants you out of the race would not be satisfied with that."

"Yeah, you're right."

"Tommy, do we have the right to quit so our kids are safe?"

"I've thought of that too. Would we be letting them down if we cut and run?"

I snuggled close to him, now wanting love.

"They are who they are and who we made them. They're adventurers. It may be in their genes. They liked Mexico. They like the campaign. If we pull out now because this adventure is dangerous, what will it do to them?"

His fingers found my breast.

"We betray them no matter what we do?"

I groaned as his lips touched my nipple.

"We trust God."

"Who makes no guarantees?"

God talk really turns me on.

"Don't stop, Tommy!"

"I wasn't planning on it."

"God's guarantees are valid only in the long run," I managed to say.

"In the long run we will all be dead anyway."

Death talk always turns me on too.

So we defied death.

The two cops survived. We repaired the house and the headquarters on Chicago Avenue. A second delegation of neighbors called upon us to urge us not to move. The bombers were never caught. The kids bounced back quickly. Tommy and I did not sleep very well. We heard from someone who would know that Rodgers Crispjin had told Bobby Bill to call off his troops. I also heard that someone has told the Senator that if this kept up his own life would be in danger. Everyone relaxed a little and we went forth *en famille* to Rockford to begin our summer-long campaign.

But the violence was not over yet.

CHAPTER 12

✝

WE REALIZED in July that the summer campaign was a waste. We still lagged seven or eight percentage points behind in the polls. Senator Crispjin remained in Washington on the Senate's business. Some of his colleagues, men in difficult races, found time to return to their constituencies. The Senator allegedly did not think that was necessary because he was so far ahead. "You don't use a tank to swat a fly," was his attitude according to the indefatigable Leander Schlenk. September and October were the only months that really mattered in a campaign.

"Next time, Tommy," Joe McDermott sighed one afternoon as we waited in the airport for our plane to arrive, "we campaign only in September and October."

"If there is a next time," I said.

I was in a mean, nasty, irritable, mood. So was Tommy, though his moods are more low-key than mine. We had been squabbling for days. We had dumped the kids at the Michigan City Airport to be picked up by their Aunt April. They needed a time out on the beach with their cousins. They had been griping and complaining all week, bickering with us and one another. When we told them we were giving them a free weekend, they had turned sullen and sulked silently on the flight from Midway to Michigan City. They hated their cousins, they had informed us when the plane landed. They were BORING!

"Brats!" I had said.

"They'll have a great time," Tommy had predicted, probably accurately.

"Adventurers indeed!" I had grumbled.

Tina had taken her brood to Green Lake. Ellie McDermott supported the campaign, as she had said, by not burdening us with her presence. I didn't argue.

I don't remember what cities we were visiting on our downstate trek, LaSalle-Peru, maybe, and Bloomington. Most downstate cities, it seemed to my urban cynicism, were interchangeable one with another—19th-century river towns in the prairies surrounded by vast fields of tall corn. Scenes from *State Fair,* two-and-a-half-hours' drive and a century away from Chicago.

It had been a hot summer, the sun, grimly implacable in cloudless skies and thick curtains of humidity, making every step an intolerable exertion. I made all of us, even the Reliables, put on sun-block cream. "No suits for cancer later on." The stress and the strain, the heat and the humidity, the dour faces and the weariness of the crowds had all taken their toll on poor Tommy. He still smiled magically, laughed at himself, joked about the kids hating us for forcing them to take a weekend off. He still gave his standard talks with his usual verve, still worked the crowd like a Chicago ward committeeman. Yet there was no light in his eyes when the show was over or when we drove from the next airport to the next rally.

"You go south of I-80," Chucky had warned us, "and you're not quite in the South, but you're not in the North either. Marymarg, jeans and T-shirts for you, and only moderately classy. Tommy, you can wear a tie and a jacket but you take them off when you begin to speak."

We did as we were told. I also wore a sombrero. When there were enough Hispanics in the crowd to respond to Tommy's brief greetings in Spanish, he might ask me to sing a song or two and apologize for not having the whole band. One of the Reliables would give me my guitar.

None of us could tell how they were reacting. They applauded enthusiastically and laughed quietly at Tommy's jokes. Even the anglos loved my songs. (I always said that my voice was not as good as Rosie's. Everyone else in the family, herself included, insisted that, as a torch singer, I was a little bit better.) They shook hands eagerly with Tommy and the women shook hands with me. They were Democrats of course or they wouldn't have been there.

After the rally, there would be the usual press conference with the usual questions and Tommy's usual smile and effective answers. Often we'd take a brief ride to the local television station for a longer interview. The only tough question would be

MEDIA: Why should people here vote for you, Mr. Moran, instead of Senator Crispjin?

CANDIDATE: Well, because I'm a Democrat and am more likely to be on the side of poor and ordinary folks than a Republican would be. It's time for a change in Washington, to give the workers and the farmers and the middle class their rightful say.

MEDIA: You never criticize the Senator, do you?

CANDIDATE: I don't think you should win elections by vilifying your opponents.

MEDIA: You've experienced a lot of negative ads this summer and a couple of attacks on you and your family. How do you explain that?

CANDIDATE: I don't. I can't. They haven't frightened us off.

MEDIA: Do you think there are people who don't want you to win?

CANDIDATE: I hope not.

Nothing very exciting, but a chance for a lot more people to see and hear Tommy and to realize, we hoped, that he was an intelligent young man and not the wimp or the inexperienced demagogue that the attack ads, growing more relentless as the summer went on, claimed.

There were a lot more questions about the violence than we would have expected. Clearly that concerned a lot of people. Nor did they seem to accept the argument that we had brought it on ourselves.

Anyway as we waited in that tiny airport with inadequate air conditioning, drenched in perspiration, and with cleansing showers a long way off, we discussed the folly of a summer campaign.

"In England," Joe said, "they only permit four weeks of campaigning for a general election. Makes a lot of sense to me."

"Senator Crispjin, as always, has made the right decision," Tommy said wearily. "He campaigns effectively by remaining in the Beltway and tending to his senatorial responsibilities while his ads beat up on me. An unknown candidate has to travel all over the state so people can see him on the television news on Saturday or Sunday night. We have no choice. This a holding action. We haven't gained on him, but we haven't lost either. September and October will be the critical months."

"What will we do then?" I asked.

"I'm not sure . . . I think the race will be won in the Chicago area. We'll do well in Chicago, though we will have to do the Black churches as often as we can. Victory is in the suburbs and the collar counties, especially suburban Cook and DuPage. So we concentrate there. Lots of challenges to the Senator to debate. Some stations will schedule debates. Of course he won't come, but we'll show up every time."

Joe nodded.

"I think you've learned the game pretty well this summer, Tommy. What do you think, Ric?"

"You've created a lot of enthusiasm among my people, Tommy. They think you're really on their side. You have to keep pounding on that. This time we will get out the votes, I promise."

I wondered if that would really happen. Latinos had yet to be mobilized in American politics, except in a couple of California districts.

"Mary Margaret?"

"There are an awful lot of soccer moms out in the suburbs. Don't forget them."

"Soccer moms and Hispanics," Tommy worked up enough energy to laugh. "Well, that's where the research shows the new Democratic majority is supposed to be . . . What's Crispjin going to do, Joe?"

"He'll go for his downstate base, especially the Evangelical churches. And he'll fight us tooth and nail in DuPage county."

"So that's where the battle will be, fair enough! There's a lot of people out there who should be Democrats . . . Does the St. Luke's women soccer team have any games in September, Mary Margaret?"

"You bet and your daughter is the star."

"Whom do we play?"

"Our arch enemies—St. Vincent!"

"Just so long as we don't have to defeat a team from DuPage county."

"I'll do my best to look like a soccer mom . . . How do we cope with the violence question?"

"Do you think we can make anything out of it?"

"It's on everyone's minds . . . I don't know what to do with it."

"The plane is landing, Senator," a Reliable whispered softly.

We flew to another city, Peoria, I think, met the media at the airport, went to another rally, and did our best to fight the good fight despite the scorching heat. It was late in the afternoon when we finished. We Chicagoans expected a bit of cooling breeze from off the Lake. But we were too far from the Lake and there were no breezes off the sluggish rivers which crisscross middle western America.

"I have an idea," I said to Tommy as we tried to sleep that night despite the noisy air conditioner in our motel room.

"We need them."

"Does it violate our norms if we use that tape of you in front of our ruined house in which you say that you simply don't know who was responsible and hate to think violence has become part of the American political process. Then you hug all of us as you did that day and the voice over says, 'Who wants to keep Tom Moran out of the Senate so badly that they would kill himself and his whole family?' "

He thought for a long moment.

"Of course we know who was responsible—Bobby Bill."

"No one else does. We have never accused anyone. You have explicitly said that you don't believe the Senator had anything to do with it."

"I mostly believe that anyway."

"So you're pointing the finger in another direction—at mysterious, conspiratorial forces who are ready to use violence to defeat candidates they don't like."

"I could say on camera that I have no reason to blame my opponent who is not that kind of man and talk about mysterious forces."

"Why not?"

"Sounds good . . . Let me think about it . . . Good night my loyal love."

He kissed me very gently.

The St. Luke–St. Vincent soccer match was Labor Day itself. Not much for the news that night. The cameras would be out in force at the park.

It was a clear and blessedly cool morning. Mary Rose promised us that they would win.

"We will totally beat those brats and I will totally score two goals!"

"Young women are taller and stronger these days, aren't they?" Tommy said. "And far too aggressive and competitive?"

"They'll grow up to be pushy wives and mothers."

Our team was dressed in red and white and the bad guys in black and white because it was a Dominican parish.

"Our guys are better looking," I announced.

"Naturally," he agreed.

Well we did win 3–1 and our reckless young heroine, her red hair a flaming comet trailing behind her, did score two goals. I thought that the bitches from St. Vincent's had roughed her up unnecessarily.

"Are you proud of your daughter, Tommy?" A TV woman asked.

"Frightened of her," he murmured.

"Will you permit her to play soccer in high school and college?"

"How could I stop her if I wanted to . . . Which I don't."

"You approve then of women playing violent sports?"

"I think that crowd of amazons out there will scare away teenage boys for a long time . . . Which may be a very good thing."

The camera also picked up a gloriously sweaty redheaded young woman with a huge grin.

"I told my daddy that we would win just like he will win the election."

Then she modestly ducked away from the camera.

Could this be the little newborn babe I held in my arms only yesterday?

The next morning we met at our reconstructed office and laid out the plans for the next two months. Our experts pointed out the issues in the various county towns (as they're always called in Chicago politics) and suburban bastions—Elmhurst, Hinsdale, LaGrange, Lisle, Naperville, Oak Brook—and the location of Mexican concentrations. We constructed a tight, tight schedule which covered white suburbs, Latino concentrations, and Black churches. We would appear in shopping malls (especially the huge one in Oak Brook). We would go on every radio or TV program that would take us. We would do band sessions anywhere and everywhere. We would issue repeated invitations to a debate in which we would tell the opponent that we would meet at a place and a time of his own choosing.

"We have to be prompt at every one of our scheduled appearances," Dolly McCormick insisted. "My husband here is my enforcer. He is in charge of getting people to the Church on time."

Randal McCormick, her towering bear of a man, was an investment banker with a reputation as tall as he was. He grinned happily. "I like this. I never knew politics was this much fun."

We met that afternoon with Chucky and his friend who was doing the ads for us. They were mostly shots of my Tommy talking about his policies and convictions. They were put together either from TV tape or from shots made on the spot. He was flawless the first time around on every ad—the charming articulate witty trial lawyer, even when he made a joke about being Mr. Mom.

"Some say that only a wimp could stay in the house all day long with three little girls. Well, let me tell you, you have to be really tough to cope with three little kids of either gender. Besides they let me out of the house occasionally so long as I was home before dark."

"How could anyone vote against him, huh, Marymarg?" my father said . . . "You think that's too much of the candidate?" he hollered at Ted McManus, the PR man making the ads.

"How could there be too much of that candidate?"

"Let's do the violence one now," Chucky insisted, brimming with even more than his usual enthusiasm. "This one is really neat."

"We'd say totally cool, Chucky."

We did it and then redid it several times.

"Perfect," Ted McManus said finally. "What do you think, Chucky?"

"What do you guys think?" he bounced the question at us.

"It was my idea, so naturally I like it."

Tommy hesitated.

"You're going to try it with your focus groups, Ambassador?"

"Certainly."

"It gets by them, go with it."

It did and we did.

We got a quick reaction from Leander Schlenck

Tiny Tommy Takes the Low Road

Even Tiny Tommy Moran can sink lower than he is. His early ads, pedestrian in every other respect, now suggest that the distinguished Senior Senator from Illinois, H. Rodgers Cripsjin was behind the bombing at his campaign headquarters this summer. With his ratings in the polls falling precipitously, Tommy has forgotten about his own pledge to eschew negative ads. He is now a completely dead duck.

Dolly issued the usual "correction" that she did after every such column and after every new Crispjin ad. She sent them to all the media outlets. Sometimes the *Daily News* or one of the TV stations used them.

CHAPTER 13

✝

THERE WAS a terrifying incident in Spingfield at the end of September. It was Democrats' day at the Sangamon County Fair. We had, according to the *Daily News* poll, come within four percentage points of our opponent, 48 percent to 44 percent. Other polls showed no change. However, the *News* polls were the most reputable in the State. The *News,* increasingly sympathetic to us, announced that my candidacy clearly had gained momentum. It added that Senator Crispjin's mostly downstate campaign was listless and that his attack ads seemed to have little influence in the Chicago Metropolitan Area.

After that news was published—and reported on all the TV stations and in some of the national media too—my brother Tony phoned.

"I won't take any of your time, Senator," he said, a sneer in his voice. "I want you to know that I'm praying to Jesus and the Blessed Mother and to our own parents in heaven that for the good of the country and your own good and the good of your poor family, you'll lose."

He hung up before I could answer. Just as well.

However, the atmosphere in the County Fairgrounds in Sangamon County was heady. Sangamon has been Republican since Mr. Lincoln. However, its Democrats are tough and noisy. There probably weren't many votes to be gained there, but I had to be present. We put on the full show, the band with trumpets and drums included. The Sangamon

Democrats went wild, even those who hated immigrants sang along with us.

Johnny Dale, the bright young chairman of the Sangamon County Democrats, enveloped us in his genial smile.

"You folks sure are game," he said, "flying all the way down here. You can see that we folks already love you."

I noticed that even halfway down the state, there was a trace of a southern accent.

After I had finished, Johnny Dale thanked me.

"The people of Illinois will be proud of you Senator when you are sworn in on the Hill in January . . . Especially the people of Sangamon County."

I waved my thanks to the ovation, and turned and shook hands with the chairman.

"Daddy," Mary Ann shouted.

I turned to look for her just as a sharp bark came from somewhere and then immediately after a second one. Something whizzed by my head.

Behind me, Johnny Dale cried out and slumped to the ground. The Reliables and the state cops threw us all on the ground.

"Easy does it, Senator," my Reliable said. "Everyone in the family is OK." I didn't believe him.

Next to me, Johnny Dale was bleeding, two state cops were bending over him, his wife was screaming. A couple of medics appeared from nowhere and bent over him. The crowd was screaming wildly.

"Tommy?" my wife cried out.

"Alive and well."

"Kids are all OK!"

State cops and sheriff's deputies were trying to restrain the crowd.

"We gotta get him to hospital, now!" one of the medics pleaded. "Where the hell is the fucking ambulance!"

As if in response an ambulance siren wailed as it tried to pick its way through screaming spectators.

"Please, please, make way for the ambulance!" cried someone on the public address system. "We have a wounded man up here."

Finally two stretcher carriers and two more medics pushed their way through the crowd, which was now turning ugly. They picked up Johnny Dale and carried him through the crowd towards the ambulance, while the state cops used their nightsticks to beat the crowd out of the way and to protect Mrs. Dale.

Squad cars were now forcing their way into the arena.

"State police captain here. We ask everyone to quietly leave the grounds. We will arrest and charge with disorderly conduct anyone who does not comply."

They just laughed.

"We're going to bring you downstairs under the platform, Senator. We'll be all around you. That rifle shot was aimed at you."

"Tell me about it, Sergeant."

Beneath the stands was our whole bedraggled gang. The Reliables were ringed around them protectively. Confused state cops were striding around, nightsticks in hand, as though they were looking for someone to belt.

I then embraced my weeping family and all my colleagues in highly emotional moments.

"Who do you think did the shooting, Mr. Moran?"

"I don't know."

"They were aiming at you, were they not?"

"I don't know."

"Do you think Senator Crispjin was behind the attempted assassination?"

"Certainly not."

"If you and your party would get into your vans, sir, we will escort you to the airport."

I glanced at my sergeant.

"I think that would be best sir."

"I don't suppose you've apprehended the gunman, Captain?"

"I have no information about that, sir."

"And you don't know anything about Mr. Dale's condition?"

"I have no information about that, sir. Now I must order you to leave these grounds. We don't want any more assassinations here."

I wanted to hit him. I wanted to insult him. But that would have been wrong, even if the TV camera had not been rolling.

I climbed into our armored van on which Mike Casey, the president of Reliable, had insisted and embraced my weeping wife again.

"Someone tried to kill you, Tommy."

"They would have if Mary Ann hadn't warned me."

"It smelled terrible out there," she wailed.

The state police cars ahead of us turned on their sirens. We emerged from the arena to find people milling about.

"Are you in communication with those idiots in front of us?"

"Yes, Senator."

"Warn them that I don't want them to run over anybody and tell them that's for the record."

"Yes sir, Senator!"

He passed the message on.

"They're not bad guys, Senator."

"Ask them where Mr. Dale is . . . Mary Margaret, did you call your mother and father?"

"Of course, dear."

"Good! Call Dolly and tell her to issue a statement . . ."

"Senator, Mr. Dale is in Sangamon General and his condition is critical."

At the airport I made a decision.

"All of you get on the plane and fly back to Midway. Joe, make sure that Commissioner Riley has vans there too. Then bring the plane back here. I'm going to the hospital. Don't argue with me, anyone. That's what I'm going to do."

"Sir," said the state cop in the lead car, "you should be on that plane!"

"No, I shouldn't. I should be in the hospital with Mr. Dale and that's where I'm going. If you want to escort us fine . . . But I'm going there anyhow. Understand?"

"But, sir . . ."

"And if any asshole tells you that I can't do that you tell them they'll have to arrest me to stop me."

"Better do it, officer," said my Sergeant Reliable.

"Yes, sir."

So, sirens blaring we barreled into the emergency entrance of Sangamon General. Two state cops and a doctor were waiting for me.

"Good news, Senator," the doctor said. "We haven't upgraded from critical yet, but he's going to make it."

"Thanks be to God!"

"Amen to that, Senator."

The MD was clearly both a Catholic and a Democrat.

"Mrs. Dale knew you were coming. She wants you to go up to him so that they can all pray over him."

"Certainly."

Johnny Dale was a man in his early forties, handsome, a lawyer with clear gray eyes. His wife Hannah was blond, perhaps real blond. Her careful make-up was stained with tears. There were four kids, a couple of them teens, looking helpless and distraught.

Hannah embraced me.

"It was so good of you to come, Senator. You shouldn't have. That crazy man might still be around . . ."

Johnny Dale opened his eyes.

"Hey, Tommy. I'm glad it was me not you!"

"You know who that's from?"

"Sure, Chicago's Mayor Anton Cermak when a crazy man aimed at Roosevelt and hit him instead."

"Only he died and you won't."

"Thank God for antibiotics," he smiled wanly.

"We have to get to know each other better, Johnny Dale!"

"You'll never see the end of me at Capital Hill."

"Will you pray with us, Senator?" Hannah asked.

This was a Christian situation. I didn't know what to do, so I followed the safe route.

"Let us join hands and pray as the Lord taught us to pray and remember especially the part about forgiving those who sin against us."

I had lifted it all from Jimmy O'Malley.

Then I decided that I liked the priest role and would try some more.

"Heavenly father, who gives us life and hope, look down on this brave family which has just endured a shattering experience. Strengthen their hope and bring peace and forgiveness into their souls and take good care of them for their long lives. We ask this in the name of the Father who created and Son who saved and the Spirit who inspires. Amen."

"Now I gotta get back home and calm my own family down. We'll be seeing you, Johnny Dale!"

Hannah and two girl kids kissed me, the boy kids shook hands vigorously.

"God bless you, Senator," said the little girl.

"Amen," they all responded.

I choked up as I thanked them.

The doctor walked me back down to the emergency entrance.

"We've upgraded him to 'serious' and we're saying that we expect him to recover. Will you tell the media outside?"

I walked out and encountered a horde of questions.

I held up my hand for silence.

"The doctors have asked me to announce that they have upgraded Johnny Dale to 'serious' and they expect him to recover."

There were some cheers from the bystanders.

"Did you see him, Tommy?"

"I did. He was conscious and, astonishingly in good humor. I joined the family in praying over him."

"Did he know you were the target?"

"I think so. He quoted the mayor of Chicago who was shot by some-one who was aiming at Franklin D. Roosevelt. As you know Mr. Dale is very interested in political history . . . Now I have to get home to calm down my family."

I jumped quickly into my armored van, just in case the shooter was hanging around.

"Mrs. Moran is on the phone, Senator. Calling from the plane."

"Marymarg, I'm all right."

"Rosie said it's all live on television and they just had a picture of you going into the hospital."

"They probably will have one of my coming out by now."

"How is the poor dear man, Tommy?"

"They've upgraded him to serious and expect him to live."

"Thanks be to God!"

"Amen . . . How is your crowd?"

"Traumatized, Tommy, especially the little girls. They're still crying. We're landing now. The plane will come back for you. Be careful."

"Count on it."

When I arrived back on Lathrop Avenue, all the lights in our re-stored residence were out. But the media were waiting outside.

"What happened, Tommy?"

"You've seen it all, more clearly than I could. Someone apparently took a couple of shots at me and hit Johnny Dale by mistake."

"Did the state police order you not to visit Mr. Dale in the hospital?"

"The last time I heard visiting the sick was a corporal work of mercy."

"Do you think that Senator Crispjin was involved in the assassina-tion attempt?"

"Certainly not. I repeat in case some careless journalist tries to mis-quote me, certainly not."

I tiptoed upstairs, all the women in my family were sound asleep. I went down to our basement workroom, found the Bushmill's bottle and poured myself a moderate amount—that is a full glass.

I sipped at it slowly, put my feet up on the desk, and tried to think.

The phone rang.

"Thomas Moran."

"Rodgers Crispjin."

"Senator," I said politely. "It's good of you to call."

"I want you to know," he spoke quickly and in an uncertain voice, "I had nothing to do with that terrible event in Springfield. Nothing whatever."

"I know that, Senator. I've said it at every opportunity."

"I know. I appreciate that. I don't know who would do something like that."

"Perhaps your good friend Bobby Bill?"

"I doubt it. I thought I had put an end to that nonsense back in the spring. He denies it though he's not a very good liar."

"I'm happy to hear that."

"I just wanted you to know that I had nothing to do with it."

"I appreciate your calling, Senator."

"Yes."

The poor clown did not know how to end the conversation.

"Good luck, Senator."

"Hmn, oh yes."

He didn't say either "thank you" or "good-bye."

I put my feet back on the desk, sipped some more of my whiskey, and thought some more. Why was Senator Crispjin so eager to persuade me of his innocence, almost beg me to absolve him? I didn't get it.

Then I had an idea.

I called the Ambassador's house.

"O'Malley's. Rosemarie."

"Tommy here. Is the Ambassador still awake?"

"Yes indeed. Here he is—you were wonderful, by the way. The angels were taking care of you."

"And your psychic granddaughter."

"Witches run in our family. Every other generation."

Had I interrupted love-making? At their age? Well, why not?

"Hi, Tommy, you were splendid—lots of votes!"

"I had a phone call from the Senator a few moments ago. He was scared."

"Really? How interesting!"

"He wanted to insist that he had nothing to do with the little affair down in Springfield."

"You've already said that several times."

"I know and I'll say it tomorrow."

"Good! Our little ad becomes all the more important."

"He seemed to be in fear for his own life."

"Why would he feel threatened?"

"Because somehow it was suggested to him that if anything happened to me, he was roadkill."

"Hmm . . . Well, he never was in any danger as far as I know."

"He believes he was."

"How interesting . . . You remember what your good friend Joe Goebbels said?"

"I wasn't alive to meet the man, but didn't he say something like if you're going to tell a lie, tell a big one?"

"Yeah. Same thing is true of a bluff."

I paused to absorb what was being said.

"I understand . . . Sleep well, Mr. Ambassador."

"You too, Senator."

"The Senator called me last night to express his sympathies and to assure me that he had no part in the attempted assassination yesterday. I thanked him and said I was absolutely certain that he did not."

That was my first statement in the morning when we walked out of our house at 8:30 to bring the kids to school. My good wife was with me and she looked terrible. I imagined that I did too.

"Tommy, how do you feel this morning?"

"Scared."

"Me too," Mary Margaret agreed.

"You're going ahead with your scheduled campaign appearances?"

"Of course."

"Is that wise?"

"I have written in my book which is appearing in the book stores today that our contemporary uncivil politics will eventually lead to violence. There are some Americans who imagine they hear God telling them to liquidate the bad guys. The violence this summer could be the tip of the iceberg."

"We've tracked the bullet, if you hadn't turned away when you did, it would have hit right above your eye."

"We're not heroes," I said firmly, "but we're not going to run away either. Now we gotta get our daughters to school."

The young folk were solemn faced.

"We're not quitting either," Mary Rose intoned.

"Like totally," the other two agreed.

So we began again our marathon race through the Chicago Metropolitan Area—The Oak Brook mall, Operation PUSH (several times), Black churches in Chicago, Maywood, and Joliet. A parish priest in Hinsdale warned us that if we tried to receive the Eucharist at his church, he would refuse it. Dolly issued a statement that we had no intention of making such an effort. However, we would greet commuters at the Hinsdale station that morning and evening. The cameras were there to catch the hundreds of folk who pushed their way to shake our hands. Then up to North Chicago for a rally at a Hispanic community center (with kids who did their homework in the van, up and back). Our final stop was a prayer service at a Black church in Waukegan. Then, in a fearsome thunder shower we drove back to Chicago, the kids finishing up their homework and my wife and I trying to nap.

We were surrounded by security everywhere—state police, county police, city police and of course the Reliables. I didn't mind their constant presence one bit because I was still scared. My wife turned fatalistic. "If they're going to get us, they're going to get us. This is a country that kills presidents. Why not kill a few senatorial candidates too?"

I saw no need to tell her about my late night conversation with her father. I suspect she already knew.

Then the Ambassador himself was in trouble.

CHAPTER 14

†

FEDS INVESTIGATE TOMMY'S IN-LAW

Reports leaking out of the United States Attorney's Office suggest that the Feds are taking a hard look at Tiny Tommy's mysterious campaign fund, one about which he pretends to know nothing. His father-in-law, Charles O'Malley, whose claim to be an ambassador is forty years out of date, is apparently running the fund with the same recklessness he has demonstrated in his years as a sensationalist photographer. Indictments are expected even before the election.

The Ambassador appeared on television with his own rebuttal.

I'm Chuck O'Malley. I never call myself ambassador, well, hardly never. I am, however, an unpaid member of the senior executive service of the State Department with the title of Ambassador. I'm called in several times a year for consultation. Now that the secret is out, I think the Administration will probably get rid of me. As for journalism, I'll compare my Pulitzer prizes with Mr. Schlenk's any time he wants. So far he is shut-out. As for the campaign fund, Mr. Elihu Kunkel, formerly chairman of the National Election Commission and a card-carrying Republican, is monitoring the fund. Every day. If the U.S. Attorney is interested in anything more than engaging in campaign leaks, I invite him to come into my office to-morrow morning and take a copy of our books with him.

He then called the U.S. Attorney and asked him if he were familiar with the libel laws. That worthy denied that any investigation was "un-der contemplation." The Ambassador then demanded that he come and look at the books anyway.

"We're not in the business of clearing people of charges that have not been made."

"You'd better be in the business of protecting yourself from a libel suit. Bring all your retard accountants to look at the books. My attor-neys are ready to seek relief."

"I am not responsible for Mr. Schlenk's reports."

"That would make an interesting point of law, sir."

The Ambassador was bluffing again of course.

And he won. The State Department confirmed his role, said that he was a very distinguished diplomat, and denied that they were thinking of removing him. The U.S. Attorney showed up at his office and said, after a day of inspection, that he wished all campaign funds were kept in such neat order.

"Incorrigible," Rosie said to me. "He's been that way since he was ten."

None of this interfered with our manic campaign. Tommy, his head reeling with ideas, was unable to sleep at all. But he was still the cool, charming little Mick whom everyone loved.

It's odd that I'm the only one talking about issues in this campaign. My op-ponent's ads affirm that he is experienced and mature, allegations which I will hardly deny. There is also a hint in a lot of discussion in the media that I am inexperienced and immature. My years of defending the poor and the innocent apparently don't count. But that is not what the campaign should be about—it's about the economic royalists, Big Oil, Big Insurance, and Big Pharma. It's about corporate America, the rich and the super rich are taking money from the poor and the middle class and giving it, with the help of the Republican party, to the rich, to CEOs who earn a hundred and forty million dollars after they're forced out of a company when it's losing money. It's about defending pensions from corporate bankruptcy tricks and your private property from eminent domain to put up Wal-Marts. It's about immigration reform which puts an end to the senseless death of the poor but ambitious in the deserts of the southwest, it's about recognizing the importance of the contribution of Mexican Americans to our national culture. Even if my opponent won't debate me on these issues, I am disappointed that he acts as though they don't exist.

The talk, short and to the point, always won big applause. The *Daily News* called Tommy an interesting and exciting candidate, one that combined old though still important issues with a challenging new political style. They had already told Dolly that they would endorse us the week before the election. Lee Schlenk had already told his avid readers that an endorsement from such a "liberal" sheet and two dollars would get you a ride on the Chicago Transit Authority. I was pretty sure that he had an impact only on those who had made up their mind months ago they were going to vote for the incumbent. Tommy was less optimistic.

"OK, he appeals to the cement heads. But there are a lot of them out there and they enjoy it when Schlenk ridicules the smart young punk."

Tommy was fading, not fast exactly, but fading just the same, like a man in whom illness is slowly transforming itself into death. The assassination attempts, the tsunami of attack ads, the ceaseless contemptuous battering from the *Examiner,* the threat to Chucky, were wearing my poor dear man out.

"I hope I can hold out till it's over," he told me after a particularly dazzling performance at a rally in the town of Harvard in McHenry County. He seemed resigned to defeat, though the *Daily News* Poll showed us trailing only one percentage point, 48 percent to 47 percent among "likely" voters and taking three out of five of the voters who had not yet made up their minds.

"We're trying to win the imbeciles who haven't made up their mind because they don't know what the election is about . . . And they think I'm immature and inexperienced."

I suspected he was right. But I insisted that we were going to win easily because of the Latino voters who would vote for the first time and whom the pollsters could not persuade to respond to questions.

"That's a leap of faith," he said with a sigh.

It was of course.

There wasn't much physical love in those hot hectic days. There wasn't any time for it and we were both too tired. A hint perhaps of what would happen when we moved to the Beltway.

We scored some points at the mall in Naperville.

"How come you guys are in Naperville tomorrow morning?" Mary Alice Quinn of Channel 3 asked me in a late afternoon phone call to our headquarters.

"Why not? It's on our schedule. The book store wants Tommy to sign some of his books."

"You know that old stuff and nonsense will be there about the same time?"

"Sure, so what?"

I didn't know it. Neither did anyone else on our team. I grabbed for the paper that had the schedule of Crispjin.

"Kind of an interesting accident, isn't it?"

"We get there a half hour earlier. The Senator is at that bank, naturally."

"Their paths might cross?"

"Tommy might even give him an autographed copy of his book, huh?"

"We've discussed that possibility."

Which we hadn't at all, as Mary Alice well knew.

"Great visual, huh?"

"If someone over there sees the conflict, they won't show."

"I'm not about to tell them," she assured me. "You guys gonna win?"

"No doubt about it."

The HQ was frantically active. Our phone banks were going strong as we tried to build up precinct organizations in key suburban precincts. Ric, Joe, and the incomparable Dolly were each dashing around with sheaves of paper in their hands. Well, we looked like professionals anyway.

Then Tommy ambled in from an interview on a PBS station. Our workers cheered him. They all thought we were going to win. We couldn't let them down.

I gave him the signal that I wanted to talk to him.

"You summon me, wife of my youth?"

"And your middle age and old age too . . . You want to give an autographed copy of your book to Senator Crispjin?"

"What a grand idea!" he said, looking cheerful again. "Here is a copy of my new book about the decline of civility, about you as a matter of fact."

"Don't you dare say that!"

We huddled with Joe, Ric, and Dolly.

"Funny," Dolly said, grinning happily. "The book store wants you to show up maybe an hour early. They've had tons of calls about autographs."

"Tell them we'll be there at nine-thirty," I said.

"Suppose they're wrong," Tommy frowned. "Suppose no one is there."

"They know their own business."

"Should we give Mary Alice a heads-up?" I asked Dolly.

She thought about it for a minute.

"We're scheduled for ten-thirty, right? We're getting there at nine-thirty, right? Tell Mary A. that we'll be there at ten. They'll arrive in the middle of our triumph."

"We need more triumphs," my husband agreed.

When my poor dear man gets whimsical, I know he needs a good night's sleep.

"Does anyone know," Joe McDermott asked, "how close that First Bank of Naperville is to the book store?"

Dolly checked with a phone call.

"Maybe thirty yards."

"We'll need some mariachi sound?" Ric suggested.

"We don't take the kids out of school!" I said. "That would look terrible!"

"We'll not be able to keep Tina away. Maybe we can dig up some local talent to join you guys. If the Senator hears the noise, it'll drive him crazy."

"If they had any sense," Tommy said, immune to our glee, "they'd cancel out. He doesn't want to be seen in public with me."

"Then our TV friends will really go after him."

"I suppose."

He needed some loving. I would have to seduce him. Fortunately that's not very difficult. I knew that. I just hadn't had the time to do anything about it in the last couple of weeks. What a rotten excuse. Then and now.

So the next morning he was in a glowing mood when we drove out in our armored van to Naperville, a sprawling former farming center and now a quintessential suburb. I'd choke to death if I ever had to live there. Nonetheless there were hundreds of potential voters waiting in front of the book store. They cheered when they saw him.

"Readers and voters!" Tommy said enthusiastically.

I should note that he was not the only one who enjoyed a good night's sleep after our little romp.

Most of the people in the crowd had already purchased their books. More royalties. We were almost broke.

"Good of all of you to come!" Tommy began with his most radiant Irish smile. "This book is what the election is about. We observe the end of civilized discourse in campaigns and the increase in attack ads. That makes our politics more angry and even more dangerous. I told myself when we began the race that its goal was to offer an example of a civil campaign. I think I've kept that promise. Now I want to WIN! So I urge you to read the book and, if you agree with me get out and vote early and often!"

Cheers interrupted my fantasy recollection of the pleasures of the previous night. I wanted more.

"I brought along some mariachi music to entertain you while I'm signing books. My wife Maria Margarita is the one with the red hair and Tina Sanchez, the wife of my campaign manager Ric Sanchez, does the fiddle. The kids are in school where they belong on weekdays, even if there is an election campaign. They don't agree of course!'

Not terribly funny but they loved it.

Mary Alice and her cameraman arrived fifteen minutes into the signing.

Tommy smiled, laughed, and joked with his adoring public.

"They say they'll have no trouble selling out the four hundred books," Dolly whispered in my ear at one of our breaks.

"Save one for Rodge."

I calculated rapidly. At 15 percent royalty that was $3.25 for each book, over twelve hundred dollars for this signing. That was nice, though it wouldn't pay for the repairs to our house because of the bomb damage. The insurance company was denying liability because the explosion wasn't in the house but outside of it. They would pay eventually but they wanted to cheat us out of as much as they could.

The books vanished while there were still at least a hundred potential readers. The store promised it would have more books by noon tomorrow. The Senator promised that if you order them today or tomorrow morning he'll sign them tomorrow afternoon. And you'll be able to pick them up here in the evening.

Tommy rose from the chair.

"This has been fun! Thank you very much! And thanks also to our redoubtable musicians. Read the book early and often! I have only this one left. I thought I'd give it to the incumbent who is just down the mall. What do you think?"

He autographed the book. I glanced over his shoulder.

For Senator H. Rodgers Crispjin,
All the Best, Tommy Moran

Laughter and applause.

The cameras were ready in front of the First Bank of Naperville. Followed by a crowd of his admirers, all clutching their precious autographed copies, Tommy walked to the front of the bank, slipped through the handlers around the Senator, and handed him the book.

"I thought you might want a signed copy," he said, extending his hand. "Good luck."

As luck—and clever maneuvering by my husband—the words went out on the public address system.

The Senator was flummoxed.

"Thank you," he stammered, shaking hands. "Very thoughtful of you."

"All the best," Tommy said slipping away as easily as he had slipped in.

Our crowd cheered. The Senator's crowd, much smaller and less demonstrative did nothing. If looks could kill, the daggers from the Senator's staff would have torn my poor little man apart and his blood would be all over the floor in the Naperville Mall.

Mary Alice cornered us on the way to the van.

"Was this a coincidence, Tommy?"

"Hey, our weekly schedule is public knowledge every Monday morning. We figured it would look like I was afraid to be in the same place if I didn't show up. His people must have figured the same way."

Zinger!

We entered the van, our next stop was a Spanish language television. I would appear on camera too, the excuse being that I spoke the language better than my husband.

I maneuvered us into the last seat, Ric and Linda in front of us.

"They will attack me at this station for exploiting Latino culture," Tommy said, sinking into self-pity, as he had all too frequently lately.

"You will reply that you are celebrating it. You will say that most Anglo citizens of Illinois did not know mariachi and now they do and love it. They will say there are other kinds of Mexican music. You will say your experience is especially in Sonora and mariachi is in its origins Sonoran music. You also admire Nortefino, Banda, and Tex-Mex. They will say that you and your wife speak with Sonoran accents and that is not a very cultivated form of the Mexican language. You will say that large numbers of Sonoran natives or their children who are watching won't like that comment. They will say that your wife and children are not Mexican Americans. You will say they are Americans with great affection and respect for Mexican people and their language and their culture. They will ask whether you support bilingual education. You will say that is a decision for parents to make about their children. However, a command of English is necessary for success in American society, as every immigrant group has learned, including the Irish. They will wonder about that. And you will say that before 1870 most Irish immigrants spoke Irish fluently and they felt they were forced to give it up. In the world we live in no one should give up a language proficiency. Then you will praise their religion of festival and celebration. They will not be very gracious because they don't like gringos but they'll know you routed them."

"Same old shit," Tommy sighed. "Nothing about issues."

"They may say that most Mexican men believe that they are the head of the family."

"And the Senator will say," Tina intervened, "that most men think that too and that most women know that they are."

"The usual boring shit," Tommy sighed. "I need a nap . . . Why doesn't anyone ask about issues?'

"Say that at the end of the broadcast," Ric suggested. "Wonder why they didn't ask about proposed immigration reform. There will be legislation before the Senate in the next session. Surely their listeners will like to know that you will do all in your power to support a reform which will protect the human rights of all immigrants, no more bodies in the Sonoran desert."

"OK, good night all."

He closed his eyes and went to sleep, the creep.

Well, I'd have him to myself in bed tonight and I'd get even.

He woke up for the Spanish TV station. I was kind of glad that he had caught his nap. This would not be a taping which would be cut down for soundbites. It would be a half-hour interview to be played in its entirety. The station staff was nasty to the point of being hostile. Were they in the tank with H. Rodge?

"Why don't you Anglos give Latinos more political power?"

"I'm not Anglo, I'm Irish. I believe that is demeaning and patronizing to ask why political power is not given. Political power has to be taken and the place to do that is in the voting both. There seems to be a lot of Latino power in Cook County. If I am given a chance to serve in the United States Senate, I'll be a voice for Mexican Americans."

"You don't even speak good Mexican Spanish."

"Oh?"

"Sonorans do not speak good Spanish."

His answer for that was already prepared. He did a good job running down Ric's agenda. He would turn to me every once in a while when he was seeking the proper word. I would also smile pleasantly and as docilely as possible provide it.

The four interviewers continued to be supercilious and hostile, hinting that they did not accept any of his answers or simply did not believe him. I noticed a slight furrowing of my husband's brow beneath his wavy hair. He watched the clock and when we were down to two minutes, he interrupted a particularly nasty question from a particularly nasty woman and spoke in Spanish:

"I'm wondering why you haven't asked any questions about immigration reform. Is that because you're not interested in the issue? Or do you think that your viewers are not interested? There will be legislation before the Senate on that subject. I will fight every inch of the way for the full human rights of everyone living in this country, their inalienable rights which no one should try to take away from them. I will in particular defend the rights of families to remain intact, no matter what the Department of Homeland Security tries to do. I will do everything in my power to put an end to the mass murders which happen in the Sonoran desert every year. Poor innocents are killed by the rules of the United States Government which seduces them into the country with de facto offers of employment and then makes them risk their lives to find such employment. I will do all in my power to fight those sinful rules . . . Thank you very much for the opportunity to appear on this program."

It had been a tour de force—an outburst in his second language in a hostile context and timed exactly to end when the time of the program ran out.

The woman whom he had interrupted stormed away from the table. The other interviewers glared.

"Feliz Navidad, everyone," he said standing up.

The "host" shook his hand. "Well done, Senator."

He wanted us back some day. Or maybe some favors if we won.

Ric and Tina burst into the sound stage and spit out insults in such rapid Spanish that I couldn't catch it. My husband smiled, the kitten who had just chased his first canary.

"I've got a tape here," Ric shouted in English. "If you dare to touch a single response, you're roadkill. Come on, Senator. I apologize for the rudeness of these jerks."

Tommy smiled benignly.

"See you at the election celebration, guys!"

Suddenly it was November and there were only a few days left. The *Daily News* endorsed us in ringing terms.

A NEW VOICE FOR ILLINOIS, AMERICA

Mr. Moran ran a brilliant campaign, despite a torrent of personal attacks, including two attempts on his life. With a limited budget he fought off a hurricane of negative advertising, some of it dishonest in the extreme. His is a bright, brave new voice in American politics, a voice which the whole country needs to hear. Despite his whimsical Irish charm he is in fact one tough customer. He says hard things that no one wants to hear especially about the increased concentration of wealth in this country and the exploitation of poor Mexican workers.

To our knowledge Senator Crispjin has not responded effectively to any of these campaign issues. Indeed, he has not responded at all. His campaign consists of the frequent repetition of the catchwords "maturity" and "experience." But those attributes, unquestionably important, should not be grounds for excluding younger and more innovate men from political life. One wants to know what evidence there is in Mr. Crispjin's record that maturity and experience have contributed to wise legislation. Indeed, his "record," frequently cited though without any specific content, consists mostly of giving more money to those who are already rich. His attack ads demonstrate the vicious incivility which Mr. Moran describes in his book and create the atmosphere in which political assassinations can happen.

We urge everyone to vote for Mr. Moran to be the next United States Senator from this our Prairie State.

"How many votes will it swing?" my Tommy, now in deep discouragement, wondered.

"A couple thousand," Joe McDermott replied. "People from out of the city who can't figure out our politics and think the *Examiner* is a paper for nutcases. They are the serious earnest type who look to the media for endorsements. In a close election, they're important."

"Not as important as a Mexican turnout in the suburbs."

No one of us disagreed.

Channel 3 endorsed us, the other stations announced that they did not make endorsements, though they had in the past. Mary Alice Quinn read the announcement with considerable vigor.

It will be good for this state and for the country to have a bright, creative new voice in the Senate. The people of Illinois will be happy that they voted for him.

The polls all reported that the race was too close to call. The media also reported a dramatic increase in activity in conservative Protestant churches for "responsibility" and "maturity" and "red-blooded Americanism." They speculated that this initiative was a sign that the Republicans now, for the first time, realized that they could lose this seat in the Senate. National Republican figures also appeared on the scene, including the vice president, to urge stability and continuity in the Senate. "We don't need another liberal demagogue," the Vice President announced.

"That will help their turnout," Joe conceded, "but it won't have any effect on the Black or Latino voters."

"Hmpf," Tommy said.

The next and probably final hurdle was the debate the PBS channel was going to stage—with only one debater—on Sunday night.

CHAPTER 15

✝

O N THE SUNDAY before the election the churches weighed in against us and captured the headlines. "Christian" churches distributed brochures attacking Tommy as a killer of millions of babies. A downstate Catholic bishop issued a pastoral letter warning his people that if they voted for the Democratic candidate they were not "worthy" to receive Communion. Father Tony called to crow over this setback, sending Tommy deeper into his tailspin. My uncle, Father Ed, who knew the bishop in the seminary, told us, "No one pays any attention to him. He has one of the worst records on pedophilia in the country. He couldn't deliver a pack of starving vampires to a blood bank . . ."

During the nine o'clock Mass at St.Luke's I finally realized that I had been Tommy's escape from his family. I was passionate love, an alternative to rigid control. It was astonishing that Tommy was able to make that choice and stick with it. When the pressure and self-doubt closed in on him, he needed me.

Of course.

Why hadn't I seen it before?

Now I ask myself why I still don't get it?

As time went on I began to realize that Father Tony was something of a Dr. Jekyell/Mr.Hyde character. I had attended a day of recollection he gave for professional women at a North Shore parish where some of my legal colleagues lived. It was during the time before the

Senate race when Tommy was still Mr. Mom and writing his first book. I figured it would be interesting to see what he had to say to women and perhaps I would understand a little better why he hated me so much. I told Tommy while he and the kids were fixing breakfast for one another that I was going to a day of recollection. He seemed surprised but said only, "Say a prayer for us."

"Especially for poor Daddy," Mary Rose said with a giggle.

The church was packed with professional women and stay-at-home moms. I expected that Father Tony would come down hard on the former and praise the latter. In fact, he avoided that issue completely and talked almost entirely about hope—the need for it and the difficulties all of us encountered in hoping. His talks displayed little depth but they were humble and encouraging to women. I could hardly believe it was the same man who disrupted our wedding breakfast. Moreover, during the lunch he moved among the women with charm and grace. Not as much charm as Tommy and not as much grace either, but still he was better than many priests would have been in such an environment. I sat in the back of the Church with a veil over my head to hide the giveaway carrot top.

But he saw me in the lobby of the church as I was trying to sneak out.

"Mary Margaret," he said, reaching out to shake hands, "how good of you to come! I wasn't expecting to see you . . . I'll walk with you to your car."

This was not the same priest who almost ruined my wedding breakfast.

"Your talks were very good," I said somewhat primly.

"Thank you! I feel so inferior to the women who attend these days. They are so good and work so hard at being a wife and a mother and a career person. I don't think that they realize how much God loves them. Maybe my words will help them to understand that women like you are saints of the everyday."

Honest, that's what he said. I wrote it down before I started my VW.

Maybe that's who he really was most of the time. Only when he was talking to his "little brother" did he go over the top. I remembered his words to me at the end of his father's funeral, a stricken man reaching out for comfort from his family. Maybe that's who he really wanted to be. Perhaps he still felt, however, that with his parents gone, his obligation to protect his "little brother" was even more sacred. It had become an obsession and he was Mr. Hyde, poor man.

So some of the time on some occasions and as angry as I was at him, I did feel a touch of sympathy for my husband's brother. When I told Tommy about the day of recollection, he did not seem surprised.

"He's a good priest, Mary Margaret. He has just one blind spot—me."

Later Tommy had taken an enormous beating during the campaign, attacks from every side, from the media, from the churches, from his family, from the would-be killers, and from the attack ads. How had he been able to hang in there and remain his articulate, charming self?

How did he survive people like his brother or Leander Schlenk or Lupe Gonzalez, the bitch on the Spanish language TV station, both of whom would be on the "debate" panel this evening. My poor, dear man was incredibly resilient, but he needed more passion from me. I had not understood that when the world closed in on him, he suppressed his emotions, perhaps fearing to risk rejection from me.

I'd never done that.

But I must take the initiative. That ought not to be a problem. I love the man and I desired him. Why did I back off when he plunged into one of his moods. God forgive me for it, but my body became aroused at the Eucharist as I was thinking of it. Well, really, there was nothing to forgive. God expected spouses to lust after one another.

So when we went up to our room after Mass and I closed the door, it was time. I slipped out of my dress, kicked off my shoes and stood there in my bra and pantyhose, a pose which usually turns him on.

He was reading again the attack brochure of the "Christians."

"Well?"

He turned, looked at me, and gulped. Well, I could still make his eyes pop.

"Do I see an invitation?" he asked with a sly little grin that always turns me on.

"A demand."

"Warriors take their women after victory in battle," he said.

"I read somewhere that the ancient Irish took them both before and after."

"That seems like a good idea."

We progressed from there.

"I'll wipe them all out tonight," he said after we were finished and while we were clinging desperately to one another. "Then I'll come back here and settle matters with you."

"I might just fight back."

"So much the better."

Love as campaign strategy? No, just love as love.

As time would tell, I still had a lot to learn about love.

The panel Channel 11 had assembled for our mock debate were not a promising bunch for our side, Leander Schlenk from the *Examiner,* Lupe Gonzalez from Spanish-language TV, Graham Grayson from the *Defender,* Mary Alice Quinn from Channel 3, and Harold Honeywell from the *Daily News.* The last two were on our side, but they wouldn't cut us any slack. The first two hated us. Grayson would probably complain that we had ignored the Blacks.

Tommy was in great form as we road over to the Albany Park location of PBS. He whispered obscene suggestions into my ear, including his intent to tie me up and torment me all night long.

"You'll be lucky if you're able to do it twice in one day," I shot back.

We both giggled like newlyweds, though quietly so as not to offend the Reliable driving our armored van.

The air was more caustic than electric at the station. Our crowd was there in the control room—Joe, Ric, Dolly and their respective spouses. No one there representing the invisible candidate, though the producer had left an empty podium for him. Thirty or forty people in the audience, mostly young people.

SCHLENK (a lean and hungry man without any hair on his head): Well, Tommy, it looks like you're going to lose. The polls show you slipping, don't they?

CANDIDATE: Mr. Schlenk, I'll bet you a hundred dollars that we will win by somewhere between five and fifteen percentage points.

SCHLENK: I'm not a betting man, Tommy . . . The churches have turned against you, haven't they? What right do you have to win? You lack maturity, experience, and even common sense. You're not half the man Senator Crispjin is. You can't even tell me one good reason why people should vote for you instead of him.

CANDIDATE: I doubt that the belated involvement of some clergy will have any effect on Tuesday. I have consistently refused to compare myself with the incumbent because I have eschewed personalities in this contest. The one good reason to vote for me is that I'm a Democrat and it's time for a change in Washington. The ordinary middle class and working people of Illinois need someone in D.C. who will defend their pensions from greedy corporations, their property from greedy local officials, their health from greedy insurance companies, and their future from the rich and super rich who have cut them out of the American dream.

(Applause from the crowd)

Ms. GONZALEZ (a petite, very sexy woman, with burning eyes. She speaks in Spanish): You now do not have your wife here to help you with your poor Spanish. Why do you patronize the Latino people? Why do you exploit them to win their votes? Why do you produce fake photographs which show Our Lady of Guadalupe at the door of your house? Why do you speak our language in a Sonoran dialect which is insulting? Why do you ignore all other Mexican music besides mariachi which is for peasants? Why should any self-respecting Latino vote for you?

CANDIDATE: (in Spanish in the first sentence) That is a litany of hostile questions, Senora, all of which are based on false assumptions (turn to English). Ms. Gonzalez attacks me for exploiting the Latino voters. Whether I have or not is for them to decide on election day. Let me answer only one of her questions which illustrates the tone of all the others. In the background as we come out of our house, the TV cameras have recorded a life-sized statue of Our Lady of Guadalupe. My daughters fell in love with her on our first trip to Hermosillo and we brought her home with us. They made the sign of the cross and touched her every day when they went off to school. They don't anymore because she was blown to pieces by the explosion in front of her house—which demonstrated how deadly attack politics can be. I presume that those Latinos who vote for me on Tuesday will do so because they know that I'm on their side.

(More applause and now cheers. We owned the audience, but young people don't go out and vote.)

GRAYSON (a large handsome Black man, not quite as big as the Shaq): A lot of people in the African-American community resent the fact that you have neglected them in your enthusiasm for the Latinos. What would you say to them?

CANDIDATE: I would say that a competent United States Senator must respect and devote this attention to both Latinos and Blacks. He should say both . . . and instead of either . . . or. We were very careful to make the same number of appearances in both groups and to address ourselves to the concerns of both. If some African Americans feel neglected, I am sorry but I think the record shows that we were evenhanded in our appearances. We were at Operation PUSH so often that they had good reason to be bored with us.

GRAYSON: You don't sing African-American spirituals.

CANDIDATE: I'm afraid that you weren't around for our appearances at Black churches. My music-mad family sang spirituals with enthusiasm and verve. I think the kids will be offended at the suggestion they did not.

GRAYSON (big grin): I been there, Senator, I heard them.

Ms. QUINN: (a handsome woman in a stylish blue dress) Are you really broke, Tom?"

CANDIDATE (laughs): Where did you hear that, Mary Alice? But the answer I'm afraid is that we are. There's enough money in the campaign fund to pay for the victory celebration on election night, but not much else. Our personal coffers are presently bare. We took out a second mortgage on the house, turned in all the accounts for our kids' college educations, sold all our insurance policies, used most of the advance from my book. We haven't been able to pay for the reconstruction of our house yet.

Ms. QUINN: Wasn't it insured?

CANDIDATE: The insurance company denies liability. That's what they do. They'll pay eventually, but they'll try to cheat us. We'll survive. My wife will go back to the practice of law when we move to Washington. The publisher wants to negotiate a contract for three books. Don't plan, Mary Alice, a tag day for us just yet.

HAROLD HONEYWELL (a quiet, tweedy man, with sandy hair and the haggard look of someone who has had to meet too many deadlines): Tommy, this has been a pretty vicious campaign, has it not? I'm wondering if the nastiness has had any effect on your wife and family?

CANDIDATE: Are you suggesting, Mr. Honeywell, that I have contributed to the viciousness?

HONEYWELL: Not all. All you did was to run on a platform which rejected negative campaigns.

CANDIDATE: As to my wife and family, how could they not be affected by the corrosive atmosphere of hate which has invaded American politics? They're tough and resilient folks. They respond by offering to fight anyone who attacks their husband and father. However, they were almost blown up by a bomb in our battered old Chevy van and saw a rifle bullet fell Johnny Dale in a shot intended for me. If I may refer to my book, I accuse the media of fomenting some of this malignity. Hate, attack, scandal is what the media offer instead of conversation about political issues. Consider the five questions that you have asked me—am I the man that my opponent is? Why do I exploit Hispanic voters? Why did I neglect Black voters? Why don't I have any money? How do my wife and family react to the viciousness? That's attack journalism, not responsible political discourse. Not a single question about the issues in the election. The media are trapped in the miasma of hate which they have helped to create.

(Standing ovation from the crowd)

SCHLENK: You still don't get it, do you Tommy? I can't believe that you're so naïve. The voters don't care about issues. They want red meat. They want to see politicians cut to pieces and their blood spilling on the streets. They know that pols are liars and crooks and they delight in their downfall. If you're broke they think you deserve to be broke because you're a naïve fool. The media and the attack ads give them just what they want. It's all about entertainment, not about issues. What would we fill up space with if we didn't have elections all the time? You're not winning any votes this evening. You're just providing alternative entertainment to *Law and Order*.

(Boos from the crowd)

CANDIDATE: Mr. Schlenk, that's a very wicked statement. If it is true, our Republic is in deep trouble. I am prepared to admit that there is a great deal of truth in your cynicism. But it is not the whole truth. Americans do care about political issues. They care about their pensions and their homes and their insurance policies and their medical bills. Cynicism like yours is all too typical of your profession, but it's pernicious and evil and untrue.

(Long standing ovation from the audience)

The "debate" continues. There are no issue questions. Candidate sneaks some issue responses into his answers.

The moderator permits three questions from the audience.

FIRST QUESTION (young woman in jeans and Loyola sweatshirt): Do you think when you go to Washington you will be able to change American politics?

CANDIDATE: I like your word "when!" I won't be able to make much difference by myself, though winning the election will show that one does not need a lot of money or negative advertising to win an election. For twenty years now American life has been dominated by greed and arrogance in reaction to the social concerns of earlier decades. I think the cycle is about to change. I hope to be part of that change. I hope the Democratic party appeals once again to the working and middle class American families and not just the East Coast Liberals. So change is in the making but it will take a while.

SECOND QUESTION (Young man in a business suit): Isn't your emphasis on poor versus rich a return to Marxist class conflict politics?

CANDIDATE: Marx did not invent every poverty or greed. Opposition to the power of the very rich and the super rich is part of the American populist political tradition. I didn't make up the statistics about the increase in concentration of wealth in this country. Finally in a democratic society you create change at the ballot box, not in the streets.

THIRD QUESTION (young woman in jeans and University of Illinois sweatshirt): What is your opinion of the current immigration reform legislation in Congress?

CANDIDATE: It's not a perfect reform by any means. In the anti-immigrant feeling of the country today it's probably the best we can get. I'll fight for amendments that better protect the rights of immigrant workers. I don't know whether we can push such amendments through Congress.

QUESTIONER: Thank you, Senator. I hope you continue your excellent Web page. It was a great response to all those negative ads.

CANDIDATE: Thank you, ma'am. My good wife and my eldest daughter are responsible for the Web page.

(Cheers)

Afterwards the crowd swarms up to shake his hand. Some request autographs. He urges them all to vote on Tuesday. His wife hugs him. His staff surround him. Quinn kisses him, Honeywell and Grayson shake his hand, the other two panelists drift away.

CHAPTER 16

†

O UR LOVE-MAKING was gentle and affectionate when we returned to the apartment. I established that two sessions of such
a day was well within my capability. Afterwards, my wife's head on my
chest, we relaxed and reveled in a few moments of serenity.

"I'm not sure how I ever found a wife like you," I said.

"I found you, Tommy Moran."

"You're astonishing."

"You mean I'm not so bad in bed?"

"That too. But I mean your faith and your loyalty and your courage.
Not once through this terrible year, did you complain. It was my crazy
idea, but you made it your crazy idea too. I never could have done it
myself."

"We haven't quite done it yet."

"We will. Ric tells me that we will carry DuPage. He says that even
the Republican leadership out there says we will."

"Then that's the ball game . . . Like I said, you were great this afternoon."

I was silent for a few moments.

"You know, I think Schlenk was right, not completely but mostly."

"Cynicism, Tommy love, is a luxury that a democratic society cannot afford."

The next day all of us were out and running with the crack of dawn.

Except you couldn't tell it was dawn because it rained intermittently all day—rallies in Black neighborhoods in Chicago, malls in the suburbs and the collar counties, elevated and train stops at the evening rush hour, TV pleas for people to vote. Ric's predictions about DuPage seemed reasonable enough. There were a lot of Latino women at the malls and a lot of soccer moms too.

On election day, we went to the early Mass at St. Luke's, the Monsignor blessed us, and gave the kids permission to miss school the next day, "but only if we win." We didn't tell him that we had already asked the principal.

Our next stop was at the polling place, just down the street from the parish. There was a huge crowd there already—turnout in our neighborhood was always way over 90 percent, sometimes, as Ambassador O'Malley often joked, over 100 percent. They cheered enthusiastically for us, shook hands, congratulated us, praised our stamina.

"And this," I said to my wife, "is in our own country and among our own people. It doesn't seem right."

"River Forest will be solidly Democratic today," a neighbor said. "That doesn't happen too often."

The cameras were there to catch us. It was a warm sunny day, weather which was supposed to be Democratic weather. My wife wore a beige autumn suit with an orange and black scarf and a jeweled pin which said simply "Tommy." She was more radiant than ever, completely confident that we would win. I wavered during the night long count. She never did. Next we appeared on some TV spots at the Lake Street L and the Burlington commuter line, begging people to vote. The spots would appear on the noon news.

Then we went over to our campaign headquarters, still suffering from the aftereffects of the bomb. The Ambassador and his wife were waiting for us.

"Too bad that Schlenk guy wouldn't bet you," he said. "You would have won."

"What an evil man!" his wife exclaimed.

Only Dolly and Joe were around from the staff. They were on the phone every second, collecting reports from our new and not always efficient precinct organization. They both seemed worried.

All we could do was sit and wait, listen to the news on the radio, and follow the voting reports from around the city and the state. The word was that there was a surprisingly large turnout in the Chicago suburbs. The noon news said that would be an advantage to Senator Crispjin who lived in suburban Sycamore, where he had made a lot of money in dubious land development, a subject from which we stayed away, though the *Daily News* had devoted some attention to it. Not enough as far as Ric and Joe were concerned. We didn't expect to do much in that county anyway.

The quiet supporters for him and his wife when they voted was in sharp contrast to the disorderly behavior at our River Forest polling place.

Ric and Tina, exhausted but jubilant arrived about twelve-thirty.

"I absolutely guarantee that we will carry DuPage," he insisted. "No doubt about it. That's a revolution in Illinois politics."

"How much?"

"Rodge will do well downstate. Those Christians will throw a lot of votes his way. But we Catholics will turn it around."

"Listen to him," Tina chuckled. "When this all started, he was an agnostic."

"Si, but an agnostic *Catholic!*"

"Now he wants to order a Guadalupe statue just like the one you've ordered."

"Patroness of all the poor peons," he insisted. "And we're only a generation away from being poor peons . . . I hope you're feeling confident, gringo, we've won it for you."

"My head is confident. I'm not sure about my stomach."

My wife who had slipped out for an expedition returned with a tray of malts and sundaes.

"Lent starts Thursday morning," she informed us.

I drank two of them, proud that I had put on no weight during the campaign. I hadn't eaten much during the last six months.

Ric and Tina joined the others on the phones. All news was positive.

"What if we win, Tommy? What will we do?"

"I was thinking the same thing myself."

When deep down in the sub-basements of your soul, you know that you can't possibly win, you don't pay much attention to that question. At two o'clock we and the Suarezes picked up our kids at school.

"Who's winning?" they demanded. "Who's winning?"

"Too early to say," I said.

"Uncle Ric says we're ahead," my wife said cautiously.

"Gringos are doubters."

We all laughed.

We then drove downtown to the Hotel Allegro, once a luxurious German-American place called the Bismarck, and now the least expensive spot for a victory party. It had been refurbished, but much of the old, if somewhat tattered, baroque German patina survived.

Mike Casey, tall, slender, white haired, and elegant, was waiting for us in the ballroom.

"Thank God, it ends here in Chicago," he said. "You'll be surrounded by Chicago cops, both on duty and off duty."

"No assassins lurking in the kitchen?" Ambassador O'Malley, who had been in Los Angeles when a nutcase had gunned down Bob Kennedy, asked.

Mike Casey glanced at him with a wry grin.

"This is not Los Angeles."

We went up to our suite, three rooms for eating, drinking, entertaining the important people. The suite was not exactly run-down, but it lacked the elegance of the Hilton or the Four Seasons.

"The food will be great," the Ambassador assured us. "I owe that to the memory of Marymarg's grandparents, as will the drinks. We save money on the hotel."

"Anything left in the fund?" I asked dubiously.

"Some," he grinned at me. "Enough for an emergency . . . Incidentally, the good Rosemarie says I should tell you that I own a townhouse in Georgetown, right down the street from the university. I bought it during the Lyndon Johnson mess, because I knew, short of nuclear war, property values there would keep going up. I've been renting it ever since. Nice income. The family that lived in it, grain lobbyist, is going back to Omaha. So I'm offering it to you guys for a hundred dollars a month. Don't even think of arguing."

Applause from everyone in the room.

"Done," Mary Margaret beat me to the punch.

We had never discussed where we would live in Washington, much less if the family would relocate. I felt queasy. This couldn't be happening, could it?

The game wasn't over quite yet.

The polls closed at seven. The first tallies showed senator Crispjin jumping into a fifteen-thousand vote lead. Silence fell on the room.

"Only one glass of whiskey, Senator," my wife warned me.

Leander Schlenk appeared on screen from the Crispjin headquarters at the Fairmont.

"It looks like poor little Tommy Moran is going to be buried," he chortled.

Joe McDermott got off the phone.

"It's mostly small rural counties south of I-80."

I felt a bit like Moses who had seen the promised land and then lost it.

The kids dug out their instruments and began to sing.

The night dragged on. By midnight we had caught up and the lead swayed back and forth. The media said the race was too close to call.

Ric reported that the news was good from DuPage.

The mayor and his wife had joined us, unobtrusive and low key as always.

"In the old days, they used to take the ballot boxes home out there and count the votes in their basements," the mayor said, "then when all the others were in, they'd report their tallies. A lot of Democratic candidates lost in those basement tallies. Then in 1960, Mayor Daley held back some precincts along Milwaukee Avenue where the Polish people voted. After DuPage gave Nixon the lead, we reported those precincts and won by seven thousand votes. It's changed a little out there."

As the night turned into morning, neither of us led by more than a thousand votes. The talking heads on the tube talked on as they must, though they had nothing to say. It was one of the closest senatorial elections in Illinois history. Still too close to call.

The kids put away their musical instruments and went to sleep. Claims of victory continued from the Crispjin headquarters. We were silent. I told my staff I didn't want anyone down in the ballroom trying to spin the numbers.

"There's lot of people down there waiting to hear from you, Senator," Dolly warned.

"They'll have to wait till the Senator has something to say."

At two-thirty there seemed to be a little movement in our favor. We were ahead by fifteen hundred votes and that lead seemed firm.

Leander Schlenk complained that it looked like another Cook County election theft.

Then Channel 3 reported that given the unreported precincts it was mathematically impossible for Senator Crispjin to win. They declared me the apparent winner.

"Dolly," I said, "go downstairs and tell them we'll proclaim victory when the lead looks safer."

Inch by inch, with agonizing slowness and occasional setbacks, we crept further ahead. Three thousand votes, thirty-five hundred, four thousand votes.

"He'll never concede, Joe," I said. "I don't blame him. He thought he had it all sewed up. His people told him it was a cinch. He's shattered. He'll demand a recount, so would I if I were in his position."

"It's all punch cards," he said. "He can't turn around this outcome."

At five thousand votes the remaining Chicago TV stations agreed that I was the winner. At fifty-five hundred, national TV agreed and the *Daily News* joined the fold.

"We carried DuPage by twenty-five thousand," Ric shouted.

The kids began to sing.

When, at four-thirty we reached a lead of six thousand, I said calmly, "I think I'll go down and join the celebration!"

Then an angry Senator H. Rodgers Crispjin appeared on the screen.

"I want to assure all my supporters here," he stumbled as he tried to read the text of a handwritten statement, "that I do not accept this rush to judgment. I am convinced that the Daley organization has stolen another election. We will demand a recount and go into federal court to seek an injunction. I do not propose to accept this crime without serious protest."

"His poor wife is crying," Mary Margaret said.

The mayor congratulated me.

"Same old stuff, Tommy. He didn't say what relief the injunction would seek."

"Overturn the DuPage County vote, probably! . . . Come on guys!"

So we paraded down to the grand ballroom in triumph. The board said we were ahead by 7825 votes with 99 percent of the vote counted.

The kids led the way, playing some kind of Mexican military march.

I confess I exulted in the cheers. The great unknown lay ahead. But we'd won. Mary Margaret hugged me fiercely.

"I'm here to claim victory," I said simply. "I understand that Senator Crispjin is not conceding and is demanding a recount. That is certainly his right. In his position I might do the same thing. However, if he is looking for fraud, he should consider his old stronghold of DuPage County which Mr. Sanchez tells me we carried by twenty thousand votes! That, folks, is a revolution in Illinois politics."

All the women in my family were hugging me and weeping. I had a hard time not sobbing with them.

"We set out, without much expectation of winning. We wanted to demonstrate that one could do well in a state-wide election without spending a lot of money, without my soliciting any contributions, and above all without any dirty tricks, any negative campaigning, and without any attack ads. I'm sure that our victory is substantial enough that it will not be overturned. But at least we proved that it could be done."

Then I thanked everyone beginning with my resilient family. Mary Margaret gave me a list so I wouldn't miss anyone.

I concluded by saying it was time for all of us to go home and get some sleep because tomorrow would be another very busy day. I also told my kids and the Sanchez kids that both the Monsignor and the Principal said they didn't have to go to school tomorrow.

Laughter and cheers.

So far I hadn't let anyone down.

The media cornered me as the cops and the Reliables led me towards the back exit.

"Will you move to the Beltway?"

"I think so. Have to talk it over with the family."

"Have you chosen your staff yet?"

"No time to think about it."

"Is Senator Crispjin a sore loser?"

"I would never say anything like that."

"What do you expect the results of the recount to be?"

"Maybe we'll pick up a few more votes."

Actually we won by more than ten thousand votes. Despite the daily stories in the *Examiner* and the constant complaints of the Crispjin staff, it was a clean victory. Nevertheless, his lawyers went into federal court and requested an injunction to invalidate the election on the grounds of vote fraud. The court rejected the plea. The United States Attorney did his own investigation and could find no evidence of serious fraud. Yet the litigation persists even today. The Supreme Court turned down the case twice.

Was my opponent a sore loser? Everyone seemed to think so. They also thought he would try to unseat me six years hence. When asked about that I said I would not make up my mind about running again for a long time.

CHAPTER 17

✝

Y OU'RE NEW HERE in the Senate," said the minority leader, slumped deeply in his huge chair. "Just elected and all with some new and interesting ideas."

He reminded me of the late "Tip" O'Neill, a New England Democrat with red face, white hair and twinkling blue eyes, not quite as tall as Tip, but in better shape. Like all of his kind, he eliminated the letter "r" from the middle of his words (his son had attended "Fodham" down in New Yok) and compensated for it by adding the letter at the end of words ("Atlantar Geogiar").

"But quiet and harmless," I said, sparring with him as I had done for a half hour.

"Got a lot of phone calls from Senators the day you were elected?"

"Only Democrats."

In early December my election was actually certified. Senator Crispjin and the *Examiner* had struggled mightily to prevent certification on the grounds of "blatant and systematic fraud" and demanded that the courts intervene to change the outcome. They first had sought an injunction that the state election commissioners show cause why they should not reverse the outcome. The federal court ruled that it lacked jurisdiction. They then turned to the state courts which summarily dismissed their motions that there was no persuasive evidence.

In the meantime the *Examiner* had begun a drumbeat demanding that to end the "confusion" I should concede the election.

My brother phoned from Panama to urge me to concede.

"It's the only honorable thing to do Tommy. Everyone knows that Senator Crispjin won the election. You should be a good loser. When we were kids I tried to teach that you should always be a good loser. People respect you when you do that. You'll earn a lot of respect if you concede."

"We won fairly," I replied.

"That's not true, Tommy. You know it's not true. If you do go to Washington you'll always be under a cloud."

The conversation ended when he said, "I've got to get to work. There's a lot to do down here. I'm sure you'll do the right thing."

Every time a new motion was filed, Leander Schlenk had claimed triumph for honest elections.

APPEALS COURT LIKELY TO RULE FOR SENATOR

Veteran legal observers are saying that the attempt of little Tommy Moran to steal the election from Senator H. Rodgers Crispjin will not survive an emergency hearing in the Illinois Appellate Court tomorrow morning. The Court is not subject to the political power of the Chicago Machine. It has always supported honest elections. It is likely to rule unanimously that Senator Crispjin was reelected.

A week later I was talking to the Minority Leader who apparently did not take the legal battle seriously. Neither, for that matter, did I. It was, however, a nuisance, though I wasn't the direct target of any of their motions.

"I've got a nice, large office for you on the second floor of the Dirksen building, facing the Capitol."

This was an unheard-of prize for a freshman Senator.

"I won't turn it down."

He laughed, he had laughed a lot during our conversation.

"Are there any special committees on which you'd be wanting to serve?"

"If I had my druthers, I'd like Judiciary and Armed Forces."

He wrote the names down on a small sheet of notepaper, the only item on his vast oaken desk.

"Judiciary because of immigration and Armed Forces because of the routine raping of women in the military."

It was a statement not a question.

"I'm told that there is a lot less work in Judiciary than in other committees."

"That's true . . . Now you won't be flying back to Chicago every weekend, I hear. Moving your family here, I'm told."

"I gather a lot of my colleagues spend two or three nights here and the others at home with their families."

He cocked a suspicious eye, "Well I don't know how important that is. They spend a lot of time with their constituents and raising money."

"I don't raise money."

"So they tell me—no negative ads, no asking people for money, and no campaigning till after Labor Day . . . Interesting ideas . . ."

"They might not work twice."

"And if they do it will be hard on a lot of people," he laughed again. "Generally, the first thing a man thinks about when he arrives here is reelection. After the first one it's not so difficult."

"I don't know whether I'll like it here and whether I'll do a good job. I won't make up my mind about reelection for a few years—like five."

He sighed and squirmed in his desk. "They said you were different and I'm beginning to believe them."

"Irish Catholic kid from the west side of Chicago. Haven't been many like that around here."

He grinned. "That's for damn sure . . . Mind if I make a few suggestions?"

"I was hoping you would."

"Your lobbyists are all over the place."

"Tell me about it. Three of them have already offered to do a nice reception for my swearing-in. I declined."

He smiled thinly.

"First time does no harm."

"Slippery slope."

"Just the words I was about to use . . . They're nice friendly fellas, most of them. And they'd do anything to please you and make you happy. And your wife and kids too. They don't ask all that much either. Except maybe to own your vote."

"Pick up their markers, as they say in Chicago."

"The point is not to leave too many markers around for anyone to pick up."

"I think I've dropped a few already this afternoon."

His whole body shook.

"I figured you being Irish and all, you'd be into loyalty no matter what favor I offered. Still and all, it doesn't hurt to sink some roots, does it now?"

"Whenever you need my vote, Senator, you got it!"

"That makes things a lot easier."

"If you don't stand by your friends, who will you stand by," I repeated a Chicago political adage.

"You'll find a lot of people wanting to be friends, Senator. Lobbyists, business leaders, people with lots of money, media folk, people over at the White House, cabinet people, everyone. And yourself with a beautiful wife."

"I noticed that too."

"Everyone needs friends. The trick of it is to realize that a lot of them will eventually want something from you."

"More markers."

"You got it."

"I'll be careful."

"A United States Senator is one of the most powerful men in the world. He has a lot less money than he has power. There will be minefields of bribes lying in wait for you. I think you're smart enough and agile enough to recognize them and turn them down."

"God help me if I don't."

"No one else will, Tommy. No one else will. They'll spoil you rotten too. Weekend trips to the best golf courses in the country. Skiing in the Alps. A trip to Africa during recess. A lecture in St. Petersburg, Super-bowl tickets. The Kentucky Derby. You name it, you've got it, all expenses paid and expensive souvenirs for your wife and children. A dozen bottles of expensive wine. Anything you want."

"I'd be a sucker for the occasional bottle of Bushmill's Green. Beyond that I don't want anything on your list. And when I fly somewhere I'll pay my own fare."

"We don't pay senators enough money. One hundred and sixty-five K in a city like this for men, most of whom would earn at least a half million any place else . . . We're dirt poor compared to the men we have to associate with: lawyers, lobbyists, corporate executives, oil people. We have little tricks now in which an outside committee recommends tiny wage increases. Our opponents in elections use that against us. If the country wants to eliminate the worst corruption here, they have to give us as much money as the typical lobbyist. That's not going to happen, Tommy."

"If we can't make a go of it on my wife's billable hours and my royalties, then we'll go home."

"Your wife has the same convictions?"

Bluntest question yet.

"All she wants is to buy things that are on sale, better yet to get them wholesale. Seriously, her convictions, as you call them, are stricter than mine."

"Daughter of that fella who takes pictures?"

"I'm sure you've talked to him already, Senator."

Another big laugh.

"She's working for her law firm here. Supreme Court kind of stuff?"

"Appeared there several times. Won her cases."

Long pause.

"You are a talented and attractive couple. I presume you don't fool around?"

"Wouldn't dare."

"There will be a lot of attention focused on you. I've seen older men than you lose their balance. I don't want to sound like that Polonius fella. You seem to have your head screwed on proper. I just thought a word from me might be a little help."

"Word of warning."

"Something like that."

"Point taken . . . and gratefully."

We both stood up.

He extended his hand.

"When you get settled in, Eileen and I would like to have you over for supper sometime. Nothing elaborate."

"We wouldn't miss it for the world."

Of course his wife's name was Eileen. What else would it be?

He walked me to the door of his office, opened it and then stepped out in the corridor with me.

"It's been bad days for us in the last twenty years. We did some dumb things and missed some great opportunities. Should never have let the insurance people torpedo Hillary's health insurance thing. The tide is turning, though it will take the next four to six years to do it. Then we should have a good long run. They wouldn't be far from wrong who might say that you can do a lot."

Properly vague, as Irish predictions tend to be.

"Sounds like fun," I said being equally vague.

I took a taxi back to our new house on Q Street where my wife and mother-in-law were reveling in the decoration and furnishing of the place. The Ambassador was playing gin rummy with Mary Ann—and consistently losing to our Good Witch of the West Side. I was constrained to recount in full detail the conversation with the minority leader.

"He likes you, Tommy," my wife said, her eyes wide in admiration. "He really likes you."

"What's not to like?" the Ambassador asked.

"Gin!" squealed our middle child. "You lose again, Gramps."

* * *

Our next big initiation meeting was with my Chief of Staff and media person, both women, both five or six years older than us, both handsome, both veterans of service in the senate, both recommended by the minority leader and both a little skeptical of us. My campaign staff all had personal and professional reasons for staying in Chicago, though Joe McDermott had taken over my Chicago office.

Christine Taliaferro (pronounced Tolivar), our Chief of Staff—once called administrative assistant when the job was a lot easier—was a Protestant from the hill country, Eastern Kentucky just at the end of West Viriginia.

Manny (short for Emanuela) Rodriguez was Dominican, hence both Black and Hispanic and Catholic.

They were especially skeptical of my wife, who had taken them seriously when they said it would be an informal Saturday in my new office, and dressed in jeans, tee shirt, and windbreaker for the warm mid-December day.

"I don't know of any freshman senator who had ever had an office like this," Chris said with a touch of disapproval. She was even taller than my wife.

"We Irish stick together," I said.

We were seated around my impressive desk. My wife watched and listened, her natural exuberance hidden behind what she called her "appellate face."

"You've seen the minority leader already?"

"I was summoned to his holiness's chamber for an hour pep talk, which was in fact a sage warning about all things I might do wrong. I assured him that I would always be polite to lobbyists and take nothing from them, not even a swearing-in party."

"He said *that*?" Chris asked, just a touch of the smoke of the hills in her voice. She was a tall, slender woman with the body of an accomplished athlete. A golfer and a marathon runner, it would turn out. Her husband was a retired Colonel who worked as a civilian in the Penta-

gon. She was given to pacing back and forth on the office floor, an out-
let for a tremendous store of nervous energy.

"I told him that I'd already declined three such offers."

"Well, that settles one office policy early on."

"We don't do lobbyists."

"That's very wise, Senator," Manny said almost reluctantly, the music of the islands still strong in her accent. "They'd be very generous to
you and your family, but they'd end up . . ."

Manny was about my height, maybe a little shorter, as laid back and
relaxed as Chris was manic. She hummed calypso songs when she was
thinking. The only way to describe her figure was to say she was luxu-
riant. Her husband was a retired relief pitcher who had played for the
New York Mets and now worked in Baseball's national office in public
relations. The leader had chosen two strong and attractive women to
mother me. It was clear from the approbation in Marymarg's eyes that
she approved of both of them.

"Owning us," I said finishing Manny's sentence.

"Something like that . . . the first thing we need to decide is what to
hang on the wall of these offices. The waiting room, first of all."

"I hadn't thought much about that. The hangings should shout Illinois! Right?"

"Preferably."

"What about some glorious color photos of the Prairie State by a
Pulitzer-winning photographer? Put some of them in the main office?
Change them every once in a while?"

"That sounds striking. Would they be expensive?"

"Get 'em wholesale."

"Free," Marymarg spoke for the first time. "My daddy."

"And in my office same kind of pictures of my family. Also free.
He'd hang them for free too."

"You'd be surprised, Senator, how many problems freshmen senators
have with this issue."

"Your relations with the media?"

"Back home? I don't know anyone here yet."

That morning Leander Schlenk had struck again.

CORRUPT BOOK DEAL FOR TOMMY

Little Tommy Moran has already profited from his attempt to steal the senatorial election even though the outcome is still before the courts. The Examiner has learned that Tommy's publisher has secretly awarded him a three book contract "in excess of seven figures." His first book appeared to thunderous bad reviews all over the country and has already disappeared from the nation's bookstores. The publisher is obviously hoping for clout in the United States Senate in the unlikely event that Tommy is actually seated.

Dolly issued the usual denial. The contract was not a secret, the book was in its third printing and was in fourth place on the national best seller lists.

"Back home is important, Senator," Manny said as they were prepping me for my role as a senator. "That's where your voters are."

"Generally they are no more hostile than to any other public figure. They want to entertain the audience by trapping you. A couple are very hostile, particularly Leander Schlenk of the *Examiner* and a woman named Lupe Gonzalez of a Spanish language TV station. Both are probably in the tank with the former senator who is already running for re-election. And in turn Bobby Bill Roads is likely subsidizing both of them . . ."

"An oil man from Oklahoma," Chris was up and pacing, "who thinks his money can buy anything he wants."

"So far," Manny continued, rolling her jet black eyes, "no one has proved him wrong."

"We have a tape of my pre-election interview on PBS . . ." I said tentatively.

My wife handed it over.

"Excellent. It will give us an idea of your style."

"Or lack of it."

Manny was silent for a moment.

"Bad people," she finally said. "There's a lot of bad people out there. They blew up your car, right, and someone took a shot at you? We'll have to talk later about your security here. The Beltway media are not much better. They're also in decline as the papers curtail and combine their bureaus and focus more on features about people instead of news and analysis."

"You're a hot property now, Senator," Chris said, as she gave up her pacing. "Every small city paper around the country will want a profile on you. It should help your presidential visibility."

Ah, a trick question.

"What was it General Sherman said?"

"I will not run if nominated and not serve if elected?"

"Yeah."

"You agree, Ms. O'Malley?"

Herself was startled to be dealt into the game?

"Huh? Oh, I wouldn't divorce him if he tried that. I'd kill him."

They laughed uneasily, still not having figured my wife out. She went to the main office and came back with the coffee pot, cups, and rolls we had brought over. I was not worried that she would win my two school marms over. Rather I feared that she would make common cause with them against me.

"So then we are generally reluctant to grant interviews that are not about issues and are not with major papers—*L.A. Times, San Francisco Chronicle, Chicago Daily News, Boston Globe,* and of course the *Times* and the *Post.*"

"And maybe the *Post Dispatch* which is read in downstate Illinois," I added, "and the Chicago TV stations and PBS."

"That will make our work a lot easier."

"Our Chicago people created a pretty good Web site for the campaign. You might want to look at it. We could put any of our stuff on it. They tell me it gets a lot of hits."

"We'll surely coordinate with them. Those sites become more

and more important. Maybe you could write a little message every week . . ."

"Why not?"

"You can't expect to write everything yourself. You'll need a speech writer and one of your Legislative Assistants will draft the bills you will propose . . . Oh, I forgot, Senator, you're a writer . . . I'm sorry . . ."

"Da nada. Let's have the speech writer."

"Did the minority leader indicate anything about your committee assignments?" Chris continued the interrogation.

"I think he said that he thought Judiciary and Armed Services would have room for me."

Dead silence.

"You asked for them?"

"And got them?"

"Yeah."

"You know what that means, Senator?"

"Along with this office?"

"I think so."

"Manny, our new Senator is really a hot property!"

"Don't let it go to his head," my wife murmured, as she cut the rolls into conscience-salving little bites.

"The leader will expect loyalty, you understand?"

"He knew he'd get it anyway. We Irish are a clannish crowd."

They were beginning to like both of us.

Did that matter? You bet your life it did.

"The size of a Senator's staff grows bigger every year," Chris began her main lecture, doubtless carefully rehearsed. "In the absence of any other system, he has become an ombudsman for his constituents against the federal government. You will receive a huge amount of mail every day, some of it hate mail . . ."

"Round file."

"Right! Much of the mail from constituents who think they have been cheated by the federal government, and in many cases are quite properly angry. They expect us to get their lost Social Security check, to pay for the damage a Postal Service truck did to their front lawn, to prevent the IRS from hassling them about taxes already paid."

"Ward committeeman work."

"That will take a lot of time and people in your office, mostly smart young people who like the idea of working for a Senator for a while. They will normally handle these kinds of complaints themselves. They will call the offending agency and investigate the case. You'd be surprised at how responsive the bureaucracy is when they get a call from a Senator's office. Only rarely will you have to intervene. Most of the time, our young person will straighten out the mess and write a letter in your name to the constituent and sign it with one of the robot signatures we will have available. An enormous amount of mail will come in every day. Only a small amount will reach your desk. You may have to sign two or three letters every day and personalize them with a little note. The only alternative is to do hands-on mail, which would drive you crazy!"

"Crazier."

"You will have several legislative assistants who will coordinate with the LAs of other Senators on matters of joint interest and on drafting legislation. They are very bright young lawyers, just out of law school, who are desperately eager to earn a name for themselves. We have to moderate them a bit."

"Better you than me. When I was a Mr. Mom, I couldn't moderate three sweet little girls."

"I assume you've already received invitations?"

"First one is tomorrow night."

"Soon you could have six invitations for every night. Sometimes you can do two, a reception in late afternoon and a dinner party every night. There are also lecture invitations that would add to the burden. There are some parties and receptions to which you should go and an occasional lecture you should accept. For the rest we can provide quite acceptable excuses, hand written by our robot . . . Unless Ms. O'Malley you would want to handle this responsibility?"

" Marymarg . . . God forbid! Can your robot provide a handwritten note for me?"

"It would be happy to try . . ."

"Good robot."

"You will also need a scheduler, Senator, in addition to this gentle robot. Someone who will try to see that you don't find yourself caught in two places at the same time. Uh, Marymarg, she will need to coordinate with you."

"Maybe we can have an electronic calendar on our respective computers. That's how we kept himself from getting lost forever in Kendall County."

She refilled the coffee cups.

The conversation droned on. I was growing weary. However, I had to let them go on with all the dreary details of how a well run senator's office is run. They seemed to know what they were doing, thank heaven, because it would take me years to figure it out. Finally I tried to absorb the rules about our hiring and firing policy and sexual harassment in the office.

"It is unlikely, Senator that you will harass anyone . . ."

"Wouldn't know how," the good Mary Margaret observed.

"Which does not mean that charges won't be made. However, even among the staff there have to be clear-cut rules."

"I should hope so."

"Anything more? Manny."

"I think we've covered all the bases."

"We are honored to be asked to serve you, Senator. And we'll do our best not to seem bossy . . ."

"Irish men are used to it. Usually they don't even complain. I am the one who is privileged to have such good staff planning. Otherwise I'm not even sure I could find my way from here to the Senate Chamber."

"Marymarg, it's hard to read your face . . ." Chris said carefully. "I hope you are not offended by our detailed instructions for the Senator."

"It's my lawyer face, which is much less revealing . . . I'm glad some people are taking charge of him, especially people that know what they're doing and I'm fascinated by the complexity of a Senator's life. It would seem that like the monarch of England and perhaps the father of the family, he reigns but does not rule. I promise to stay out of your way. I don't believe in Mom and Pop shops. I may show up occasionally to cadge a lunch . . ."

Then Chris said something that I would later learn Chiefs of Staff rarely say to their Senator's wife.

"Some day we might want to have you around all the time."

That was a real compliment for the O'Malley woman. The flush that spread across her face showed that she realized it.

"That probably wouldn't work, but it's nice of you to say it."

"Then you won't mind if I say something to you and the Senator about your children?"

"Not in the least."

"They'll be going to Gonzaga and Ursuline."

"The oldest to Gonzaga this year. Two of them next year."

"Both fine schools. Our kids are there too. It's difficult to be a teen and a Senator's child. Our kids are quick to say 'stuck-up.' The child must be careful not to talk about their father or any of the perks, like ice cream socials at the White House or tickets for early viewings of new films."

"Our kids," Marymarg said firmly, "will never go into the White House for ice cream socials or anything else. They're *Republicans* over there. We don't take any favors from anyone, unless it is a bigger office with a nice view and the right committees and great staff, and neither will they. We'll make that clear to them. They're adventurers. They like new things and new people. No one will ever push them around a second time."

"She's right," I said. "They're throwbacks to Irish nobility or Phil Sheridan's cavalry riding down the Shendanoah."

We had a heart-to-heart with the kids when we returned to our new home. They listened impassively.

"Like we don't know those things already," Mary Rose said with a frown.

"We totally will not be pompous," Mary Ann protested.

"Who's going to hang out in bars with creepy boys anyway," Mary Therese, our nine year old sophisticate, added to the consensus. "We got more sense than that."

"Really!"

"Point taken?" Marymarg pursued the issue.

"Yeah."

"Fersure."

"Totally."

I don't know what else we expected.

Manny asked my wife to put in a few hours several days later to help them sort out mailing lists, e-mail addresses, and the Internet.

"We worked it all out," she reported back to me. "All you have to do is to write a reflection of some sort every week and we'll put it on our Web page, send it out on e-mail, and mail to our list of major donors, if we have one."

"Sure we do. Chucky keeps it . . . I don't want to see it."

"Who says you have to? Chucky also gave us a list of people, not necessarily all major donors, who deserved more than a robot letter and an answering call if they phone. If they tell you someone is on the line they will also add that that person is on Ambassador O'Malley's list. I also gave them a list, a short list, of people who should have your personal phone number. Like Dolly and Tina and that bunch."

"My brother?"

"He'll be flagged for a call back."

"How did the work go?"

She frowned as Mary Rose did when we tried to promulgate our new rules. "Fine. They're very able women and already dedicated to you. They say you have the best Web page in the Senate, though we have to keep updating it. The Internet is the new big thing in politics and it doesn't cost much."

"They expect you to work with them on it?"

Again the frown.

"Why not? I can do it all by phone or by e-mail."

Later in the office I was informed that my wife was a remarkable woman and that I was a very lucky man. I didn't disagree. They had bonded already.

CHAPTER 18

✝

THE NEXT DAY I attended a seminar at Wie House out in Virginia, a civil war hospital and an old Virginia landmark with elegant porches around the whole building. The Brookings Institution would spend the day teaching the five freshmen Democrats (four men, one woman) how to act like Senators. The Republicans had far more elaborate seminars, but then they had the task of civilizing the poor white trash that they had elected. Or so I told my wife that night as we cuddled in bed. There was also a parallel session for senatorial spouses. The good Mary Margaret declined with thanks. She had an appearance before the Supreme Court.

We were taught about the mores and the customs of the Senate— "unanimous consent" (that the leaders of both parties granted consent in the name of the rest of us to call up a bill for consideration, a process which involved intense haggling and trade-offs), senatorial courtesy, the right to put a "hold" on a nomination, seniority (you have to stay around a long time to build up privileges, "hideaways," small private offices just off the floor of the Senate where those with power or seniority could read, write, think, sleep and possibly make love in private without fear of interruption, save for a quorum call).

However, the main focus of the seminar was on how an up-to-date senator in the television age should behave. He should first of all remember that the camera was everywhere and that he was on stage all the time when he was out of the sanctum of his office (or the hideaway if he was fortunate enough to have one). He should never carry a brief case, but rather swagger confidently down a corridor with aides all around him to carry his impedimenta. He should never turn to an aide because that would make him look weak. Rather the aide should whisper in his ear and he should nod, as though he already knew what he was being told, though in all probability he did not. He should never pick his nose, scratch himself, rub his eyes, yawn or shut his eyes in public. He should avoid obesity which looked terrible on television. If he were to appear on one of the morning programs or the Sunday morning shows, especially the Jim Russell program, he should always practice with his staff beforehand in the Senate TV studio. He should never use obscenity, scatology, vulgarity or blasphemy in his public comments and never take the name of God in vain. He should never counter-attack the media even though for the most part they sought to destroy him for their own fame or pleasure. Sarcasm or irony were dangerous and should be used rarely. He should never be caught on camera in sustained and apparently unnecessary conversation with an attractive young woman, he should always be polite to other Senators though he might despise many of them.

I realized that I would have to concentrate on the confident swagger because that was not how I thought a lawyer should enter a courtroom, at least when a jury was seated.

We would be completely dependent on our staff. We should pay them well—the Chief of Staff and the top Legislative Assistant were worth six figures—and permit them extra days off when they asked. We should be loyal to them. When they make mistakes that cause us trouble, we should never blame them in public or snub them in private. We should strive to be pleasant and collegial with them and avoid arrogance. We should reach our offices by eight or eight thirty in the morning and do our best not to look and act like we had a hangover on arrival. Therefore we should be out of bed by six, especially if we wanted to exercise and read the *Times* and the *Post*. We should remember that a morning exercise postponed till later in the day would be an exercise lost.

I took copious notes, though more for my next book than because I doubted my ability to remember them.

I did ask whether bells rang for morning and evening prayers and what was the time for spiritual reading. This implicit comparison of the Senate with a monastery occasioned only a weak and delayed laugh.

Then there was a remarkably candid discussion of Sex and the Senate. Some Senators on occasion indulged in adultery and fornication, as was well known, sometimes even in the Senate itself or the office buildings. How prevalent such behavior was problematic, most likely less than gossip or folk lore would lead us to believe. The senatorial day was long and difficult and left very little time for seduction. There were many attractive women around the Senate, some of them potential groupies. The Senators present for the seminar would have to make their own personal decisions on this matter based on their existing commitments and their personal code of morality. Nonetheless, it must be observed that such intimacies always carried some element of risk, more in these days of the ever-present media eager to destroy as many Senators as they could. There is a tight-knit gossip network among the Senate staffs. A seemingly secret and private relationship consummated in the office after hours or in a hideaway can easily become common knowledge the next morning. If you want to make love in a hideaway, it might be better to bring your wife.

Nervous laughter, though not from me. I thought it an excellent idea and I thought the virtuous Marymarg would agree.

Not yet.

The speaker, a woman, drove home the point. An affair, even a brief one, could lead to swift destruction of a Senator. You'd have to be a gambler, even a reckless one, to risk it.

OK. I wasn't planning one. Or so I thought then.

After I was sworn in and we had our little party at the house in Georgetown, my first assignment from my staff was to attend both prayer breakfasts, Protestant on Tuesday morning and Catholic on Wednesday.

"You don't have to go ever again," Chris said. "At least they'll see you there. You won't be branded an atheist."

The Protestant prayer breakfast turned my stomach.

The Evangelicals have the right to their own convictions and rhetoric. However, I don't have to feel at ease with them, any more than they would feel at ease if I took out my rosary and began tolling the beads. The preacher enjoyed pronouncing the name of the lord as if it were "JAYZ-zus," with musical variations around both syllables. The BIBLE was also subjected to such rhapsodic enunciation. I felt like someone was rubbing a ruler against a blackboard.

"You're a Roman Catholic, aren't you Senator?" Wayne Bates, the Senior Senator from Kansas sitting at my left, asked when the praying and preaching were over.

"Yes, Senator," I said not wanting to dispute that I didn't find the adjective demeaning.

("You're a real shanty Irish bigot," my wife insisted as I told her the story.)

"Then you really haven't been saved yet, have you?"

"I think I have."

"Not unless you have experienced faith in the love of the lord JAYZ-zus who covers our sins with the blood of the lamb."

"Oh."

"My dearly beloved wife is a Roman Catholic. It makes me sad to realize that when we die, I will have to look down from heaven and see her burning forever in the fires of hell. Yet I'll see in her torment the fires of divine justice and I'll cry out, 'Praise the lord!'"

"I hope you are pleasantly surprised," I murmured.

He quoted several verses from scripture with which I was unfamiliar. Then someone else rose up to pray that the Lord would grant us the strength of faith during the coming term to snatch the Yewnited States back from the edges of hell by fighting against the horrendous sin of homosexuality. There were cries of "Amen" not unlike those I had heard at the Rainbow Coalition in Chicago.

"Don't take all of that seriously," Senator Hatfield McCoy said as I walked out of the breakfast. "I'm a Christian, but I'm not an extreme Christian, if you understand my meaning."

"There is but one tragedy," I said, falling back on a quote I had heard in college, "and that is not to be a saint."

"I suppose," "Hat" answered. "Take old Wayne for example. He'll screw any pretty girl he can get his hands on. Doesn't bother him at all. Everyone knows it. He's drunk half the time too. Yet the piety flows out of his lips like he was a preacher man . . . I'd say he's an extreme Christian."

"I'm sure there are many sincere and devout Christians in the Senate," I replied, "even if they're Republicans."

He slapped me enthusiastically on my back.

"Hell fire! You Irish are really quick with words!"

"Hypocrisy is a part of the human condition, Senator."

"You shouldn't let all that piety in there trouble you, Tommy. It's part of our culture. Like I say, I'm not an extreme Christian, but I don't fool around, though it's pretty easy. My wife would de-ball me."

"I know the type, Hat. I'm sure we have our share of hypocrites in the Senate too. The spirit is willing but the flesh is weak."

"You shunuff sound like a preacher man, quoting the scriptures . . . You ever think of being one of them celibate priests?"

"I gave it some thought. My brother beat me to it."

"He approve of you?"

"Occasionally."

"Does he find celibacy difficult?"

"He's utterly dedicated to his work."

"Nice to talk to you, Tommy. We gotta see more of one another."

"Good idea, Hat."

Hands across the two great divides.

I felt more at home at the Catholic breakfast. The minority leader signaled me to an empty seat next to him. He was leaving no doubt that I was a man approved.

"Heard you went to the other side yesterday. Enjoy it?"

"I wouldn't say that. I don't doubt the sincerity of their piety, it's just not mine."

"I heard you got thrown out of Church by that asshole priest over at St. Ethelreda."

"My whole family. Sins of the parents are visited on their children. A lot of the congregation walked out with us. It was towards the end of Mass anyway, maybe they just wanted to go home and work through the Sunday editions of the *Times* and the *Post*."

"Jesuits take you in?"

"They almost had to. My wife and I both had seven years of higher education with them. My oldest daughter is going to Gonzaga prep."

"So I hear."

"Not much you don't hear."

"My job," he laughed. "Some of the bishops expect us to vote the way they tell us to vote. I hear your brother is on their side."

"Again you hear right. I'm my own man, Senator."

"Didn't doubt it for a moment."

You just wanted to know where I stand with my brother. Legitimate question. Honest answer.

The Catholic breakfast was much less frenetic though there were some manifestations of piety, prayers for guidance and faith and patience and persistence. I had no trouble saying "amen" to all of them. I wondered whether God had time to listen to such breakfasts or to our prayers. He had said that he did. Did he ever get bored with us I wondered? Did I ever get bored with my three Marys?

"Why do you think after all these years the Bishops are after us?"

"It helps their careers. They think they'll win back some of the authority they lost with the pedophile mess. Kidding themselves."

The speaker for the morning was, naturally enough a Jesuit. He did not drop his 'r' and then add it elsewhere. Rather there was the flavor of the prairies in his voice. Gary Cooper playing the Plainsman in an old western. He argued that much of the religious response to science didn't work because it assumed that God was subject to the same kind of rhetorical proof as the Big Bang or evolution. That, he said, was a language mistake. Any God that could be proved that way might be the great Unmoved Mover but he was not the God of Abraham, Isaac, and Jacob, not my God and your God. The Catholic philosophers in their arguments in favor of God had given the game away by ignoring the "religious," that is mysticism, saints, devotion, faith, stories, music, art—all the resources for which science had no room and could not have room. Who believes, he asked, in God because of one of St. Thomas's five ways and who believes because of devotion of a mother or father, the patience of a grandparent, the goodness of a parish priest.

I talked briefly to him afterwards.

"Good points," I said. "We've been giving the game away on lots of things."

"Descarte, Kant, that bunch."

"And religion teachers."

He laughed.

"I hear you're already in the hands of the Society here in D.C."

"There was no room in the other inn . . . and let me assure you that my brother has little effect on my thinking or acting."

"Why does that not surprise me?"

I promised I would be back for future breakfasts, a promise I kept occasionally.

The next day Schlenk was after us again.

SOFT CORE PROVIDES DC HOUSE FOR TOMMY

Supporters of cute little Tommy Moran were embarrassed to learn yesterday that his palatial house in the tony Georgetown district in Washington was provided free by his father-in-law, Charles "Chucky" O'Malley, who is famous for his soft core porn photos of women. O'Malley, who likes to call himself "Ambassador" because of a post in Germany forty years ago, allegedly bought the home during the Johnson administration. Convenient isn't it? Especially, despite his big seven-figure book contract, Tommy doesn't have much money to spend on housing. Will he ever stop embarrassing the people of Illinois?

We put a "clarification" on our web page and in my newsletter and sent it to the *Daily News* which often printed such replies. We had a hard time talking the Ambassador out of a suit. His lawyers demanded that the *Examiner* issue an apology. They admitted that his rank was valid, that he had won Pulitzer prizes for his photography, and had photographed every president since Dwight Eisenhower. Neither the house nor our family were mentioned.

"He's a smart man," Manny admitted.

"Been at the game a long time."

"Best office art in the building. A lot of staffers come by to look. Can I show them the family pictures in your office?"

"Free of charge."

One day, it must have been about that time, I brought in a five-foot statue of Our Lady of Guadalupe and put it in the corner of our reception office. No one complained. So there she stayed.

I began to learn many facts, some of them distinctly unpleasant, about my job.

I rarely spent much time on the Senate floor. No one did. When someone demanded a quorum call—usually a delaying tactic—we'd race over to chamber and register our presence. Most of us would immediately go to the subway which runs from the office building to the chamber, answer "present" when our name was called, and then hurry back to whatever we were doing. Senate debates were rare—only when a major piece of legislation was up for a vote and many of us wanted to say something for the record. There was very little give-and-take argument on the floor. We said what we wanted to say, then yielded to others who would say what they wanted to say. Debates didn't affect the outcome of the voting in the slightest. We'd all long since made up our minds how we were going to vote. Even when an actual vote was taken, we'd often not be present—unless it was on, let us say, a major cabinet-level appointment about which there was controversy and on which the media would be focused. On lesser issues, Senators would leave immediately after their vote was cast. Some of us would come in, catch the eye of the clerk, and give him a thumbs up or thumbs down.

Committee meetings were another matter. Usually they were not hearings for which the TV cameras would be present. In those cases we—or more often our LAs—would hammer out the issues and we would argue and fight about them and either send the bill on to the floor or let it die. It was a rare bill that came before the committee and an even rarer one that went up to the full Senate. The other party had the majority of votes, so in theory they should dominate the committees. But not infrequently some of the nominal Republicans would vote with us. So, as much as it offended the Republican ideology to compromise on anything, they would sometimes have to hammer out a compromise. I turned out to be reasonably good in those situations and earned a reputation as a tough but honest negotiator. All those years as public defender had served me in good stead.

Most Senate speeches are made for the record, written and televised. One wants to establish what one is for and against and for many reasons—most of them having to do with keeping the constituents happy. On occasion we might want to leave a minor record for history. We'd all put the text of our remarks on our web page and quoted them in our newsletters. Sometimes our speeches were intended to impress our colleagues. Occasionally we spoke out of passionate conviction. I can't sort out which motivations affected me whenever I rose in that august chamber (and it really is august) to tell the world or whoever was present what I thought.

CHAPTER 19

✝

M Y TOMMY's maiden speech in the Senate was on St. Patrick's day, chosen in part because the kids would be out of school and they could sit in the galleries and be proud of him. His topic was to be immigration, an appropriate subject for the day. He had worked very hard on the draft, argued with me about some of it, then gave it to his speech writer, a bright kid from Notre Dame, who looked at it and said, "I wouldn't change a word."

He would speak at about noon, so he would appear on the evening news. We would eat lunch in the Senate dining room, from which we had hitherto been barred, after the talk. The kids were dying to see "daddy's office" and "the place where daddy works." That this was the United States Senate didn't matter in the least. We all wore green dresses of course. And I bought Tommy a very special green silk tie, which look truly bitchin' on C-SPAN.

Tommy is a cool one when he has a major speech or plea or anything of the sort. I can never tell if he's nervous, not until afterwards and even then only sometimes. He seemed especially cool this time. Maiden speech in the Senate? So what!

We showed up in the office at ten, two hours after he arrived. After we had gone through security, Capital Hill cops escorted us to the second floor of the Dirksen building and down the corridor to his office. The pretty receptionist stood up to greet us when we came, a bit nervous in the face of the four solemn redheads in brilliant green dresses—womanly druids.

My kids either had inherited it from Rosie or had learned how to be gracious and charming in all possible circumstances and from their father how to take in everything with a glance and store it.

"Gramp's pictures," they said, noting the art work in the outer office. "Cool!"

"Guadalupe," they said as they touched the statue with the respect and reverence they had learned from their Sonoran friends, perhaps more than reverence. "Neat!"

Tommy met us at the door to the large office. Everyone on the staff looked up, stopped working, and cheered.

We blushed and smiled and I said, "We're grateful to all of you for keeping our daddy out of trouble this long."

Then in the inner office, the kids rushed to the window to look at the dome of the Capitol.

"Out of sight!"

"Excellent!"

"Outstanding!"

A bright young man took charge of us on a brief tour of the office building, the capital, and the Senate. A plainclothes cop trailed behind us.

We ascended to the visitor's gallery where a cop viewed our credentials and let us in. Two or three Senators were on the floor, talking to one another, while a fourth was reading a speech to which no one was listening. The acting President Pro Tem seemed to be snoozing in his chair. The various senate staff members looked bored. The pages in their uniforms also looked bored.

"Where is everyone?" Marytre demanded.

"In their office working just like Daddy."

"Will there be more when Daddy talks?" Maran wondered.

"There had better be."

"The page uniforms are yucky."

"What a boring job!"

"I'd never want to be a page."

I confess that the four of us garnered a lot of attention as we wandered around. Juno and her daughters come to listen to the paycock.

We walked around the rotunda under the dome and looked at the statues of the famous people from each of the states on the House of Representatives side of the Capitol. Most of them I had never heard of.

Then we took the subway back to the Dirksen building.

There was hubbub in the crowded main room. The Senator was about to deliver his first address. Most of the staff would watch it on C-SPAN.

"Do you think your daddy will give a good talk?" a woman staff member asked, like she was talking to five-year-olds.

"Daddy has a lot of practice telling us what to do around the house," Mary Rose answered.

Then an entourage formed and my Tommy emerged from his inner office, face freshly scrubbed, hair neatly combed, suit buttoned, smile in place. My heart skipped a beat. I remembered him in sixth grade when I had my first crush on him.

"Shall we go?" he asked.

Chris, who had been pacing up and down, a bundle of high powered nerves, offered him a folder, presumably his talk.

"I don't think I'll need that . . . Ted, you already have the text. Note any ad libs I may have to defend."

"Yes, sir, Senator."

He handed the folder to me.

"Your cell phone, Senator," Chris said with a perfectly straight face.

"Thank you, Ma'am," he handed it to her with a guilty grin.

Everyone in our family touched Guadalupe and made the sign of the cross on the way out. Some of his staff looked at us like we were savages from the Amazon jungle who might be carrying blow guns with deadly darts.

"Why the entourage?" I asked.

"So no one will accost me. Security. Superstition, I suppose."

We went up to the gallery and he went into the chamber. Manny hummed one of her calypso melodies which reminded me of a very old Harry Belafonte record. I hummed it along with her.

"He looks cute, Mommy," Marytre informed me.

"Daddy always looks cute."

There were perhaps twenty-five senators on the floor. When the presiding officer recognized Tommy, they all quieted down. They wanted to listen closely to their new young star.

Chris sat behind me in the visitors gallery, my kids sat on either side, serenely complacent.

"He's one stubborn Irishman," Chris whispered, the mountain smoke in her voice, just as Tommy had described it. "He's supposed to read from the manuscript, he's supposed to have an aide in there. He just smiles and waves me off. They're putting a podium on his desk which he won't use. He could make a fool out of himself."

"Bet?"

"You're as bad as he is!" she laughed anxiously.

We were in the first row of the visitor's gallery. We could barely see Tommy on the floor, in the last row of the chamber. A senate staff member hooked a lavalier mike around his neck. Tommy smiled graciously. My stomach became very tight.

"I recognize by unanimous consent the Senator from Illinois for a period of thirty minutes."

"Thank you, Mr. President. I think I can promise that I will speak well within that limit."

The President Pro Tem, a junior Republican, sighed in evident boredom, opened a book and began to read.

"I rise to speak, Mr. President, about the immigration reform bill that we are discussing these days. I do so with some embarrassment on the festival day of the patron saint of my ethnic group. I am not embarrassed to be Irish, heaven knows, but I am embarrassed to be speaking on this holy day in favor of an administration bill. My family has been Democratic for four generations. I hope the spirits of the past do not complain about my lapse from virtue, not till this body adjourns for the day. I also hope that St. Patrick does not object, though as we all know, St. Patrick was a Democrat."

The laughter on the floor was genuine. Who the hell was this punk kid to joke so calmly at his first speech—and where was his typescript?

Chris opened her copy and I opened mine. Mary Rose peered over my shoulder.

"I support the administration bill and I congratulate the White House on it. It is not a very good bill. In fact it is a very bad bill, but it is the only one that has a chance of getting through Congress in the present immigrant-hating mood in our nation of immigrants. It may well diminish the slaughter of innocents in the upper Sonoran desert next year. Any legislation that accomplishes that deserves our strong support.

"Let me be honest about the matter, Mr. President. It will not diminish the flow of labor across our southern border. It will regularize it somewhat, nothing more. But such regularity will save some lives. Any legislation that accomplishes that deserves our strong support.

"Let us be even more candid. If the goal is to choke off the flow of immigrants, we ought not to waste our time with punishments like denial of driver's licenses, education, and health care or breaking up families. The payoff of immigration to the United States is twelve dollars an hour compared to ten cents an hour if you don't migrate. If we really want to protect our borders, to seal them off, then we should define all illegal immigrants as invaders and shoot them on sight, and I fear some Americans would like to do just that.

"As it is, hundreds and now thousands die of hunger, thirst, heat exhaustion and sunstroke in the Sonoran and the Chihuahuan deserts every year. Many Americans feel that's their problem not ours. They break our laws, they take responsibility for the consequences. However, the truth, Mr. President, is that American business seduces them to cross the border by the promise of better wages and a better life and the American government winks at this seduction. Their blood is on our hands. Mr. Jefferson wrote that all men are created equal and endowed by their creator with certain inalienable rights such as life, liberty, and the pursuit of happiness. Mr. Jefferson did not say that these rights were limited only to American citizens. The right to life of a ten-year-old child who dies on the desert not far from Tucson, Arizona, has been alienated by American society. Our corporations need them. Some segments of the American economy would grind to a halt without them. So we say to these indispensable workers, we will pay you more money than you had dreamed possible if you break our laws and cross our border. In return you must put your life in jeopardy. It is a bargain Dr. Faust would have understood."

I was following the manuscript. He was speaking it word, for word, a phenomenon not surprising to me. He did that all the time. He was also his usual relaxed self, confident and charming, even when passion pervaded his voice. My cute little Irish superhero. Around me the staff were quiet and attentive. Down on the floor, the other Senators had turned to listen and watch. They too were very quiet. Even the President Pro Tem closed his book. A new senatorial orator was a borning. Danny Webster look to your laurels.

"We should realize, speaking of Dr. Faust, Mr. President, that the arguments that they are taking away American jobs are the devil's work. They are dishonest justification for the flagrant violation of human rights in this new slave trade. Employment rates not only in this whole country but even in the border states have not declined. Moreover these migrant workers make a major contribution to our economic health, not only by their work but by the money they spend in this country. They also contribute money to our Social Security system, money they will never see again because their cards are fraudulent, another violation of rights. The answer, Mr. President, to any problems the Social Security system may have is to permit all the undocumented immigrants to pay into it. They are young and they will be contributors for a long time.

"With this fact in mind I have proposed one amendment to the bill under discussion. I oppose the requirement that those who come over as guest workers pay a two thousand dollar fine to acquire a green card. If we gave them the green card a year earlier, they would pay more than two thousand dollars at the end of that year in taxes.

"Finally, Mr. President, we must reject the absurd myth that those who wish to stay in America are engaged in an invasion which will restore to Mexico the territories taken from them in the Treaty of Guadalupe Hidalgo or at the Battle of San Jacinto or in the Gadsen Purchase. All the research evidence indicates that those who stay have exactly the same goals as did the children of the saint we celebrate this day. They want to become good Americans. They want themselves and their children to enjoy the American life. They have a rich and joyous culture to share with us. We will be fortunate to have them, Mr. President. We should not be as wrong-headed as those a century and a half ago who thought there were too many Irish pouring into this country.

"Finally, speaking of that good saint, I want to remind you, Mr. President, once again of Mr. Jefferson. He wrote that *all* were created equal. These undernourished, furtive, frightened, hungry, and thirsty little men and women who risk death in the deserts are God's people just as we are. It is not a stretch of the imagination to hear the Lord saying to us today what Moses said to the Egyptians. LET MY PEOPLE GO!

"Thank you, Mr. President, I believe I have honored the time limits you requested."

There was silence, dead silence, for a moment. Then our gallery, led by the four redheads, erupted in a standing ovation. We were crying and so were many of the women staff members who were with us, including Chris and Manny.

The President Pro Tem looked up in dismay. We were interrupting the peace of the Senate.

"If the disturbance in the galleries does not cease immediately, I will order the Sergeant at Arms to clear the galleries."

We shut up. I felt like S'ter had caught me whispering in a grammar school class. My face grew very warm. I had given a bad example again.

"That glorious son of a bitch," Chris whispered as we hugged one another, "letter perfect."

"Do we get our ice cream now, Mommy?" Marytre demanded.

There were cheers down on the floor. The Democratic senators who were present were embracing him. They knew a star had been born. I thanked God and Guadalupe that we had finally found a place for which my cute little Tommy was destined.

"I'm Eileen," a handsome gray-haired woman said to me as we walked down the stairs. There were tears on her face too. "You must be so proud of him, Mary Margaret. We have needed someone like him for years."

Minority Leader's wife. I said, "Thank you very much. Now you've started me crying again."

Contrary to the decorum expected of a senator's wife and the whirling of the TV cameras I pushed my way through the surrounding Senators in the corridor outside the Senate and embraced my husband. His heart was beating rapidly and his face was damp with sweat.

"Top of the morning, Senator," I said to him as I kissed him.

"And the broth of the day to you, Mary Margaret. I need a splash of Bushmill's."

"So do I!"

He introduced me to the Minority Leader and the other Senators. I memorized their names carefully.

"Danny Webster better look to his laurels," the Leader said.

"My very thought, Senator."

"Hat" McCoy introduced himself.

"I'm a Republican, Ma'am, but there's some Irish in me too. So I'm wearing this hyar green tie legitimate enough. Your husband shunuff is a powerful preacher man. He gonna be a real trial to us on our side of the aisle."

"When do we get the ice cream?" Marytre demanded.

"I think Daddy will have to go back to his office to thank his staff. It's a big day for them."

"OK. They're real nice people."

We were greeted with cheers on the second floor of the Dirksen building. Three bottles of champagne were produced, paper tumblers were filled and Chris proposed a toast.

"Happy St. Paddy's day to the Senator."

My daughters, who love Champagne—in limited doses, mind you—turned up their noses but sipped the coke anyway. We were not about to contribute to the delinquency of minors in the Everett McKinley Dirksen Senate Office Building.

The staff were ecstatic. They now knew for sure what they had begun to suspect—they had a winner.

I hummed a note softly. The kids picked it up.

"When Irish eyes are smiling they'll steal your heart away!"

While we were singing several other senators, attracted by the noise joined us. They wore green too. On St. Paddy's day everyone is Irish.

"Double celebration, huh, Ms. O'Malley?" one of them said to me.

"Sure," I replied in my best phony brogue, "blarney is alive and well!"

"And living in the United States Senate, thanks be to God," the Senator replied.

Then we went for lunch. The kids all ordered hamburgers and French fries, diet Coke, and two kinds of ice cream. In the evening Tommy and I drank our toast to the day in Bushmill's before we collapsed into bed and celebrated again.

CHAPTER 20

✝

MY STAFF had downloaded the speech from C-SPAN. It was available on my Web page that evening along with the text for those who wanted to follow along. DVDs went out the next morning to our core mailing list and a note was printed in our newsletter telling the readers that DVDs were available of the talk. We had more than five hundred requests.

I came down to earth very quickly the next morning. We had a meeting of the full Armed Forces Committee the next morning to examine the newly appointed Chairman of the Joint Chiefs, a spit-and-polish Navy admiral with thick brown hair, a tense red face, a jacket laden with ribbons, and a brusque tone of voice as though he were barking out responses on the bridge. He glared at the junior Democrat on the committee as though he were a seaman third class or whatever their lowest rating is.

"Admiral, I'm sure you have heard of the Powell Doctrine, even though it was enunciated by a soldier."

"Yes sir, Senator."

"And didn't General Powell argue that the United States should engage only in wars in which it would bring to bear massive force?"

"Yes sir, Senator."

"Was not his argument based on the long and drawn-out war in

Vietnam? Was not his idea that wars should be concluded promptly and successfully."

"I believe it was, yes sir, Senator."

The poor idiot didn't see it coming. Neither did his handsome and polished aides who were seated on either side and behind him.

"Do you subscribe to the Powell Doctrine?"

"Certainly."

"What would you estimate to be the proper size of an overwhelming force?"

"It would depend, Senator, sir, on the war being contemplated."

"What would have been the proper size for the war in Iraq?"

Got him.

"I wasn't involved in that decision," he stumbled.

"But surely you have given some thought to it?'

He glared at me.

"I'm sure that those responsible for the decision about force levels were satisfied with the size of the force."

"Are you aware that General Sheneski, one of your predecessors, should you be confirmed, estimated before this very committee that a force twice the size of the one actually used would be needed to secure Iraq?"

"I believe I heard that, yes, sir."

"And that the Secretary of Defense ridiculed and humiliated him in public for that suggestion and subsequently dismissed him?"

"I can't recall that."

"Did the force actually used in Iraq promptly and successfully end the resistance there?"

"Of the Iraqi army."

"Our troops are still there, Admiral."

"One more question," the committee chairman said irritably.

"One's all I need, Senator. Tell me, Admiral, if the Defense Secretary contemplates another war without massive and overwhelming force, will you resist such a plan?"

"It will be my duty to obey the Secretary."

"I was afraid of that."

"That's enough, Senator."

"You should not have embarrassed the Admiral, Senator," the chairman said when the meeting ended. "We're hoping for a unanimous approval."

"Forget about it," I replied.

"We have to support our troops."

"The best support would be a leader who can protect them from harm's way."

The senior Democrat on the committee was not pleased with me either.

"You don't know much about the armed services."

"Enough to know about the Powell Doctrine."

"Now we will have to vote against him in committee and on the floor of the Senate. A freshman Senator should not embarrass us this way."

"You didn't tell me that I shouldn't ask him a tough question."

"You ought to have known that."

I shrugged and walked away.

Then Manny told me that I had been invited to appear on the Jim Russell program on Sunday morning.

"We will have to take you over to the Senate TV studio for prep. He's the best and the most difficult."

I had watched Russell and found him intelligent and articulate, hardly difficult. I thought it would be fun. However, I wasn't about to challenge my staff. Manny, Chris, a couple of Legislative Assistants and some friendly media people gathered around the table and fired mean, nasty, tricky and difficult questions at me, some of them very personal (How much do you drink? Is marital fidelity a problem? How did you wheedle your way into such high-profile committees? Was the chairman of the Armed Forces committee upset with you for your question? Don't you think your maiden speech was inappropriately strong?) They were, I assumed, hostile questions from friendly people who wanted to prepare me.

I put on my urbane persona and fended them off.

"You did well, Senator," Manny assured me.

"Cool under fire," Dermot Kane, my senior LA, agreed. "I hope you understand that we didn't enjoy it."

"Not too much," I laughed. "But he won't ask about those things, except at the end. He'll ask about the campaign."

Russell was exactly what I thought he would be and he asked the questions I had expected.

RUSSELL: Are you on a one man crusade, Senator, to reform American electoral politics? This fine book of yours makes a powerful case for such reform.

(He holds up the book)

MORAN: That would be what the Greeks call hubris, Mr. Russell, intolerable pride. I merely wanted to test a theory that one might win an election in my state without attack ads.

RUSSELL: It looks like you proved your theory. And you didn't have a campaign fund?

MORAN: We did, but I didn't ask anyone for money and I don't know who the major contributors were, if there were any such.

RUSSELL: An election on the cheap. How much money did your committee raise?

MORAN: I'd rather use the word "collect." One of the rules I made for myself was that I did not want to know how much. I'd guess it was under five million dollars.

RUSSELL: How much do senatorial campaigns normally cost in Illinois?

MORAN: I have been told upwards of thirty million, ninety percent for television. I hate to cheat the networks out of revenue . . .

RUSSELL: You're not busy raising money for your reelection bid?

MORAN: If I run again—and I'm not at all sure that I will—I'll follow the same rules. I'll add a new one: The campaign begins on Labor Day. Last year, since people didn't know me, we had to start in

January. If there is an "again," never again. The never-ending campaign provides great material for you media folk which I don't begrudge you, but I don't want to pay for it. Besides I think people grow bored with it and politicians.

RUSSELL: Senator, do you think there will be many candidates who will be willing to imitate your asceticism?

MORAN: All I wanted to do was show that one could win despite making such a pledge. If someone wants to win badly and has the money available, it would be hard for him to give up negative campaigning. Should both major candidates agree to a truce before the campaign, then it might work.

RUSSELL: And in a presidential campaign?

MORAN: A presidential campaign in which both candidates would forswear attack ads! No attacks on each other's virtue, intelligence, character, or marital and military history? Mr. Russell, that would be almost un-American . . . Did you know that there was once a blessed time in our country's history when it was customary for a President not to campaign? Mr. Lincoln sat on his front porch in Springfield and never once budged.

RUSSELL: Senator, you'd put me out of a job . . . So you were subject to many attack ads? Didn't you ever want to fight back?

MORAN: Certainly I did. With the help of God, the saints and the angels, I resisted the temptation.

RUSSELL: You're saying that the thirty million dollars which your opponent spent was a waste of money?

MORAN: I don't know how much he spent. All I would say is that he didn't win the election.

RUSSELL: He claimed that he did and that you and the Cook County machine stole it.

MORAN: And he's still fighting in the courts. Besides the election was won by my twenty-thousand-vote margin in his Republican bailiwick DuPage County.

RUSSELL: I hear that he's already running against you six years from now.

MORAN: New attack ads are appearing every week.

RUSSELL: Where does he get his money?

MORAN: I never asked him.

RUSSELL: Some say there's Oklahoma oil money behind him.

MORAN: I hear that too but I have no way of knowing whether it's true.

RUSSELL: In this book you quote the late Mayor Daley as saying that attack ads hurt the kids of a candidate. Do you believe that?

MORAN: Sure. What does a child think when she hears every day that her father is an immature, inexperienced demagogue? And the other children get on her at school about it. Yah, yah, you're Daddy's a demagogue. Or worst still he is an immature, inexperienced, LIBERAL demagogue?

RUSSELL: Did your children react that way?

MORAN: My wife and kids are pretty tough. I don't think many people harassed them twice. But it's still not right.

RUSSELL: And there was an assassination attempt?

MORAN: Two of them.

RUSSELL: Your car and home were blown up and a rifle bullet barely missed you?

MORAN: I began to think I was running for office in Lebanon.

RUSSELL: I hear that you escaped because one of your lovely daughters is a psychic.

MORAN: Oh, I wouldn't believe that, Jim. I'd rather think it was my guardian angel. My mother-in-law says there's a tradition of witches in her family, every other generation. Good witches of the West Side, of course.

RUSSELL: And the insurance company wouldn't pay for the house?

MORAN: Anyone who has ever tried to collect an insurance claim knows how hard that is. However, they paid this one finally.

RUSSELL: Before or after you were elected?

MORAN: What do you think, Jim?

RUSSELL: You're in trouble with the Catholic Church aren't you, because of your toleration of abortion?

MORAN: Not in my own Archdiocese of Chicago. A bishop downstate
  issued a pastoral letter on the Sunday before the election. We carried his county just the same.

RUSSELL: Weren't you denied Holy Communion here in Washington?

MORAN: My whole family. We went over to the Jesuits and are doing
  fine now . . . Let me say something about that, Jim. The leaders of
  the Church lost all their clout with their people because of the pedophile scandal. Now they're trying to win back some of their authority by going after politicians. That's self-destructive too
  because they're making the Catholic Church look like a de facto
  wing of the Republican party. They should return to their old
  policy of leaving to us moral decisions made in the complexity of
  the American political system about which they know little and
  care less. They want us to impose Catholic teaching on the whole
  country, which we can't do. They are making the Church look as
  bad as some of the bigots say it is.

RUSSELL: Do you expect to hear from your brother the priest because
  of that statement?

MORAN: Perhaps.

RUSSELL: When you run for the presidency will you test your theories
  in that race?

MORAN: I believe that a President or a Presidential candidate demeans
  himself and the Office when he permits attack ads. I have no intention to run for it, by the way . . .

RUSSELL: Thank you, Senator . . . Senator Thomas Patrick Moran
  of Illinois, one of the most interesting new faces in American
  politics.

My family and my three top aides were waiting for us in the Green
Room.

"We'll never doubt you again, Senator," Chris said.

"You were great," Manny added.

"You need a stiff glass of Bushmill's," my wife said as she kissed me.

My daughters, unpredictable as always, rushed after Jim Russell to collect his autograph.

"I'm the Good Witch, Mr. Russell," Maran announced. "Sometimes I smell bad things. Only not all the time."

"Certainly not in this studio!" he laughed.

"Totally, no way!"

A genial representative of the insurance industry stopped by my office on Monday morning. "You ought to talk to him, Senator," Manny said. "You don't want them to say you won't talk to them."

"You're the boss," I said reluctantly.

I put on my own genial face and shook hands with the man, waved him to the chair, and sat next to him on the couch. He opened his brief case and placed thee copies of my book on the coffee table.

"Would you mind signing one for my mother and one for my mother-in-law? And the third one for myself and my wife?"

A bit obvious. However, I asked for the names of the three women.

"Is there anything the insurance industry can do to make peace with you?"

"I doubt it."

"We did straighten out the problem about your house?"

"As I said yesterday, only after I was elected. That was a bit obvious."

"An overzealous adjuster, I'm afraid."

"If an adjuster wasn't over zealous, he wouldn't be an adjuster for very long."

"That's a little harsh, isn't it?"

"People cheat on you a lot, I'm sure. But they cheat on you because they think you cheat on them. Which you do of course. The first thought of your industry when you see a claim is to calculate a technicality which will make it possible for you to deny liability or curtail the payment. Every dollar taken from a customer is one more dollar for your profits. My own broker said that insurance companies are whores."

He gulped.

"I hope you're not planning to say that on television."

"Only because my media people wouldn't let me."

"What would we need to placate you?"

"No small print. In big letters at the top of a homeowner's policy, 'WATERS DRIVEN BY HURRICANE WINDS ARE FLOODS NOT STORMS. WE ARE NOT LIABLE FOR FLOODS.'"

"I take your point."

"Then set up a system of ombudsmen to whom your clients can apply when they know they've been cheated but not by enough to justify hiring a lawyer. The ombudsmen would lean over backwards to defend equity, not the letter of the contract."

"Risky . . . We might lose a lot of money."

"Only if your adjusters didn't know that too many awards from the ombudsman would affect their promotions. I'm talking about small claims. The big ones would still have to go to court. Our house wasn't a big claim. Your adjuster was engaging in legerdemain. If we hired a lawyer, the adjuster would have settled for something less than our damages so we wouldn't have to go through the motions of getting ready for a suit—an offer which would cost us something to which we had the right, but not as much as a lawyer. From where I come from that might be good law but bad morality."

He nodded agreement.

"I know that there's nothing we have that you want, Senator. No rides on the Potomac for important people from Illinois. No weekends at golf resorts, no vacations in Spain . . . I won't even ask if there's anything we might do for you. But could we ask you to meet with some of our senior executives for an informal, off-the-record brainstorming session on these matters? These wouldn't be CEOs but a somewhat younger generation who are increasingly worried about our public image. They may be hostile, but I'm sure you can take care of yourself. Now the stipend . . ."

"Should be made to Catholic Relief Services."

There would be no payoff for me in such a seminar. It would take time and effort and even at this stage of my Senate career I realized that I had very little of either and I was already getting tired. Nor would I collect any votes if I should run for reelection. Why do it?

My brother used to tell me that a priest never turned down an opportunity to teach. OK, I wasn't a priest. Maybe deviant United States Senators had a similar obligation. That evening my wife insisted, "Of COURSE, you do! I'm proud of you."

That made if official.

Since I knew he would call before the morning was over, I thought about my brother. He was certainly a hard working, zealous priest, a bit like the fire marshal of the Clementine Order—racing around the world at breakneck speed to put out the fires. He had become a trouble shooter and apparently a satisfactory one or they would have taken his fire marshal's baton away from him. When he was a recently ordained priest, I was deeply impressed by his piety and zeal. His opposition to my marriage startled me. I didn't think he was serious. He couldn't possibly be serious. Mary Margaret was such a wonderful woman . . . But he was and I still don't know why. It could not have been his displeasure at her father's clearly modest pictures of women. Yet he didn't seem to like the O'Malleys—his odd behavior at the rehearsal and then at the wedding dinner astonished me. To this day I can't get over the embarrassment. Somehow, I thought, his zeal for traditional family standards and his dislike for Mary Margaret combined into an obsession. I'm not sure even now that he was sexually attracted to her, as she thinks, but it is certainly a possibility.

Something was wrong with him, however. It broke my heart. Any possibility of friendship between us or between him and my family had died somewhere along the dusty road which somehow we had traveled in the opposite direction.

"I know you don't care about your reputation or your family's reputation," he began with me in that morning's phone call, "but I'd like to think you care about the Church and care just a little about me."

"Oh," I said my body tightening, as it always had when he was bawling me out in the old days. I had done something wrong and it was his solemn duty to correct me.

"Your tirade on TV yesterday was an absolute disgrace, a vile play for media approval. Is that man Russell a Catholic?"

"I believe so."

"Did he have to tell the whole world you are barred from the Eucharist?"

"I'm only barred in one church here in the District."

"And then you let him bring me into the conversation!"

"How was I supposed to stop him?"

"I've already had a phone call from the Vatican . . . to say nothing of bishops in this country and my own brothers in the Order of St. Clement!"

Mary Margaret was right, he was narcissistic. He had become the center of my problem.

"What did the Roman say?"

"He asked me if I thought you were in the state of grace! That's what happens when you condemn the whole hierarchy!"

I guess I had done that.

"And you told him?"

"I told him that I hope you made an act of perfect contrition every night before you went to bed."

He must know that it wouldn't do any good unless I was serious about changing my mind about bishops and politics.

I was now sick to my stomach and would be for the rest of the day.

"I'm sorry I embarrassed you," I muttered.

"I wonder how long this will continue."

"Maybe until the people who tried to kill me last year are successful."

"You are such a disappointment to me, Tommy. I can't figure out where I went wrong or how I failed you."

He hung up. I rushed to the little bathroom in my office and vomited.

After I had told Marymarg about my visit with the insurance lobbyist, I did not tell her about the call from Tony. She had probably guessed anyway.

CHAPTER 21

✝

W E H A V E the votes for your amendment," Dermot Kane told me
a couple of weeks later. "The other side doesn't like it, but they
need a lot of our votes to pass the legislation. It's top priority at the
White House. We have them over the barrel for the moment."

"Then in the conference committee we can stonewall the delegates
from the House."

"You're a quick study, Senator."

"An exhausted study," I said.

"You'll learn to pace yourself."

"I hope so."

I seemed to be stumbling around in a fog every day. My sleep was
untroubled, except for dreams about blood pouring from Johnny Dale's
chest. There was so much to do every day, even those days like Monday
and Friday when most of my colleagues were home fund raising.

"The leader wants you to speak for the amendment. Two minutes
maybe. Four-thirty if we're lucky."

"Of course."

"His LA tells me that the leader was very pleased with your questions
at the Armed Forces hearing."

"The Chairman wasn't."

"We shouldn't worry too much about him."

That was about as close as a good, professional LA would go in criticizing one Senator to another, a relic of the past when the Senate was a more gentlemanly place. Younger LAs were less reverent.

Dermot was Montana Irish, a tall, lanky Plainsman with a strong touch of the Mick mixed in.

"I'm glad to hear that. My instincts said we shouldn't."

"Not that you would have behaved differently."

"Not on that Admiral."

Voting on the Immigrant Reform Bill would be late on Thursday evening. Thursday was the day when the Senate tried to clean up all its business for the week before many of the members dashed to National Airport to fly back to their constituencies, their fat cats, and perhaps their families. Thursday was the one day of the week when voting on legislation was likely to occur, the one day during which the real business of the Senate transpired. Not that, I had discovered to my dismay, the other days were not horrendously busy.

The leaders would meet in the cloakroom before the session and work out the final schedule and the mechanics. Since both leaders supported the bill, there would be little conflict in the cloakroom. The difficulty would be controlling the many dissidents in both parties who wanted to go on record against anything tainted with the word "immigrants." We would be fortunate if we could adjourn before midnight. Few senators would dare leave for the airport before the final vote on this bill.

Our leadership would make sure that there were enough votes on the floor for my amendment to pass. The other side wouldn't much care. They wanted to pass the bill, go home, and leave its fate to the conference committee where it would languish till just before summer adjournment. Then the White House would become nervous and insist on a report from the conference committee and a vote on the last day of the session. The members of both houses would hope that it would be lost in the other last minute measures and their constituents wouldn't notice.

My amendment was called at 7:30.

"I recognize the Senator from Illinois for two minutes to speak in support of his amendment."

"Mr. President, I will be brief. The requirement that immigrants from Mexico pay two thousand dollars for their green cards, disguised as a 'fine,' is blatantly punitive and violates the Constitutional provision for equal justice under the law. Will we charge immigrants from Western Europe, England and Ireland, let us say, for their green cards? Moreover, the income tax and Social Security they will pay in their first year will be much more than two thousand dollars. If the Treasury needs income, we could make the green cards available after five years instead of six. Thank you, Mr. President."

"Will the Senator from Illinois, yield, Mr. President?"

The vast mound which was Richard "Poor Richard" Yardley from Oklahoma rose unsteadily at his desk. Dressed in western boots, a snow white "Western" suit that Cowboys might wear to court pretty ladies from the East, a string tie, but not wearing his cowboy hat, Poor Richard started to drink at noon every day, was incoherent at the Thursday Republican caucus lunch, and slept most of the time when he was in the Senate chamber. He was a figure of fun even among his fellow Republicans, but he still had one percent of the vote in the United States Senate.

"The Senator has already finished his allotted time, Senator."

"I demand a Senator's right to respond."

"Two minutes, Senator."

I remained standing.

"These illegal criminals belong in jail, that's where they belong. Why are we giving them illiterate vermin the right to come into our country, take our people's jobs, send American money home to their vermin families in Mexico, and ruin our country? We should horsewhip them all and send them back to where they belong, that's what we should do. We should shoot them on sight at the border, that's what we should do. If we don't protect our borders, this won't be America any more."

He babbled on for five more minutes—the C-SPAN camera grinding away and the members growing restless. I wondered if anyone from Oklahoma were watching. Would they be ashamed of him or proud? Bobby Bill Roads who had doubtless poured millions into his campaigns would surely be very proud.

The President Pro Tem touched the handle of his gavel to his desk, a gentle hint. Poor Richard became more incoherent on the subject of vermin, but did not take the hint.

Finally, after half way through eternity, the President Pro Tem spoke up.

"The Senator from Oklahoma has exceeded his time. Will he yield?"

"Poor Richard" simply collapsed into his chair and fell asleep.

"Does the Senator from Illinois wish to respond?"

He didn't.

"There being no other speakers, we will proceed by unanimous consent to voting on this amendment."

No one requested a quorum call. The amendment passed by nine votes, what we had expected. Was it all a charade? Was the whole long afternoon and evening a waste of time because everyone knew the bill would pass by five or six votes, many of them reluctant?

We voted and went on to the next amendment which would mandate health examinations prior to the awarding of green cards.

"These people are sick," the supporting senator argued. "We can't give them permanent residence unless we are sure they won't bring contagious diseases into our country and infect our people."

The research showed that, on average, the immigrants were more healthy than average Americans. However, everyone knew what wasn't true. Nonethless the amendment was doomed because it didn't have the votes. It lost by five votes—the size of the majority that the two leaders had created against the will of their respective caucuses.

A page, Asian, pretty, with braces, brought me a note from the Minority Leader. He wanted to see me in the cloakroom.

"You did good, Tommy."

"Thank you, Senator."

"Sorry you had to put up with 'Poor Richard.'"

"He's a member of the United States Senate. He has the right to be heard, poor dear man, as my wife would say."

"As does the Senior Democrat on the Armed Services Committee."

He laughed.

"I figured you and he wouldn't get along when I put you on the committee. It's so easy for those guys to sell out to anyone with stripes and ribbons. They'll be more careful about who they send up to the committee now that they know they have you to contend with . . . How do you see the Conference Committee on this bill?"

"There'll be two of us from the two houses on the committee and three of them. We're down six to four. And we hold all the cards thanks to the White House."

"Right, they want immigration legislation and they know—or at least they've been told by my friend across the aisle—that they're going to get the legislation only if they can hold the Democrats in both houses. So if our guys hang tough the Conference will report out mostly our bill."

"An opportunity to be seized."

"Would you mind seizing it?"

"Not at all if you want me to."

"You'll have to spar all through the summer up to recess with the nativists."

"I'm prepared to do that."

"Everyone will see the handwriting on the wall when you hang tough. So they'll probably only schedule a meeting every week. Not all of them will come either."

"It should be interesting. Poor Richard will be there?"

He grinned. "No way, but guys that are sober most of the time with the same ideas."

"Will the White House stick with us?"

"They're notorious for cutting the ground out from under us. This time my friend across the aisle will probably hold their feet to the fire."

The Immigration Reform Bill passed at 11:55. Many of the Senators had left for the airport. We still had our six-vote majority. I went home exhausted and depressed. So much fighting, so much fooling around for a law that would not help very much, but was better than nothing. That is the burden of democracy, I told myself.

My wife, with a gender-discrimination case before the court, one in which she had little confidence because of mistakes at lower levels, was sound asleep. I didn't bother her.

CHAPTER 22

✝

THE FIRST MEETING of our Conference Committee was a rhetorical slugfest. The chair of the House Delegation, a Congresswoman from Texas was Ms. Anita Bell Landry, a true, artificially blond southern Belle. She was a mean, snippy woman with a giggly, passive manner which hid both her tenacity and her acute dislike of "our little brown brothers" as she called them—in the presence of Representative José Maria Espinoza from California. My chairman from the Senate was my old friend Hat McCoy who treated her with the deference a southern gentleman owes to a Texas Belle—without conceding anything in the argument.

"The Senate will have to concede many points to the House if this bill is ever to get out of conference."

"Not to be offensive, ma'am," Hat responded, "we're not fixing to give up much."

"That amendment Senator Moran introduced must be deleted and replaced with our text. We simply won't report out a bill that does not fine those who have come to our country illegally."

"No way," I said simply.

Most of the time I simply sat and listened while the immigrant haters and the immigrant supporters, including Representative Espinoza, traded insults. My friend Hat maintained a brave front though

I didn't think that many of his actual voters were Latino. He was there because the Majority Leader wanted a bill he could get to the President.

Vile woman that she was, Ms. Landry knew the same thing. We would spend spring and summer sparring for the benefit of our respective constituencies both in Congress and around the country and then end up with legislation that had to please Senate Democrats for a change. Everyone around the table knew that, more or less, but the losers wanted to go back and tell everyone that they had fought the good fight.

I began to draft the early chapters of my book *Political Show Trials,* under the guise of taking copious notes at the discussion.

"At least you found something useful to do," Dermot protested as our entourage returned to the Dirksen building. The entourage routinely included Dermot, Pat Coogan, a recent product of the Golden Dome, and Roberta Becker, our new assistant press secretary, a disturbingly gorgeous young woman—model beauty—three years out of Columbia. I noted the look of sympathy in her eyes when I had to tangle with the Texas Belle. Sympathy is always welcome, especially from a beautiful woman, but, I told myself, this is someone of whom you should be a little wary. She might develop a crush on you.

Ordinarily I ignored the sallies of La Belle, partly because I'm a gentleman (usually) and partly because if I were rude the word would leak out and there'd be trouble with the media, not that as summer wore on I cared much about the media. However, one day a riposte slipped out, one which had surged up like a geyser from my Irish sub-basement.

"I wouldn't be so hard on your little brown brothers, Congresswoman. The way they assimilate to American society in three generations they'll be voting Republican and joining country clubs."

"Not my country club," she snapped back, as Hat and José and my staff guffawed.

That story would get around. It wouldn't hurt our side, but it would hurt theirs.

So we finally adjourned, having agreed on nothing.

A couple of TV cameras and some bored reporters were waiting outside.

"Any progress, Senator?" someone asked.

Robbie tried to protect me by hustling me down the corridor. Mother Hen, I thought.

"Not one bit."

"Do you expect any during this session of Congress?"

"If the White House is serious, we'll start seeing progress a couple of days before the August recess. The Senate has given them pretty much the bill they wanted. The question now is how badly they want it."

On a dull news day, that might be a useful clip for our side.

A critic of the media and the political game, I had nonetheless succumbed to its techniques. I was a trial lawyer, however, and I love to score points for our side.

"Saw you on C-SPAN," Chris said when I dragged myself back from my lunch with Hat in the Senate dining room. We had discussed a bill we proposed to bring to the floor in January, a can't-miss bill for both of us. We were going to follow the advice of the Supreme Court and forbid municipalities to condemn private property so that they might zone them for shopping malls and other income-producing enterprises. Only the lethargy of both houses had delayed it this long. It would certainly help Hat in his reelection bid. I hoped for a Democratic majority, but I feared we'd have to wait several more years for that turn of the tide. The high tide, King Alfred cried, the high tide and the turn! But we also needed Republicans like Hat who were not "extreme" Christians.

"Debil made me say it," I muttered.

"You're getting a reputation for quotable one-liners," she said.

"That's bad?"

"So far that's good. I am kind of afraid what you might say when you lose your temper."

"I have a long record for self-control, too much maybe."

"I also heard about your remark about little brown brothers voting Republican."

"That was bad?"

"That was naughty, but it was good . . . When was the last time you really blew up?"

"Probably back in high school. Maybe junior high."

She probably wondered what kind of a freak her Senator was.

"What do you think of Robbie?"

"Competent . . . Perhaps a little too protective . . . Maternal."

"I was afraid of that. I'll deal with it."

"Carefully, I hope. She seems a little fragile."

"A lot fragile."

That night Marymarg, as worn down by Beltway heat as I was, and the kids and I discussed our plans for the August recess. To our surprise the kids were not interested in going back to Hermosillo. They were tired of the heat in Washington. They wanted to spend the month with their cousins in Grand Beach.

"Swim!"

"Water ski!"

"Sail!"

This was good news for us. Security questions had been raised about a United States Senator and his family living as a private citizen in a Mexican city. They would be easy targets for kidnappers. A luxurious beach resort with lots of guards might be acceptable.

Grand Beach sounded fine to me too.

"What about your Spanish?"

"There are kids in our classes who speak Spanish," Mary Rose informed us. "They laugh at our accents, but we get tons of practice with them."

"What did you make of that?" Mary Margaret asked me as we were getting ready for bed.

"They took counsel among themselves and decided that their parents needed time at the lake."

She chuckled.

"I wouldn't be surprised at all. Soon they will outnumber us."

"Already they do."

As June turned into July, the only other exercise was the first important meeting of the Judiciary Committee to hold hearings on the appointment of Judge Marsha Barnard of Tuscaloosa, Alabama, to the Court of Appeals of the 5th Circuit. The senior Democrat on Judiciary gave me a stack of her opinions.

"She is to the right of Catherine the Great," he confided. "If we cause enough trouble, she won't even get out of committee. I don't think she has anything near sixty votes. If her hearing record is bad enough, we could mount a filibuster if we had to."

"Is she an African American?"

"How did you guess that? She's also a born-again Christian. Will you handle the religious issues in her rulings?"

"If that's what you want."

"We have to protect the wall between Church and State. She doesn't believe in it."

"The wall is a metaphor, Senator. One doesn't base good law on metaphor."

"You're in favor of prayer in public schools?" he said, looking puzzled.

"My kids don't go to public schools. I'm not sure that prayer makes them any better than they would be if they were 'publics' but it wouldn't make them any worse either."

"You want vouchers for Catholic schools?" he asked even more astonished.

"You bet I do. I want freedom of choice for minority parents. Catholic schools are the only ones in the country that provide that choice for most of them. If a bill ever comes before the Senate, I'd vote for it. To hell with the ACLU and the AFT."

"I don't necessarily disagree with you, Tommy. If you don't want to tackle her on these matters, we'll let you do gender."

"I'll look over her rulings."

I realized as soon as I read the first couple of them that I'd have no problem at all. The poor woman was articulate, indeed very articulate.

But she was out of the main stream of American legal convictions and apparently didn't know she was—a Clarence Thomas in the making.

There is a solemnity about the hearings of the Judiciary Committee of the United States Senate. It is not exactly as portentous as sessions of the Congregation of the Holy Office of the Inquisition (in my imagination, never having appeared before that tribunal)—no crimson robes, no holy water, no incense. Yet the wood panels, the red hangings, the solemn faces of the Senators all imply that nothing the Senate does is more important than approving a lifetime appointment from one of our separated powers to another separated power. Such a hearing focuses two hundred years of American constitutionalism into single issue on which the survival of the framers' delicate balances may be put in jeopardy. Senators take themselves seriously. All right, we Senators take ourselves very seriously, but never more than when we consider judicial appointments, especially of someone on the inside track to the Supreme Court, an institution whose members take themselves even more seriously than we do.

For which God forgive them, comments my irrepressible wife.

After her initial description of her life—welfare poor up to a law degree—we began our questions gingerly. The other side tried to emphasize her "American grit and determination." We emphasized her rulings. It was clear to everyone in the room that she wasn't very bright, probably not even bright enough to be serving on the district court. She was someone's Republican token appointment, African-American skin but not much legal ability.

The senior Democrat had questioned her about equal rights for women and affirmative action. She responded by asking whether he wanted to put men and women in the same "restrooms" and whether he thought black children were not as smart as white children.

I began as cordially as I could. "I want to ask you some questions, your honor, about Religion . . ."

"I am proud to be a Christian, Senator, very proud. My God sustained me all through my education. I am not likely to turn my back on Him."

She was a tall, slender, gray-haired woman, tense and charming before the grand inquisitors. She responded to our questions in the manner of a kindly schoolmarm explaining simple matters to a class of likeable but not very bright junior high boys.

"An admirable sentiment, your honor, with which I agree completely. But I had more in mind what we call in this country the separation between Church and State . . ."

"This is a Christian country, Senator. Always has been, please God, always will be. You can't separate God from daily life . . ."

"Are you saying, your honor, that there is no such thing as separation of Church and State in the Constitution?"

"Don't you have a chaplain in the Senate? Doesn't he pray over you every day? Does he separate God from the daily life of the Senate?"

"You believe, if I read your decisions correctly, that such prayers should occur every day in all our schools?"

"How can praying ever hurt anyone? What harm can it do to children?"

Up to that point she had answered me in a manner that African-American people around the country, especially women, would have approved enthusiastically. She was one of their own. She had taught them in school.

"Won't it offend the children who don't believe in God or whose God is not the Christian God?"

"This is a Christian country, Senator. People who come to it realize that they have to make certain adjustments."

That sentence would do her in. She had just breached the wall. I could imagine the fury of the *New York Times* editorial board.

"There are, as you know, Judge Barnard, many divisions even among Christians. Some parents might want a prayer like those they experience in their Pentecostal church and some like those they have heard in their Quaker meeting halls. Would not Congress and the courts have serious difficulty trying to regulate the kind of prayers which would occur in the classroom?"

"No more than there are problems regulating the prayers in the Senate."

I could hardly say that very few Senators ever heard those prayers.

"I also note, Judge Barnard, that you have ruled that school boards might mandate the teaching of intelligent design in the classroom biology courses."

"I think that's the only fair way to deal with the controversy, Senator. It's the American way. It provides an opportunity for the children to hear both sides of the argument. I was quite disappointed when the Appellate Court overturned my verdict."

"Thank you, Judge," I said with my most charming smile. "You have been very clear and forthright."

And destroyed your chances, I added to myself.

"Thank you, Senator, you are a very courteous and Christian young man."

Titters from the media and from my own staff who hovered behind me.

I felt wretched. As a responsible member of the Judiciary Committee I had to ask the questions I did. She was a good and kind woman who should never have been appointed to the federal bench. The White House had sent her name over to us without any preparation at all. They knew we would turn her down. They wanted us to turn her down. They would pick up points and we would lose them. They played the race card in reverse. Dirty politics.

I would let the senior Democrat make that point.

"Will you want to talk to the media when we adjourn, Senator?" Robbie leaned over my shoulder and engulfed me in the smell of very expensive scent.

"I don't think so. Senator McAfee has the priority."

Wilson McAfee from Wisconsin was blunt.

"She is a lovely woman," he said, "and honest and trenchant in debate. But she is not qualified to serve on the Fifth Circuit. The Administration knows that. They did not even prepare her to answer questions in a way that would resonate with the current state of constitutional interpretation. They played the race card again, this time to embarrass us."

Black people would ask me hostile questions about "Marsi" Barnard every time I spoke to them in the months ahead. All the more reason to turn down more talks back home.

"They mouse-trapped us," I said wearily when I had returned to my office.

"Maybe you should have crossed them up and approved her," Chris suggested.

"Then they'd be back in a year with a Supreme Court appointment. How about the Black people out there?"

"They were embarrassed by her, Senator. But they also liked her."

"So did I."

"They laughed when she said you were a good Christian young man and you blushed."

"I didn't think any of the adjectives were accurate."

That night Mary Margaret and I attended yet another Georgetown dinner party. We were both dead tired and irritable. I looked tired, but my wife in her new gauzy white summer dress looked like she had just returned from a spa. I complained about the contrast.

"My job is not boring. Yours is, poor dear man."

"I feel very much like a poor dear man."

The party was like a liberal caucus. I was praised for the courteous effectiveness of my questions. The White House was damned for its dirty political trick.

"They hoisted us on our own petard. We invented affirmative action to salve our liberal guilt. Race and gender, we said, deserve a discount to expiate for our past sins. So they provided us with both discount claims and then suddenly we had to argue what they always do—only ability matters. We will reject the very discounts which we have created."

"But . . ." a woman columnist argued, "surely there is an upper limit to your discount?"

"Who sets that limit?"

No one had the answer.

As July wound down and my morale with it, the Conference Committee came alive again. The Belle charged in one day, denounced us for stalling, and presented a list of nonnegotiable demands. They were mostly trivial. We gave in on the health examination for green cards, warning that as the amendment stood it demanded such exams only from immigrants across the southern border. Obviously that would violate the principle of equal protection under the law and would quickly be rejected by the courts.

"You can have it if you want it, but it's unconstitutional."

"We'll take our chances on that," she snapped back.

I looked at José. He shrugged.

"OK. You got it. You want to place a little bet on how the courts will rule."

"I don't gamble, Senator. I'm a Christian."

There were so many comments I might have made. I was too tired even to be mean. She could go back to her colleagues and claim a victory while giving us everything else we wanted.

After squabbling later in the day about wording we finally had a conference report to pass on to the whole Senate.

"Well done, Tommy," the Minority Leader said to me. "A long and tough fight."

I shrugged.

"White House made 'em do it."

The bill was approved by voice vote in both houses on the last day of the session. That way no one could take the credit and, more important, no one would be blamed.

That night, as I was on my second whiskey, a hand-delivered invitation came from the White House to be present at the signing the next afternoon.

"They're still Republicans over there, aren't there?" Mary Rose asked sarcastically.

"They sure are," her mother agreed.

I called the leader.

"I have to go over there," he admitted. "It's up to you."

"Have fun," I said.

I called the White House and said that I had to catch a plane first thing in the morning."

"We're outta here!" I informed my cheering family.

Grand Beach was healing. At the end of our interlude there I was not exactly a new man, but at least one ready to return. The kids had a grand time with the cousins who all looked much older than they had the last time we saw them. Siobhan, Marymarg's "little" sister, much to everyone's sigh of relief was engaged. An MD who had done medical missionary work in Africa, she had violated the family custom of young marriages. Moreover, she was marrying a "foreigner." But since he was Irish and also a doctor no one complained. For refined skills at the purest blarney he was at least the equal of Ambassador O'Malley.

We had become celebrities of a sort. Our family and friends wanted to hear stories about life in the Beltway. I complied, using all my seanachie skills, subject to correction for inaccuracy by Mary Margaret. The stories were greeted with laughter and cheers. We were surrounded by Democrats, Chicago Democrats, among our own kind. Naturally they liked the stories.

Then came Labor Day and the party was over.

CHAPTER 23

✝

THE CHRISTMAS BREAK was almost as good as the Grand Beach break. I had only ten days of escape from my Senate office which I now considered a prison, from which I emerged for breakfasts and lunches and committee meetings, quorum calls, unpaid lectures around the country (for no good reason save for a sense of vocation), receptions and dinner parties, the last two somewhat more enjoyable because I was accompanied by Mary Margaret with whom I had a chance to talk that otherwise would not have occurred. She too was a prisoner of her office and the courts, Appellate and Supreme. In retrospect we were both out of our mind. We had been swept up in the madness of doing good. At least she received a decent salary for her efforts.

In a city of neighborhoods (and River Forest, if it wasn't always a neighborhood, became one when the Catholics moved in), Christmas is a neighborhood event—front lawns dense with light displays, not all of them vulgar; kids' Mass and midnight Mass at the local church, carillon playing Christmas Carols, carolers patrolling the streets, snow perhaps on the lawns (but not on the streets!), excited kids, candles in all the windows, wives and mothers and daughters exhausting themselves in their culinary efforts, God bless every one. Then there are pilgrimages to see the Marshall Field's Christmas decorations—those pilgrimages have declined since the store acquired a New York name— and the Mayor's Christmas Tree in the Daley Plaza (complete with a crib scene and a menorah and a "Deutchfest) and the lights in Millennium Park.

I know that Christmas is like that all over the country, but in the intense community of Chicago neighborhoods it is especially magical.

Compared to Georgetown anyway.

The O'Malley clan is exuberant and by and large have married exuberant people, myself alone a partial exception. Even Shovie's new husband from Ireland, for all his Trinity College background is a firm believer in *craic*, as the Irish call it—it's not his fault that he looks like an IRA gunman. Their festivities are always exuberant, and their Christmases transcend exuberance and approach madness—though no one dares to take too much of the creature, a rule enforced by stern womanly disapproval. You don't have to be exuberant and no one, not even my wife, minds if I stand at the edge, smile happily, and hum mentally while they are singing.

During that Christmas which marked the end of my first year in the United States Senate, however, I became as crazy as all the rest. I was happy to be back in my own neighborhood and my own kind of people, a place where the TV camera wasn't picking up my every mood and my staff were not monitoring my every move.

I thought to myself as I sang an amateur duet with my wife that at last I had left behind the bleak Christmases of my childhood. I had learned, mostly because of Mary Margaret, how to celebrate.

Unfortunately for all of us, my brother showed up just before dinner on Christmas night.

The Ambassador heard the doorbell, slipped away to the door, and opened it.

"Good evening, Father," he said in a tone of voice that commanded attention from the rest of us.

My heart sank. The wet blanket had arrived.

Everyone stood, stricken into immobility, as he entered the huge parlor, his jacket (no overcoat, not for the fire marshal on the move), covered with snow flakes.

"I expected my brother to be at his home with his wife and children and that I could join with him to celebrate the Feast of the Incarnation."

"You must stay and have supper with us, Father," my mother-in-law, as always gracious approached him and offered a hand. He did not take it.

"No, no, not at all," he replied. "I know where I would not be welcome."

Msgr. Ed, the Ambassador's younger brother, broke the stillness.

"Please stay, Father. At Christmastime everyone is welcome."

"I expected to find my brother and his family at home. The next-door neighbor said he was here. I will not intrude."

"You're not intruding at all," the Ambassador insisted, making the invitation absolutely official.

"No, I will return to the Clementine house and say my Christmas breviary."

And out the door he went, without a "Merry Christmas" or a word to me and my family.

The exuberant O'Malleys were still frozen in one place. There was cold fury in Mary Margaret's green eyes. April Nettleton, Mary Margaret's big sister, played "God Rest You Merry Gentlemen" on the piano and we joined in, hesitantly at first and then heartily. The Grinch was gone.

"I'm so sorry, Tommy," my wife took my hand, "so very, very sorry."

"You did nothing to be sorry for," I said. "Nothing at all. I'm sorry that my brother threw a wet blanket on our celebration."

"I'm sorry," she hugged me, "that he has tried to throw a wet blanket on your life."

However, the O'Malleys are nothing if not resilient. The celebration of the Lord's birth began again. We who believe in Him have much to celebrate all the time, but especially at Christmas. I slipped away to the bathroom and returned to the celebration with I hope no signs of my desolation.

As we fell asleep in each other's arms, Mary Margaret whispered to me, "I'll always love you, Tommy. Never doubt it."

That was, I thought, an effective response to my brother the wet blanket. But I was still in thrall to him. I probably always would be.

I returned a day early to conspire with Hat McCoy about our "Defense of Private Property" Bill. A city in Connecticut had exercised the right of eminent domain, not to build a highway or a bridge or even a school. Rather it confiscated a whole neighborhood of elderly but elegant homes from the people who owned them in order to build shopping malls and new homes which would bring far more revenue than the current property taxes. It was theft, pure and simple, greed by vote of a city council. The Supreme Court rejected a suit against the city council, ruling that there was nothing in the legislation about condemnation proceedings which prevented an attack on property from which a municipality might be able to squeeze more tax revenue. Several of the justices opined outside of the Court that Congress ought to change the law to prohibit such a misuse of power.

"That's nonsense," my good wife sputtered. "They could have found ample grounds to rule for the homeowners. They're just showing off their restraint."

Legislation was proposed in both Houses, but somehow never quite made it to the floor because lobbyists for the municipality organizations persuaded important people to drag their feet. Hat McCoy and I decided to join forces and go after those evil men who were stealing homes just to enhance their tax base. We both talked to our respective leaders and they agreed to call up our bill, which had cleared committee unanimously during the first week of Senate business. They would arrange for unanimous consent in their morning negotiations and bring it up.

Such cooperation was not all that usual in the Senate in our highly polarized era. The reason they were willing to cooperate this time around, according to Hat, was that national sentiment against what happened in Connecticut was overwhelming and that neither party could afford to seem to go against that sentiment. The White House was indifferent, probably because no one had called it to the President's attention. We would strike before the lobbyists, not the most powerful to begin with. Finally we had drafted our bill—or rather our Legislative Assistants had with advice from scholars who specialized in the Court and covert advice from a couple of justices who have voted reluctantly to reject the suit brought by the victims of eminent domain. It said simply that the right of eminent domain did not extend to the condemnation of property to improve a municipality's tax base.

"Slick," my wife admitted. "You'll catch the lobbyists by surprise."

Mary Margaret and I had returned from snow-covered Chicago to snow-covered Georgetown with firm resolutions to amend our lives. I would restrict the number of speeches I accepted and she would not take as many cases. We both would instruct our respective schedulers to limit us to two dinner parties and one extra reception during the week. We pledged that we would have more time for our daughters, two of whom were now at Gonzaga Prep. We also meant more time for each other. I'm not sure we really believed that it would be that easy.

It wasn't.

My staff had a party to celebrate my return. Robbie continued to stare at me with soft eyes of adoration. I didn't like that, but I did not want to hurt her feelings. I wished there was some reason to fire her, but she was a first-class Assistant Press Secretary. I resolved I would not provide any encouragement. Unfortunately my hormones, never completely under control, began to protest my attempts to feign indifference to this readily available prize.

"Did you really think I wouldn't come back?" I asked them.

Silence for a moment. Then Peter Doherty, my junior LA, said, "We were afraid you might do the smart thing and quit the job."

No illusions about the Senate of the United States in my staff.

Peter reported from conversation with Hat's LA that we would go with the bill on the Tuesday of the second week of the year.

Much to the surprise of most of our colleagues the Fairness for Private Property Bill was called up from committee in the first moments of Tuesday afternoon. There was an immediate quorum call to stall the process.

Hat ambled over to my side of the aisle like he wanted to make predictions about the outcome of the Super Bowl.

"This should be easy if we all keep our cool. I'll speak fust, then you say a few words. If no one wants to reply, and unless their LAs tell them what to say, no one will, we'all will call for unanimous consent that there be a vote. It will be history before the afternoon is over. They can lobby against in the house all they want and we may not get it out of conference till the end of August again, but no one is going to fight too hard against it."

Once a quorum was established, the "debate began."

"By unanimous consent," the President intoned, "Hatfield" McCoy stood at his chair, "five minutes for the Senator from Kentucky."

"This hyar piece of legislation, also called the McCoy-Moran bill— please note whose name is first—has a unique origin. It is sponsored by two Irishmen, one who kicks with his left foot and one who kicks with his right foot. This is clearly an ecumenical age, Mr. President. Its aim is to prevent local governments from stealing the property of ordinary citizens so that developers can put up malls and town houses and condominiums that will enhance the local tax base. The Supreme Court didn't like what a certain municipality did along these lines, but bounced the ball back to us. Happen someone would try to condemn a little farm community along one of our lovely rivers in Ole Kentuck so that a developer could put up big box stores and pay the county more taxes than these poor farmers, those farmers would want to skin my hide off because I hadn't protected them. This hyar bill would protect my hide."

The President Pro Tem yawned, glanced at his notes, look out to see if I were standing and said, "by unanimous consent, the Senator from Illinois is recognized for five minutes.

"I do not know, Mr. President, if the distinguished Senator from Kentucky has ever visited the land of our common ancestors, but I say to him that there'll be no need to kiss the blarney stone. He already has an ample supply of that commodity. I can add to his remarks that it is important we move rapidly on this legislation before unscrupulous developers all over the country make more pot-of-gold promises to venal and corrupt local governments so they can steal the homes of poor people, elderly people, and hard-working middle class people, all crimes that in my religious tradition call to heaven for vengeance."

"Will the Senator from Illinois yield?" Jeremey Cline from Oregon.

"The Senator from Illinois gladly yields to the distinguished Senator from Oregon."

A small man from a small town in eastern Oregon who wandered around the Senate with the perpetual frown of someone who thinks someone else is trying to put something over on him.

"Will the Senator from Illinois please explain the reason for all the rush about this piece of legislation? Why didn't we get a chance to read it before today and to discuss it?"

"The Senator from Kentucky already explained the urgency. We fear an epidemic of such misuse of the right of eminent domain all around the country unless we act quickly. Moreover as the Senator from Oregon doubtless remembers we had extensive debate on this legislation before the holiday recess. Comments were, I'm sure the record will show, quite favorable. There simply was no time to vote on it. My colleague from Kentucky and I think it is important that we complete Senate action on the legislation before we are caught up in the tumult of legislation that we will have to consider as we prepare for the election in November."

"Thank you, Senator."

I noticed that both leaders had enough dependable men on the floor to win easily. During the voting men moved in and out of the Senate to signal the clerk, thumbs-up, thumbs-down how they wanted to vote. There were only a handful of thumbs down. No one loses many votes by opposing venal local governments and greedy developers.

We carried the day. I was elated. Immigration and eminent domain were two promises I had made during the election campaign. I had delivered on both of them. As long as there was a semblance of bipartisanship in the Senate, one could move quickly on an important issue.

There were some handshakes of congratulations. The two leaders appeared together to commend us.

"We'd better watch it," said my guy, "these two connivers might have their eyes on our jobs."

"I don't think so," said Hat's guy, who was notorious for the fact that his wit was a vestigial organ. "Still they work well together."

"It's the blarney, Senator."

At the door of the chamber, Robbie waited with a warm smile of congratulations.

The woman was flirtatious, but it was hard to prove it. Also very distracting. My imagination was unruly whenever she was near.

"Will you speak to the media, Senator?"

I looked at Hat.

Why not?

"I want it to be clear to everyone," Hat began, "that I have not been taken in by this conniving Democrat from Chicago. However, he's not a bad man for a Democrat. He's a man you can work with on matters that pertain to the common good of all Americans."

"I'm delighted by the passage of the McCoy-Moran bill and to have my name on with that of Senator McCoy. I think many of our colleagues who are running for re-election will be happy when they realize how popular this act is."

"Do you think Senator it will be signed before the November election?"

"I wouldn't be surprised at all."

There was another celebration in the office.

"All you guys want to do is drink champagne on the Senate's time!"

"Not bad, Senator," Chris said, "not bad at all. You work well with folk from the mountains."

"As long I'm a going along with whatever they a telling me to do."

"It will probably be the last victory until the next session in January."

"I know that, Chris, so everyone enjoy your champagne."

My personal phone rang. I picked it up. I knew who it would be.

"I'm not sure, Senator, that I could vote for you again. What kind of Senator is it who keeps two promises during his first year in office?"

"A Senator who gets the best legal advice possible from a member of the Supreme Court bar."

We both laughed. How long had it been since my wife and I had laughed together.

Chris's prediction was correct. The election was close, but we lost. Democrats have to win by substantial majorities in key states or one way or another they lose. That's just the way things work out. We picked up a couple of seats in the Senate. We were in striking distance. When we adjourned for the holiday recess, the Minority Leader caught me in the dining room after I had lunch with Mary Rose, who had walked over from Gonzaga.

"Bye, Daddy. The Boss wants to talk to you."

"That child gets more like her mother every day," he said to me.

"Funny, I noticed that too."

"You're moving up in seniority in both committees, Tommy."

"I'm not sure that's a good idea, though maybe I'll get to ask my questions earlier."

"I'm wondering if you would be willing to become part of our leadership team, Assistant Minority Whip for a start. You're affable and charming, but you're also as tough as they come. We need people like you in the Congressional leadership. We could offer you one of those hideaways where you can work on your books."

"I'd be happy to do so, Senator. I'll learn more about how the Senate works."

"Our day is coming, Tommy, our day is coming."

When I told my wife about the new job on our way to a reception at the British Embassy, I said apologetically that I knew I should have asked her first.

"Tommy love, you knew what I would say. You don't have to ask me anything when you know what I will say. I'm proud of you!"

I realized that she thought I was much better at the job than I really was. She thought I was becoming a power in the land. I didn't want that to happen, but I didn't want to disappoint her either.

CHAPTER 24

†

I WAS HAILED as a success as an assistant during the next year and a half. The national news magazines described me in the very words the leader had used (and apparently given them). I was charming and affable but as tough as they come.

I wasn't ashamed of that label. My good wife was ecstatic, though we were having less and less time for one another. I knew that after the off-year election, we would be only a vote or two from taking control of the Senate. Then I would have to make up my mind about re-election. I kept telling myself that it was a wise idea to quit when I was ahead.

Three and a half years after our trip to the Beltway and the beginning of my term in the Senate they went after my daughter—the *Examiner*, Leander Schlenk, and Bobby Bill Roads. And eventually my brother. The costs of being a Senator had become unacceptable. I made up my mind I would not run for reelecton.

Mary Rose had creamed—her word—Gonzaga. She had become a young woman who in most ways was a clone of her mother, though her hair was even brighter and her poise even more self-assured and she lectured us daily on what we should do. We were proud that she would be the valedictorian and did not dare suggest what she might say in her address—unless she asked, which she certainly would not do.

There then appeared an article on the front page:

DID TOMMY'S KID CHEAT OTHER GIRL
OF HIGH SCHOOL HONOR?
Mother Alleges School Cooked Records

The ethical problems that have dogged Cute Little Tommy Moran since he was elected to the United States Senate have now tainted his daughter, Mary Rose Moran age 17. Mrs. Cordelia Burton Mulholland has charged that the Tom Cruise of the United States Senate has conspired with the Jesuit Fathers at Gonzaga to cheat her daughter Agnes of the valedictorian prize to be awarded at the school's graduation ceremony next week.

"My Aggie is smarter than the Moran girl," Mrs. Mulholland said, "and has better marks."

"Aggie's a nice kid," Mary Rose told us. "Kind of shy. Her mother's a pusher. Everyone knows that I had better marks."

I was reassured until the evening news the next day reported the "controversy" over Senator Moran's daughter.

Standing in front of the old Victorian pile of bricks that house the Prep, Aggie's mother, a thin, perfervid woman with disorderly blond hair and a rapid-flow voice made her claim.

"Everyone in the school knows that they have cheated my Aggie. The poor kid is brighter than that little slut. She had better marks and should be valedictorian. She needs it to get into Harvard. She is not lucky enough to have a Senator for a father. I'm going to sue the Jesuits and Senator Moran and make them appoint Aggie as valedictorian."

Then Burton Braxton, a high-powered and high-priced Washington lawyer replaced her on the screen from the book-lined sanctum of his law office.

"It would seem there's prima facie validity in Ms. Mulholland's claim and she has the right to seek relief. Her daughter's grade score is 3.68, surely high enough for a valedictorian. We're going to file a motion asking the school to show cause why it should not reveal the scores of both young women."

Finally Fr. Michael Crosby S.J., the president of the Prep, stopped in mid-flight while rain poured down.

"As a matter of policy we don't reveal the grades of our students," the young priest said. "However, I do know that Ms. Moran has had the highest grades in her class for the last four years."

Robbie Becker, leaning very close to me as I watched, was irate.

"Did they call for a comment?"

"No, Tom, they didn't."

Even beautiful young women should not call me Tom. It's either "Tommy" or "Senator."

"We should issue a statement. 'Senator Thomas Moran denied that he had ever spoken to the Jesuits at the Prep about his daughter being valedictorian of her class. He also denied any knowledge of a conspiracy.'"

"You could sue her for calling Mary Rose a slut."

"What good would that do?"

When I returned home about nine-thirty, the four women in my life, all wearing the standard issue of jeans and sweatshirts, were gathered in a solemn high conference. The eldest partner was in high dudgeon, the others, as they would say were "like totally cool."

"Chill out, Mom," the eldest daughter was saying in the tone of voice of a patient grandmother reproving an out-of-control teen. "It's no big deal."

"That bitch called you a slut."

"That's not a word we use around this house," said little Mary Ann, not so little any more.

"Two words actually," Mary Therese added.

"Everyone knows she's off the wall," Mary Rose insisted. "What difference does it make?"

"It will be on national television tomorrow!"

"My fifteen minutes of fame."

Mary Margaret turned to me.

"I suppose you think we should just let it go?"

Those were fighting words.

"Which one of your colleagues will represent us in court?"

I knew that she'd already laid court plans.

"Jack Ahern."

"Ah, a true fighting Irishman. You have doubtless recommended to him that he warn Braxton Burton . . ."

"Burton Braxton! You always do that!"

"I beg the court's pardon . . ."

Giggles from the daughters.

"That unless there is an apology for the use of the term slut, his clients will seek relief."

"I don't want to have to prove that I'm not a slut!" Maryro sighed, "It's all too heavy."

"You can show them that you're still a virgin," Marytre chortled.

"Brat!"

"You'll be on national TV tomorrow," her mother insisted.

"I can take care of myself."

"Since you're your mother's daughter, we have no doubt about that."

In bed that night as we tried to sleep, Marymarg sighed, "It's Bobby Bill again."

"Of course. He saw the piece in the *Examiner* and moved in with big bucks for the legal heavy."

"Do we want our children to live this way?"

"A good argument for not seeking reelection."

Leander Schlenk was at it again the next morning.

LIKE FATHER LIKE DAUGHTER

Polls show that the people of Illinois would like to have H. Rodgers Crispjin back in the United States Senate. Small wonder. Cute Little Tommy Moran, the Tom Cruise of the Senate, is back in court again with the charge that he and his daughter conspired to steal the valedictory at her high school from another young woman who had earned it. Tommy is always in court, it seems. He has been charged with stealing the senatorial election three years ago, living illegally in a multi-million-dollar house in Washington, demanding an increase in the advance on his clunker of a book after he was elected, and using Senate funds for his annual trip to a high-toned Mexican resort. With good example like that, one can understand his daughter's legerdemain with her grades.

There was no truth in any of these allegations and in fact there were no active suits, save for a motion for a rehearing in Supreme Court on the outcome of the Senatorial election. Already rejected once, this motion would certainly be rejected again. But it did keep alive the myth that we had stolen the election from the distinguished H. Rodgers Crispjin.

We had made the decision to refrain from any direct replies to Schlenk and simply issue statements denying the charges, as I had yesterday. But trying to fight back would be to play his game. It was, however, hard not to.

As usual the *Daily News* picked up the denial and printed it the day after the attack. I'm not sure how many would read it, however. People don't read denials.

"Well," said Maryro at breakfast, "I'm going to see the president and the headmaster this morning."

"Ah?" I said.

"And . . . ?" my wife wondered.

"I'm going to settle the matter."

Beyond that deponent sayth not.

Nor did her parents ask her.

"So chill out," she said as she left for school, her junior partner trailing after her.

"We'll cream them," Maran assured us.

At noon a call came to the office.

"Mary Rose?"

"Who else?"

"Well?" I said to the phone.

"Like Maran said we creamed them. And, Daddy dear, your daughter will be on all the networks tonight."

"Did you tell your mother?"

"Of course! You'll both be proud of me. Gotta run now. Bye!"

At six o'clock all the four TV monitors in the office went on. My daughter was the lead off on all of them. In her school uniform and accompanied by another stern Irish goddess (as in Biona or Siona or Erihu) she strode out of the red brick building and faced the media with poised confidence.

MEDIA: Mary Rose, is it true that you met with the school authorities this morning?

MARY ROSE: Ms. Moran, please.

MEDIA: What did you talk about? Did you admit that Aggie Mulholland had higher grades?

Ms. MORAN: Hardly, I told the president and the headmaster that I would not give the valedictory address. They said I had to. I said again that I would not. They said that I couldn't graduate and that I wouldn't get a diploma.

MEDIA: What did you say?

Ms. MORAN: I told them that I didn't care. I already had a President's Scholarship to Georgetown University because I'm a National Merit Scholar. So I was out of there.

MEDIA: You scared them?

Ms. MORAN: I hope so. My grades are my business—and my parents' and God's. I'm not in competition with anyone and I don't want to get into a public argument about them. That defeats the whole purpose of knowledge being a good in itself. I won't do it.

MEDIA: Do you think the Jesuits conspired to make you the valedictorian?

Ms. Moran: I trust the integrity of the Jesuits. I know what my grades were. I don't know Aggie's and I don't want to know. But if she wants to be valedictorian, that's fine with me. Like I say, I'm out of here.

(The two solemn goddesses stalked away.)

Media: Ms. Moran . . . One more question. Were you accepted at Harvard?

Ms. Moran (glaring over her shoulder): Yes.

Media: Why are you going to Georgetown?

Ms. Moran (wicked grin): Because my poor family needs me here!

My phone rang.

"Tommy, who is this child!"

"Her mother's daughter!"

Then my brother called.

"Tommy, it's what I've been warning you about all along. That girl is so proud, so hard. You have to make her give the prize to the other poor child."

My stomach twisted as it usually does when I get one of those calls from Tony.

"You didn't watch very carefully, Tony. She did just that."

"There's no gentleness, no femininity, no grace in her. You and Mary have really failed her."

"On the contrary, I thought she was very graceful."

And then, my gut turning over and over and over, I hung up.

Needless to say the two little witches were inordinately proud of themselves.

That night as the five of us watched a repeat performance on the evening news, Mary Rose, serenely proud of herself, was embarrassed.

"I was a little brat," she exclaimed.

"You were wonderful," I said.

"I could never do that when I was your age," her mother added.

"She could too, couldn't she, Daddy?"

"She never had to, but she did some equally gutsy things like the day your great-grandmother died."

"We've never heard that story," Maran complained.

"Ask your grandmother when she's here for the graduation."

The next news item was the president of Gonzaga Prep announcing that if necessary he would appeal any court order forcing him to reveal the grades of his students all the way to the United States Supreme Court.

We cheered.

Then he added, almost as an afterthought, that because of the unfortunate controversy there would be no salutory or valedictory address at the graduation.

"You really did scare them!" Mary Margaret said hugging her first born.

"Poor Aggie, she would have been happy with a chance to talk. Now she doesn't get anything because of her bitch of a mother."

"We don't use that word!" all of us said together.

My wife and I made love in bed that night, our usual stress eased by the sense that we had at least done something right. We didn't even need the usual symbolic glass of Bushmill's.

As we expected, Lee Schlenk had his usual twist on the scene the next day.

TOMMY'S DAUGHTER YIELDS PRIZE IN CONTROVERSY

Both Mary Margaret and I, however, were relieved. The controversy was over. Nothing would spoil our first high school graduation. Alas, it is never that easy in the Beltway.

CHAPTER 25

✝

SATURDAY MORNING we were eating breakfast with Ambassador
and Ms. O'Malley (Rosie and Chucky) when Mary Rose entered
the nook in her pale-blue graduation dress. I started the applause.

"It's Mom's dress," she admitted. "I stole it from her closet."

"Without asking permission," my wife complained, not seriously.

"Look at how much money we're saving!"

The Ambassador was destroying his usual huge breakfast. Mary
Rose leaned against the fridge.

"What can we expect today, hon?" my mother-in-law asked.

"Nothing special. They're going to give a big cheer for me when I
walk on the stage. I told them not to but I can't stop them. They
wanted to boo Aggie. I absolutely forbade it."

"You're class president, aren't you?" the Ambassador asked.

"I guess so."

"And the boys voted for you?"

"They call me 'The Boss!' "

"And they do what you tell them to do?"

"Of COURSE!"

"May it always be that way dear," my wife said piously.

"You and Grams don't have any trouble!"

Laughter around the table.

Pushy little brat!

"No one special among the boys?" Rosemarie asked.

"Nope, and I know you and Moms had already chosen your husbands at my age! I'm in no hurry."

So we drove over to Gonzaga under the crisp blue sky, a gentle Beltway spring day, with only a hint of the humidity that would soon drench the city.

It was a nice ceremony. An ancient Jesuit, of whom the University had an apparently limitless number, delivered a fine short talk based on Cardinal Newman's *Idea of a University*—knowledge as an end in itself without ever saying the words. It was a nice nod to our daughter.

Then the graduates were awarded their diplomas. Each of them, wearing the red and gold academic gowns without which one cannot have a Jesuit graduation, waited on the steps to the stage until the name was called by the headmaster. Then they walked across the stage to the president of the school and accepted the diploma while the next one in alphabetical order waited on the stairs. The president asked that we refrain from applause which most of us did. Typical Catholic event.

"Mary Rose Helen Moran," the headmaster intoned.

The students jumped to their feet, applauded, cheered, and otherwise misbehaved. Both the president and the headmaster smiled.

Our daughter, slightly flushed, touched the top of her academic hat, much as Tiger Woods would have after sinking a thirty-foot putt.

"Agnes Lourdes Mulholland," the Headmaster announced.

There was a hint of displeasure from the class which had returned to their seats. Mary Rose waved her hand in a quick little sweep and silenced the disobedient.

"What a wonderful mother superior she would make," my mother-in-law whispered.

Aggie, a slender little blond with a hint of beauty, was weeping as she walked across the stage, paying a big price for her mother's ambition.

I noted that our daughter had not left the stage at the other side, but stood waiting for Aggie. The two children, for that's all they were, embraced and walked down the steps arm in arm. Their classmates cheered and applauded again. The president, the headmaster, and the faculty joined in. Smiling through her tears, Aggie touched her hat àla Tiger.

Mary Margaret and her mother were crying too.

Our child had learned something about civility—or Christianity to call it by its proper name.

The game was not over, however.

Outside, the cameras were clicking and the families cheering. Graduations were for the families even more than for the graduates. My wife and her father, a Pulitzer Prize winner, were banging with SLR cameras, none of these little digitals for the real pros. However, both their cameras were digital. At the end of the street there was a small line of pickets, mostly women, a man with a roman collar. Waving placards with endearing slogans like "Jesus Hates You, Slut" and "Your Daddy Murders Babies" and "Don't Kill Children." Bobby Bill Roads had unleashed his furies. A line of cops were keeping them at bay. The Jebs must have had a hint that something was going to happen.

The girl graduates were shedding their gowns to reveal their graduation dresses. The cameras continued to click away.

"Look how much money we saved on that blue dress," I said to my wife.

Chucky O'Malley, whose ears and eyes were those of a brilliant photographer, turned suddenly. A woman from the picket line had broken through the police and was rushing towards the graduates. Thin, angry, clad in jeans and sweatshirt, she clutched a transparent plastic bag in one hand.

"Slut! Slut!" she shouted as she knocked Chucky down.

It all went into slow motion for me. She brushed Mary Margaret aside and threw the bag at my wide-eyed and frightened daughter!

"Slut!" She yelled. "Your daddy murders babies!"

The bag exploded as it hit Mary Rose and covered her with human excrement. The smell quickly permeated the air around us. I tried to move but my feet didn't know where to go. Chucky, who had been taking pictures for at least sixty years, bounded back to his feet and continued shooting. TV cameras were all around us. Cops were shouting.

"Mary Rose," a reporter shouted, jabbing a mike at her, "what are your feelings about what has happened?"

My daughter's lips were quivering, she was about to burst into tears. Mary Margaret and her mother were trying to push through the wall of journalists. The cops were wrestling the screaming assailant away.

"I'm Miss Moran," she said firmly. "The dress is my mom's. I borrowed it from her closet. I'm sorry it's ruined . . . I'm sorry too that people who claim to follow Jesus are so mean . . . Now I want to go home."

For the second time that day people cheered her. The cops finally pushed the media people aside.

Her mother and I took our daughter home.

"I can't say this when we get in the house," she said with a laugh as we walked to our van and turned towards her angry classmates, "but now I am really full of shit!"

Later in our parlor while my wife and her mother repaired the damage, Ambassador O'Malley was flicking through images on his camera.

"This one, Tommy," he handed me the camera. "If you folks don't mind I can get in on the AP wire and on the front page of the *New York Times* tomorrow morning."

It was an incredible shot of a furious woman slamming a bag of excrement against the breasts of a beautiful and astonished young woman.

Her mother and grandmother looked at it.

"You're still really good, Chucky," my wife said.

"He just holds his finger down on the shutter button," her mother said. "Anyone can do it."

"Mary Rose?" I asked.

"Huh? . . . Oh, go with it, Gramps. Fersure."

She was coming down from the high she'd experienced when she had heard the cheers at the crime scene, aware perhaps for the first time in her life how much ugliness there was in the world. Soon, I hoped, she'd come to realize that she had, if not exactly won the battle with ugliness, pushed it back a little bit.

Joe McDermott called from Chicago. There was unimpeachable evidence that the shite kickers (as he called them) were members of Mothers Against Murder, a group funded by Bobby Bill Roads and that Bobby Bill himself had met with them at his mansion outside of Shawnee before they left for the Beltway.

"I'm sure the D.C. police know that already, but thanks for the heads-up. I'll pass it on if they ask me."

"No objection if I leak it to the *Daily News?*"

I hesitated.

"Sounds to me like a legitimate news option."

We had not, at Mary Rose's imperious command, planned for a big graduation party. Just the seven of us and a few guests who might stop in . . . Mary Ann had whispered to her mother that there might be tons of people, so we secretly had stored sandwiches, soft drinks, and a huge cake in a freezer in the basement among the exercise machines.

It was a wise strategy. In the middle of the afternoon the guests began to arrive: Tina and Dolly and a delegation from my office, the senior Senator from Illinois and five other senatorial colleagues (one of them a Republican), and most of the senior class from Gonzaga. The latter visitation, our daughter asserted was, "like, you know, a total surprise!"

However, she turned on her charm for everyone. I understood now why she was class president, indeed why her classmates of both genders called her "Boss." Mary Rose was a beautiful young woman whose laughter and grace were contagious. Who wouldn't love her?

"Aggie?" she asked the boy who seemed to be the head of the first delegation to arrived.

"Her mother wouldn't let her come. She sends her love . . . In so many words."

Mary Rose nodded sympathetically.

"Well, I think we won that one, don't you, Steve?"

"Fersure, Boss!"

We cut the graduation cake which disappeared almost at once. I drove the O'Malleys to National—which I dared not call Reagan in their presence. A grandchild was making her First Communion on Sunday afternoon.

"She's an astonishing young woman, Tommy," Ms. O'Malley said as we pulled up to the curb.

"Dazzling," I said.

"Photogenic," the Amassador said, "decidedly photogenic, especially under pressure. The photo, by the way, is already out on the wires."

I was not sure that was good news.

I became melancholy on the ride back across the Key Bridge. Every parent is astonished when their child becomes, quite suddenly, a young person. Only yesterday . . . Why didn't we notice what was happening when it was happening? Why had we been too busy to enjoy her progress towards the cusp of maturity? Were the satisfactions of being a member of the United States Senate worth missing the excitement of her dramatic climb to young womanhood? Why was a high school graduation party our first clear glimpse of who she was becoming?

At home the party was still raging, singing, dancing, youthful laughter. The celebration had overflowed the house into the patio. Mary Rose was the center of it all, enjoying the time of her life. These thoughts made me even more melancholy.

The smell of sweaty human bodies and beer-laden human breath was everywhere. The dance music was jarring. I wanted to go home, even though I was home.

A second cake had appeared from nowhere, this one an ice cream cake. My wife shoved a cardboard plate with a large slice into my hand. "Eat sourpuss and forget the *weltschmerz*."

"Irish melancholy," I argued.

"Same thing."

"There's no beer here, is there?" I asked.

"Not a drop. The Boss says absolutely not. Some of them had a splash of it before they came here . . . Finish your cake! I want to dance!"

So I finished my cake and we danced.

"You had a splasheen of something yourself."

"A tiny sip of Bushmill's Green."

So we would make love that night. Twice in one week. That was un-usual in those days, unthinkable later on.

When the mess was cleaned up, with enthusiastic help from the three daughters, and they had gone to bed, Mary Margaret and I sat on the couch in the parlor.

"Is the Senate worth all of this?" I began.

"Good question, Tommy. I was thinking the same thing."

"I haven't had much success in introducing civility into American political life."

"Some progress," she agreed, "but not much."

"The work is taking its toll on both of us. We haven't been able to watch our kids grow up. They're suddenly strangers in the house."

"That might have happened even if we were practicing law in Chicago."

"That's true," I agreed.

"Look, Tommy, I supported your decision to run for the Senate. I didn't think you'd win, but neither did you. A reelection campaign is likely to be hellish. All of Bobby Bill's people and money will be thrown into it. Rodgers Crispjin must be salivating at the prospect. I'll support you either way."

"I guess I take that for granted . . . Maybe I shouldn't."

"Yes, you should . . . Are you leaning towards stepping down?"

"Sometimes."

"Me too," she sighed.

Our eldest daughter padded down the stairs, in pajamas, terrycloth robe, and floppy slippers. She eased her way between us.

"I want to cry now," she said simply. "Get it out of my system."

So we huddled together as our first-born daughter sobbed and tears streamed down our cheeks.

Finally she was sobbed out.

"OK, I think I can sleep now," she kissed us both and bounded up the stairs.

Halfway up she stopped and bent over the railing so she could see us. "Thanks! I love you both! Night!"

"Night, Boss," I said and we all laughed.

The next morning the picture was indeed front page in Sunday papers all around the country, including the *Chicago Daily News*.

In the *Examiner,* however, the headline on page four, bottom corner, announced.

Mothers Against Murder Assail Tommy's Daughter
Protesters Call her Partner in Crime

However, the brief article, in which the leader of the protest called it a huge success, had no byline. For once we had shut up Leander Schlenk.

Copies of Ambassador O'Malley's picture must have made it to the Italian papers. My brother woke us up at three in the morning to report that he was acutely embarrassed to see his niece "displayed" on the front of the "sensationalist" Roman press (I didn't even know he was in Rome.) His friends in the Curia sympathized with him, he assured us. Why didn't we consider the shame that such pictures brought to him and to the whole Church?

I listened and then asked him if he knew what time it was in the United States. He replied that it was three in the afternoon.

"Three in the morning," I said and hung up.

One outcome of the controversy was that the *New York Times* wrote a generally sympathetic account of my efforts to improve civility in American political life.

Senator Pushes for Civility but Encounters the Opposite
A Don Quixote from Chicago

Despite the Don Quixote label, it was a reasonably fair and accurate piece, especially from the *Times* when the subject was Chicago. It celebrated especially my wife and daughters. It described the machinations of the *Examiner* and Bobby Bill Roads. It doubted that I could triumph over the elaborate campaign already launched by former Senator H. Rodgers Crispjin to recover the seat that he claimed he had never really lost.

The Times article may have influenced a lot of people who didn't live in the state of Illinois, but it would not have much effect there. However Joe McDermott leaned hard on the editors of the *Daily News* to reprint it. Cautious and careful as always, they hesitated, thought about it, hesitated again and finally published part of it.

Joe said that it would help a lot. That I doubted.

However, the *Times* article delighted my publisher because my second book *Political Show Trials in America* was about to appear.

All right, we had won that one. Who would they go after next? I would resign in a solemn high fashion and settle to writing, a neater—and much cleaner—way to earn a living.

CHAPTER 26

✝

DURING THAT SUMMER RECESS we decided that the kids, one in Georgetown University, the other two now in Gonzaga, might want to visit Spain. They debated Grand Beach versus Spain and finally decided somewhat reluctantly that they had never been to Spain before. They also informed us that the Spanish kids at both Ursuline and Gonzaga were "snobs" and "stuck-up" and made fun of the way we talked Spanish . . .

"We don't lisp the way they do," Marytre insisted. "I hate it."

Also in their experience Spanish boys were totally not cool. They thought they were irresistible but were "gross" and "creeps."

Mary Rose said she had met an occasional "nice" Spaniard at Georgetown but she agreed that even the nice ones were snobs who looked down at "Mexicans like us."

"The woman from Spanish TV thought we were dolts," I said, "because we talked with a Sonoran accent. Who can we look down on?"

"Tex-Mex," Mary Margaret said and we all laughed.

We traveled on official passports so the Spanish government knew we were coming and had security forces waiting for us at the airport and keeping track of us all through the trip. Not cool. We were invited to a round of dinners every night for a week. Even less cool, especially since the Spaniards have the bizarre habit of eating dinner at eleven PM.

Least cool of all was an invitation to speak to the Cortes, the Spanish parliament. Mary Rose informed us that in various forms it went back to the 13th century. She had become our expert on Spanish history. She also spent a lot of time on her cell phone with a fellow Hoya named Daniel (NOT Dan or Danny) who was a Chicagoan but, heaven protect us all, a South Sider and a White Sox fan.

"I'm only a very junior member of the Senate," I said. "I don't represent the American government or the Senate. I think the State Department would not approve. Moreover, as you will note, Señor Presidente, I speak with a Mexican accent, indeed a Sonoran accent. Your members will of course be polite, but they will want to laugh."

"We do not want you to talk policy," the President of the Upper House of the Cortes argued, "but only describe how the American Senate works. The American Ambassador says he would be delighted. You are already very well known in Spain. They say you will be President some day."

"They are mistaken."

I called my office to make sure there was no objection from the State Department. Chris called back and said they would like to see a copy of my text, after I gave the talk. That didn't seem unreasonable.

I wrote out a twenty-minute address in Spanish and gave it to Mary Margaret for correction of my mistakes. She approved of what I intended to say. My wife, by the way, attracted quite a bit of attention in Madrid. Some of the locals claimed that she was a true Spanish beauty. "Pre-Visigothic," my know-it-all daughter claimed. "We are throwbacks to the original Celts, the kind you can still see up in Galicia."

Our hosts nodded their solemn agreements.

"These people don't look like Latinos," Maran complained.

"They're not, silly," her sister informed her. "They're Spaniards, a mix of Celts and Romans and Goths and Arabs."

Anyway I was sweating profusely when I rose to the podium of the Cortes. I sensed that there was an undercurrent of anti-Americanism in the group. Who did this little punk think he was, daring to address one of the oldest parliaments in the world!

"Because Spaniards are an infinitely polite and courteous people, I presume you will not laugh at my atrocious Mexican accent. I grant my permission for you to smile discreetly. When I speak in Chicago, I am accused of not speaking good Mexican because my family and I learned the language of Cervantes and Lope de Vega in Hermosillo where we spent some of our summer months learning the language and studying the culture of that infinitely fascinating and infinitely complex country. We are happy now to expand our experience of the wonderful heritage with which Spain has painted much of the world, such that the political entity in which our Congress works is called the District of Columbia. We are very grateful to the Admiral of the Sea for discovering us."

There was polite laughter, not particularly forced, I thought. In the gallery my good wife gave me the thumbs-up sign.

"I have been asked to explain to you how our Congress works. My answer is that we work very hard much of the time and that the institution works barely if at all, and most effectively on the last day before recess. My feeling is that there is no such thing as an efficient parliament in the free world. If a parliament works efficiently, then some power behind the scenes is manipulating it. Inefficiency, incompetence, frustration are all necessary consequences of representative democracy. So, if you think you have problems, let me tell you some of ours."

To my surpise much of my humor did survive translation. The applause at the end was genuine enough as were the handshakes and the comments over the wine we drank afterwards. In fact, however, the Spanish parliamentarians were considerably more interested in conversation with the women in my family. I couldn't blame them.

We were about to leave for Toledo, Sevilla, and Granada and then double back through Barcelona and the Costa Brava. I knew my children would think it was not as nice as Grand Beach. Just as we were about to leave our hotel, Chris was on the phone.

"Let me read your very good friend Leander Schlenk."

Tommy Goes on a Junket, Speaks to Parliament without Permission

Cute little Tommy Moran, the Tom Cruise of the Senate, is reported to be thinking of a run for President two years from now. However, according to reports from Spain, Tommy already thinks he is President. Without seeking permission from the American Embassy or the State Department, he talked to the Spanish parliament the day before yesterday, something that is usually reserved for visiting heads of state. Tommy attacked Senatorial junkets while he was running for the Senate, but now apparently he is changing his mind. His wife and children are traveling on the junket with him, including the daughter who allegedly cheated one of her classmates out of the valedictorian role. That case is still before the courts.

I felt sick to my stomach again. One can never escape from Leander, not even in our castles in Spain.

"What do you and Manny recommend?"

"The usual. We point out that once again Mr. Schlenk is careless with the facts. You are paying your own way. The invitation was cleared by the American Embassy and the State Department. The case before the courts is against the Jesuits and has been repeatedly turned down because of lack of evidence. Your daughter withdrew from the race. We print the text of your speech on our Web page. We deny that you are considering a Presidential race."

I thought about it. I wanted to attack him, to destroy him. That would be a mistake.

"Go with it."

"You want to see a proof for the Web page."

"Not necessary."

"Have a good trip."

"I'll be looking for castles in Spain."

"Leander?" Mary Margaret asked.

She was wearing pantyhose and a bra, a costume that used to turn me on. Not any more. My fault.

"Same old stuff, junket in Spain on taxpayers' money."

"Does he believe that stuff?"

" 'Course not. It's what he does for a living."

I do not, I told myself, have the stomach to be a United States Senator. I really don't. Let Crispjin have it back.

During the exploration of Spain beyond Madrid, the kids vied with one another to see who had piled up the most knowledge, especially about El Greco. I opined that the man was sick and really thought people looked that way.

Daddy!

They loved Sevilla, Granada, and especially Toledo. If the purpose of the trip was to expose them to Spanish culture, it was a huge success, though they briskly dismissed Spanish boys as narcissistic creeps. They also were not enthused by the rambla in Barcelona and rejected the concept that what bordered the Mediterranean in the Costa Brava was a beach.

"A beach has sand, DAD-dy!"

"Not gravel!"

"And there's no room to walk!"

"It's gross!"

"Grand Beach is nicer!"

"Let's go home now!"

I tried to explain that not all the beaches in the world were like those in the Indiana and Michigan dunes.

Anyway, they managed to put on their bikinis and suntan cream and lie under an umbrella to protect themselves from the sun, which didn't last very long anyway.

"We were never that way when we were kids," I protested.

"I was! They're fun kids. Enjoy them!"

"I do that!"

"They like to bait you, though this Costa Brava really doesn't compare with Grand Beach."

So we went home and went up to the Dunes for Labor Day and I was wiped out by some kind of Spanish bug and carried off to St. Anthony's hospital on Labor Day Sunday. My stomach settled down and my fever went away and I returned to the Beltway furnace, more than ever convinced that I did not belong there.

One more year and I'd be able to announce my retirement in October and begin to relax.

I did have some fun at an Armed Forces hearing with the Secretary of Defense on a budget hearing.

"Why should we have any confidence in these budgetary projections, Mr. Secretary? They've been wrong so often, that I can't believe any new ones."

"Senator," he said, trying to be patient, "war is an unpredictable event."

Here was another burned-out case. He would be glad to escape from the mess he had created for himself.

"Like your prediction that the United States could win the war with a hundred and thirty thousand men?"

"We did win the war. Now we're fighting an insurgency which we will defeat."

"An insurgency which might not have happened if we had the force that General Sheneski recommended."

"I'm not going to go through that argument again."

"Why not, Mr. Secretary? I don't think you've admitted yet that the General was right and you were wrong. Why did you think you could abolish the Powell theory of overwhelming force? Why didn't you plan for a war which would continue into an insurgency?"

"Time, Senator," said the chairman.

"Saved by the bell, Mr. Secretary."

I walked out of the hearing and returned to my hideaway to work on the new book which didn't have a title yet but was about the themes I had discussed in Madrid. My tentative title was "Why Democracy Doesn't Work."

Then Robbie surprised me when I was most vulnerable.

CHAPTER 27

✝

I WAS HALF ASLEEP in my hideaway pondering in a hazy—and unproductive—reverie Winston Churchill's wise comment that Democracy is a bad way to run a government until one considers the alternatives. Someone knocked at the door, against the rules I had imposed on my staff. Maybe it was Hat McCoy. I opened the door. It was Robbie with the top two buttons on her blouse open.

Well, it had to come sometime. The question I told myself was how I would react.

She walked in and closed the door. I leaned against the desk, trying to recoup my resources. She unbuttoned the blouse down to her skirt, her sumptuous breasts constrained tightly in a lacy bra. She looked at me shyly, fragile, vulnerable, as open to my pleasure as if she were my slave. A sense of sweet opportunity, the beginning of a wonderful experience fell on me like a cloak of golden gauze. Why not? There would be no costs. I could enjoy her, make her happy for a little while and then be free. It was only an interlude, joy and bliss with no serious repercussions. Wasn't it? Mary Margaret need never know.

I prepared to seize the gift she was offering me, a gift of herself in all her youthful glory, a chance I might never have again.

Instead I buttoned up her blouse.

"You shouldn't be here, Robbie," I said as gently as I could. "Don't come back here again."

The light went out of her face, her shoulders slumped. I had crushed her.

"I appreciate the gift you offer me," I stumbled on, "but it is a gift I cannot accept. I'm a married man and I love my wife. Please try to understand."

She turned and quickly fled the little office. I heard her sob as she closed the door.

I fell back into my chair, spent, shaken, unclean.

Had I really turned her down? How could I have done that? I had broken her poor confused heart.

That's not what the script had called upon me to do.

I was a fool.

Maybe it was all my fault. Maybe I had led her on.

Thank God my brother would never find out.

The next morning I went over to the set of "Fast Pitching," a rough and tumble interview program. I had met the anchor at a party which seemed to be mostly loud, contentious, and interesting Irish Catholics. He begged me to come on the program. Like an idiot I agreed. Chris and Manny said it would be a tough interview. I said it would be fun. It was both. I brought a copy of the tape back to the office, so we could excerpt it for our Web page.

INTERVIEWER: Don't you think, Senator, that you have an obligation to the Democratic party to announce your candidacy for the presidency?

MORAN: I'm not running for the presidency. I haven't even made up my mind to run for reelection to the Senate.

INTERVIEWER: Are you waiting for the convention to draft you?

MORAN: If the angel Gabriel came down from heaven and recommended me, the convention wouldn't draft me. Should they do that I'd turn them down.

INTERVIEWER: Do you think the Democrats will lose again this time? Are you waiting four more years?

MORAN: I am convinced that the Democrats will win easily.

INTERVIEWER: Then you'd be eight years older before you get your chance. You'd no longer be one of the bright young Democratic faces.

MORAN: I'm not sure that my face is so bright or young even now.

INTERVIEWER: If the Democrats win and you're reelected, you could have your choice of either Armed Services Committee or Judiciary, wouldn't you? Have you decided which one you would take?

MORAN: I haven't thought about it. Should that develop it would be up to the leadership to decide.

INTERVIEWER: Aren't you part of the leadership?

MORAN: Assistant Minority Whip. Back in Chicago that plus two dollars would get me a ride on Mayor Rich's subway.

INTERVIEWER: Let me ask you a hypothetical. If you found yourself running for President would you continue your policies of no negative campaigning and no personal fund-raising?

MORAN: Certainly.

INTERVIEWER: Your presumed opponent in Illinois is already running attack ads, isn't he?

MORAN: So I am told. He has been running them since the last election.

INTERVIEWER: Have you seen any of them?

MORAN: I don't watch them. They're bad for my digestion.

INTERVIEWER: How will you run against them?

MORAN: I think it would be pretty hard to overcome six years of a negative campaign.

INTERVIEWER: I hear that your presumed opponent has already spent forty million dollars on these ads. Where does get his money?

MORAN: I have no idea.

INTERVIEWER: Some people say that most of it comes from Bobby Bill Roads, the oil tycoon.

MORAN: Oil tycoons have a lot of extra money lying around these days.

INTERVIEWER: Well, good luck to you, Senator Moran. I still think you'd make a very good President.

Moran: You and my daughters.

With Maryro at Georgetown, Maran, a junior at Gonzaga, was the designated weekly luncheon partner in the Senate dining room. Some of my senatorial colleagues, especially the Southerners who fantasy themselves courtly, always paid homage to the daughter with a polite bow.

"How do, Miss Maryro, nice to see you again."

"Maryro aw gone. Me Maran."

Our middle child, besides being a witch, was also the comedian of the bunch.

"Do you smell any bad things here today?" I asked.

Her nostrils twitched as though she were scanning the dining room.

"No *really* bad smells. Just the ordinary ones."

"Does your boyfriend know you're a witch?"

"Jimmy?" she dismissed him with a wave of her hand. "He's such a nerd. He keeps wanting me to do something like that dweeb Buffy does on television."

"Are there any vampires in the dining room, Maran?"

She glanced around.

"I'm not sure that I really do vampires, Daddy, but I don't see any, just Senators."

"You can tell the difference?"

"Oh, sure . . . Now about next August . . ."

She and her siblings had decided that it would be "nice" if we went to Paris and Vienna and studied Napoleon and the Hapsburgs. We couldn't do anything the following August recess because we'd be singing in the campaign.

Even my children presumed I'd run again. Which meant that my wife did too. I was in a trap that I'd better escape before it was too late.

"Do your friends at school know where you eat lunch once a week?"

"Sure! They want to come along. They think you're totally cool."

Kids that age didn't recognize a burnt-out case when they saw one.

"We'll have to do that some time."

"Bitchin'!"

She pecked at my cheek in front of my office and dashed off to her BORING afternoon classes.

Why did the young have to possess so much more energy than their parents?

Robbie was not at her usual desk in the bullpen. I would have been surprised if she were.

I gave the tape to Manny.

"How did it go?"

"He nominated me for President. I thanked him but declined."

She giggled.

A couple of letters waited on my desk for real as opposed to robotic personalization. I signed them.

Chris came into the office with a sheaf of work for me.

"Robbie Becker resigned this morning and left, never to come back I assume."

"I noticed that she wasn't here."

"She hit on you real hard and you turned her down?"

"Something like that."

"Good for you."

"Maybe."

"I'm surprised it lasted this long . . . She's not so much a predator as a groupie who is an incorrigible romantic. She was so much in love with you that she could not believe that you didn't love her in return. She told one of her friends that you have a heart of stone."

"Did I encourage her?"

"No one in the office thinks so. You were pleasant to her as you are to everyone. Do you want to tell me what happened?"

"She knocked on the door of the hideaway and came in with two buttons on her blouse open. She opened the rest of them. I told her that was against the rules, buttoned her blouse, and said thanks but no thanks and I loved my wife. She left sobbing."

Chris nodded.

"Not many Senators would have done that."

I shrugged.

"Chris, I knew it would happen. I keep asking myself what I could have done to discourage her."

"Nothing, Tommy, absolutely nothing, except firing her and that would have been a mistake."

"That's what I thought too."

"She had two friends in the office to whom she whispered her love and her frustration. She even confided to them this morning what happened. Pretty much as you described it."

"Will there be trouble?"

"There's always a chance, but I don't think she could admit to herself that she had been rejected. Both the women have given me an affidavit. I will type out one for you and I'll witness it and put it in a file."

I sighed and agreed.

"I don't need this aggravation right now."

"You're not over that flu yet."

I was in fact over the flu. I was sick of the United States Senate. Maybe my brother was right. I didn't belong here.

Joe McDermott called from Chicago.

"Some interesting rumors going around, Tommy. The feds have started an investigation of your good friend Bobby Bill."

"That surprises me."

"There's a new federal prosecutor down there, out to make a name for himself."

"I think I just published a book about that kind of person."

"Bobby Bill is very popular down there. He's given money to lots of folks, especially to Christian churches and schools. The feds better have the goods on him before they make any charges. I hope it takes them a long time."

"Oh?"

"So the news will break during the election campaign."

"We won't be able to use it."

"We won't have to . . . By the way, you were very good on 'Fast Pitching.' "

"They got the tape to you already?"

"Very efficient staff. That forty million figure that he had is the same one we have."

I found myself hoping that if there had been violations down there in Tulsa, they would break soon. It would get Lee Schlenk off my back.

I was thinking like I would be running for re-election. I must avoid those kinds of thoughts or I would be dragged into a race which everyone but me seemed to want.

I walked over to the chapel at Georgetown after I had delivered my two younger daughters home.

You got me into this, I told God. I can't believe that you want me to stay here. I survived yesterday. But I do not have the temperament for this kind of life. Maybe it was the way I was raised. Maybe it's my problem with my brother. But I don't have the energy or the motivation to keep this pace up. All right, I got some decent legislation through. Maybe that's all you expect me to do. Isn't it enough? Do you have any signs in mind to make it clear to me what I ought to do next? Otherwise maybe I should go back to being a public defender with a rich wife.

There were no answers. There never are.

Or maybe there was.

That night we went to a reception and a dinner, the former for the American Civil Liberties Union, the latter for the Latino-American Alliance. I was a hero with both of them. Hence they would pressure me to run for President.

"These are nice people," Mary Margaret said with a sigh as we dressed, "but I'd just as soon stay home and watch college football."

"You look scrumptious, Mom," Maryro looked up from a history book in the parlor which she was reading while a football game went on in silence on the TV. "You too, Dad . . . Come home early. You both look tired."

"No date?" I asked as we got in our car, the Chevy van which had replaced the one that Bobby Bill had blown up.

"Daniel's parents are in town. She's having supper with them tomorrow night."

"Is it that serious?"

"A lot less than we were at the same age, counselor."

I wished we were that age again. I would have done a lot of things differently.

There was enthusiasm for the two of us at both affairs. Mary Margaret had won another gender case at the court five-four. And my performance on "Fast Pitching" had made me a presidential candidate. It did me little good to protest that I had no intention of running.

Then that night I was seduced. By my wife, a lot more polished and ingenious a seducer than poor Robbie Becker. Anger, frustration, disappointment, passion suppressed too long, desperate need–all made our romp wild, demanding, implacable. We grasped recklessly for pleasure and then achieved it in a final explosion of love.

Then something strange happened. As we both relaxed in the floating sensation that comes often at the end of satisfying sex, something else invaded our bedroom. Or, to be honest, someone else. Or even more honest, Someone else.

The room seemed to fill with light, luminosity that flowed from us and then bathed us in a tidal surge of joy and peace and love. We knelt on the bed in a terrified but happy embrace, crying and laughing, caught up in a pleasure so intense that we felt that if it increased even a little we would be torn apart, not that we would have minded.

The Transcendent had invaded our marriage bed and joined in our game.

That's a reflection we had afterwards. At the moment itself—maybe a half minute and maybe an hour, it didn't matter, we only knew that we had temporarily left time and space behind and had been caught up in a demanding power that held us and did not want to let us go, a power that loved us and was consuming us with the fire of its love. His love. Her love. Whatever.

Then slowly it seemed it released us, but not without the promise that we three would meet again.

OK, Tommy Moran, you wanted a sign. Was that enough?

We collapse into prone positions. Mary Margaret, always the modest matron, pulled the sheets over us.

"Who was that?" I gasped. "What did he want?"

"She."

"OK . . . What was it all about?"

"She wanted us."

"No right to invade the privacy of our love-making."

"She owns us, Tommy love. Delights in us. Created us to enjoy one another and then decided to join the fun."

"Do you really believe that?"

"What else could it have been? God delighted in us." .

"Why?"

"Ask her!"

I buried my head against her breasts. She caressed my head with her fingers.

"Will it ever happen again?"

"The afterglow will always be with us, Tommy."

"All your fault for attacking me!"

She laughed.

"I thought I was pretty good at it . . . then the Transcendent taught us both how to do it."

Then we both said together, "I'm sorry."

Then we argued about who was to blame for the loss of passion in our lives, each of us claiming responsibility, each of us promising that we would never let it happen again.

Then we went to sleep, peaceful sleep, sleep which was a grace of all the goodness in the world.

We slept till ten o'clock Saturday morning. The daughters had made brunch for us, at the suggestion of Maran, who had decided at lunch in the Senate Dining Room that I looked like I needed a good night's sleep.

Did they realize that we had made love together? Who knows what such smart and perceptive young woman might guess. However, they would never know the half of it.

They went out shopping together. My wife and I, still in robes, retreated to the library, not to talk about our ménage à trois from the previous night, but merely to talk to one another.

"Well," she said, "I'm glad we got that out of the way."

"It's only the beginning, woman," I replied. "I have plans for you for every night of the week."

She blushed.

"I realized I was risking something like that."

"In fact," I said, closing and locking the library door, "I have plans for you right now!"

I pulled away her robe and peeled off the gown she had donned when we got out of bed.

"Tommy," she protested weakly, as I pinned her on the couch.

"We have to make up for lost time."

"There's that!"

Our love-making was very gentle and sweet, despite my pose as an attacker. She was right in her prediction there was a distinctive afterglow from our night visitor.

We went to our bedroom, dressed in jeans and Loyola sweat shirts, returned to the library, and poured ourselves some champagne.

"I suppose," she said toasting me, "I can be available most nights of next week, especially since I'm taking a temporary leave from the firm."

It was none of my business, but I still asked, "Why?"

"I'm going to work in your office as a volunteer for a while anyway."

She spoke as though this was just a minor change in my fortress prison.

"Chris knows?"

"Of COURSE! She and Manny said they needed me around there to deal with the increase of press attention and Illinois politics . . . Unless of course, you object?"

"You will be a substantial distraction in my work, but I'll love the distraction."

"I figured you would," she said complacently.

"How long have you women been planning this coup d'état?"

"We had lunch two weeks ago at the Monocle. I had to rearrange some of my work at the firm. I'll have to plead a couple of cases in the spring, but that won't restrict much my volunteering."

So before the Robbie matter had occurred. A scheme to prevent it?

What did I know?

Our daughters returned, laden with purchases.

"How come the champagne?" Marytre asked.

"Celebrating that I'm going to work in Daddy's office!"

"Finally told him, huh?"Marytre, said. "He couldn't say no anyway."

"It had nothing to do with Robbie," Chris told me on Monday. "We just felt it would be useful to have her around. She's terribly bright and everyone likes her and her presence always cheers you up."

"Lately I've been in need of cheer," I admitted.

"I know that the conventional wisdom is that a wife shouldn't be anywhere near the office . . . no mom and pop stores as you once said. But this is a different kind of wife."

"Tell me about it."

What Ambassador O'Malley calls, misquoting John Knox, the "Monstrous Regiment of Women" had taken over. The Senate job had hammered the poor little Senator's morale into the ground. So they would take steps to salvage the poor dear man.

Saturday night Mary Margaret and I, both a little tired from our activities of the past twenty-four hours, were watching NFL on TV, my excuse being that the Senate was for all practical purposes quiescent till the election in the first week in November when a third of its members were compelled to submit themselves to reelection.

Maryro bounced into our media room in high dudgeon.

"Daniel is a dweeb, a nerd, a flake," she announced as she sat in the easy chair.

"You broke up with him in front of his parents?" I asked. I would never have dared break up with my teenage date in front of her parents.

"He didn't tell them my name until he introduced me to them at dinner, like I was a brand-new pet puppy."

"Irish wolfhound bitch?"

"Don't be gross! He tells them that I'm Mary Rose Moran . . ."

"Your real name!"

"They take one look at my hair and they know who I am. So all we talk about all evening is my parents, whom they, you know, totally adore! BORING! I have to tell them what you're like . . ."

"And what did you tell them?" Mary Margaret asked.

"I said that my father was born with the gift of wit and my mother with the gift of laughter which made a great combination, except that he worked at the Senate where laughter wasn't permitted and she at the Supreme Court where the only wit was dry legal jokes that were not very funny."

"You had prepared that beforehand," Mary Margaret observed.

"Of COURSE, I did. I knew what would happen. Mrs. Leary said that I clearly had inherited from both sides of the family. And Daniel there beaming proudly at his prize bitch."

"I assume they're Democrats," I said.

"Worse even than you . . . Now they want to have dinner with you the next time they're here in D.C., like I'm going to permit that."

"We'd be happy to meet them, dear."

"Not yet," she said firmly.

"You're not breaking up with Daniel, are you?"

"Just because he's a dweeb? I'm not THAT dumb! . . . And their grandparents knew your grandmother, Mom, back in St. Gabe's during prohibition, whatever that was."

"Were they sure?"

"April May Cronin is not a name you'd forget . . . She must have been quite a woman . . . I told them how you found her dead in her bedroom and said a decade of the Rosary and were even younger than I am and Mrs. Leary started to cry, like I'm doing now."

She rushed up stairs to finish her crying in privacy.

"A lot of heavy emotion in the family this weekend," I remarked, only to discover that my wife was weeping too, silently.

"The little brat had us down cold, didn't she, Tommy?"

"Even if she prepared it beforehand . . . Am I correct in assuming that dinner with the Learys went well?"

"Certainly. Rather better than she had expected."

CHAPTER 28

✝

I WILL NEVER FORGET the lunch with Chris and Manny. It changed my whole life and made me realize what a dweeb I had been.

We lunched at the Monocle which was filled with Democrats and their friends and constituents. Tommy's two aides did not follow the Irish procedure of waiting till dessert before discussing the reason for the lunch. Rather they dove right in. We want you to work in the office. We need you to help out with the media and constituents. In the latter to liaison with Joe McDermott of the Senator's Chicago office, You know that scene better than we do. We can't pay you a salary because it would violate the nepotism rule. We need you as a volunteer.

Does my husband know about this scheme?

We haven't told him yet. We thought you would ask him about it if you decide to come on board.

Tell him about it.

Whatever. There are other reasons. The Senator is one of the great men here in the Beltway. There hasn't been anyone like him in a long, long time. Yet he is not happy here, though he enjoys the game and is very good at it. When he comes into the office, it's a prisoner returning to jail. He still smiles. The geniality is so much part of his personality that he smiles no matter what is happening in his heart and his gut.

That's my Tommy.

But he never laughs. Except when you are around.

So my job would be to keep the Senator laughing.

Happy and therefore laughing. Joe McDermott says that the campaign would have folded early if it wasn't for your laughter. We haven't asked about finances. You could work part-time and maybe do some cases before the court too. Not at the first but as time goes on.

I can't promise to deliver a reelection decision. He has to make up his own mind on that. He should do what he wants to do.

We agree, of course.

Sometimes I think Tommy married me because of my shanty Irish laughter.

If you need time to think about it, it's OK. We don't want to rush you.

I won't have to think about it. I'd love the job. If I get out of line—all Irishwomen are bossy—let me know.

All *women*. You won't get bossy.

I can't guarantee that he'll run again, I repeated . . . He has to make that decision himself. If he asks me what I think I'll tell him, but I won't argue.

That's the way it should be.

I was trembling when I left the Monocle and not because of the cold wind blowing in from the north. I was trembling because I now understood something about our marriage that I had never grasped before. These two women and, later, my daughter Maryro had seen it immediately.

Tommy, my sweet, cute little Tommy had married me because there was tons of laughter in the crazy O'Malley clan and none at all in his own family. He had married into laughter, laughter I had always taken for granted. It did not enter into my adolescent head that this boy wanted, indeed needed, a wife who would laugh at his jokes and at him. I was his escape from his elderly and respectable parents and an obsessive brother into a world of comedy. That model didn't explain everything about our love. There was considerable sexual attraction too. Or there used to be. And it is my fault I've let it diminish. Even if it takes two to tango, it should have been obvious to me that I'm the musician in the family.

I ducked into the St. Joseph's Church. I had to straighten out this mess with God before I straightened it out with Tommy.

Why didn't You tell me that I'm supposed to be an audience for a stand-up comic? I would have taken the job a lot more seriously. Were You afraid that it would offend my feminism? My husband is a wonderful man and I'm grateful for Your sending him my way. I like to laugh. That ought to have been icing on the cake. Instead I missed the point. I didn't appreciate after the campaign how essential my laughter was to him, how he couldn't really be the United States Senator he wants to be and can be and should be unless I were around to laugh at him and to protect him from his creepy brother. So I deserted him for the Supreme Court where people only smirk.

I'll defend myself on the grounds—see what a good attorney I am—that I thought I shouldn't intervene in the work of his office. That's good advice for most senatorial wives, but no good at all for my Tommy.

Well, all's well that ends well, isn't it? His staff had to appreciate that they needed me before it would work. It will be tons of fun! So will the renewal of our romance . . . Look at me laughing—and dirty laughing at that—in Church!

So all I have to do is seduce my husband and bring a little laughter to his life in the Dirksen building. No problem. And the firm will be happy with whatever cases I'm willing to work for them.

And, like I told them at lunch, I can't guarantee he'll run for reelection. Like them I think he should. But he has to want to do it. When it comes to decision time, he'll ask me what I think. I don't know what I'll think. Whatever, it's his call. Right?

I talk to You like I'd talk to Chucky. Is that reverent? If it's not, it's Your fault for giving me a father like him.

It's up to You to give me some kind of sign that this is the right road. I'll count on You for that. OK?

I'm going home now to take a nap before supper. I want to be wide awake when we begin this new phase of our life.

I had a lot of fun seducing him and a lot more fun in what became a violent romp. Then the night visitor intervened and the change was written in fire.

"Tommy, I asked him the first day we had lunch in the Senate Dining Room, 'what was the name of that gorgeous young woman who had the crush on you? Am I a replacement for her?' "

"Robbie Becker?"

"That's right."

"No, Chris and Manny had already made up their minds to bring you on board before she left."

"You broke her heart, I assume?"

"I told her thanks but no thanks."

"Poor dumb kid. She should have realized that you're not that kind of Senator."

"You think I'm immune to temptation?"

"Certainly not! Just immune to that kind of temptation. You don't exploit the helpless and the lonely . . . Only the wild and the crazy!"

He threw back his head and laughed.

So, I whispered to the night visitor, we were both right, weren't we?

Then something quite unexpected happened. I developed a crush on my husband and I was not a lonely and helpless arrested adolescent. I found it hard to concentrate my thoughts on our Web page and our mailings and our DVDs. My imagination flooded with memories of making love with Tommy and desires to make love again as soon as possible. Women my age in life are prone to love affairs, imaginary more than real, but with their own husbands? Wasn't there something, well, transgressive about these daydreams?

I wanted to spend the whole day with him, naked in his arms, in some place warm and cozy with the sound of surf in the background. Failing that, our marriage bed would do.

You are not a teenager, I told myself, you are a member of the bar of the United States Supreme Court. Grow up and act your age.

I called Rosie—my mom—and in an indirect fashion asked her about this, uh, syndrome.

"You're goofy over poor Tommy?" She said, clearing the air of all obscurity. The word "poor" in our ethnic group is affectionate and has nothing to do with income or possible victimization.

"All the time . . ."

"With any luck, it will last for the rest of your lives."

"Will he get tired of it?"

"A man get tired of a woman who is obsessed with him? Don't be silly, Marymarg. He'll think he's died and gone to heaven."

I didn't ask her whether it was that way between her and Chucky. I guess I didn't have to.

Worse still, Tommy seemed to know that I belonged to him completely. He never said that, of course. He wouldn't dare. But he didn't have to. He'd occasionally catch my eye in the office with a special cat-that's-got-the-canary smile which would melt me. Or he'd touch my arm when we were marching down the corridors towards a press briefing and set me on fire. I wanted to take off my clothes then and there. He'd grin slyly. Or I thought it was a sly grin. Maybe I was imaging it all. But he'd have no trouble ravishing me when we finally made it to our bedroom.

It still seemed transgressive, but nice transgressive.

I find myself slipping into transgressive day dreams in the office. No one really supervises me, I'm there as a wife object, though they're delighted when I produce something intelligent. I recreate in my imagination our last encounter and fantasize about the next. Then my body gets involved and I have to stop. I know that this interlude of passion not quite adolescent, but not unlike adolescent either, will shape or maybe reshape our marriage. I tell myself prudishly that we ought to grow up, that we're too mature to be playing silly games. Only I don't listen to myself because the silly games are so much fun and because I love him so much. He is unfailingly tender with me, though I find that the paths of tenderness are many and varied and lead through glorious and mysterious and multi-colored lands.

Then one day we slipped over the boundary of transgressive and became decadent.

It was a Monday after Thanksgiving, just before the holiday recess. My Tommy had just added his voucher proposal to the Distributive Justice Amendment. He was having a grand time with it. Win or lose it would make lots of trouble for the other side. Like Chucky says, "You gotta remember that for us Micks, politics is a game!"

After our Monday lunch in the Senate Dining Room—a custom we had quickly established—he took my hand and said, "Let's go over to my hideaway."

'Why?" I asked.

"Why do you think?"

"I'm not sure that's a good idea."

"You don't have to join me."

Of course I did and he knew that I did.

"Dreary place," I said, glancing around, "like Mother Superior's office in a Catholic grammar school. It doesn't look very sexy to me."

He touched the zipper on my dress. I gasped as I usually do when he uses that approach.

"Tommy, we shouldn't be doing this. It's decadent, dissolute, and debauched."

"Transgressive too," he said as my clothes fell to the floor.

I tried to cover myself with my arms. He laughed and pulled them away.

"This is the place where you rape innocent matrons!"

"There are very few such wandering through the corridors here."

My protests were for the record, weak and ineffectual. I wondered what it would feel like to make love so close to the Senate Chamber.

His love play was interesting and original. I was groaning even before he pushed me back on the couch. Ever so gently I might add. I abandoned my pro forma objections.

Would our mysterious night visitor intrude on love even in this unlikely venue? I was aware that She was around.

When we were finished, I huddled in this arms, my body covered with sweat, my soul filled with joy.

"Well, at least we won't have to do it tonight after the Christmas party at Senator Hewitt's."

"This a bonus card," he said, kissing me delicately. "A new senate rule. Monday lunch and ravish a matron in my hideaway."

"You should come down here to work on your book . . . No shower here, not even a towel. I'll remember to bring one the next time."

He watched me with an approving leer as I dressed.

"There's one other thing," I said.

"Ah?"

"Your brother . . . He called you yesterday and you went into one of your slumps."

The pleasure went out of his face.

"I get over them."

"You shouldn't have to . . . I could tell the switchboard that calls from him should be relayed to me and I'll deal with him . . . that is, if you want to."

"He's my bro, Marymarg."

"He has a powerful negative influence on you. He has no right to ruin your life."

He frowned and shook his head sadly.

"He told me that he would certainly campaign against me if I run for reelection."

"The bastard!"

"I'm surprised at such language within a whisper of the United States Senate."

"If you don't want me to brush him off, Tommy, I won't."

He zipped up my dress.

"Let's try it and see if it works."

We did return to the game after the noisy party at Senator Hewitt's house in Capitol Hill.

"You're a satyr," I told him.

"You're a temptress."

"Slander," I laughed as I drifted off into pleasant sleep.

The next morning, my phone rang.

"Mary Margaret O'Malley."

"I want to speak to my brother."

"The Senator is in conference now, Father."

Actually, that was true. He and his LAs were working on a final version of the Distributive Justice amendment.

"I want to talk to him NOW."

"I'm afraid that is quite impossible, Father. I'll tell him you called."

Click.

It was the first barrage in what could easily be a long war.

CHAPTER 29

✝

M ARY MARGARET'S arrival in my office generated more cheers and applause than one of my triumphs on the floor of the Senate. She was assigned a desk in the rear of the room, as far as possible from the one vacated by Robbie, from whom nothing had been heard, according to Chris, except that she was looking for a job at the State Department.

I had to admit, though only to myself, that I felt less oppressed by the job than I had been in weeks. Maybe I did need to hear her laughter more often. Looking back on the campaign, I had hardly noticed it, but it had kept me going. Our eldest child had it all figured out.

My new staff member did not escape the eagle investigative eye of Leander Schlenk of the *Examiner*.

TOMMY CHARGED WITH NEPOTISM
Hired Wife as part of Presidential Fantasy

Little Tommy Moran is apparently showing presidential ambitions. He has hired his wife, Mary O'Malley—daughter of the soft-core pornographer—to work in his Senate office. Since no one thinks he has a chance in a rerun election next year with Senator Rodgers Crispjin, a presidential bid might be an easy way out of that race. Unfortunately for the Tom Cruise of the United States Senate, he has violated the Senate rule against nepotism.

His double-dipping wife may have to quit her job at a prominent Washington law firm.

With Manny on one side and Chris on the other, Mary Margaret, in a clingy mauve dress which left no doubt about the durability of her figure, responded with her own little press conference in the lobby of the Dirksen Office Building.

"Mr. Leander Schlenk would not make so many mistakes in his 'Under the Dome' column if he had time to check his facts. I am not double dipping. I have taken a temporary leave from the firm of Brown, Berger, Bobbet, and Butts to work in Senator Moran's office. I am a volunteer, as this ID shows, and I will receive no salary. I am listed on the rolls that Senate security keeps as a volunteer. I am, alas, not even single dipping. Finally, the Senator has said repeatedly that he will not run for the presidency and that he has not made up his mind about reelection. Other than that, Mr. Schlenk hasn't made any mistakes."

REPORTER: What about his claim that your father is a soft-core pornog-
     rapher?
MARY MARGARET: Ambassador O'Malley is quite capable of defending
     himself, but if I might quote one of his remarks on this subject, in
     the Pulitzer contest he leads Mr. Schlenk five–zip.

I had lunch with the Leader that same day. I was a bit uncertain about his reaction and fearful that he might object.

"Smart idea bringing herself into the office."

"My staff's idea. They didn't even tell me about it till it was a done deal!"

"You might have put the kybosh on it. Nepotism and that kind of thing."

"She's a volunteer."

"She's just not your typical senatorial wife . . . I hope you give her charge of Lee Schlenk. Serve the little so-and-so right . . . But I did not invite you to lunch just to praise Mary Margaret. I'm thinking of making a little trouble when our friends get back from the election. We'll pick up two or three seats, just a shade short of our majority . . . We might just bring up a couple of issues that could stir up the pot for the presidential election . . . Catch up on some of our issues, if you take my meaning."

"Embarrass the other side for a change?"

"That bill of yours to repeal the tax benefits for those making more than two million a year is languishing in committee, isn't it?"

"We'll never be able to pass it, will we?"

"We might come close. The President would veto it of course. We could make a great hue and cry that his whole administration has concentrated on giving more money to the rich . . . You're right that it probably won't get through this year or during the next session. But it will be fun to watch all the efforts of the other side to protect their fat cats . . . You aren't earning more than that are you, with your royalties and her billable hours?"

"Not with her working as a volunteer, but even if she were we wouldn't come close. Mind you I wouldn't mind paying more taxes in the name of fiscal responsibility. I'd still have more money after taxes."

"There's a lot of people in this building who would be furious at paying more."

"Your bill says that the money could be earmarked for education?"

"That would be up to the House to decide, but it's one of the arguments."

"We have an appropriations bill coming over from the House before the election. We'll vote on it after the election but before the new session begins in January. By then it will be a big issue."

"It's good politics and good government," I argued. "The Democrats balanced the budget then the Republicans created the biggest deficit in history. It's time to return to a responsible budgetary policy. No reason to sell our children and grandchildren's lives to the Chinese and the Saudis and the Venezuelans."

"We could add an amendment for a small increase in the gasoline tax to promote further development of hybrid cars as a conservation measure? . . . Your man Peter Doherty is your tax specialist, isn't he? . . . First rate . . . Have him get together with my guy and we'll put it on the agenda the day after the election—with solemn high publicity."

"Any support from the other side?"

"The fiscal conservatives over there might like it, but that would mean repudiating their president."

"Co-sponsor?"

"George Hewitt from Montana, prairie populist. I'll have his LA get involved in the drafting. He's on the appropriations committee and will be sympathetic, but he isn't the alley fighter you are."

"We'll get on it right away."

"Mind you, it's still secret. Tell your AA and LA—and herself of course and tell them to keep it quiet."

"AA"—administrative assistant was the term some of the old timers used for "Chief of Staff." It dated to the time thirty years ago when a Senator needed only one or two aides and not a crowd of them.

I had always told the good Mary Margaret what was going on—good lawyer that she is, she knows how to keep secrets, though silence violates her ebullient personality.

Did I really need her laughter as a response to my wit? Maryro thought it was self-evident. I hadn't thought about it that way. No one laughed much in our house when I was growing up. My parents were quiet, serious people. My dad had a dry wit, I guess you'd call it, but the most he expected from one of his low-key jokes was an appreciative smile. My brother was a noisy, serious presence overshadowing me and my life. In school my teachers and classmates, on the contrary, laughed frequently at my attempts at humor, so I played the game often, earning a measure of popularity which I never found at home. The red-haired O'Malley girl laughed more loudly than the rest. Indeed she seemed to be laughing all the time, though she was the smartest kid in the class. The O'Malley's, it was said, were a crazy family. I fell in love with her, of course, a silly junior high school crush. I was also terrified by her.

I'm not sure that primitive adolescent reaction to her has changed all that much.

When I attempted humor with Tony and his friends, it earned me ridicule.

"Shut up, Tommy," he would tell me, "we don't need your silly comments."

If he didn't need them, then none of his friends would dare laugh.

Had Mary Margaret saved me from my family, rescued me? She saw only my smile and heard only my jokes. She could not imagine me as a repressed little boy and never paid attention to him when he tried to surface during our marriage.

Maybe that's why I relaxed in my responsibility-heavy Senate office when I heard her laughter. It was, I concluded, medicine for me and for everyone else. No wonder they were delighted to have her around.

Was it her laughter which attracted God in our marriage bed? Did He find her laughter irresistible too? If so, God had good taste. Who was I to deny Him that characteristic?

I began to lay plans to seduce her in my hideaway. Exorcise my memory of the temptation by Robbie, poor lonely Robbie. Such plans were pure delight.

We picked up enough seats in the November election for a virtual tie, 49–51. It was not difficult to find a few people from the other side of the aisle who were really closet Democrats when we needed a majority. Better, the leader said, that we didn't quite have control yet because that way the Republicans couldn't blame us for the "politics" that went on in the chamber.

As though politics were something bad, a point to make in my book on democracy as a failure (though still the only way!).

On the Thursday morning after the election, Senator Hewitt, the Leader, and a dozen reelected Democrats and I met the media to announce the "The Distributive Justice Amendment"—also the Hewitt-Moran Amendment—to the appropriations bill.

"It is a statistically demonstrated fact that for the last thirty years," I began, "that the poor in our society have grown poorer, the rich have grown richer, and the middle class has not improved its share in national wealth. The present administration has devoted its major efforts to make the rich richer, witness the President's remark that his people were the haves and the have-mores. We proposed three items in our amendment that will be the first steps in modifying this situation. We will repeal the tax relief that was given to the rich in the last tax reform package. The tax rates for those who make more than a million dollars will return to what they were when the present administration came to power. The income level above which no taxes will be collected will increase by ten thousand dollars, and we will add a dollar to gasoline tax which will also become an income tax credit. The last proposal will be to enforce conservation by other methods than urging people to drive less. The funds collected will be used to subsidize the purchase of such gas-saving vehicles as hybrid cars.

"These reforms will bring somewhat more equality to our country and to serve notice that the days of free yachts are over for the rich and the super rich."

"Will rates for you and your wife go up this year, Senator?"

"I doubt they will this year. If my wife continues to work as a volunteer in my office, then our income will fall under the magic number. If my book royalties dry up, then we might start having tag days."

"Will these reforms be part of your platform in the Presidential election two years from now?"

"I hope they will in the platform of the Democratic candidate next year, whoever it may be. However, I won't be the candidate as I have said repeatedly. I also hope this amendment will serve notice on everyone in America that the inequality in our society is intolerable and that we Democrats intend to do something about it. It will also be a first step in restoring some sense of fiscal responsibility to the nation, so that our children and grandchildren will not be in hock to the Chinese and the Saudis and the Venezuelans for the next hundred years."

"Do you think you have the votes for the amendments, Senator?"

"I refer that question to the Minority Leader."

"After the Thursday election, yes."

"Won't these changes cause a decline of ambition in America?"

"Gimme a break. If I earn an extra million dollars on a book and have to pay a little bit more of it in taxes, I'm still a lot better off than if I didn't earn it. There was a lot of ambition back in the nineties when the proposed rates applied."

"The administration will say that increased taxes will hurt the economy."

"I didn't notice a lot of increase in the economy during the last eight years of give-aways to the super rich."

"Aren't you stirring up class war by turning the poor against the rich, by creating resentment against those who have worked so hard for their success in this country? Isn't this amendment somewhat Marxist in orientation?"

"Who are the poor? They're the people who cut your lawns, who collect your garbage, who clean your homes, who sweep the sidewalks in front of your stores, who empty your bedpans and make your beds in the hospitals, who don't own cars, who have to take public transportation to work, even in the worst weather, who have no life insurance, no health insurance, no pension plans, who often can't get medical care in hospitals where they work, who can't pay for the medicines to stay alive, who live in the homes that are the first to be swept away by storms, who can't afford good education for their children. They are the people who are all around us, but we don't see them. They are not about to throw up barricades in the streets or come after us with baseball bats. They are not revolutionaries. They are more likely to feel beaten down into the ground than resentful. All we're asking is to give them a bit of a break, a better chance for their children than they themselves had. This is Marx, only to someone who hasn't read him!"

The last couple of sentences made one network and CNN. As usual we put it on our Web page and sent DVDs out to our mailing lists.

"We could assemble a collection of these comments," Mary Margaret suggested, "and send them to Chucky. They'd make great ad copy for the next campaign."

"If there is a next campaign . . . Doesn't he get the newsletter?"

"Sure, but, if you don't object, Manny and I can cut them down a little and put them all on one disk."

"Fine," I said without too much enthusiasm.

They were all taking away from me the right to make my own decision about running again. Now that my wife was around the office most of the day, I had actually begun to enjoy being a United States Senator. I must be suspicious of that reaction.

"You and Mommy are really happy these days, aren't you, Daddy?" Maran, our wide-eyed little witch said to me one day while we were walking home from weekday Mass.

"You smell good things too, sweetheart?"

"Uhuh."

"What does happiness smell like?"

"Like flowers."

I wasn't sure that I liked my marital relationship being monitored by a good sniffer.

After our first highly rewarding tryst in my hideaway—I was intolerably proud of myself that afternoon—I had an idea for the Distributive Justice Amendment. Only the brave deserve the fair, right?

I walked over to the Leader's office to see what he thought. He listened to me carefully, nodding his head as I talked.

"We'll have trouble with the teachers' union," he said.

"And the ACLU and the AJC and the editorial board of the *New York Times*. But where else do they have to go?"

"No place. They'll all have to support you for reelection, regardless . . . Should you run of course . . . In Illinois they certainly don't want Crispjin back . . . It might win some Catholic votes and some Black votes too . . . Yeah, why not . . . I'll clear it with Hewitt. I'm sure he'll enjoy it too."

The idea was to use some of the funds from our tax increases on the wealthy to provide a five-thousand-dollar tax grant to poor people so they could choose an alternative to public schools. The alternative school would have to be certified by some educational certification institution. No mention was made of religious schools one way or another. The Administration supported such ideas but never had to worry about implementing them because the Democrats would be afraid of the teachers' unions. But in the fluid times between the last election and the next one, we might just sneak it by. Many Democrats felt just as I did. If the Catholic schools in the poor neighborhoods were providing better education, they deserved help in staying open.

"Is this a payoff to the Catholic bishops so they won't deny you the Sacrament?" a very angry woman reporter demanded at a press conference.

"Only one bishop has denied me Holy Communion. If anything it is a payoff for the poor people who desperately want a little more choice. That seems to me to be a very liberal idea. The rich can make choices about the education of their children, why can't the poor be given choices too?"

"Doesn't your proposal violate the wall of separation between Church and State?"

"I don't think you can base laws on metaphors. But there's no mention of churches or religion in the proposed amendment."

"But in fact, only Catholic schools provide alternatives for most poor people?"

"Is that wrong? Do you want to punish the schools for trying to educate the very poor? Moreover with this law on the books, other groups, religious and secular, will undoubtedly form their own schools."

"Is it fair to demand that public schools compete?"

"Ours is supposed to be a capitalist society. Why shouldn't the public schools compete?"

So it went. All the ideological forces weighed in against us. I dismissed them. "There are enough votes in both houses of Congress to approve this amendment. Let the courts decide whether it's constitutional or not."

"I want to note," I said in one of my remarks from the floor, "that every Republican administration since that of Richard Nixon has promised help to Catholic schools. Now it is Democratic senators that are supporting a measure to which the present incumbent has already paid lip service."

The *New York Times* editorial harrumphed that I was merely courting the Illinois Catholic ethnic vote.

I took the opportunity to reply. Or rather to direct my assistant in charge of media relations to reply.

> To the Editors:
>
> It is interesting that your editorial writers see a Catholic ethnic plot behind the amendment to the appropriations bill proposed by Senators Hewit and Moran. Most Catholic ethnics with European backgrounds earn much more money than the limit for tuition grants. Hispanic Catholics have shown so far little inclination to seek alternative educational opportunities for their children. The group of poor people most likely to benefit from the Distributive Justice Amendment will be African American. Should Senator Moran decide to seek reelection, he doesn't need this amendment to gain their support. He is surprised, however, that so many who are eager to help the poor are opposed to the first major attempt to aid them in the last ten years.
>
> Cordially
> Mary Margaret O'Malley
> Assistant to Senator Thomas P. Moran

The White House applauded this part of the amendment but condemned the "typical liberal trickery to increase taxes."

Their era was winding down and they knew it. Vouchers for private schools were something to add to the legacy.

All four amendments to the appropriations bill passed at a session which ended at two AM three days before Christmas. The house, weary from the long wait, passed the bill by voice vote the next day, though some of their old-fashioned members protested that we had taken away their power to initiate tax reform.

The president signed the bill on Christmas Eve. Senator Hewitt was invited to the signing. I had flown home with my family that morning. They didn't invite me because, as they told the media, I had turned down a previous invitation. We nonetheless had a Christmas party at my house, a modest and quiet one, despite the presence of the O'Malley redheads. However, we did toast to "The Beginning of a New Democratic Era."

"If you decide to go for it," the Leader told me, "you're a shoe-in."

"Which 'it'?" Mary Rose asked with mischievous eyes.

"Either 'it.' "

CHAPTER 30

✝

"WELL, what do you think?" I asked my wife as she lay content on the couch in the hideaway, her clothes in dishabille because of the vigor of my love-making.

"You've got about six months to decide," she said. "You should make up your mind tentatively before we go to Ireland this summer. Then confirm it when you go back and announce a year beforehand. That will keep all presentable Democrats out of the primary. Then the election campaign will begin on Labor Day, especially on weekends because of your responsibility here in this building. It won't be as hard as it was last time, but you'd use the same kind of techniques and run now on your record. You have to hope that the Party nominates an effective candidate for the Presidency."

I reached over and tickled her ribs.

"Cut that out!"

"And you think I should do all these things?"

"I didn't say that. I said that's the schedule you'll have to follow . . . I said cut that out . . . We've already made love."

"Just a little afterplay."

"Oh, *that!*" she sighed. "Anyway, it's your call. I'll support you whichever way you go."

"But what *should* I do?"

"It's a free kick, Tommy dear."

I touched her breast.

"That's better . . . You have become an effective Senator. You like the job, though it wears you out. You can't do it forever, but we're not talking forever."

"I liked it more since you came on the staff."

"We can't do this transgressive stuff back in River Forest. No secret hideaways there."

"By the time we're finished with the next election, Marymarg, we will have an empty nest."

"They'll all go to graduate school, Tommy, not such an empty nest."

"What about your career?"

"In any objective measure," she laughed, "your job is more important than mine. More fun too. I can still take the occasional case to keep my hand in. Besides I love the Court, but, Tommy dearest, I love the Senator more."

"I didn't think you'd be much help," I muttered, permitting my lip to touch hers. "Who wants freedom!"

"There is," she sighed, complacently, "the problem that you'll probably be running against your brother."

"That won't be easy . . . But I'm used to him by now. I declared my independence when I married you. He won't take away from me anything I want."

"So the question is not what you *should* do, but what you *want* to do?"

"I don't want to risk your lives any more—you and the kids."

"So much miserable stuff, Tommy," she said as she began to reassemble her garments. "But I think we've left that behind us."

"There's still Bobby Bill and Leander Schlenk."

"Unless I'm mistaken the public is sick of hearing about them. And sick of the negative ads of the last six years. They've written H. Rodgers off as a poor loser."

"Maybe."

"I'm sure of it. This campaign would be a cakewalk."

As she had often said of her mother, my wife was rarely in error and never in doubt. As time would prove, this time she was in error.

"Come on,"she said, adjusting her bra. "We should get home. Dan Leary is going to take out our eldest on their first real date."

"So we get a look at him. He's Dan now? Is that significant?"

"Probably."

I didn't want it to be.

Dan turned out to be a big, handsome kid, a good six inches taller than me with unruly black Irish hair and the gifts of both wit and laughter, a combination of both sides of our alleged family structure. He did not seem ill at ease with us, despite his black eye. He treated Mary Rose with infinite respect and her parents with great courtesy.

"I collected this souvenir," he said with an easy laugh, "from a Harvard guy on the field of combat."

"Daniel," Mary Rose said, as though she were admitting a fault in her date, "plays rugby. He says it is the ancestor of the NFL."

"He's right," I said. "They get five points for a touchdown and they have to literally touch the ball down and two points for a PAT but they have to kick it from where the player crossed the goal line."

"And is not nearly as dangerous as the NFL," Danny chuckled. "Except when you play Harvard."

"A very well-behaved young man," I said to the rest of family when they had left.

"Totally cute," Maran opined.

"Extremely gorgeous," Marytre agreed.

"Time passes too quickly," Marymarg said, tears streaming down her cheeks.

"Well you didn't have to put up with such a big galoot anyway."

Her tears turned to laughter.

The next week I called in Chris, Manny, and my three legislative assistants.

"I know all of you are wondering whether I will run for reelection. I am too. All I can say now is that I have an open mind on it. I have not made up my mind not to run. I will tell you off the record when I come back from the summer recess and make my formal announcement in November as our crazy Illinois primary requires. I won't keep you guessing any longer than that. I must say again what I've said many times before. If I have become at all an effective Senator the credit goes to you and to the rest of the staff. Thank you for your help and support."

"What does herself think?" Chris asked.

"She pretends to be neutral and even persuaded herself that she's neutral. But she's not, she likes her job here too much to be neutral. But she genuinely says that it's up to me."

"As it should be," Peter Doherty commented.

"The *Examiner* reports a state-wide poll showing Crispjin ten points ahead with only eight points undecided," Manny said, "but we know what confidence we have in their polls."

"Ten points ahead," I said, "and after spending maybe fifty million dollars over the last five years. Hardly worth all the money."

"I'd guess that in a real poll," Manny said, "you'd be ahead. They're afraid of too obvious a distortion."

"I'm going to run, if I run, on my record. I kept my promises sort of thing. Only way to do it."

"And the rules are the same this time," Chris asked, "no attack ads, and no personal requests for donations. This time we add that you don't start the campaign till Labor Day."

"And you'll have to fly back and forth because of your Senate duties?"

"Precisely . . . If my record isn't good enough to get me reelected, then I don't deserve it."

"We'll draw up some preliminary memos about your record and draft some materials for the Web page and the e-mail mailings, just in case."

"That's a good idea, but I want to make it clear, my decision is still in doubt."

"That's the way it should be," Chris said as she stood up. "And like Marymarg we're all completely neutral."

"Sure!" I said with my best witty Irish grin.

My heart sank as they left the room. Their reactions had been perfectly correct. But they had invested many years of their lives in my career with complete selflessness. I did not want to let them down.

I called Mary Margaret's cousin, Margaret Mary Antonelli Corso at her law office in Chicago.

"Hi, Cousin," that lovely Sicilian woman said. "What's going down?"

"How's your file on the *Examiner* coming?"

"I have twenty absolutely clear issues of falsehood in reckless disregard for the truth. You want I should seek relief?"

"Not quite yet . . . How are the kids?"

"Flourishing! . . . From what your wife tells me your eldest finally brought a date around the house, rugby player of all things . . . Serious?"

"Maybe . . . My best to himself . . . See you at Easter."

I asked myself as I hung up why I had made that call. No point in it. My instincts said that I should win easily, Rodgers Crispjin had become a bore. Yet a tiny voice in the sub-basement of my mind warned me that there would be one more dirty trick, this one perhaps decisive.

The next day Leander Schlenk struck again.

Will Tommy Quit?

Rumors are circulating under the Dome that cute little Tommy Moran, now pumped with pride in his role as Majority Whip, is thinking of giving up on the United States Senate, a decision which will be greeted with a sigh of relief both by Senators and by voters in Illinois. The recent scientific survey by the *Examiner* has acted like a bucket of cold water in the face for the swaggering little man who appears to think that he owns the Senate. Rather than risk a stinging defeat by the resurgence of Senator H. Rodgers Crispjin, it is said that Tommy might accept a vice-presidential nomination if it were offered to him or a cabinet position, though it is not certain which post would be low enough for Tommy's meager talents. Stay tuned, this should be an interesting year.

Mary Margaret told me that Tony had called several times begging her to talk me out of running again. She said that she had laughed and assured him that the decision was completely mine.

She wouldn't quote his words because she said she couldn't remember them. And herself with a photographic memory.

We had a grand time in the first session of the new Congress, beating up on the faltering and often incoherent Republicans. Indeed we took control of the Senate because of the departure of two Republicans, one to a better world and the other to become president of a college in his native state. They knew a sinking ship when they were on one. In both cases the governors appointed Democrats to replace them. I became majority whip that summer. We pushed through legislation for health insurance for children under twelve and limitations on corporate golden parachutes. The President vetoed both of them and we overrode in both Houses the health insurance veto. We were making progress towards a more just and equitable society without becoming the welfare society that had hampered economic progress in Europe. I thought that we had come a much longer way than there was any reason to expect five years ago.

Before we left for Ireland, I met with Joe McDermott, Dolly, and Ric Sanchez.

"What's it going to be?" Joe demanded "You're having too much fun to quit now that you're ahead."

"I'm not sure I'm ahead," I said cautiously.

"Don't believe all that junk in the *Examiner*. They fudged the actual numbers. You're eight points ahead. Besides we have evidence that they've been faking their surveys for several years."

"You have a great record, Tommy," Dolly said. "You just have to point at that. And if you've got a lot of things for Illinois. As eventual majority leader, you can get a lot more."

"The Demographics have changed, Tommy, since you went away . . . Not only more Latinos in the state, but more citizens and a lot more registered voters. They're solid for you all the way."

"I presume that Mary Margaret is not opposed," Joe asked cautiously.

"Hardly," I said with my patented grin when my wife's name came up. "She maintains complete neutrality. But she loves the job more than I do."

Silence all around the lunch table at the Chicago Yacht Club. Outside, the lake, the graceful boats, and the skyline against a clear blue sky looked like a retouched travel poster. This time around, if I won, I could come home more often and with my wife.

"We'd be proud to help again," Dolly said, breaking the silence.

"Thanks for your patience," I said, rising from the table, "and thanks Ric for the lunch. I'll let you know right after Labor Day."

I was sure that all three of them would bet that I would decide to run again. Why would anyone quit when they were ahead?

Perhaps because he really didn't like the job. Perhaps because he was afraid of some final devastating attack.

What could such an attack be? My personal life? Robbie? She was married and living in San Francisco with an affluent banker husband. She even sent me a Christmas card.

I couldn't quit because of a nameless fear, could I?

Ireland was wonderful. Mary Margaret had been there with her parents when they were in Germany for Jack Kennedy.

"I remember only the awful poverty," she said. "How did it get to be one of the richest nations in the world?"

"Hard work and good education," I said. "I don't know why we can't do the same thing in America."

I knew why we couldn't. That could be one of the main themes of my campaign.

The daughters started out skeptical about Irish men, but soon found them charming, "even if they talk some strange foreign language."

They also thought that the young women their own age were "stuck-up" and without morals.

I think our daughters scared the locals. They were too beautiful, too bright, too sophisticated, and too intelligent. Yanks weren't supposed to be that way, if you take my meaning. Then the kids took over a song fest in a Galway pub and did mariachi music.

"Would those young women," a man asked me, "be Spanish, if you don't mind me asking?"

"Yanks," I said

"I was telling meself that, but they sing in Spanish."

"Mexican."

He shook his head in bafflement.

"Well, whatever they are, aren't they brilliant altogether?"

"Aren't they now?"

Ireland brought laughter to the four women in my family. It depressed me—too much rain, too many clouds, too many resigned sighs. I think I covered it up pretty well.

"You're sleeping a lot, Thomas Patrick Moran," my wife informed me.

"Jet lag."

"Fersure," she said skeptically.

The kids were responsible for my depression. They weren't kids any more, they were young women—tall, smart, sophisticated, quite able to take care of themselves in almost any situation. More sophisticated than their mother was at the same age, and she was quite sophisticated. Or so it had seemed to me. What did I know? My five years in the Senate had transformed my family and I had not been there to watch them grow up.

That wasn't true, was it? I had been around all the time, hadn't I? I had a good relationship with them, didn't I? They still laughed at me and called me Mr. Mom, didn't they?

Six years, I told myself, were a long time in a man's life. I was growing older, that was the problem. Did I want to give up six more years of my life to the folly of the United States Senate? What would I do instead? Write more books? That was a lot easier but often boring.

My talk to the Dail (pronounced Doll) the Irish parliament started out badly. They were even more hostile to the "friggin' Yank" than I had expected. I struggled on with comic stories about how the world's second oldest parliamentary body (a title we unjustly claim for ourselves) tied itself up in knots. There were a few weak laughs. Then I began to describe the tragicomedy of the last day before recess. I think my wife and kids started the laughter but everyone joined in. They overwhelmed me with laughter and cheers as I wound down.

"I'm sure in this nation of distinguished poets and even more distinguished storytellers and in this august body of surely the best storytellers if not the best poets, you avoid the confusion and chaos that we suffer every day. But come to the District of Columbia and see how we just barely manage to keep democracy alive and I'll explain to you then that 'just barely' is the most one can expect in democratic rule—of which as your man across the Irish Sea once remarked is the only alternative to tyranny."

Thunderous applause.

The reception afterwards was great *craic* as the Irish would say, enlivened by the charm of my four womenfolk.

My depression lifted for an hour or two.

Finally, we were sitting in the Club lounge at Dublin Airport, contemplating the green grass and the blue sky from which rain clouds had just disappeared and *the* question surfaced.

"Daddy," said Marytre, "you are going to run again aren't you?"

There was only one possible answer.

"You guys want me to?"

Enthusiastic agreement from my four womenfolk, wife included.

"That settles it."

They took the decision out of my hands, didn't they?

CHAPTER 31

✝

SCENE: In front of refurbished Moran home in River Forest.
TIME: Early November, trees still red and gold.

CANDIDATE: My family took a vote on whether I should run for reelection. The vote was four to zero with one abstention. I was the abstainer. So I will claim that I was drafted.

In my last campaign I made promises of what I would try to achieve as a Senator, not guarantees, but promises of efforts. I will run on my record—immigration reform, pension reform, protection of private property from greedy municipalities, and tax reform which moves towards greater equality among Americans. I have obtained for Illinois our fair share of funding for roads and parks and especially funding for progress on the remodeling of our airport, a necessity for our city and for the whole country. I've also managed to win enough confidence from my colleagues in the Senate that they elected me Majority Whip, kind of an assistant Majority Leader in charge of counting the votes, something we have learned to do very carefully in Cook County. I am not so much proud of my record as reasonably satisfied with it. It represents a good beginning.

We are in the midst now of one of those epochal swings in American political life. The Democratic party, the party of the poor, the working people, the middle class, is returning to power to replace the party of the rich and the super rich. We must improve the quality of American life by setting aside the values of greed and profit which have dominated it for the last decade and replace them with values of equality and concern. We must make it possible for all Americans to share in the good life, no matter what their income is. I am convinced that the most important concern for most American families is quality education for their children. We have had six years of No Child Left Behind and in fact there are more children left behind than ever before. If reelected I will do my best to improve the quality of American education. I will establish committees of experts and committees of parents to advise me in these efforts.

Finally, I will keep the promises I have made about my campaign. I will not engage in negative campaigning of any sort, including attack ads. I will not ask anyone for a contribution to our campaign and I will not inquire of my campaign the names of contributors. Finally I will start my formal campaign on Labor Day. Two months is more than enough time for the people of Illinois to see my face on television. Thank you.

REPORTER: Tommy, how can you hope to overcome Senator Crispjin's massive lead in the polls?

CANDIDATE: We overcame it last time and now I have a record on which to stand.

REPORTER: Senator Crispjin is reported to have a campaign fund of fifty million dollars. How can you hope to compete with that?

CANDIDATE: We can't hope to compete with it.

REPORTER: Given the record of your family in Washington, why should the people of Illinois vote for you again?

CANDIDATE: What record?

REPORTER: Your wife is double-dipping and your daughter stole a high school honor.

CANDIDATE: You don't have your facts right. When my wife works in my office she does so as a volunteer. My daughter renounced the valedictorian role because she didn't want her academic record to be a matter of public debate. Since then there have been five court decisions that the Jesuits did not conspire to cheat the other young woman of the prize.

REPORTER: Do you still deny that you are hoping for a draft as vice presidential candidate?

CANDIDATE: Absolutely. I'll quote General Sherman again. I will not run if nominated. I will not serve if elected. Every time your question is asked, I'll give the same answer.

REPORTER: Do you expect us to believe that?

CANDIDATE: I hope the people of Illinois believe me.

REPORTER: Tommy, will you make an issue of Senator Crispjin's relationship with oil tycoon Bobby Bill Roads?

CANDIDATE: As I said in my remarks, I will not engage in attack politics.

REPORTER: Tommy, does your staff resent your wife's presence in the office?

CANDIDATE: They recruited her without telling me, not that I had any choice in the matter.

REPORTER: You enjoy being called the Tom Cruise of the Senate?

CANDIDATE: I'm flattered to be compared to such a handsome and skillful actor. I'm not sure he feels the same.

REPORTER: Senator, do you resent being called Tommy when reporters always refer to your opponent as Senator Crispjin?

CANDIDATE: No.

(Mariachi musicians appear and sing and play two brisk and stirring songs. Then they change their ethnic group and sing "When Irish Eyes Are Smiling")

I restrained my eldest daughter who would have attacked the punk who accused her of cheating. Daniel Leary, who had flown to Chicago for the announcement, held her back too.

"Chill out Mary Rose. Don't act like your mother!"

She rested her head on my shoulders and wept bitterly.

"Liar, liar, liar."

"How can they get away with it?" Dan demanded. "Isn't there a law?"

"Sure there is, Danny, but the Supreme Court has ruled that you have to show actual malice if you defame a public person. Alas, Maryro is a public person."

"I'd like to . . ."

"So would we all, Danny. So would we all."

Rosie joined us. She had been commissioned by her magazine *(The New Yorker)* to write an article about Tommy's campaign.

"I can't believe what I heard," she said. "That was vicious."

"The adversarial media," I replied. "They were trying to make Tommy lose his temper. They now know that the charges against me and your granddaughter can't drive him to the edge. They'll keep trying."

"Dolly can give me their names?"

"So we get even with him, hon, in *The New Yorker*."

"He's an illiterate dork," Maryro grumbled. "He doesn't read *The New Yorker*."

"I'll send him a copy," Rosie said.

I was the only one who was not surprised, much less angry.

"We can't afford to let those buffoons make us angry," I said to Tommy as we walked over to Petersen's for our ice cream fix.

"We were set up. Many of those guys were from the *Examiner*. They didn't want to risk Schlenk in a head-to-head, so they sent copy boys, interns, stenographers over here to ask questions."

The high command gathered around a table.

"I think we have a problem on our hands," Tommy said.

"We have five years of attack ads with which to deal," Joe McDermott agreed. "And a limited budget."

"We could get some feature pieces on Mary Rose, if she doesn't mind, in the papers or even the national magazines . . ." Dolly suggested. "I'm sure she can handle herself."

Tommy hesitated.

"I don't think I want my daughter exploited that way . . . Marymarg?"

"She'd love to set the record straight," I said. "She certainly won't lose her cool. I could ask her."

"OK," Tommy agreed. "I don't like anything about today. They have a campaign outlined and they're going to go after us on every possible occasion."

"Amigo!" exclaimed Ric Sanchez, "We will sing 'When Irish Eyes Are Smiling' right into their faces."

CHAPTER 32

✝

WE WENT BACK to Washington the day after I announced my intentions to seek reelection. I met with Manny and Chris in my office. There was no choice. I had to press ahead with all my Senate duties and responsibilities. The Republicans, faced with considerable losses, were fighting bitterly against us. The Majority Leader decided that we would do our best to create the impression that we were not being obstructionist. There was not much point in blocking most presidential appointments which would not last more than a year and a half. Even if a Republican should win the presidency he would want to put his own people in key offices. We would make trouble for some of the military appointments and block the Administration's judicial appointments. We would substitute our own budget and our own legislation for his and on some occasions maybe even override his vetoes. At no time, however, would we be rude or discourteous or even reply in angry fashion to their accusations. Our theme song would be that we wanted to restore the old civility to the Senate relationships. There were five or six Republican Senators we could count on, many of whom would flock to our side of the aisle after the election if our margin of victory was big enough. Some of us wanted to get even quickly but most of us thought that we could afford to play a waiting game.

"They have a campaign plan down to the last detail," I told Chris and Manny. "They will harass and block us every inch of the way and they know I won't fight back in kind. It's going to be very tricky."

"The Ambassador is doing his focus groups? What do they show?"

"In general, people don't like Crispjin much. They think he's a poor loser who trying to buy his way back into the Senate. They're just not sure about me. The ads have had some impact as does the constant sniping from the *Examiner*. On the other hand, they are more likely to know my record than the other side thinks. We don't have much choice to use that strategy. We will have to be prepared for disruption everywhere we turn. They've finally figured out that disruption is a better tactic than assassination."

My two colleagues were silent. They had been around long enough to know what the odds were.

"The best polls still show that I'm ahead and that the majority of the uncertain lean in my direction."

"You don't sound very optimistic," Chris said cautiously.

"I'm not. I never thought it would be a cakewalk. They will try to find more ways to attack my family. And they have unlimited funds to do so."

"This is not the best time to do so, but you'd better look at. 'Under the Dome' for today."

TOMMY LIES AT ANNOUNCEMENT

Cute little Tommy Moran, the pathetic excuse Illinois has for a junior Senator, deliberately fibbed at the "announcement" yesterday of his alleged decision to run for reelection to the Senate seat that many think he stole from Senator H. Rodgers Crispjin. He flatly denied that he would accept a draft to run for the vice-presidency. Everyone knows that Tommy, a failure in the Senate, has little chance to defeat Senator Crispjin. Everyone knows that the offer of a shot at the vice presidency would appear to be an "honorable" way out. The next president may well be a Democrat. He may think that Tommy would help him carry Illinois, always a swing state. Tommy would then be only a single heartbeat away from the presidency. That's scary.

The next day the *Daily News* wrote an editorial saying that it decried the fact that another Chicago paper had sent six "reporters" to Senator Moran's announcement of his reelection campaign and that these reporters had dominated the question period afterwards. This, the *News* contended, went far beyond an editorial position on a campaign and became actual participation in the campaign. It raised questions which ought to trouble everyone in Illinois. It then listed the names of all six of the "reporters," none of whom had press credentials.

Mary Margaret issued a statement the next day which denied Schlenk's allegation that I had lied and quoted extensively from the *Daily News* editorial. "There may have been some lies at the campaign announcement but they came not from the Senator but from the pseudo-journalists."

"Do you want me to cut that last sentence?" she asked.

"What does Manny say?"

"She loved it."

"Then go with it."

"You bet. . . . Are we still having lunch next Monday?"

"That is a provocative question, Ms. O'Malley."

"It was meant to be."

"Have I given any indication that I want to abolish that custom?"

"No."

"Then we will have lunch in the Senate dining room at the usual time."

"I will look forward to it . . . Oh, your brother called this morning. I told him you were in conference. He was very angry."

The muscles in my body tightened up, as they usually do when Tony is mentioned.

"The usual?"

"This time the public humiliation of your daughter."

"And you said in reply that neither the young woman in question nor her mother or father thought she'd been humiliated?"

"You're a mind-reader, Senator."

On the first Sunday in Advent, the *Daily News*'s magazine section carried a feature article on our child.

Not So Wild an Irish Rose

It was a delightful piece whose theme was that despite her red hair and her green eyes and her great beauty, Senator Moran's daughter was, like her father, a very relaxed and even conservative young woman—all of this despite her feverish activity on the basketball court. She dismissed the hubbub about the valedictorian issue, claimed that she and her rival were still good friends, and said that, if your father is in public life, you're a target for creeps and she could deal with that. Yes she was dating a young man from Chicago whose privacy she would respect by not revealing his name. It could not be termed "serious" at least not yet. Yes she was going to graduate school and she wanted to become an expert on the education of kids and teens. Yes she was very proud of her parents because they were active in public life and at the same time totally cool parents. Her grandparents were totally cute too.

"I didn't know she was doing this interview," I said to her mother at our Monday lunch.

"Neither did I!"

"Dolly must have called her and assumed that she would ask us."

"Dolly is too smart even to imply that."

"She did it on her own?"

"That bother you, Mr. Mom?"

"No, it's the sort of thing her mother would have done. Does her grandmother know about it?"

"Certainly."

"Is there any chance of that *New Yorker* piece appearing before the election?"

"I asked her that. She says they wouldn't hear of it."

"I was afraid of that," I nudged her thigh with my knee.

She stiffened in response.

"You know too damn much," she whispered, "about turning me on."

"I've had a lifetime to study your reactions."

Life went on in the United States Senate. A southerner was winning presidential primaries around the country. He seemed all right to me because he sounded like a Democratic Hat McCoy.

"What do you think of this guy?" I asked Hatfield one day when I met him in the corridors.

"Don't like him one bit. He's the kinda fella y'all should be putting up all along. Bill Clinton without the libido. I'm glad I'm not up for re-election. Y'all might carry ole Ketuck this time."

The Governor dropped into my office unannounced one morning, "jest to say hiyah."

"Always welcome here, Mr. President."

He grinned like a mischievous elf.

"I see by the papers you might like to be vice president."

"The papers lie, Mr. President."

A quick spasm of disappointment flashed across his face.

"I want to make sure you carry Illinois," I added. "Besides I gave my word."

"I understand, Senator, I understand. I admire your integrity. If I should win, you'd be more help to me h'yar. Still I won't take this 'no' for a definitive answer. Now I'd be pleased to meet that pretty woman out thare with red hair, your wife, I presume."

I thought of Rhett Butler as played by Clark Gable in *Gone With the Wind*.

He turned on all his cornpone charm for my wife who replied with all her West Side Irish charm. Everyone in the office stopped working. They applauded when he left the room.

"Right nice y'all cheering!" he bowed as he left.

"I told him no way," I announced as soon as the door closed. "Now y'all get back to work, ya'hear!"

"Will he win, Daddy?" Maran asked that night at supper after my wife had celebrated the governor's charm.

"I think so, dear. But he has to carry Illinois to be sure."

"We're a blue state!" Marytre protested.

"That's right."

How to stop the plan to prevent Bobby Bill from stealing Illinois?

I could lose the presidential election for the Democrats.

"I hyar the man came to call on ya, the other day," Hat McCoy said to me as we filed in for a quorum call.

"Shunuff?"

"He offer ya anything t'all."

"He did remark that, should he be nominated and elected, I'd be a heap of help to him right here in this building."

"He's right on that. He a going to win, Irish, he a going to win."

"He's Irish too," I said, "another one of your left-foot kickers."

The convention was in Chicago. We came back for it because I was a delegate and because we wanted the kids to see it. Our guy was the heavy favorite, but it was not a sure thing. It would be an exciting event. He won unanimously on the third ballot and we sneaked out and went home.

The Reliable woman who was guarding the house greeted us at the door.

"The President is on the line, Senator, sir."

I picked up the phone.

"Tom Moran."

"I promised I'd ask you once more, Senator, so I'm asking."

"I'd love to do it, Mr. President. I really would. But I can't."

"I understand. I admire your integrity. See y'all in Washington in January."

"You bet, Mr. President."

I hung up, feeling sad and empty. Virtue is rarely its own reward, in the short run anyway.

"He said he'd see us uns in Washington in January."

Applause from all, even the Ambassador and Mrs. OMalley who just came in the door.

Mary Margaret hugged me fiercely.

"I'm so proud of you, Tommy. So proud."

"I hope he mentions that he called you," the Ambassador said.

"Why should he?" I asked.

" 'Cause he'll need you when he gets there."

The nominee did mention me.

"My first thought was to round up your Yewnited States Senator from Illinois and put him on the ticket. He said that because of his commitment here he couldn't do it. I'd like to have had him, but I admire his integrity. He made the right decision. If we win this race, I'll be confident of one very loyal and honest ally over on the Hill and y'all in this great Prairie state will have one of the finest men I've ever met as your senator."

"Didn't your man kiss the blarney stone?" Ambassador O'Malley chuckled.

His wife was busy scribbling in her notebook.

"What are you thinking, Tommy?" she asked.

"Just now feeling that virtue is not necessarily its own reward!"

"It's worth twenty thousand, maybe fifty thousand votes," the Ambassador chortled. "We've canceled them out."

I could not shake my conviction, now almost absolute, that there would be some massive dirty trick at the end.

I confided this to Joe McDermott after the acceptance speech.

"Do you have anything in your life that could create a scandal?" he asked, almost like a clinician. "A love affair, maybe?"

"Only one bed partner all my life and no complaints about her."

"I figured."

So we went back to the Beltway for August. No recess now until Labor Day. The big game was on. I worried about my own campaign. I had heard they were going after me with a phalanx of Catholic antiabortion campaigners. Petitions were being signed in every diocese in the State, requesting the bishops to excommunicate me.

Father Jim, Mary Margaret's brother, called me in mid-August.

"I have a message for you from the Cardinal," he said.

"OK."

"You know he disagrees with your stand on abortion . . ."

"I haven't taken a stand in the six years I've been in the Senate," I replied hotly.

"He knows that. He also says that he accepts your good faith in the matter and he does not believe in using the Eucharist as punishment."

"He's said that in public," I said, still a little angry.

"Therefore he will head off this excommunication nonsense, even in the diocese that threatened you the last time."

"Oh," I said cooling down. "Does he expect a response from me?"

"It might be a good idea."

"Will a 'thank you very much' do?"

"Just right. I'll pass the word on."

Still we weren't prepared for the assault of the "pro-life" brigades.

Our first rally was on Labor Day, sponsored by Chicago Unions, at Gately Stadium in South Chicago near the site of the massacre at Little Steel in 1937. The labor people filled the stadium. I spoke after the crowd had been called to order and a local priest—who shook my hands warmly—had prayed the invocation.

"The murders at Republic Steel are history," I began, "as are the crimes against humanity by the steel companies lead by the notorious Tom Girdler."

I was interrupted by a crowd of maybe two hundred placard-waving, hymn-singing men and women who poured in from one of the entrances of the stadium, overcoming the cops who were there, and rushed towards the raised platform on which I was standing. Their theme seemed to be that Tommy Moran was as bad as Adolf Hitler. They swarmed on to the platform, tore away the mike, and pushed me off the edge.

"You should die and go to hell!" one of the two women who pushed me off the platform shouted.

I landed on the ground in one piece or so I thought. Several other women pounced on me and began to beat me. I lost consciousness with the ironic thought that I might die at the hands of those who were part of the household of faith.

I woke up in a hospital bed, opened my eyes, and looked around. A doctor and a nurse hovered over me, four women with intolerably red hair watched me anxiously.

"The script calls for me to ask where I am," I muttered, my voice hoarse.

"You are," the doctor, a handsome man with dark skin and an English accent, said, "in South Chicago Hospital. I am Doctor Ragiv. And who, sir, are you?"

I thought about it.

"Thomas Patrick Moran, attorney at law."

"And what work do you do, Mr. Thomas Patrick Moran?"

"I don't work. I'm a United States Senator."

The four women with the tear-stained faces laughed. That was part of the script.

"What happened to me?"

"You were assaulted at a political rally, pushed off a platform, and beaten viciously. You have had a mild brain concussion and may have suffered internal injuries. We will keep you in the hospital for twenty-four hours to make sure that you are able to go back on your campaign."

The four women insisted on kissing me, the oldest quite demonstratively. She was undoubtedly my wife.

"Can you identify these women, Senator?"

"I think so . . . If I may read from left to right, Mary Rose Moran, my daughter, Mary Margaret O'Malley, my long suffering wife, Mary Therese Moran, my youngest daughter, and Mary Ann Moran, my middle daughter."

"You are very fortunate, Senator," the doctor frowned in disapproval. "They might have killed you."

"Do you wish to show him the tape now, Ms. O'Malley?"

My good wife pressed a button.

The tape revealed me speaking to a crowd of people in an unfamiliar sports arena. Before I could work my way into the talk, a swarm of angry women erupted out of one of the entrances to the arena and rushed the platform on which I was speaking. They were comparing me to

Hitler. Two of them pushed me off the platform and into a crowd of milling women who began to beat me with placards they were carrying. Then the camera switched to some dozen women who are assaulting my three red heads. They fought back with commendable vigor and gave better than they received. A police ambulance, blue light whirling, forced its way into the arena and pushed towards the platform. The women who had beaten me fled, but were captured by angry cops and angry people from whoever it was I had been talking to.

I closed my eyes.

"This is still the United States of America?" I asked.

"I fear so, Senator."

Then my brother was on the monitor.

"I am terribly disturbed that my only brother was injured this afternoon. Yet I can't fault the attackers. They were fighting for what they believe. Tommy should never have run for the Senate."

Then a short man with flaming eyes.

"If Catholics had done this to the Nazis, the holocaust would not have happened."

Then the Mayor of Chicago in a sports shirt with the Lake behind him.

"All my sympathies and those of my family go to Senator Moran and his family. They are my friends and neighbors. I am ashamed that this happened in Chicago. I'm sure that the State's Attorney will want to prosecute these rioters to the fullest extent of the law."

"What would that be, Mayor?"

"Attempted murder. What else?"

Then Sean Cardinal Cronin, resplendent in red cummerbund, zucchetto, and cloak.

Cardinal Cronin stared at the camera for a minute.

"I will not judge the rioters. But I will certainly judge their behavior. They have disgraced the Catholic Church. If we want to change people's minds, we do so by prayer, patience, and good example, not by trying to kill them. Senator Moran is a distinguished Catholic gentleman. He has never voted on abortion legislation. The attack on him, his wife, and children is objectively a serious sin for which the rioters must do appropriate penance. I am driving out to the hospital now to visit them."

"His brother is a priest, Cardinal."

"I am not unaware of that."

"He said that the Senator had brought it on himself."

"Father Moran does not speak for the church or for the Archdiocese and I do. I believe his words are as dangerous to the peace and civility of American life as were the despicable acts of the rioters."

"And this time," the Cardinal appeared in the doorway of the hospital room, "I really mean it!"

He was wearing the same garb as we had seen on television.

Trailing behind him was his self-effacing little auxiliary bishop Blackie Ryan, attired in his usual Chicago Bulls jacket and an open clerical shirt.

"In the old days, Tommy Moran, we would gather together a bunch of our guys and beat those people up. I concede that the new days are better but not so satisfying."

We all laughed. Doctor Rajiv bowed to the Cardinal and kissed his ring, which is a no-no in Chicago. Sean Cronin was nothing if not graceful.

"Your Beatitude," he said, "would you tell the swarm of people down stairs that the Senator is recovering and will probably be able to leave the hospital tomorrow afternoon. And will the rest of you, Mrs. Moran excepted, please join the Cardinal for his report. We must permit the Senator to rest."

"Cardinal," I called after him, "tell them that when Doctor Rajiv asked what my work was, I said that I didn't work; I was a United States Senator."

"I will tell them that and then assure them that many think he is the hardest working Senator in Washington."

"I'll sing you a lullaby, Tommy love," the incredibly lovely woman who was apparently my wife said, "and you can go to sleep."

CHAPTER 33

✝

Leaning on Mary Margaret's arm I ambled cautiously out of the
elevator the next afternoon. The lobby of South Chicago Hospital
was filled—the whole O'Malley clan, with musical instruments, my
campaign staff, Chris and Manny from Washington, the media, a mass
of uniformed cops, and a similar mass of the off-duty Reliables.

"Senator, do you blame Rodge Crispjin for the attack on you?"

"I have no reason to do that."

"Did you know, Senator, that he said that while he disapproved of
violence, he could understand why people are angry?"

"I did not know that."

"Would you comment on his comment, Senator?"

"It needs no comment."

"Are you going to withdraw from your campaign?"

"Not a chance."

"Did you know that the police are charging the protesters with attempted murder?"

"I had heard that, yes."

"Do you approve?"

"The police must do what they have to do to prevent riots."

"Don't you think that the protesters are doing the same thing that
the civil rights protesters did forty years ago?"

"I don't think that the followers of Dr. King ever tried to kill anyone."

Dolly interrupted the questions.

"That's the end for now. The Senator needs to rest."

"When will you continue your campaign, Senator?"

"Tomorrow."

My wife helped me to a couch in the lobby. Cops and Reliables formed a ring around us, my staff sat in chairs next to the couch.

"Where are the kids?" I asked Mary Margaret,

"Home, binding up their wounds."

"I feel awful, Mary Margaret."

"The trouble with you, Tommy Moran, is that you always look great even when you're feeling awful."

We both laughed. I discovered that my chest hurt when I laughed.

"What's the plan, Senator?" Joe McDermott began our conference.

"Full steam ahead!"

"Are you sure you're up to it?" Dolly wondered.

"No, I'm not up to it, not now. But I'll be all right in a day or two. What's on for tomorrow?"

"Rockford in the morning, Sangamon County Fair Grounds in the afternoon, East Saint Louis in the evening. The next day there are rallies at three malls where you sign copies of your books, then a Hispanic Community Center in DuPage. Not the one at the Catholic Church we used the last time. The local pastor banned us."

"OK. We'll take it one day at a time. This is the way we will do it. If I'm dizzy, confused, have a headache or otherwise not my sterling self my good wife will read my talk. Well, actually, she won't have to read it because she can give it from memory, but it will look better if she brings a paper to the podium. The people will like looking at her better than they like looking at me. I'll sign books until I can't see the page any more and then she can sign them for me . . . OK, Mary Margaret? Maybe I should have asked you first?"

My good wife was laughing so hard that she couldn't reply. I felt better.

"Whatever you say, Boss man!" she said finally.

"The security will be very tight, Tommy," Mike Casey informed me. "We don't have any choice. City, county, state police, and my guys everywhere. We hear that the priest down in Tennessee who organized the protest yesterday is backing off, especially because Cook County has issued a warrant for his arrest. Still there may be local imitators . . ."

"Let me guess. The priest is on the list of Bobby Bill's charities."

"It would seem so . . . I hear on the street that the feds are very interested in Bobby Bill."

"However belatedly . . . Wife of my youth are you going to drive me home from this violent city to the safety of River Forest?"

I had never been seriously sick in all my life. I figured an act of will power was all that was needed to continue full speed on the campaign. I had figured wrong. The first two weeks of the campaign were a waste as far as my input. The headaches faded only in October. So my wife became the candidate. I would introduce her and warn the people that they should not try to write in her name as a candidate because that would split the Democratic votes. I admitted that in every respect she would make a better Senator than I would. Much laughter and then much applause afterwards. She would always add a few sentences in Spanish.

"It's not fair," I would say. "Mary Margaret 'took' elocution in grammar school and I didn't. Remember when you look at the ballot that my name is spelled t h o m a s!"

The crowds were larger and more boisterous than the last time. They easily drowned out the hecklers. On the weekends the kids all showed up, along with the random O'Malley cousins to do the mariachi and "Irish Eyes." Also "My Wild Irish Rose" and "Mary, It's a Grand Old Name."

"We have the big mo, Senator," Dolly assured me. "The real polls showed you ten points ahead and solid."

"I'm not sure about the momentum," I said. "They've still got something up their sleeves."

Lee Schlenk weighed in again.

Tommy Chickens Out

Cute little Tommy Moran seems to be chickening out of the Senatorial race in Illinois. Never one to display a profile in courage, Tommy is using the excuse that he was too badly injured in the South Chicago Protest to deliver his canned campaign speech. So his wife, Mary Margaret O'Malley, stumbles through it, almost incoherently. She is, readers may remember, the daughter of "Ambassador" Charlie O'Malley, the well-known pornographer.

That segment from "Under the Dome" pushed Ambassador O'Malley beyond the breaking point. His lawyers promptly sued the *Examiner* for twenty million dollars. I was not mentioned again in Schlenk's column.

"Calling me Charlie is the worst insult of all," the Ambassador complained. "I am not a Charlie. I am a *Chucky*."

The lawyers at the *Examiner* did not laugh, however. They had warned the editor often that they were in grave danger of losing a suit. The *Examiner*'s tone moderated, though their editorial endorsement of "Senator Crispjin" over "Tommy" was in the same tone as Schlenk's columns and their polls were generally dismissed as rigged.

Most of the other polls showed that I had a "commanding" lead, though some downstate surveys reported that the tide was beginning to shift towards Senator Crispjin. I was still convinced that the other side had one final dirty trick up its sleeve.

We avoided the media mobs, save in the small cities downstate. My answers were always the same. No I didn't think that Senator Crispjin was behind the attack in South Chicago. I would not comment on his response after the violence. I had no idea who was funding the various attacks on me and my family. No, I was not embarrassed by the endorsement of the gay and lesbian alliance.

No questions on the issues. No, of course not.

The crowds were friendlier this time around, the African Americans and Latinos especially. The people on the commuter platforms and in the malls were very nice. They praised Mary Margaret's taste in clothes and told us how wonderfully brave our daughters were. Priests showed up and thanked me for our efforts on behalf of Catholic schools.

"They like us, Tommy," my bride insisted. "They really like us."

The Cardinal, who was also from the West Side, stopped in our campaign headquarters along with the ever present and ever insightful Bishop Blackie Ryan. They both accepted an invitation for a snack at Petersen's.

"They've got an ace up their sleeve," I said to the little bishop who was on his second malt. "They'll play it just before the election."

He sighed loudly.

"Arguably. Yet I suspect that you will have a trump."

A few days later, we were offered a trump.

Joe and Dolly took Mary Margaret and me back into the corner where we had our private conversations.

Joe began.

"The feds will indict Bobby Bill the week after the election, Senator. They're going to throw the book at him. He has spent a hundred million dollars on Crispjin's campaigns. He organized the assassination attempts, the attack on Mary Rose, and the demonstration at Gately Stadium. He pays a fee of a hundred thousand dollars a year to Leander Schlenk. He cheats on his income tax. They have enough to indict Rodge Crispjin too and will do so if he loses. Moreover the *Daily News* has the story and will run it."

"After the election, I presume?"

"Naturally."

"However," Dolly continued, "the writer at the *News* who did the story is willing to leak it to us."

"Leak it or sell it?" I asked. "Not that it matters."

"Sell it."

"We don't want it," I said firmly. "I'm not going to break my promises now."

Joe sighed.

"I didn't think you would."

"It's a dirty game," Dolly added. "Thank God you won't play it that way."

"They will," I said, "and we will have to be ready for them."

"When?" Dolly asked.

"Friday afternoon late. We need everyone here to plot our response."

When they left, Mary Margaret hugged me.

"I'm so proud of you, Tommy. You are my gallant night of the Holy Grail."

"Or maybe the Holy Sepulcher."

As the election approached, some African-American congregations were singing "Irish Eyes" and "It's a Grand Old Name." The Latinos followed suit. I began to think that maybe they really did like us. I still feared the final blow on the final Friday evening.

Henry Honeywell of the *Daily News* stopped me on the Brown Line L platform the Wednesday before the election. He handed me a copy proof of their editorial endorsement.

"We're going to run it on Friday."

I glanced at it quickly.

"Very nice, Henry," I gave it back to him. "Dolly McCormick wouldn't have been more generous."

"I'm not sure our endorsements make any difference."

"With some folks, I think they do."

"I hope so."

"Henry," I said, "you folks over at the *Daily News* talk a lot about the people's right to know."

"That's part of our prime directive," he said with a thin smile at his illusion to Star Trek.

"Yet the people of the State of Illinois don't have a right to know what's happening down in Oklahoma before they vote next week?"

He stiffened.

"You know about that?" he said, frowning.

"A lot of people know about it."

"You've got the story?"

"No. And I don't want it . . . If I were to use it now it would violate my prime directive. But if you don't use it you're violating your prime directive, are you not?"

"We didn't want to exercise undue influence on the election."

"Neither did the prosecutors in Oklahoma . . . When the story comes out, how will you explain your silence on a matter to which the people of Illinois have the right to know—no matter who wins next Tuesday."

"You're way ahead, Tommy. You don't need this to win."

"Maybe we do, Henry, and maybe we don't. That's not the point is it?"

"We stand by our decision, Tommy," he said averting his eyes.

"I'll be interested next week to see how you explain it."

I turned and walked away from him.

I realized I shouldn't have said what I did. However, I was fed up with media and their hypocrisy.

We continued our reckless and feckless campaign. Everyone said we were going to win big. I was waiting for Friday afternoon.

We gathered together at campaign headquarters on Chicago Avenue at four forty-five to wait for the five o'clock news and the axe to fall.

Everyone, even the good Mary Margaret, thought I was wrong.

Then, right on schedule, the axe fell.

CHAPTER 34

✝

ANCHOR: We have a breaking news story which will have a tremendous impact on next week's national election. Amanda Crawford, a former staffer for Illinois Senator Thomas Moran, has filed a paternity suit against the Senator. She contends that her three-year-old son, also Thomas, was conceived in the Senator's office in the Senate four years ago during the August recess. We take you to Tamar Montcrief in Washington.

MONTCRIEF: That's right Luci. Twenty-four-year-old Mandy Crawford brought her son with her when she and her lawyers entered the Federal Court House in the District of Columbia. She was obviously a very distraught young woman.

CRAWFORD (a pale, pretty blond in jeans and sweatshirt. In tears. She is surrounded by lawyers, security, and public relations): He wouldn't talk to me. He wouldn't return my phone calls. He wouldn't answer my letters. I had to think of my poor Tommy here.

(Her handsome son with dark red hair stares at the camera)

See, doesn't he look like the Senator? Isn't he cute? The Senator told me that he wasn't happy in his marriage because his wife wouldn't make love with him and that he would divorce her and marry me. He was very nice to me at first but then when the August recess was over, he seemed to lose interest. I still love him, but he's let me down.

REPORTER: Did you consent to sex, Ms. Crawford?

CRAWFORD: Not at first, no.

REPORTER: Where did you have sex with him?

CRAWFORD: Usually in the closet in his office.

REPORTER: When?

CRAWFORD: At the end of the day when everyone else went home.

REPORTER: Why did you wait till the week before the election to reveal your affair with the Senator?

CRAWFORD: I wrote him last week and told him I would sue him before the election unless he talked to me about poor little Tommy.

(The baby begins to cry)

PUBLIC RELATIONS PERSON: I think that's enough questions for now. Mandy finds this all very painful.

MONTCRIEF: This sensational news is likely to have a profound impact on next Tuesday's election, especially since her little Tommy was born in District General Hospital exactly nine months after Ms. Crawford's affair with Senator Moran. We now go to our Congressional correspondent Marty Gordon. Marty?

GORDON: That's right, Tamar. Most senators are not in Washington on the Friday before an election. However, we do have Senator Winston Evergreen available for comment . . . What do you think of this shocking scandal, Senator?

EVERGREEN (rotund and almost clerical): I've been in the United States Senate for a long time and I've heard just about everything. Yet as a devout Christian man, I am shocked by adultery. Senator Moran was a young man on the make, a typical new Democrat who wants to run the country. He was hoping to continue his mischievous role as a member of the Democrat leadership. Now it looks like lust has destroyed him. I for one won't miss him.

GORDON: Now for a view from the White House, we go to John Kramer at the White House. John, what are they saying over there?

KRAMER: They're not saying much on the record, Marty. But off the record they're pretty pleased. Senator Moran has been a thorn in the side of the administration since he came into the Senate almost six years ago. The White House thinks he's a slick and dangerous operator and that his now certain defeat in Illinois will signal a return to Republican control in the Congress and here in the White House.

ANCHOR: Sorry to interrupt, John, but we now have a reporter who is interviewing Senator Bartlett McCoy in Kentucky. Senator McCoy has sponsored several legislative measures with Senator Moran. We take you to Joan Merton in Lexington Kentucky.

MERTON (breathless): Senator McCoy do you have any comment about the scandal involving Senator Thomas P. Moran?

McCOY: Yes, I do, ma'm.

MERTON: And what is that comment, Senator.

McCOY: My comment, ma'am, is that it is all balderdash!

MERTON (baffled): Balderdash, Senator?"

McCOY: Yes, ma'am, pure balderdash, not to use a more scatological term. A cheap election trick, in which I am sure the Republican Senatorial Campaign Committee is not involved, because I'm a member of it. Tom Moran simply isn't the kind of man who would engage in that sort of behavior. He is a true gentleman . . .

MERTON (cuts him off): Back to you, Luci.

ANCHOR: Now we turn to our chief political correspondent, Arthur Kincaid in Washington. Arthur, what's this scandal going to mean for the Democratic party next Tuesday?

KINCAID: I'm afraid it will mean defeat, Luci. Senator Moran, one of the most promising younger Democrats in the Senate, faced a tough election challenge from former Senator H. Rodgers

Crispjin. Now he will certainly lose by a large margin, thus threatening the Democrats' paper-thin advantage in the Senate. A more serious question for those who see this election as a Democratic revival is whether Senator Moran's negative coattails will drag down their presidential candidate in Illinois which has always been a swing state in presidential elections. I suspect that the Democrats are thanking heaven that Tom Moran didn't accept the vice presidential nomination.

ANCHOR: We have just learned that the *Chicago Daily News,* which had endorsed Senator Moran in today's edition, will withdraw its endorsement in the Sunday edition. We have also learned that Senator Moran will hold a press conference tomorrow afternoon. It is expected that he will withdraw from the race . . . Now for weather and sports.

CHAPTER 35

✝

News Conference

Place: Senator Moran's reelection headquarters
Time: 3:30 Saturday afternoon.

(The Senator stands in front of the room. His family and staff are behind a long table on which there are many stacks of paper)

Senator (solemnly and grimly): It is rather late in the day to fight off the feeding frenzy which has enveloped me and my family in the last twenty-two hours. I have already been judged and executed without a chance at self-defense. I will begin by saying that there has been only one woman in my life and that I have been faithful to her since we were married. All allegations to the contrary are crudely crafted lies. I will now endeavor to demonstrate that they are lies.

First, I dismiss as frivolous the allegation that red hair of the unquestionably adorable Tommy Crawford is proof that he is my son. A minute's thought would suggest that the red-haired genes come from the other side of the family—my wife, my father-in-law, my wife's grandfather, and several earlier generations of west of Ireland Irish.

Secondly, my staff did a very careful search of Ms. Crawford's governmental employment. She was never a member of our staff. I never met her. I do not know her. Nor did she ever work for the staff of another senator. Quite the contrary, at the time of her alleged relationship with me, she was in fact working as a stenographer in the Department of the Interior. I have here on the table evidence of these facts which we have labeled "Exhibit A" in case any of you want to take copies with you.

Thirdly, young Tommy's blood type is A as is evident from his birth certificate, copies of which are available as "Exhibit B." My own blood type is O. It is impossible for someone with my blood type to have a child with the A type. My blood test is here in "Exhibit C."

I note in passing that the lawyers, security guards and public relations personnel around Ms. Crawford in front of the district courthouse are all, in one way or another, associated with the so-called Oklahoma oil tycoon Bobby Bill Roads who has opposed me on various occasions. Here in "Exhibit D" are their names.

Fourthly, it would have been physically, indeed metaphysically impossible for me to have carnal relations with anyone in Washington at the time alleged. Ms. Quinn, where was I in August five years ago, do you remember?

QUINN: You were in Spain, Senator, all month. I saw you speak to the *Cortes* and meet the king and queen.

MORAN: And you so reported on your station?

QUINN (sadly): Yes Senator.

MORAN: And you played clips from Spanish television of our peregrinations through Spain?

QUINN: Yes, Senator.

MORAN: Indeed. It would have been impossible for Chicagoans who paid attention to the media to miss the fact that I was in Spain. Did not even the wondrous Leander Schlenk complain that I was violating protocol by speaking to the *Cortes*?

QUINN (softly): Yes, Senator.

MORAN: To prove that I could not have jumped on a plane, flown to Washington for some quick illicit sex and then flown back, we have here on the table Exhibit E, a photocopy of my official passport which shows one entry and one exit from Spain and one re-entry to the United States and a record of hotel charges throughout Spain during our month of travel.

I repeat, Mary Alice, that allegations made on your station last night were demonstrable lies and indeed made with reckless disregard for the truth. Moreover, they have done grave harm to my reputation and that of my family. I hope everyone will offer quick apologies and retractions.

Are there any questions?

REPORTER: Senator, how do we know that you are really type O?

MORAN: I thought someone would ask that, Mr. Hollander. Nurse . . .

(Moran takes off his jacket and rolls up his shirt sleeve. Nurse draws blood from his arm into a vial and corks the vial. Moran rolls down his shirt sleeve and puts his jacket back on)

MORAN: Here you are, Henry. Do your own test of my blood. Incidentally, your paper will look pretty dumb tomorrow morning when it withdraws its endorsement and denounces me and then has to backtrack on Monday.

REPORTER: Are you alleging, Senator, that there has been a plot against you?

MORAN (shrugs his shoulders): There is the evidence. What do you think?

REPORTER: Are you serious about suing the media?

MORAN: I certainly am. My lawyers on Monday morning will go into the Cook County Court and file a slander charge against Ms. Crawford and her unnamed associates. We will be asking relief in the amount of a hundred million dollars. The Chicago media will be next unless retractions and apologies are immediately forthcoming.

REPORTER: Don't you feel any obligation to Ms. Crawford?

MORAN: I feel that she has already been amply rewarded for her efforts. I don't believe in paying blackmail.

REPORTER: Do you think this is a plot to defeat you in the election?

MORAN: What other motive would there be for monstrous and false allegations so close to the election that there is really no way to effectively refute them? I add that the plotters effectively seduced the media to rush to judgment without a careful investigation of the facts.

REPORTER: Do you believe that Senator Crispjin was involved in the plot?

MORAN: I have no knowledge that he was.

REPORTER: You suggested that Bobby Bill Roads was involved with the plot and we know that he is close to the Senator.

MORAN: I pointed out that the people around Ms. Crawford frequently worked for him. I didn't say he was involved in the plot. Moreover, as I said, I have no knowledge of Senator Crispjin's involvement. I don't believe in guilt by association.

REPORTER: Do you think this scandal will defeat you in the election?

MORAN: It certainly won't help.

REPORTER: Do you regret your decision to seek reelection, Senator?

MORAN (shrugs again): What man in his right mind would allow his family to be put through the horror of the last twenty-four hours?

CHAPTER 36

†

(Russell is in Washington in his usual studio. Senator is in Chicago with skyline background)

Russell: You certainly have been the victim of a very crude plot, Senator.

Moran: Crude, Jim, but very effective politically. One can't imagine a better way to steal an election than a media scandal over the final weekend of a campaign.

Russell: Both a senatorial and a presidential election . . .

Moran: Precisely.

Russell: Did you see something like this coming?

Moran: I knew they would try something at the last minute. I wasn't smart enough to suspect what it would be.

Russell: Who are *they,* Senator?

Moran: I don't know Jim, not for sure and I'm not going to make any accusations.

Russell (smiles): Sticking to your principles?

Moran: Trying to.

Russell: They are the people who blew up your car and your campaign headquarters, fired rifle shots at you, and organized the riot in South Chicago?

Moran: There seems to be a pattern . . . The politics of a banana republic, appealing from the ballot to the bullet—or a poison dart.

RUSSELL: Do you see a banana-republic trend emerging in American politics?

MORAN: Do you remember when a group of Republican thugs intervened in the vote-counting in Dade County, Jim? Yes I think there is such a trend.

RUSSELL: Do you think that your chances will improve because Ms. Crawford has admitted she was paid ten thousand dollars to lie about you?

MORAN: Cheapskates! . . . I think it's too late, Jim, to make any difference. *The Daily News* in Chicago endorsed me on Friday and revoked its endorsement this morning. I'm told they will apologize tomorrow morning. That may well be too late. *The New York Times* spread the story on its front page yesterday, didn't report my press conference today. What will they do tomorrow?

RUSSELL: Can they deliver many votes in Chicago?

MORAN (grins for the first time): Probably not, but they have contributed to the atmosphere of scandal. One of their people called me yesterday to ask me about the obligation I felt to Ms. Crawford. I tried to persuade her that the charges were lies. She didn't want to listen. No one from the *Times* came to my press conference.

RUSSELL: Do you think you will lose on Tuesday?

MORAN: I wouldn't bet against such an outcome. Before this phony scandal, we were probably way ahead. I don't know and I don't think anyone else does how the people of Illinois will react.

RUSSELL: Will you be sad if you lose?

MORAN: If it were my fault, if I had blown it, if I let people down, yes I'd be sad. But I don't think it will be my fault.

DEBATE ON CHICAGO PUBLIC TELEVISION

Similar cast of characters, Senora Gonzalez is absent as is Leander Schlenk. They have been replaced by a reporter (woman) for a national news magazine named Lorene Philippi.

MODERATOR: Well, Senator, it looks like you've been cleared. Ms. Mandy Crawford admits that she lied on Friday.

SENATOR: Yeah? Who gives me my reputation back? Mandy Crawford was a victim too. So, I suppose, were the media who were suckered in by the taste of blood.

HONEYWELL: You sound bitter, Senator.

SENATOR: Speaking of blood, Harold, did my blood type turn out to be O as I claimed yesterday?

HONEYWELL (embarrassed): I thought we had to be sure.

SENATOR: You're sure now?

HONEYWELL: We will apologize tomorrow morning and restore our endorsement.

SENATOR: How much good will that do?

HONEYWELL: Frankly, I don't know.

QUINN: Do you have any thoughts, Senator, on how this could have been avoided?

SENATOR: Not running in the first place.

PHILIPPI: Have you heard Senator Crispjin's comment on the so called scandal?

SENATOR (brightens): No, what did Mr. Crispjin have to say?

PHILIPPI: He said that he did not believe you had answered all the unanswered questions.

SENATOR: Did he say what were the unanswered questions I didn't answer?

PHILIPPI: No.

SENATOR: Well I guess I can't answer them can I?

GRAHAM: There is a lot of anger in your heart, isn't there, Tommy?

SENATOR: You got it, Grayson. I'm angry at the conspirators but also at the media who gobbled down the bait the conspirators provided. Anger in the present circumstances is justified and even virtuous.

HONEYWELL: It is your opinion that in matters like this the media should not rush to judgment?

MORAN: It is also my opinion that Lake Michigan shouldn't turn cold in the winter.

QUINN: You are hinting that once the media have a possible sensation, they don't pause to see if there's any truth in it?

MORAN: I'm not hinting at it Mary Alice. I'm asserting it bluntly. Surely somewhere in the feeding chain of the networks there ought to have been someone that asked whether this might be a last-minute election dirty trick.

QUINN: I wasn't working that day. As soon as I heard the five o'clock news, I called our news director. I tried to tell him you were in Spain at that time. He didn't have time to talk to me. We're going to apologize tonight.

MORAN: I hope they don't fire you, Mary Alice.

QUINN: I don't think they will, no way.

MORAN: My lawyers, and there are many on the O'Malley side, will be listening very carefully. They may still demand payment. But I'm glad you will still be around.

HONEYWELL: There just wasn't enough time.

SENATOR: So you rushed to judgment. You did not exercise due diligence. I'm not sure that excuse will satisfy my lawyers. Moreover your comment is an admission of moral bankruptcy.

PHILIPPI: My magazine wants to put your picture on its cover next week.

MORAN: Nothing is more successful than martyrdom.

PHILIPPI: Win or lose? Will you accept?

MORAN: Talk to my media director, Dolly McCormick.

PHILIPPI: I would like to hear what your wife and daughters have to say, if you give them permission.

MORAN: They don't need my permission. If this goes down, you'll find them prepared to talk all day and into the night.

GRAHAM: I went to a couple of churches out on the South Side this morning. African-American people won't forget their friends.

MORAN: That's very good news.

HONEYWELL: You're denouncing the media because we didn't check facts.

MORAN: I think the courts might decide that fact checking on a charge like the one you made was a failure of due diligence and hence actionable. At Ms. Quinn's channel, they didn't want facts, they wanted to feed on raw meat . . . Now, we have had two rounds of questions about the Crawford Scandal. Could we now have just a little time for issue questions. Senator Crispjin and I differ on most of the issues which face the country. Isn't anyone interested?

QUINN: What was your most important achievement during your term?

SENATOR: Immigration reform and that was, oddly enough, an administration bill. Second one has to be pension reform. Third is vouchers for poor kids.

QUINN: Those are pretty good achievements for a first term. And you're slated to be Deputy Majority Leader when you go back.

MORAN: If.

HONEYWELL: Are you ready to forgive those who organized the scandal?

MORAN: Forgiveness is at the core of my religious faith, Harold. But I want to be able to cut the cards in the future.

PHILIPPI: One more family question?

MORAN (a touch of a smile, for the first time): Sure.

PHILIPPI: How did your wife and children react?

MORAN: Fury.

PHILIPPI: At you?

MORAN: At the conspirators and at poor little Mandy.

PHILIPPI: They didn't believe the possibility that you might have strayed from the path of virtue?

MORAN: My daughters were very angry at the claim the poor little toddler's hair was the same as their red hair. My wife tells me that I am a one-woman man, which I guess is the truth.

MODERATOR: One more question, Graham?

GRAHAM: In your heart, Senator, don't you believe that you'll win?

MORAN: I'll have to examine my heart later, Graham. In my gut, where
the politics emotions rise up, I think that it could go either way.

"No questions about issues," my wife and my daughters hugged me
when I left the sudio.

"You totally gotta win, Daddy," Maryro informed me. "I have a lotta
big bets with Georgetown dweebs."

We drove up to a rally in an affluent neighborhood where the parish
precinct had voted Democratic for the last four presidential elections.
We sang the Mexican and Irish songs, promised the beginning of a new
era. Our next stop was in Lake County, and after that out in DuPage,
both for Mexican Americans. Everywhere there were cheers. A lot of
people were pleased with us. When we returned, Chucky and Rosemarie were waiting for us, as were a number of the family lawyers.

"We're getting apologies, guys," Chucky chortled. "We're getting offers for settlement from the media, not generous enough. So we're playing hard guys. Oh yes, Tommy, Mandy called."

"Poor thing was sobbing," Rosemarie said, a touch of sympathy in her
voice. "She claimed that she didn't have a hundred million dollars. We reassured her by saying that since she has apologized we have forgiven her."

"Nothing from the Senator?" I asked.

"Not word, Tommy," Chuck chortled. "He must have realized that
it didn't work.

"We go after Bobby Bill," I said, "because he has to be stopped. We
don't sue the former Senator, however. By now he knows that no matter who wins, he loses."

The next morning with daughters and the Sanchez kids in tow, we
hit three more malls, a very useful place to meet former Democrats who
were in the process of returning and were bringing me books to sign.

I was exhausted and collapsed into bed.

"Day after tomorrow," I said, "and it's all over."

"And we turn to our usual lifestyle," she said as we hugged each other.

CHAPTER 37

✝

THOUSANDS OF PEOPLE waited for us at the polling place. Mary Rose and Mary Ann were voting for the first time. "Good deal that I can vote for my dad."

Many of the people were not our neighbors. They had come because they liked Tommy and wanted us to know that they were loyal. Immediately I decided that we would win. Most people would see through Bobby Bill's trick. It had been close for a while but Tommy's tough talk won us a lot of votes we might not have had and even, I think, some Republicans. Then we went to five crucial L train stops and asked people to vote. We also passed out "Holy Cards" with a picture of the family on the cards.

Chucky's photo of course.

Voters knew the L stations we would visit. So we were mobbed by people wanting us to autograph the picture cards.

Tommy seemed his usual cheery ebullient self, confident of victory. I could tell, however, that the confidence was an act. He was still recuperating from the campaign traumas—Gately Park and the Friday afternoon massacre. If we lost, as he thought he would and I vigorously denied, he'd go through an interlude of near-depression.

"So," I had told the Lord, "he's gotta win."

We shared wonderful love during our afternoon nap. Then we picked up the kids at Rosie's house and rode down to the Allegro for our second victory as Chuck had assured both of us. The rain poured down and lightning crackled against the skyscrapers as we rode down on the Congress Expressway. Just like six years ago.

The night started out badly.

The polls closed at seven. By seven-fifteen, Crispjin's spokesperson was on the air claiming victory.

"We have sophisticated scientific surveys which enable us to predict the outcome of the election very early in the evening. We now believe that Senator Rodgers Crispjin will carry Illinois by fifty-three percent of the votes. As soon as Tommy Moran concedes, Senator Crispjin will address his followers here at the Fairmont hotel."

"How can they know so early?" Mary Rose demanded.

"They can't have data this soon," Joe McDermott said. "It's another one of their frauds."

"Is there any sign around the states that exit polling was going on?" I asked Joe.

"None that we have heard about."

"They're faking things," Tommy murmured. "They figure that it will be a close race and they can more credibly claim fraud when they've been ahead all night. We're going to win!"

Then Leander Schlenk appeared on the monitor.

"Mr. Schlenk, you are a veteran observer of American elections. Are you surprised that Senator Crispjin is winning so easily?"

"Not at all. I've taken for granted that people would grow tired of Little Tommy and his noisy family. The people of Illinois should be grateful that this is the last roundup for the drugstore cowboy senator."

One of the national networks reported that the Illinois Senate race had added one seat to the Republican contingent in the Senate. A check appeared after Crispjin's name, even though he was trailing in the returns by five thousand votes.

"Asshole," Maran muttered.

I did not find it in my heart to reprove her for the language which seemed just then to be appropriate.

Then Father Tony appeared on the tube.

"How do you feel about Senator Crispjin's victory, Reverend Moran?"

"I feel a great relief. My little brother is a clever little fellow, but I have been telling him all along that he shouldn't try to play with the big boys. I hope and pray that God will turn him away from empty celebrity and he will return to being the good Catholic he used to be. Then, I hope he will concentrate on saving his immortal soul."

I screamed several obscene words which I would not permit to my daughters.

Tommy seemed unaffected.

"Poor Tony," he said. "He'll be terribly disappointed by morning."

The atmosphere of a large room in which election returns are watched is odd, a mixture of hope and fear, victory and defeat, joy and sadness. Every change in the tally you're watching increases the dread and the expectation. One is either a little bit closer or a little bit further away. The neurosis which pervades the room makes everyone edgy, both laughter and curses inappropriately vigorous. An anteroom perhaps to a mental institution in which everyone was eating and drinking too much.

Oh, when is it going to end!

Two of the national networks had now ruled Rodgers Crispjin as the victor, mostly on the flashes emanating from the newsroom of the *Chicago Examiner*. The *Daily News* on the other hand reported with its usual caution that the race was much too close to call while Channel 3—which was receiving the same tallies showing up on our monitors—said that Senator Moran was edging away from Senator Crispjin.

We had in fact never lagged behind the opposition from the very first tallies on the monitor. With 20 percent of the ballots we were 13 percentage points ahead of the opposition.

"We can't be that far ahead," said a very anxious and somewhat overweight South Side Irish woman.

Our own interests were frustrated by the national interest in the presidential election.

Joe and Dolly would appear periodically in the family group around the candidate's easy chair. He himself remained relaxed and serene, occasionally muttering something barely intelligible after he'd done some calculations.

About eleven thirty we picked up five thousand more votes.

"DuPage," Joe intoned.

"Truly?" my poor little Tommy asked.

"Then we have it . . . We'll win by maybe 100,000 votes! Women of the house, the champagne please!"

Rosie and Maryro and I popped open the bottles and filled the plastic goblets we'd brought along.

"Gentlepersons," Tommy stood on a chair, which I held steady, not quite convinced that his sense of balance had returned. "I proclaim victory. We're going to win bigger than anyone had expected. The scandal of last Friday evening backfired. A hundred thousand votes, a veritable landslide."

Quite sober, as he would remain all evening, he began "A Grand Old Name." Then the kids grabbed their instruments and did "When Irish Eyes Are Smiling." Chucky and Rosie sang "Rosmarie," their favorite theme song.

I was afraid to count our chickens before they were hatched.

A phone rang, the one next to Tommy's chair. I picked it up.

"Mary Margaret," I whispered.

"How y'all doing down there," the President-elect said. "Having a little celebration? You're entitled to it. Do you think you can get the Senator?"

"I'll just snap my fingers, sir."

"The President is on the line, Tommy!"

He jumped off the chair and came running.

"Congratulations, Mr. President! I'm glad ABC is about to call it for you. I hope I can ride along on your coattails. You on mine? I don't see it . . . Hey, you're right . . . It doesn't much matter so long as we're both winning. I'll look forward to it . . . Your first call? . . . I really appreciate it, sir. Have a good vacation."

The room turned dead quiet.

Tommy took a deep breath.

"That was the President-elect. ABC will shortly proclaim him the victor. Apparently we carried Illinois by more votes than he did . . ."

A mega cheer exploded. Then on the TV monitor Channel 3 put a check after Tommy's name.

I answered another phone.

"Yes, Dolly, I'll tell him . . . Boss Man, Dolly says we should come right on down!"

The young people, cousins, aunts, uncles, and friends, led us down to the main ballroom playing "Happy Days Are Here Again!" They struck it up the second time as we entered the big hall. Then "Mary, a Grand Old Name," which opened my tear ducts. Finally as Tommy reached the podium, myself dragged along, they turned to "When Irish Eyes Are Smiling."

Finally the crowd settled down.

"You'll excuse me if I don't get too close to the edge of the platform," Tommy began. "And if I hold on to my wife so I won't fall off again."

After another wave of cheering, Tommy brought the crowd under control.

"The President-elect called me ten minutes ago and assured me that we both had carried Illinois. He thanked me for providing coattails. I don't think that's true. But he did say that I was the first one he called after ABC declared him the winner. I thanked him in the name of all of you who have worked so hard. Happy days are indeed here again!"

Our pickup orchestra played that again and then its favorite Mexican serenade, during which my husband kissed me like he meant it. I have little recollection of the rest of the evening until we were home in bed about three in the morning. I won't, however, forget our romp of love. Together we'd beaten the bad guys. We had proved that we were smarter and stronger than they were.

Happy days were indeed here again.

EPILOGUE

B EFORE THE WEEK was out Bobby Bill and a dozen of his aides and beneficiaries were indicted, including Senator Crispjin. The editor of the *Examiner* was fired and his replacement announced the "retirement" of Leander Schlenck. Tommy flew back to D.C. on Thursday for a conference between Democratic congressional leaders and the President. Marytre went with him because the Ursuline Academy was less tolerant than Gonzaga was with missing class days. The rest of us moved in with Chucky and Rosie for a few days. We'd go back on Monday. Maryro spent a lot of her time on the cell phone with Daniel Leary.

Then on Saturday morning, I received a phone call.

"Mrs. Moran?"

"Yes."

"I'm Father George of the Clementine fathers. I have been searching for your husband, but I have learned he is in Washington. Father Anthony has had a very serious accident. I am here with him at Little Company of Mary Hospital. His condition is critical but stable. He would like it very much if you could come here and visit him. Now."

"Yes, of course . . . Where is that hospital?"

"Little Company of Mary, Ninety-fifth and Central Park."

"I'll leave right away. Should I bring one of my daughters?"

"Yes, by all means, Father Anthony would very much like to see her ."

Maryro and I were both in jeans and blouses. We grabbed windbreakers.

"Why are we going to visit that man, Mom?"

"Because he is badly injured, maybe dying, and he wants to talk to us."

"God will like that, won't he?"

"She."

We both laughed.

Father George greeted us at the door.

"Mrs. Moran, so good of you to come . . . And I believe you are Mary Rose—the one in the song."

"Just as my mother is the grand old name."

"Briefly, Father Anthony had a terrible accident driving home from Joliet the other night. He probably fell asleep at the wheel. He was pinned in the car for twenty-four hours before the state police found him. His condition is critical but stable. The doctors think he will recover. He most strongly wanted to talk to someone in the family. Just for a few minutes."

"Of course, Father."

We stood at the side of the bed. A young Asian woman was watching the monitor. She smiled politely at us.

"Father Anthony," I said softly.

He opened his eyes, blinked and then smiled.

"Mary Margaret," he said reaching out to take my hand. "I'm so happy to see you. And, let's see you . . . Yes, you are Mary Rose. I believe I baptised you."

My daughter walked around to the other side of the bed.

"Yes, Father."

He held both our hands.

"I'm sorry to have disturbed you. They didn't think I was going to survive. So I wanted to make peace with all of you, especially you, Mary Margaret. I have behaved very badly towards you for all these years. God is displeased with me. I begged him to give me a chance to talk to you. I had much to think of when I lay in that car . . ." He closed his eyes and breathed deeply.

I looked at the nurse. She smiled, as if to say there was no immediate danger.

"Maybe later, if I really recover, we can get together again, this time as friends instead of rivals. All I want to do now is to beg your forgiveness. I am very sorry for what I did and said. Tell Tom that I beg his forgiveness too. Please, please forgive me!"

Tears rolled down his cheeks.

"Yes, Father Anthony," my daughter spoke first, "of coure we do and we love you very much."

She kissed him on his forehead.

"We begin a new life, Father," I said. "Let the past be as if it never were."

I pecked at his cheek.

A wonderful smile crossed his face,

"Thank you," he murmured. "Thank you very much."

Father George met us in the hospital corridor.

"That room was filled with grace, Father," my daughter said.

"He is a different man," I added.

"We have noticed that too. Perhaps he had some sort of near-death experience. He is very aware of God. Thank you for coming."

"I'm sure Tommy will drive out here tomorrow when he returns to Chicago."

"Thank you both once again . . . I am not unaware of past tensions."

"Like Mom said to him, Father, the past is now like it never was."

"I'll drive, Mom," my child said. "You call Daddy on the cell phone."

So I did what I was told and dialed my husband.

I finally found him as he was leaving the hotel where the Administration to be was setting up camp.

"You're crying, Mary Margaret," he said. "I hope it's not bad news."

"No, Tommy love, unbearably good news."

"I hope you're not driving . . ."

"Our stalwart eldest is driving . . . You'll find this hard to believe."

I told him about our encounter at Little Company of Mary Hospital. He listened in silence.

"Tommy, are you there?" I asked when I was finished with the story.

"You know our friend the night visitor?" he said in an unsteady voice.

"Yes."

"She really has a strange sense of humor!"

And we both laughed. And laughed, and laughed.

Grand Beach/Chicago

Feast of the Holy Rosary

2005